GEORGE SAND was born Amantine-Aurore Lucie Dupin in Paris on July 1, 1804. She was brought up at Nohant, the family's estate in Berry, which Sand inherited at age seventeen. She married a young officer, Casimir Dudevant, in 1822 and had two children. In 1831, she separated from her husband and went to Paris to earn her living by her pen, doing translations, drawings, and articles for *Figaro*. She collaborated on a novel, *Rose et Blanche*, with noted novelist Jules Sandeau, from whom she borrowed her famous pen name. George Sand's first novel, *Indiana* (1832), was an immediate success and was quickly followed by the novels *Lélia*, *Valentine*, and *Mauprat*. Sand was a prolific novelist, renowned throughout the world not only for her talent but also for her bohemian lifestyle, masculine attire, and celebrated love affairs—which included long-term relationships with the poet Alfred de Musset and the composer Frederic Chopin. Sand was a close friend to such great figures as Balzac, Eugène Delacroix, Heinrich Heine, Franz Liszt, and Gustave Flaubert. She participated in the Revolution of 1848, and afterwards retired to her estate at Nohant, where she wrote for nearly thirty more years. The acclaimed pastoral novels *La Mare au diable*, *La Petite Fadette*, and *François le champi*, as well as the autobiography, *L'Histoire de ma vie*, are among the works of this prolific period in her life. Sand died on June 8, 1876, at the age of 71.

Indiana

by

George Sand

Translated by Eleanor Hochman

With an Introduction by
Marilyn Yalom

A SIGNET CLASSIC

SIGNET CLASSIC
Published by the Penguin Group
Penguin Books USA Inc., 375 Hudson Street,
New York, New York 10014, U.S.A.
Penguin Books Ltd, 27 Wrights Lane,
London W8 5TZ, England
Penguin Books Australia Ltd, Ringwood,
Victoria, Australia
Penguin Books Canada Ltd, 10 Alcorn Avenue,
Toronto, Ontario, Canada M4V 3B2
Penguin Books (N.Z.) Ltd, 182-190 Wairau Road,
Auckland 10, New Zealand

Penguin Books Ltd, Registered Offices:
Harmondsworth, Middlesex, England

Published by Signet Classic,
an imprint of New American Library,
a division of Penguin Books USA Inc.

First Signet Classic Printing, May, 1993
10 9 8 7 6 5 4 3 2 1

 REGISTERED TRADEMARK—MARCA REGISTRADA

Library of Congress Catalog Card Number: 92-085363

Printed in the United States of America

To David and Genie,
Daniel and Joel,
and, as always, to Stan

—E. H.

Introduction

"And, in spite of myself, I felt I was an artist." With these words, George Sand, at fifty, recalled her state of mind two decades earlier when she threw caution to the wind and embarked upon a literary career. To realize the artist within, she renounced her role as a full-time country wife and mother and, with her husband's grudging consent, moved to Paris for six months of the year.

Sand's account of her ascent to authorship, taken from her autobiography, reveals complex motivations and contradictory beliefs. On the one hand, she was, from her late twenties on, dedicated to an artistic vocation, yet she frequently denigrated her writing as a simple means of earning a living and downplayed its aesthetic merit. At heart, she held the conviction that "woman will always be more of an artist . . . in her life," while "man will be more of an artist in his work." This dichotomy was part and parcel of the nineteenth-century ideology that proclaimed women destined by God and nature for the domestic sphere, and men, for the public sphere. In crossing the divide between female-identified "life" and male-identified "work," Sand entered a no-woman's land where she had to invent the rules of the game.

Between 1831 and 1833, this fledgling author, privately known as Mme. Aurore Dupin Dudevant, acquired a succession of pseudonyms: Jules Sand, J. Sand, G. Sand, Georges Sand, and finally George Sand. These tentative pen names, all presumably masculine, reflect her initial malaise in entering a literary arena dominated by men. Her letters from this period also offer evidence of the mixed blessings publication conferred on a woman.

On February 7, 1832, Sand expressed to her friend Émile Regnault her intoxication in being, like him, an artist. Regnault was, at that time, a Parisian medical student and the confidant of Sand's secret liaison with Jules Sandeau, the man with whom she had set up housekeeping in Paris. In her letter to Regnault, the word "artist" denoted a bohemian fraternity whose signs of membership could be seen in Regnault's long hair or Sand's boots and frock coat. She had adopted this masculine attire so as to circulate more easily through the muddy streets of the capital and specifically to gain access to the cheap theater "pit" where only men were admitted. Artists, she maintained in her letter to Regnault, "don't belong to any country, to any coterie, to any sect, to any conspiracy"; they owed allegiance only to "fantasy." Being an artist was a matter of temperament, a state of rapture, a dedication to beauty—in short, the 1830 Romantic ideal. Not surprisingly, Sand contrasted the artist to the bourgeois, who was associated with such mundane pursuits as eating string beans and drinking herbal teas.

In reference to herself, she had no difficulty appropriating the term *artiste* whenever she referred to her various enthusiasms, not only for literature, music, painting, and the theater but also for nature, religion, and any other domain that evoked deep feelings. She projected that quality backward onto both her parents, reconciling their social differences according to the commonly held view that artists were beyond class. Her plebian mother, Sophie Delaborde, was presented in Sand's autobiography as an artist without knowing that she was one. Her aristocratic father, Maurice Dupin, was remembered as a Napoleonic soldier with artistic tastes. To conceptualize her parents as innate, albeit unrealized, artists fed the fantasy of a family romance more satisfying to her self-image than the objective facts. After a liaison of four years, carefully hidden from the senior Mme. Dupin, her parents had legalized their union only one month before Aurore, the future George Sand, was born in Paris on July 1, 1804. The new Mme. Dupin would never be comfortable in upper-class society, especially in the company of her highly cultivated mother-in law. After the untimely death of Maurice Dupin when his daughter was only four, Aurore became increasingly her grandmother's ward, residing with her at Nohant rather than with her mother in Paris. Her childhood years were marked by a distressing sense of divided loyalty to a mother she fiercely loved and a grandmother she profoundly respected. Though Sand attributed her artistic genes to her parents, it was probably the broad education she received under her grandmother's tutelage that deserves major credit for her ability to compete in the male literary arena.

While Sand embraced the identity of the *artiste*, she was less comfortable with the terms *écrivain* and *auteur* ("writer" and "author"), words which designate a profession rather than a temperament. Even when she was already the published author of a novel, *Rose et Blanche*—a collaboration written with Jules Sandeau—she wrote to her friend Charles Meure on January 27, 1832: "Never call me a *woman author*, or I'll make you swallow my five volumes." The words *femme auteur* are underlined, and stand out, especially in French with their contradiction of gender.

Sand had good cause for wanting to remove herself from the female literati so ridiculed by the playwright Molière in the seventeenth century and by a host of like-minded spirits in the eighteenth and nineteenth. Recall the 1793 statement of Madame Roland, the most famous memoirist of the French Revolution: "I never had the slightest temptation to become an author; I saw very early that a woman who acquired that title lost much more than she gained. Men do not like her and her own sex criticizes her. If her works are bad, they make fun of her . . . and if they are good, they deny that she wrote them." Like Madame Roland, Sand anxiously tried to disassociate herself with the woman author and to identify instead with ordinary domestic women. Her letter to Meure continues: "I drink and eat like anyone else, I wipe my children and wash my hands like a normal person. Well then, I work every day so as to deserve to have inscribed on my tomb . . . that I was a good mother, good daughter, good *wife*, good sister, good cousin, good aunt, good niece, and so that, God willing, one can add a good grandmother." Clearly, despite her new professional status, she preferred the image of a woman buttressed by family relationships to that of an independent "public" woman.

By May 1832, Sand was already sending out copies of her second novel, *Indiana*, this one written alone and to be published under the pseudonym of G. Sand. To her friend from the Berry, Charles Duvernet, she equated writing with money making: "For me, you know, the writer's *métier* consists of an income of three thousand pounds in order to buy, in addition to staples, pralines for Solange [her daughter] and good tobacco for my damned nose." Each offering of *Indiana* was accompanied by a similar note downplaying its aesthetic value.

She understood her writing primarily as a job, *un gagne-pain*, the profits from which helped to support her family and, later, a host of friends and causes. Though she absented herself for long periods from the domestic responsibilities of her country estate until 1836 when she was legally separated from her husband and could return to live permanently at Nohant, she never abandoned the belief that woman's first obligation is to "life," that is, to love and friendship, humanitarian ideals, and the countless private chores that sustain existence. Like most women in the Western world, she judged herself primarily by the quality of her human ties; however great her success as a writer, and it was very great indeed, Sand would have been a failure in her own eyes if she had failed as a "woman," that is, as an artist in life.

Indiana is the story of one woman's struggle to become the artist of her life. Given the context of her unusually oppressive marriage, the protagonist Indiana is eventually forced to oppose the prevailing laws that required a wife's submission to even a brutal husband. Ten years after its publication, Sand would recognize that *Indiana* was one of a series of novels all more or less on the same general theme—"the false relationship between the sexes." (Preface of 1842)

The husband, Colonel Delmare, is not Indiana's sole antagonist. There is also one Raymon de Ramières, an archetypical aristocratic seducer, who casts his spell over Indiana despite her best protestations. And there is also her cousin Sir Ralph, a silent soul mate, who reveals his true nature only at the end of the novel. It was characteristic of Sand at this period of her life, in keeping with the received ideas of her culture, to conceptualize a woman's life primarily in terms of her relationships with men. Indeed, she would always adhere to the belief that what distinguished women from men was the feminine capacity for boundless love. Sand's contemporary, the British poet Byron, well understood the imaginative hold of romantic love over nineteenth-century women when he wrote: "Man's love is of man's life a thing apart; 'tis women's whole existence." For men, there were other outlets.

In *Indiana*, there is a telling correlation between the three male characters and the greater political order. Each of the men represents one of the forms of government vying for supremacy in the France of 1830. Colonel Delmare is loyal to his Napoleonic heritage; Raymon de Ramières to *ancien régime* and post-Napoleonic aristocracy; Sir Ralph to the vision of egalitarian democracy. Though Indiana herself never voices a direct political opinion, it becomes clear through the unfolding of the plot that she, like her creator George Sand, favors a society based on democratic principles. Social and political considerations would increase their importance in Sand's work as she grew older, especially in the period surrounding the revolution of 1848.

But in the novels published in the wake of the revolution of 1830, despite conscious attention to political issues, the motivating forces are largely personal and psychological. We who look back on Sand and her generation of Romantics from a post-Freudian perspective are often amazed by their intuitive understanding of psychological phenomena and by their ingenuity in exposing areas of their own unconscious life, often incarnated symbolically or through the use of double characters. In *Indiana*, the high-born mistress Indiana and her low-born servant Noun are doubles representing a basic duality common in Western culture—that of the lofty spiritual woman and her fleshly counterpart. Consider the following passage:

> Noun was Mme. Delmare's foster sister, and the two young women, who had been brought up together, loved each other dearly. Noun was tall and strong, vividly alive, full of the ardor and passion of her Creole blood, and strikingly beautiful in a way that far outshone the delicate, fragile charms of the pale Mme. Delmare; but their tender hearts and mutual affection eliminated all possibility of feminine rivalry.

The words "foster sister" do not fully convey the original French expression *soeur de lait* (literally, "milk sister") which indicates that Noun and Indiana had shared the same wet nurse, probably Noun's mother. Having nursed at the same breast, they are spiritual sisters, despite the difference in their social positions. Each is endowed with the physical attributes deemed appropriate to her social station: Noun is tall, strong, healthy, and passionate, whereas Indiana is pale and frail and, implicitly, less hot-blooded than the true Creole. Individually they are stereotypes of their respective classes; together they constitute a whole person who has been fragmented by social proscriptions. Indiana's compelling sense of sisterhood with Noun far exceeds the conventional bonds between mistress and confidante; it suggests the union of a "respectable" woman and what Jung would have called her "shadow" self.

It is Noun who carries on the behind-the-scenes affair with Raymon de Ramières. She is the free, uninhibited female who delights in lovemaking with "that wild tropical lust which can triumph over the most determined . . . resisistance." She is the body fully experiencing pleasure. Raymon loves her "with his senses" but he loves Indiana "with all his heart and soul." During the day he declares his chaste and undying love to Indiana: "You are the woman I have dreamed of, the purity I have worshipped." But at night he returns to Noun to exchange "voluptuous caresses" that banish all vestiges of reason. Alone with Noun in Indiana's bedroom while Indiana is out of the house, he succeeds in confusing the two of them.

> Little by little a vague memory of Indiana began to float in and out of Raymon's drunken consciousness. The two mirrored panels that each reflected Noun's image into infinity seemed to be peopled by a thousand phantoms, and as he stared into the depths of that double image he thought he could see, in the final hazy and indistinct reflection of Noun, the slender, willowy form of Mme. Delmare.

The confusion in Raymon's mind between the two women is not accidental. They are complementary characters, each half of a full person, projections of a split self. Despite their spiritual sisterhood, they are, on the underground level of the novel, engaged in psychological warfare. That neither knows of the other's involvement with Raymon adds to the tension and suggests the hidden reality of two hostile forces operating simultaneously within the writer's psyche. How their respective fates are resolved reveals an irreconcilable conflict between the ideas of sacred and profane love.

Sand's novels provide a valuable supplement to the literary portraiture of nineteenth-century heroines. For the most part, European fiction from this period—be it that of Balzac, or Dickens, or any lesser male novelist—distinguishes between the ethereal woman who gives herself to love with a whole heart and the carnal woman who loves with other organs. The ideal woman, as she appeared in print, was virtually an angel. She had raptures of the heart but nothing so gross as physical desire. The woman who admitted to feelings of a sexual nature was treated as inferior—an outright courtesan, adulteress, or fallen woman. In France she was not obliged to wear a scarlet letter, but her fate, like that of Noun and Madame Bovary, was invariably tragic.

Many of the novels of George Sand follow this pattern, but they differ from male-authored works in that the angel and the whore are intimately related to one another. Like Jekyll and Hyde, they spring from a single psyche and vie for dominance in the same breast. In *Indiana*, as in Sand's succeeding novel *Lélia*, the double characters act out the author's conscious spiritual aspirations, as well as her repressed erotic appetite.

One may argue that the sensual self was not wont to take a subordinate role in the life of George Sand. From the time that Mme. Aurore Dupin Dudevant left her husband to live with the writer Jules Sandeau, she shared her bed with a series of lovers, of whom the poet Alfred de Musset and the composer Frédéric Chopin were only the most famous. She was certainly far removed from her English counterparts, the Brontë spinsters, who conceived their literary creations while sequestered in a Methodist parsonage. But despite the outward appearance of Sand's sexual freedom, her writing reveals that sexuality was, at least, problematic. The solution proposed at the end of *Indiana* is the least credible part of the book, though the reader is swept along to the very last word by that narrative current which was always Sand's forte.

Indiana announced the arrival of a master storyteller, who would go on to fill a hundred tomes with her novels, stories, plays, and essays. Writing was for Sand the breath of life, only to end in the final months of her seventy-second year. By then she was the best-known woman author in Europe, honored by a host of her peers, including the British poet Elizabeth Barrett Browning, the French novelist Gustave Flaubert, and the Russian writer Ivan Turgenev. She died at Nohant on June 8, 1876, surrounded by her two children, Maurice and Solange, and her two beloved grandchildren. Long before her death, she had come to represent for millions of readers the quintessential woman artist who gave unstintingly to the dual demands of work and life.

Not for Sand the model of the isolated creator, alone in her ivory tower or cork-lined room; not for her the Parnassian religion of art with its impersonal adherence to formal perfection. To the credo of art for art's sake, she countered with the dictum of life for life's sake. She expressed these views most forcefully during her last years in her remarkable correspondence with Flaubert, who was seventeen years her junior, yet infinitely more weary of existence. Sand never stopped chiding Flaubert for his obsessive dedication to literary craftsmanship and his splenetic isolation from humanity. Work so conceived and so practiced was deemed bad for his health: "What . . . you've been sick?" she wrote on November 5, 1874. "I worry about that solitude where you no longer have anyone to remind you to eat, drink, and sleep, and especially, to take walks." With the self-assurance of her seventy years, she reminded Flaubert "that there is something above art: namely, wisdom, of which art at its apogee is only the expression. Wisdom comprehends all: beauty, truth, goodness, enthusiasm . . . It teaches us to see outside of ourselves, something more elevated than is in ourselves, and to assimilate it little by little, through contemplation and admiration." In this same letter, she compared herself unfavorably, as an artist, to Flaubert and Victor Hugo, but she gave herself top marks as a student of life who had learned to "lay hold of *happiness*." Ultimately, then, Sand reconciled the division between "life" and "work" by moving to a plane that encompassed them both. Wisdom, with happiness as its side effect, was placed even above art.

If the search for wisdom still has meaning, much can be learned from George Sand. We shall have to find room, once again, for such sentiments as nostalgia, reverence, and solidarity in a world which teaches the benefits of immediate gain and ruthless individualism. We shall have to believe, as George Sand did, that literature has something to do with the lives we lead, and—dare I say it?—that it can trigger personal and social regeneration.

—Marilyn Yalom

Translator's Note

The Bourbon Island that George Sand describes so lovingly is not a figment of her imagination but a place now known as Réunion. Located in the Indian Ocean off the coast of Africa and about 425 miles east of Madagascar, it was discovered by and named for the Portuguese navigator Pedro Mascarenhas in the early sixteenth century. Though the archipelago of which it is part is still known as the Mascarenes, the island itself was annexed by France in the seventeenth century and called Bourbon Island, retaining that name until the French Revolution, when it was baptized Réunion. From 1810 to 1815, the British occupied the island, and when it was restored to France at the end of the Napoleonic wars, it reverted to being Bourbon. In 1848 it again officially became Réunion, But since *Indiana* takes place in the years immediately preceding and following the 1830 Revolution, Sand of course referred to it as Bourbon.

–E. H.

Preface to the 1852 Edition

I wrote *Indiana* during the fall of 1831. It was my first novel, and because I was at an age when one writes with one's instincts—and when in any case one's intellect only finds reasons to confirm and support those instincts—it was written out of the impulses of my heart rather than in conformity to any theories of art or philosophy. Some people chose to see the book as a carefully reasoned argument against marriage, but since that was not my purpose, I was quite astonished by all the things critics found to say about my subversive intentions. Criticism is much too subtle, and that will be its undoing: critics are never content to judge what is directly in front of their eyes but go out of their way to look for what is not there. What anguish they must cause any artist who pays too much attention to their judgments!

At all times and under all regimes, moreover, some critics have so little faith in their own literary talent that they feel they must curry official favor by denigrating that of other writers—a strange function to fulfill vis-à-vis their fellows! They have never found the government's harsh measures against the press sufficiently savage: they would like to see those measures enforced not only against the works but also against the creators, and if they had their way, some of us would be forbidden to write anything at all. When I wrote *Indiana*, Saint-Simonism was the most common charge; in later years there were others, and even today there are some authors who are afraid to say what they want lest the police agents of certain newspapers denounce their work and have them summoned before the powers that be. If such an author has a working-class character demonstrate a noble soul, that is seen as an insult to the middle class; if he shows a girl who has gone astray atoning for her sins and being rehabilitated, that is an attack on virtuous women; if a dishonest man is given a title, that is an insult to the aristocracy; if a swaggering soldier behaves like a bully, that is an insult to the army; if a woman is shown being abused by her husband, that is a rationalization of promiscuity. And so on and so on. Fine colleagues, just and generous critics! What a shame that there are no plans to establish a court of literary inquisition in which you would be the judges! Would you be satisfied with ripping up the offending books and burning the pieces one by one, or would you like to be allowed to apply a bit of torture to the writers—those who allow themselves to have other gods than yours—as well?

Thank God that I have forgotten even the names of those who tried to discourage me from the very beginning and who, since they were unable to say that my humble debut was a total failure, labeled it an incendiary proclamation against the peace and well-being of society! I had not hoped for such an honor, and I think I owe those critics the same thanks that the hare owed the frogs in La Fontaine's fable: when the hare saw how he frightened the frogs, he felt like a fiercesome warrior.

—George Sand
Nohant, May 1852

Preface to the 1832 Edition

Some critics may feel that portions of this book encourage imprudent and dangerous new ideas, but it seems to me that such a response would confer too much significance on an unimportant work. One must have either great strength of purpose or great confidence in one's talent to address the serious questions of social organization, and such presumption is totally foreign to the nature of this very simple tale in which the author has invented almost nothing. If he sometimes allows the characters to complain of the injustices they endure, or to voice their hopes for a better life, let the blame be laid on society for its inequities and on fate for its caprices! The writer is only a mirror that reflects images and an instrument that traces them, and as long as the reflection is accurate and the impression exact, he need not apologize for them.

Remember also that the narrator has not chosen as a theme any of the major crises responsible for mankind's cries of suffering or rage. He does not claim to have hidden a serious message in the guise of a story, and he is no more helping to build the society that a still undefined future has in store for us than he is helping to destroy the society of the past that is already crumbling away. He is only too aware that we are living in a time when the old morality is in a state of decay and that the human mind must be shielded from the brilliant light that is being cast upon that condition; if he had felt wise enough to write a really useful book, he would have softened the truth instead of presenting it in all its raw and crude harshness, and such a book would have served the function of tinted lenses, protecting those eyes too weak to withstand the glare.

He may yet perform such an honorable and generous-spirited task. He is still young, however, so for the moment he is simply telling you what he has seen, without daring to draw any conclusions about the great ongoing process of change from the past to the future—which is probably something no

one of this generation is capable of judging. Too conscientious
to hide his doubts from you, and too timid to pretend they are
certainties, he relies on your intelligence and refrains from
weaving any preconceived theories or judgments into the woof
of his story. Faithfully practicing his narrator's trade, he will
tell you everything, even painful truths; but any attempt to turn
him into a philosopher would only embarrass him, for he is a
simple tale-teller whose mission is to entertain rather than to
instruct.

Even if he were more mature and more skillful, he would
still not presume to probe the gaping wounds of our dying civilization, because before doing anything like that, one should
be very sure of being able to cure them! He would much rather
try to incorporate old, discarded beliefs and vanished forms of
faith than to employ whatever talent he may have in blasting
already overturned altars; and although he knows that in these
charitable times intellectual diffidence is despised as hypocritical caution and a modest artistic presentation is mocked as a
ridiculous mannerism, he also knows that there is honor if not
profit in defending lost causes.

To those who misunderstand the spirit of this book, such a
declaration will seem anachronistic. The narrator hopes, however, that few readers, after finishing the story, will deny the
morality that emerges from the presentation of the facts—a
morality that triumphs here as it does in every human en-
deavor. It seemed to him, as he ended the story, that his conscience was clear. He was proud to have described social
miseries with moderation, human passions with dispassion; he
had muted chords that were too loud, and he had tried to stifle
certain notes of the soul that should remain silent, certain cries
of the heart that are not voiced without risk.

Perhaps you will do him the justice to acknowledge that he
has shown the person who tries to free herself from her lawful
curbs as quite miserable, the heart that rebels against the decrees of its destiny as quite wretched. If he has not given the
best role to the character who represents *the law*, and if he has
been even less flattering to the one who represents *public
opinion*, he has clearly shown the third, who represents *illusion*, as suffering cruelly from the vain hopes and mad ambitions of passion. And you will also admit that if he hasn't
strewn rose petals over the spot in which the law pens up our
desires as though they were ravenous sheep, he has certainly
scattered thorns along the roads that lead away from that spot.

It seems to me that this should be enough to protect the book against the charge of immorality, but those who absolutely insist that a novel should end like an eighteenth-century moral tale may reproach me for the conclusion and disapprove of my not condemning to a lifetime of misery and scorn the character who has sinned against the laws of mankind throughout these pages. To such a charge the author will reply that he wanted to be truthful rather than moral; he will repeat that he felt too inexperienced to compose a philosophical treatise on how to endure one's life and therefore limited himself to writing *Indiana*—a story of the human heart, with its weaknesses, passions, rights and wrongs, good and bad qualities.

For those who insist on an explanation for everything, Indiana represents woman, the weak creature who represents repressed passions—or rather, passions suppressed by the law; she is desire at odds with necessity, love hurtling itself blindly against all the obstacles of civilization. But just as the serpent's teeth are eroded when he tries to gnaw through a file, so the soul's strength is eroded by the struggle against the facts of life. That is the conclusion you may draw from this story, and that was the spirit in which it was told to the one who tells it to you.

Despite these disclaimers, the narrator expects to be faulted. Some sterling souls and upright consciences may be alarmed at seeing virtue portrayed as so harsh, reason as so ineffectual, opinion as so unjust. That is a disturbing thought, for what a writer should fear more than anything else in the world is alienating the confidence of men of good will, awakening a dangerous response in embittered souls, inflaming the already painful sores that the social yoke has left on rebellious and impatient necks.

Success obtained by an unworthy appeal to the passions of an age is the easiest to achieve, but the least honorable to aim for. The author of *Indiana* has never aspired to it, and if he thought he had attained it, he would destroy his book—despite the fact that he feels for it the same sort of paternal affection that swathes all the rickety literary miscarriages of our time.

But he hopes to justify himself by saying that he thought his principles would be better served by true examples than by poetic inventions. He thinks the melancholy honesty of his tale may make an impression on young and enthusiastic minds. They will not find it easy to disbelieve a chronicler who deals with facts, brutally elbowing his way through them right and left with no more regard for one side than for another. To present a point of view as hateful or ridiculous is merely to persecute it, not fight it, and the novelist's skill may perhaps be judged by how successful he is in touching both the culprits he wishes to reform and the unfortunates he wishes to help.

Any attempt to ward off every possible accusation would give too much weight to a work that is unlikely to attract much attention, so the author simply offers himself up unreservedly to the critics. Only the charge that he wanted to write a dangerous book seems too serious for him to accept, and because he would rather remain unimportant forever than build his reputation on an unclean conscience, he will therefore add one more word as a defense against the reproach he most dreads.

Raymon, you say, is society, and therefore society, which should represent reason and morality, is shown to be mere self-interest. To this the author replies that Raymon is the *false* reason, the *false* morality, by which society is governed; the world considers him an honorable man because the world does not examine things closely enough to see them clearly. The good man is right there alongside Raymon, and he is certainly not the enemy of order since he is clearly shown as sacrificing all his sense of self and all his personal happiness to precisely that sense of social order.

Finally, you may complain that virtue is not shown to be rewarded in a particularly brilliant manner. Unfortunately, the answer is that the only place one can now see virtue triumphant is at the theater. The author will tell you that he did not undertake to show society as virtuous but as necessary, and that in these days of moral decadence, it is as difficult to be honorable as it is to be heroic. Do you think that a recognition of this truth will disgust great souls with the idea of honor? I think just the opposite.

Preface to the 1842 Edition

By allowing this book to be reprinted, I do not mean to imply that it accurately or completely represents my current beliefs about the relative rights of individuals and society. I do it simply because I feel that past opinions, frankly expressed, are almost sacred and that we may not decide at a later date to retract, belittle, or modify them in any way. However, since I have subsequently traveled along life's highway and experienced broader horizons, I owe it to the reader to explain my present feelings about the book.

When I wrote *Indiana* I was young, and my sincerity and enthusiasm led me to write a whole series of novels, most of them based on the same theme: society's responsibility for the false relationship that exists between the sexes. Those novels were all, to a greater or lesser degree, condemned by the critics, who saw them as dangerous attacks on the institution of marriage. Although *Indiana*'s focus was narrow and its grasp of the issues uncertain, it was nevertheless the target of several so-called serious thinkers, whose indignant comments I was at first strongly disposed to listen to with docility and accept as truth. But despite the fact that my intelligence was barely developed enough to permit me to write about such an important subject, I was at least mature enough to judge the intelligence of those who judged me; no matter how simpleminded the criminal in the dock or how clever his judge, the accused always has enough mother wit to know if the sentence is just or unjust, sensible or absurd.

Certain journalists who set themselves up as representatives and guardians of public morality—by what orders I do not know, since I do not know by what authority they are commissioned—strongly protested the tendencies of my poor tale, and by presenting it as an attack on the social order, they gave it an importance and a resonance it would not otherwise have achieved. A young author—a mere neophyte in the world of social ideas, one whose only literary and philosophical equipment consisted of a little imagination, a bit of courage, and a love of truth—was thus endowed with a very serious and weighty role. Sensitive to their charges, and almost grateful for the lessons those critics wanted him to learn, he quite objectively examined the indictments of his morality that were presented to the public; and thanks to this examination, carried out with no false pride, he gradually acquired some ideas—ideas that were little more than feelings at the beginning of his career but that are now basic principles.

During ten years of often painful but always sincere intellectual probing and the disturbing qualms and nagging doubts that accompanied it, during ten years of fleeing the role of pedagogue that some people attributed to me in an effort to make me ridiculous and of hating the imputation of pride and bad temper with which others pursued me in order to make me odious, I proceeded as well as my artistic talents allowed to analyze life in the hope of arriving at a synthesis; and during those ten years I managed to portray situations that have sometimes been recognized as realistic and plausible and characters that have often been acknowledged as accurately and faithfully drawn. Limiting myself to that work, I have tried much harder to arrive at my own beliefs than to destroy those of others, telling myself that if I were wrong, society would easily find voices powerful enough to counter my arguments and repair by their intelligent responses any damage my imprudent questions might cause. Many voices were indeed raised to warn the public against the dangerous writer, but as for the intelligent responses, both the public and the author are still waiting.

Long after having written the Preface to *Indiana* under the influence of a remnant of respect for society as it was constituted, I was still trying to resolve this insoluble problem: *How do we reconcile the needs of society with the happiness and dignity of individuals oppressed by that society without changing society itself?* Sympathetic to the victims and mingling his tears with theirs, trying not so much to excuse his characters' faults but to interpret them to his readers, the novelist—like a prudent lawyer who appeals on behalf of his clients to the mercy of the judges rather than to their severity—is the true advocate for the abstract beings who represent our passions and our suffering before the court of established law and the jury of public opinion. Beneath the frivolous exterior of his work there is an earnest purpose, one that he finds difficult to achieve because he is troubled at every step by those who accuse him of being too serious in his style and too superficial in his substance. I do not flatter myself that I have succeeded in this task, but I do know that my efforts were sincere; despite some hesitations caused by a conscience that was sometimes restrained by ignorance of its rights and sometimes stimulated by a heart thirsting for justice and truth, I went forward without straying too far from the path and without taking too many backward steps.

To describe all those internal conflicts would have been childish; it would have been too vain and self-important to speak so much about myself, so I refrained from doing so just as I refrained from touching on the points that were still unclear in my mind. Though conservatives found me too bold and radicals too timid, I must confess that in fact I had respect and sympathy for both the past and the future, and I had no peace of mind until I fully understood that the latter should not mean the violation and destruction of the former but its continuation and development.

After those ten years of apprenticeship—during which I was introduced to a world of broader ideas that were the result of the general philosophical progress taking place all around me, particularly in the minds of a few extraordinary men whose thoughts I explored quite assiduously, and during which I also observed carefully the sufferings of those around me—I have finally come to the conclusion that though I was right, because of my ignorance and inexperience, to hesitate to express definite views at the time I wrote *Indiana*, my present duty is to congratulate myself for having been as daring as I was, then and later: those audacities provoked bitter rebukes, but I would have been even more audacious if I had known how legitimate, honest, and holy my sentiments were.

Having now, on the eve of a reissue that will attract more attention than its previous reprints did, reread this first novel of my youth as objectively and severely as if it were the work of someone else—and being resolved not to retract anything, for one should never retract anything that was done or said in good faith, but also being determined to be the first to condemn myself if I should discover that my old ideas were mistaken or dangerous—I found instead that the feelings which dictated *Indiana* then are so completely in accord with my present feelings that if I were to tell the story now for the first time, I would do it the same way; and I have therefore changed nothing but some ungrammatical sentences and imprecise words. Many other such errors undoubtedly remain, and I unreservedly submit the *literary* merits of my work to the cavils of the critics; I admit that in that area they are much more competent than I am. Certainly I cannot deny that there are men of great talent working as journalists in the daily press, and I am happy to acknowledge it. What I do emphatically deny is that there are many moralists or philosophers to be found among those elegant stylists—and I say this though it may offend those who, from the heights of their morality and philosophy, have condemned me in the past and will do so again at the first opportunity in the future.

To repeat: I wrote *Indiana* because I had to. I was responding to a powerful instinct of outrage and rebellion put into my soul by God, who creates nothing that is not useful, even the most paltry of creatures, and who intervenes in the most trivial as well as the most significant events. But is the issue so trivial? It is the cause of half the human race—no, of the entire human race, because the unhappiness of woman entails the unhappiness of man, just as that of the slave entails that of the master, and that is what I tried to show in *Indiana*. Some said that I was pleading a personal cause—as if, even if that had been true, I were the only unfortunate person in an otherwise peaceful and happy universe! I heard enough cries of pain and sympathy answering mine to enable me to judge just how peaceful and happy the rest of the world was!

I do not think I have ever written anything for purely personal reasons; I have never felt it necessary to guard against doing so. Those who have read me without any preconceptions understand that I wrote *Indiana* out of deep and genuine feelings—not very carefully reasoned, it is true—about the barbaric injustice of the laws that still control a woman's existence within marriage, family, and society. I was not interested in writing a treatise on law but in waging war against public opinion, because that is what propels or postpones social change. The war will be a long and difficult one; but I am not the first, the only, or the last champion of such a noble cause, and I will fight for it as long as I have a breath of life.

The instinctive, unreasoned feelings that originally inspired me have been thought through and developed in response to the opposition and censure they gave rise to. Unjust and spiteful criticism taught me more than a quiet acceptance would have done, and for that, I thank those blundering judges who were responsible for my education. The motivations behind their judgments enlightened me and allowed me to enjoy a clear conscience. A sincere mind turns everything to its advantage, and that which would discourage mere vanity redoubles the fervor of real commitment.

The complaints that I have seriously and unemotionally addressed to most of the journalists of the day should not be seen as a protest against the right the French people have given them to criticize. It is clear that critics often do not fulfill—and often badly understand—their social role, but that the role itself is God-given and sacred cannot be denied unless one has no faith in progress and is an enemy of truth, a blasphemer of the future, and an unworthy child of France. Freedom to think, write, and speak—blessed conquest of the human spirit! What are the petty sufferings and ephemeral disturbances generated by errors or abuses compared to the infinite blessings in store for the world!

PART ONE

I

On a cool and rainy autumn night in a small château in Brie three people were gravely watching the wood burn in the fireplace and the hands of the clock move slowly around its face. Two of the silent figures seemed quite resigned to the vague, oppressive boredom, but the third showed signs of rebellion; he fidgeted on his chair, tried to stifle some plaintive yawns, and prodded the crackling logs with the fire tongs, clearly determined to do battle against the common enemy.

This person, much older than the other two, was Colonel Delmare, the head of the house; a retired soldier on half-pay, once handsome but now overweight, with a gray mustache and a harsh expression, he was an excellent master before whom everyone—wife, servants, horses, and dogs—trembled.

Evidently growing impatient at his unsuccessful efforts to break the silence, he finally rose from his seat and with a heavy tread began to pace the entire length of the room, making military about-faces at each end and never losing for a second either his erect, soldierly bearing or the air of perpetual self-satisfaction that is so typical of the model officer on parade.

But his days of glory, those heady days when the young Lieutenant Delmare had breathed the triumphant air of the camps, were over, and the pensioned officer, ignored by an ungrateful country, now found himself contending with a young and pretty wife, a comfortable manor house and its appurtenances, and a prosperous manufacturing business—all of which made him bad-tempered, especially on such a damp evening, for he was also rheumatic.

As the colonel paraded solemnly up and down his old Louis XIV drawing room, he would sometimes stop in front of a door surmounted by a fresco of nude cupids wreathing chains of flowers around well-mannered fawns and docile boars, or in front of a panel completely covered by convoluted carvings of capricious and complicated couplings that wearied the eye. But these momentary, vague distractions did not prevent him from carefully observing the two companions of his silent vigil each time he turned around, looking first at one and then at the other with that same watchful eye which had been guarding his wife, that precious and fragile treasure, for three years.

His wife, you must understand, was only nineteen years old, and if you had seen her—dwarfed by the mantel of that huge white marble fireplace adorned with burnished copper; slim, pale, sad, her hands resting on her lap; a young girl in the midst of that ancient household, next to that old husband; a budding flower forced to open in a gothic vase—you would have pitied Colonel Delmare's wife, and you might have pitied the colonel even more than his wife.

The third occupant of that lonely house was also sitting in the recess formed by that same mantel, at the other end of the blazing log. A man in the full, vigorous bloom of youth, his glowing cheeks and abundant golden hair and whiskers were a sharp contrast to the withered complexion, graying locks, and harsh features of the master of the house; but rough and stern as the latter's expression was, anyone—even the least "artistic" of people—would have preferred it to the young man's insipid blandness. The puffy face carved in relief on the sheet of iron lining the back of the fireplace, its eyes eternally fixed on the burning logs, was no more unchanging than that of this pink and blond character of our story doing the same thing. Aside from that, however, his well-formed figure, sharply defined brown eyebrows, smooth white forehead, clear and untroubled eyes, beautifully shaped hands, and severely correct hunting costume would probably have made any woman with an eighteenth-century sensibility find him a very attractive cavalier. But perhaps M. Delmare's young and timid wife had never yet really looked at a man, or perhaps there was no bond of sympathy between that woman who looked so frail and ill and that man who slept so soundly and had such a good appetite, because certainly the husband's tireless, hawklike eye never surprised a look, a breath, a flicker, between those two dissimilar people; and when he was finally certain that he had no cause for jealousy, he became even more unhappy than before, and abruptly plunged his hands into his pockets.

The only lively and alert face in the group was that of a beautiful hunting dog, noteworthy for her large body, powerful legs, foxlike muzzle, intelligent expression, and tawny, topaz-like eyes. At the moment, her head was resting on the knees of the seated man, and those eyes, so fiercely alive during the excitement of the chase, were fixed on her master with a kind of sympathetic sadness. He was clearly the object of all her instinctual love, which is sometimes so superior to the rational love of man, and when he would occasionally run his fingers through her silky, silvery fur, her eyes would begin to gleam with unmistakable pleasure while her long tail rhythmically swept the hearth and scattered the ashes over the marquetry floor.

This domestic scene, dimly lit by the hearthside fire, was worthy of a Rembrandt. Occasional flashes of brightness would illuminate the room and its occupants, slowly take on the reddish glow of the embers, then finally fade entirely away, leaving the vast space to darken proportionally, and every time M. Delmare would turn around and pass in front of the fire he seemed to appear and then almost immediately disappear like a ghost into the mysterious, shadowy depths. Sometimes the gilded borders of the oval frames decorated with wreaths, medallions, and inserts of wood would be illuminated, sometimes the furniture inlaid with ebony and copper, sometimes the uneven cornices of the wainscoting; but as each brand was extinguished and passed its task on to another, the objects that had been in the light would return to the shadows and others would emerge from the obscurity and take their place. With enough time, it would have been possible to take in every detail of the picture, from the console resting on three gilded tritons, to the painted ceilings that represented a sky studded with stars and clouds, to the heavy, long-tasselled, crimson damask hangings whose ample folds swayed in the flickering light and shimmered like satin.

The two people outlined in such bold relief in front of the fire looked almost as if they were afraid to disturb the fixity of the scene, as if they had become petrified, locked into place like the heroes of a fairy tale, and were terrified lest the slightest word or gesture bring disaster tumbling down upon them—and as if the grim-looking master, whose regular tread was all that broke either the shadows or the silence, were the sorcerer who held them under his spell.

The dog, having finally obtained from her master a smile, yielded to the magnetic influence man wields over the intelligent animals and gave a soft whine of timid affection as she raised herself with a liquid motion and gracefully placed her forepaws on her adored one's shoulders.

"Down, Ophelia, down!"

At the young man's stern reprimand, spoken in English, the abashed animal crept docilely over to Mme. Delmare, as if to beg for her protection. But Mme. Delmare remained lost in thought and merely allowed Ophelia's head to rest on her two white hands as they lay clasped on her knees, not even petting the animal.

"Has that dog made this room her permanent home?" growled the colonel, secretly pleased to have an excuse for a quarrel with which to pass the time. "Outside, Ophelia! Out to the kennel, you stupid animal!"

Anyone watching Mme. Delmare closely could have guessed the painful secret of her entire life from that perfectly ordinary and unimportant incident. An almost imperceptible shudder ran through her entire body, and her hands, which had been passively supporting the animal's head, suddenly tightened around the rough, hairy neck in a gesture meant to restrain and protect her.

M. Delmare, taking his hunting crop out of his jacket pocket, strode threateningly toward poor Ophelia, who closed her eyes, crouched at his feet, and whimpered in advance with hurt and fear.

Mme. Delmare became even more pale than before; breathing rapidly, she turned her large blue eyes on her husband and said, with an air of indescribable terror, "For pity's sake, monsieur, don't kill her!"

The colonel trembled at those few words, and his anger changed to embarrassment.

"I understand that you want to reproach me, madame," he said. "You've never forgiven me for having killed your spaniel in a burst of temper during a hunt. And a great loss he was, too, wasn't he? A dog that was forever rushing around and chasing the game—anyone would have lost patience with him! Besides, you never loved him so much as you did after he died. Before that you never paid any attention to him, but now he gives you a good excuse to accuse me—"

"Have I ever reproached you?" Mme. Delmare asked, with that courtesy we show those we love because we respect them, and those we do not love because we respect ourselves.

"I didn't say that you had," replied the colonel, in a tone half paternal and half marital, "but some women's tears are more scathing than other women's curses. *Morbleu*, madame, you know I don't like to see anyone weep."

"I don't think you've ever seen me weep."

"But I always see you with red eyes, which is even worse!"

During this conjugal conversation the young man had calmly risen from his seat and led Ophelia out of the room; when he returned, he lit a candle, placed it on the mantel, and once again sat down opposite Mme. Delmare.

The effect of that unimportant action on M. Delmare was immediate. As soon as the light of the candle, steadier and more uniform than that of the fire, had illuminated his wife's face, he noticed how weak and exhausted she seemed; the cheeks over which her long black hair fell were hollow, there were dark rings under her dull, inflamed eyes, and her whole being expressed an indescribable lassitude.

He made several more turns around the room, then brusquely returned to his wife and said, "How do you feel today, Indiana?" He spoke clumsily, like someone whose heart and temperament are rarely in agreement.

"About the same, thank you," she replied, with no sign of either surprise or resentment.

" 'About the same' is no answer—or rather, it's a woman's answer that doesn't mean either yes or no, good or bad."

"Then let's say that I'm neither sick nor well."

"Then I say that you're lying," he retorted with a return to his former roughness. "I know that you're not feeling well because you said so to Sir Ralph. Isn't that true? She did tell you that, didn't she, Monsieur Ralph?"

"She did," replied that phlegmatic person, paying no attention to Indiana's reproving look.

Just then a fourth person came into the room: Lelièvre, a former sergeant in M. Delmare's regiment and now the factotum of the household.

He spoke briefly to M. Delmare, explaining that he had reason to believe that for the past few nights thieves had managed to enter the property and steal some coal, and that he wanted to take a gun with him as he made his rounds before locking the gates.

M. Delmare, who saw the possibility of a martial adventure, immediately took his shotgun, gave another to Lelièvre, and started to leave the room.

"What!" Mme. Delmare exclaimed in terror. "Are you

going to kill some poor peasant because of a few sacks of coal?"

Irritated by her protest, M. Delmare answered, "I'll shoot like a dog any man I find prowling around my property at night, and if you knew the law, madame, you would know that it authorizes me to do just that."

"That's a terrible law," Indiana replied heatedly. Then, quickly subduing her fervor, she added more quietly, "And what about your rheumatism? It's raining, and if you go out this evening, you'll suffer for it tomorrow."

"You're just afraid that you'll have to take care of your old husband!" exclaimed Delmare, opening the door forcefully.

And he left the room, continuing to mutter about his age and his wife.

II

THE two people we have just described, Indiana Delmare and Sir Ralph, or, if you prefer, Mr. Rodolphe Brown, remained seated opposite each other, as silent and separate as if the husband were still there. The Englishman had no intention of justifying himself, and Mme. Delmare realized that she had no reason to blame him, for he had meant to help her by speaking as he had.

Finally forcing herself to break the silence, she scolded him mildly. "That wasn't right, my dear Ralph. I asked you not to repeat what I had carelessly let slip in a moment of pain, and Monsieur Delmare is the last person in the world I would have chosen to tell about my illness."

"I don't understand you, my dear," said Sir Ralph. "You're not well, yet you don't want to do anything about it. My only choice was to risk losing you or to tell your husband."

"Yes," Mme. Delmare replied with a sad smile, "and you decided to 'notify the authorities.'"

"You're wrong—yes, I'll say it again—you're wrong to speak so bitterly about the colonel. He's an honorable, worthy man."

"But who has said anything else, Sir Ralph?"

"Why, you yourself have, without meaning to. Your depression, your poor health, and as he said, even your red eyes—they all make it quite clear to everyone that you're not happy."

"Enough, Sir Ralph, you go too far! I've never given you permission to see so much."

"I know that I'm making you angry, but I can't help it. I'm clumsy, I don't know the subtleties of your language, and in many ways I'm not all that different from your husband. I understand as little as he does, in English or in French, about how to comfort a woman. Another man would have been able to make you understand, without words, what I've just said so awkwardly. He would have found a way to gain your confidence without your being aware of it, and he might even have been able to relieve your heavy heart, which becomes hard and distant as soon as I approach. This isn't the first time that I've noticed how much more important words are than ideas, particularly in France. For women especially . . ."

"Oh, you have a profound contempt for women, my dear Ralph, and since I'm a woman alone here with two men, I see I must resign myself to never being right!"

"Prove us wrong, my dear cousin, by getting better, by recovering your old gaiety and vivacity. Remember how it was on Bourbon Island—think of our delightful hideaway at Bernica and our happy childhood and our friendship, which is as old as you yourself are . . ."

"I also remember my father, " said Indiana sadly, putting her hand into Sir Ralph's.

They fell silent again.

"Indiana," Ralph said after a while, "happiness is always within our reach, and very often we only have to reach out our hand to grasp it. What do you want? You are comfortably well off, which is better than being rich, you have an excellent husband who loves you with all his heart, and—though I say it myself—you have a loyal and devoted friend."

Mme. Delmare pressed Sir Ralph's hand weakly, but she kept her head down and her misty eyes fixed on the magical effects produced by the flames.

Sir Ralph continued. "My dear friend, your depression is morbid. Everyone must endure some measure of disappointment or irritation. Look around, and you'll see many who envy you, and with good reason. . . . But people always want what they don't have."

I will spare you good Sir Ralph's many other commonplaces, spoken in a tone as monotonous and sluggish as his thoughts. He was not a stupid man, but he was completely out of his element; lacking neither common sense nor understanding, it was nevertheless, as he himself had acknowledged, completely beyond his ability to comfort a woman. With the best will in the world he was unable to ameliorate anyone else's unhappiness without making it worse, and because he was perfectly aware of his awkwardness, he seldom allowed himself to notice that his friends might be miserable lest he have to try to cope with that misery; he was now making an extraordinary effort to carry out what he considered the most painful obligation of friendship.

When he saw that Mme. Delmare had to force herself to listen to him, he stopped speaking, and once again there were no sounds but the thousand little songs of the crackling wood, the sorrowful murmur of the burning log expanding in the heat, the snapping of the bark as it crisped before bursting, and the faint phosphorescent explosions of the sapwood as it gave off its bluish flames. From time to time the noise of a baying dog would mingle with that of the whistling wind coming in through the cracks of the door and the rapping rain beating against the windows. It was one of the most depressing evenings Mme. Delmare had yet spent in her little manor house in Brie.

She also felt some vague presentiment weighing down her impressionable soul and making every nerve and fiber of her delicate being vibrate. Frail creatures live surrounded by terrors and omens, and Mme. Delmare had all the superstitions of a nervous, sickly Creole: certain night sounds, certain tricks of the moonlight, made her believe in certain specific events, certain impending misfortunes. Dreamy and melancholy as she was, the night seemed to speak a mysterious and fantastical language that she alone, through her fears and sufferings, could understand and translate.

"You'll say that I'm mad," she said, removing her hand from Sir Ralph's, "but I'm sure that some catastrophe is hovering over us. Someone is in great danger—most probably me. I tell you, Ralph, there is about to be a great change in my life, and I'm afraid." She added with a shudder, "I feel faint."

Her lips became as white as her cheeks. Sir Ralph—terrified not by her presentiments, which he felt were symptoms of mental exhaustion, but by her deadly pallor—tugged violently at the bell rope to summon help. No one came, and as Indiana became more and more feeble, Ralph became more and more alarmed; he carried her away from the fire, lay her down on a chaise longue, and began to run through the house calling the servants, looking for water and smelling salts, breaking all the bell ropes, losing himself in the maze of dark rooms, and clenching and unclenching his hands in a frenzy of self-contempt.

Finally it occurred to him to open the glass doors that gave onto the park and to shout alternately for Lelièvre and Noun, Mme. Delmare's Creole maid.

A few seconds later, Noun emerged from one of the darkest paths on the grounds and asked breathlessly if Mme. Delmare was worse than usual.

"Much worse," Sir Ralph replied.

Both of them went into the drawing room and tried everything they could think of to revive Mme. Delmare, one demonstrating an energetic but useless and clumsy zeal, the other all the gentle skill of a devoted woman friend.

Noun was Mme. Delmare's foster sister, and the two young women, who had been brought up together, loved each other dearly. Noun was tall and strong, vividly alive, full of the ardor and passion of her Creole blood, and strikingly beautiful in a way that far outshone the delicate, fragile charms of the pale Mme. Delmare; but their tender hearts and mutual affection eliminated every possibility of feminine rivalry.

When Mme. Delmare regained consciousness, she immediately noticed the expression on Noun's face, her damp, disheveled hair, her unmistakable agitation.

"Don't worry, my poor child," she said affectionately. "My illness is worse for you than for me. Why, Noun, you must take care of yourself. You cry and lose weight as if you weren't meant to live and be happy, but your future, my dear Noun, is so bright and rosy!"

Noun brought Mme. Delmare's hand to her lips and kissed it effusively, then looked wildly around the room and said, in a kind of hysteria, "My God, madame, do you know what Monsieur Delmare is doing in the park?"

"What Monsieur Delmare is doing . . . ?" Indiana repeated, immediately losing the bit of color that had returned to her cheeks. "Wait . . . I don't remember . . . you're frightening me! What is it?"

Her voice breaking, Noun replied, "He says there are thieves. He's making the rounds with Lelièvre, and they're both armed."

"Well?" said Indiana, as if anticipating some dreadful news.

"Well, madame," Noun continued, wringing her hands in anguish, "isn't it terrible to think they're going to kill someone?"

"Kill someone!" exclaimed Mme. Delmare, springing to her feet with the ready panic of a child frightened by its nurse's tales.

"Of course they'll kill him!" cried Noun, trying to stifle her sobs.

"Those two women are mad," thought Sir Ralph, who was watching this scene in utter bewilderment. "For that matter," he added, still to himself, "they all are."

"But why do you say that, Noun? Do you really think there are any thieves in the park?" Mme. Delmare asked.

"Oh, if it were only a question of thieves! But it might be some poor peasant just trying to pick up a bit of wood for his family."

"Yes, that certainly would be terrible! But it isn't very likely that someone would risk entering a walled property when it's so easy to steal wood from the forest of Fontainebleau, which is so close by. . . . Don't worry, I'm sure Monsieur Delmare won't find anyone in the park!"

But Noun was no longer paying attention. She was moving from the window to her mistress's chaise longue and back again, visibly straining to hear the slightest sound, and she seemed torn between the desire to run after M. Delmare and the wish to remain with her sick mistress.

Her anxiety seemed so strangely misplaced to Sir Ralph that he lost his usual self-control and grabbed her roughly by the arm, saying, "Have you gone completely out of your mind? Don't you see that you're upsetting your mistress and that your absurd fears are making her worse?"

Noun didn't even hear him. She had turned around to look at her mistress, whose whole body had begun to tremble, as if an electric shock had affected all her senses. At almost that same exact moment the report of a gun made the windows shake, and Noun dropped to her knees.

"What miserable nerves you women have!" cried Sir Ralph, exasperated by their emotions. "In a few minutes you'll be presented with a dead rabbit and then you'll laugh at yourselves."

"No, Ralph," said Mme. Delmare, walking firmly toward the door, "I tell you that human blood has been shed."

Noun shrieked, and fell to the floor in a faint.

Then they heard Lelièvre's voice calling out from one side of the park: "There he is! There he is! A good shot, Colonel, you've brought the thief down!"

Sir Ralph began to respond to the excitement and followed Mme. Delmare. A few minutes later, a blood-covered, seemingly lifeless man was brought to the colonnaded porch of the house.

"Not so much noise! Stop your screaming!" the colonel said with a kind of rough cheeriness to all the servants who had crowded around the wounded man. "It's not serious. My gun was only loaded with salt, and I'm not even sure that I hit him. He fell because he was frightened."

"But what about all this blood, monsieur?" Mme. Delmare asked reprovingly. "Is it his fear that's making it flow?"

"Why are you here, madame?" cried M. Delmare. "What are you doing here?"

"I'm here to repair the harm you've done, as is my duty, monsieur," she replied coldly.

And approaching the wounded man with a courage none of the others had as yet felt capable of, she held a light up to his face.

Instead of the common features and poor clothes they expected to see, they discovered an aristocratic-looking young man dressed in a fashionable hunting costume. He seemed to have only a minor wound in his head, but his torn clothes and deep faint indicated that he had had a serious fall.

"I should think so!" said Lelièvre, confirming their theory. "He fell about twenty feet. He was just putting his leg over the wall when the colonel took aim, and he must have gotten some grains of salt or some small shot in his right hand because he couldn't keep his hold. I actually saw the poor devil fall, and by the time he reached bottom, he was in no shape to think about running away!"

"It's hard to believe that such a well-dressed man would have any reason to steal," said one of the maids.

"And with his pockets full of money!" said another servant, who had unbuttoned the jacket of the supposed thief.

"It's all very strange," said the colonel, looking down with no little emotion at the man stretched out in front of him. "It isn't my fault if he's dead. Examine his hand, madame, and if you find even a particle of lead—"

"I prefer to believe you, monsieur," replied Mme. Delmare, who was carefully checking his neck arteries for a pulse with a self-possession and strength of purpose that surprised everyone. "He is certainly not dead," she added, "but he needs immediate attention. He doesn't look like a thief, and he may deserve our care—but even if he didn't deserve it, our duty as women is to give it to him in any case."

Whereupon Mme. Delmare had the wounded man carried into the billiard room, which was the closest. A mattress was placed over several chairs, and Indiana, helped by some of the women servants, cleaned and dressed the injured hand while

Sir Ralph, who had some knowledge of surgery, drew large quantities of blood.

Meanwhile the colonel found himself in the embarrassing position of a man who disapproves of his own behavior. Feeling that he had to justify himself to the others—or rather, to have them justify him to himself—he had remained outdoors with the servants, joining with them in the long, impassioned, and completely useless discussions that always follow upon any major event. Lelièvre described twenty times, in the most minute detail, the shot, the fall, and its consequences, while the colonel, surrounded by his servants, recovered his good humor—as he always did after he had given vent to his anger—and demanded to know what reason any man could have for climbing over the walls into another man's private property in the dark of night. Everyone agreed with the master, but the gardener quietly led him aside and assured him that the thief looked exactly like a young man who had recently settled in the area and whom he had seen talking to Mlle. Noun three days earlier at the Rubelles fair.

This information gave M. Delmare something new to think about, and a huge vein on his high, shiny forehead began to throb and swell—always a sign of an impending outburst.

"*Morbleu!*" he said, clenching his fists. "Madame Delmare seems to be very interested in this elegant young dandy who sneaks over the wall into my property!"

White, and shaking with fury, he entered the billiard room.

III

"You needn't worry, monsieur," Indiana said to him. "The man you killed will be quite well in a few days—or at least we hope so, though he still can't speak."

"That's not why I've come, madame," said the colonel, his voice full of suppressed passion. "I want to know who this interesting patient is, and why he was so absentminded that he mistook the wall of my park for the entrance to my house."

"I know nothing about that," Mme. Delmare replied, with an air of such cold and dignified pride that her formidable husband was left speechless for a moment.

But his astonishment was soon overcome by his jealous suspicions, and he returned to the charge. "I will find out, madame, you can be quite sure that I will find out," he said softly, and since Mme. Delmare pretended to be unaware of his anger and continued to attend to the wounded man, he turned on his heel and left the room so as not to explode in front of the servants.

He called back the gardener and asked him, "What's the name of the man you say looks like our prowler?"

"Monsieur de Ramière. He's just bought the little English-style house that used to belong to Monsieur de Cercy."

"What kind of man is he? A nobleman? A dandy? Is he handsome?"

"Oh, very handsome, and I think he's a nobleman."

"That must be who he is—Monsieur de Ramière!" the colonel said emphatically. "Tell me, Louis," he added, lowering his voice, "have you ever seen that fop around here before?"

Looking embarrassed, Louis replied, "Well, monsieur, last night—that is, I don't know for sure if it was a dandy, but it was certainly a man . . ."

"You saw him?"

"As clearly as I see you. He was right under the windows of the orangery."

"And you didn't go after him with your shovel?"

"Monsieur, I was just about to do that when I saw a woman in white leave the orangery and go to meet him. So I thought, 'Maybe Monsieur and Madame have decided to take a walk before dawn,' and I went back to bed. But this morning I heard Lelièvre talking about finding a thief's tracks in the park, and I said to myself, 'There's something strange going on.'"

"Why didn't you tell me about it immediately, you fool?"

"Because, monsieur, there are some things in life that are very . . . delicate."

"I see—you thought you could use your own judgment. You're an idiot, and if you ever dare do anything like that again, I'll cut off your ears! I know perfectly well who this thief is, and what he's looking for in my garden. I've only asked you these questions so I can check on how carefully you guard your orangery. Remember that I have some rare plants that Madame is very attached to, and that there are collectors insane enough to even steal from their neighbors' hothouses! But you were right—it was Madame Delmare and me you saw last night."

And the poor colonel walked away, more tormented and irascible than before, and leaving his gardener quite unconvinced that there were men who were such fanatical horticulturists that they would risk a bullet to steal a shoot or a cutting.

Monsieur Delmare returned to the billiard room. Ignoring the faint signs of life the wounded man was finally displaying, he went directly to his jacket, which was lying on a chair, and prepared to search the pockets.

Just then the invalid put out his hand and said weakly, "You want to know who I am, monsieur, but that's not important right now. I'll tell you when we're alone, but until then, please spare me the embarrassment of having to identify myself while I'm in such a ridiculous and disagreeable situation."

"I'm sorry you feel that way, but I assure you I don't much care!" the colonel responded sharply. "However, since I assume we'll see each other again, and alone, I agree to postpone our acquaintance until then. Meanwhile, please tell me where I should have you taken."

"The inn of the closest village, please."

"But Monsieur is in no condition to be moved!" Mme. Delmare interjected. "Is he, Ralph?"

"You're much too concerned with this gentlemen's condition, madame!" the colonel exclaimed. "Leave the room," he said, turning to the servants. "Monsieur is better, and he's strong enough now to explain what he's doing here."

"Yes, monsieur, I am," the wounded man said, "and I would appreciate it if everyone who's been good enough to help me would remain to hear my explanation. It's important to you to understand my behavior, and equally important to me that I not be taken for something I'm not. So please listen to the reasons for what I did.

"You've managed to establish, monsieur, by using very simple means known only to yourself, a factory that is superior in both its methods and its products to any other factory of its kind. My brother has a similar establishment in the Midi, but his operating expenses are enormous and his enterprise is about to fail. I learned about how successful you have been, and I determined to ask your advice, which I was sure you would be generous enough to give me because my brother's product is completely different from yours, and nothing you might tell me could affect your own business. But the gate of your English garden was shut in my face, and when I asked to speak to you, I was told you would under no circumstances ever allow me even to set foot in your establishment. Disheartened by such a rude rebuff, I resolved to save my brother's life and honor even at the risk of my own, so I climbed the wall of your premises at night with the intention of entering the factory and examining the machinery. I had decided to hide in a corner, bribe the workmen, get at your secrets in any way I could—in other words, to help an honest man without doing you any harm.

"That was my crime, and now, monsieur, if you feel that you haven't already taken sufficient revenge, I'm ready to offer you additional satisfaction as soon as I'm strong enough. Indeed, I may demand satisfaction myself."

"I think we can consider ourselves quits, monsieur," said the colonel, half-relieved of a great anxiety. "All of you have heard this gentleman's explanation, and you are my witnesses when I say that I feel more than adequately avenged, supposing any revenge to have been necessary at all. Now leave us so we can discuss my thriving business operations."

The servants, the only ones to be deceived by this reconciliation, left, but the wounded man, exhausted by his long speech, was unable to appreciate the tone of the colonel's last words: he lost consciousness for the second time and fell back into Mme. Delmare's arms. She leaned over him, not deigning to notice her husband's anger, while at the same time the colonel and Sir Ralph—the former livid and with a face distorted by anger and the latter as stolid and vacuous-looking as ever—exchanged glances and silently questioned each other.

M. Delmare's feelings were quite clear, and it wasn't necessary for him to say a word to make himself understood. Nevertheless, he took Sir Ralph aside and said, "My friend, this is a very carefully constructed plot, and though I'm delighted, perfectly delighted, that the young man's quick thinking enabled him to protect my honor in front of my servants, I assure you he will pay dearly for his offense. And that woman who nurses him and pretends not to know him—ah, how true it is that all those creatures are instinctively cunning!"

Dumbfounded, Sir Ralph paced methodically up and down the room three times. At his first turn, he concluded, *unlikely*; at the second, *impossible*; at the third, *proven*. Then, his expression glacial, he returned to the colonel and pointed to Noun, who was standing behind the injured man with haggard eyes and ashen cheeks, wringing her hands, immobilized by confusion, fear, and despair.

A real discovery is accompanied by such an immediate, powerful, and total recognition of its truth that the colonel was more impressed by Sir Ralph's emphatic gesture than he would have been by the most skillful eloquence. Of course Sir Ralph had had more than one clue to put him on the right scent. For instance, he remembered that when he had gone outside to call Noun, she had come from the park with wet hair and muddy shoes, which indicated a whimsical but unlikely notion to walk in the rain; he had hardly been aware of those details at the time because he was so concerned about the unconscious Mme. Delmare, but they now came back to him. And then there was her bizarre behavior when she was attending her mistress—her uncontrollable agitation, her anguished cry at the sound of the shot . . .

M. Delmare did not need all those clues. More acute because he had more at stake in the matter, he had only to look at Noun's face to see that she was the guilty one; but even so, he became more and more displeased by his wife's attentive care of the hero of this amorous exploit.

"Indiana," he said, "go to bed now. It's late and you're not well. Noun will stay with this gentleman tonight, and tomorrow, if he's well enough, we'll make arrangements to have him taken home."

There was nothing Mme. Delmare could say in the face of this concession. Quite capable of standing firm against her husband's violence, she was defenseless against his softer moods, so after asking Sir Ralph to remain a little longer with the sick man, she retired to her room.

The colonel had his reasons for arranging matters this way. An hour later, when everyone had gone to bed and the house was quiet, he silently entered the room in which M. de Ramière lay, hid behind a curtain, and was soon completely convinced by the conversation between the young man and the maid that they were indeed involved in a love affair. The young Creole's rather unusual beauty had created a sensation at the country dances in the neighborhood: the first families of the province had paid her homage, and more than one handsome officer at the Melun garrison had put himself out to please her; but Noun was in love for the first time and interested in only one man's attentions, those of M. de Ramière.

Since Colonel Delmare did not have the slightest desire to follow the development of their liaison, he left as soon as he was sure that his wife had had no part in this operatic intrigue. Still, he had heard enough to understand that there was a difference between the love of poor Noun, who was throwing herself into the affair with all the unrestrained fervor of her passionate nature, and that of the proper, well-born young man, who was indulging his impulse today but reserving the right to recover his reason tomorrow.

When Mme. Delmare woke up, she found Noun beside her bed, sad and distraught. But since she had believed M. de Ramière's explanations—especially because other people had already tried to discover the secrets of her husband's factory—she attributed Noun's confusion to the excitement and fatigue of the previous night; and Noun herself was reassured when she saw how calmly the colonel entered his wife's room and began to discuss what had happened as if it were a perfectly natural occurrence.

Sir Ralph had checked the patient's condition early in the morning. Though the fall had been a painful one, there had been no serious consequences. The wound in his hand had already closed, and he had wanted to be taken immediately to Melun. He had also distributed the contents of his purse to the servants, asking them not to talk about what had happened lest the adventure alarm his mother, who lived close by, so the story spread slowly and in several different versions; and meanwhile the colonel was able to verify that M. de Ramière's brother did indeed have a factory, which lent further support to the story the prowler had so happily improvised. Both the colonel and Sir Ralph had the delicacy to keep Noun's secret, without even letting her know that they knew it, and the Delmare family soon forgot the entire incident.

IV

You may find it hard to believe that M. Raymon de Ramière, a young man of scintillating wit, many talents, and a multitude of estimable qualities, a young man accustomed to great success in both the social life of the drawing room and the perfumed dalliance of the boudoir, could have entertained the idea of a serious relationship with a young maid in the household of a minor manufacturer in Brie and be neither a fool nor a libertine. Yet he was neither. He was perfectly aware of the advantages of his birth, and he had many high moral principles; but his strong passions often overwhelmed those principles and made him unable to think rationally or behave in accordance with his conscience, so he often did wrong without being aware of it, and his past experience never foreshadowed the future.

Unfortunately, the most important element of his character was not his principles—which were shared by many other amateur philosophers and which did not save him from inconsistencies any more than they did the others—but his passions, which his principles were unable to control. And that was what set him apart from everyone else in his corrupt society, for it is difficult to be different without being ridiculous, yet Raymon was often guilty without being despised and eccentric without being shocking—and he was sometimes even able to arouse the sympathy of those who had the most reason to complain about him! There *are* men who are spoiled that way by all who know them, often because of nothing more than a handsome face and a charming manner, but we do not presume to judge M. de Ramière so severely, or to draw his portrait before having shown him in action; at this point we are merely examining him from afar, like the crowds of people who pass him in the street.

M. de Ramière was attracted to the dark-eyed young Creole who had aroused the admiration of the whole province at the

Rubelles fair, but merely attracted and nothing more. He had probably first approached her because he was otherwise unoccupied, and his success had then whetted his desire. He had received more than he had asked for, and on the day when he triumphed over that easily conquered heart he returned home, frightened by his victory, and said to himself, "If only she doesn't fall in love with me!"

It wasn't until after he had accepted the ultimate proof of her love that he began to suspect the existence of that love. He was sorry, but it was too late; he could either allow the future to bring what it might or retreat like a coward into the past. He did not hesitate for a minute; he allowed himself to be loved, loved in return out of gratitude, scaled the walls of the Delmare property because he reveled in danger, suffered a serious fall because of his own clumsiness, and was so touched by the grief of his beautiful young mistress that he felt quite justified in continuing to dig ever deeper the pit into which she would inevitably fall.

As soon as he had recovered, winter had no icy storms, night no danger, remorse no stings that could keep him from crossing a corner of the forest to meet the young Creole, swear to her that he had never loved anyone else, insist that he preferred her to all the society women in the world, and repeat the thousand other exaggerations that poor, innocent young girls will always take for the truth.

In January, Mme. Delmare went to Paris with her husband, and Sir Ralph Brown, their worthy neighbor, returned to his own estate; Noun, who had been left behind to manage her master's country house, thus had more freedom to leave the grounds. This was unfortunate, because the ease with which she could now meet her lover meant that her ephemeral happiness would come to an end even sooner than it would have otherwise. The poetry of the forest—the elaborate traceries of frost on the branches, the magical effects of the moonlight, the mysterious little gate, the furtive dawn departures when Noun's tiny feet would leave their footprints in the snow as she walked him back to that gate, all the romantic accessories of their love affair—had prolonged M. de Ramière's infatuation. Noun in a white robe and with her black hair left loose was a great lady, a queen, a fairy; seeing her emerge from that red-brick castle, a square, squat, semi-feudal structure dating back to the early eighteenth century, he could easily imagine her as a medieval chatelaine, and in the summerhouse filled

with rare flowers, where she made him lose himself in the seductions of youth and passion, he forgot everything that he
would have to remember later.

But Noun coming to his home wearing a white apron and a
madras bandanna coquettishly arranged in the fashion of her
country, disdaining precautions and braving danger in her
turn—why, that Noun was nothing more than a maid, and
worse, a maid who worked for a beautiful woman, which always makes the maid look like second best.

Yet Noun was quite beautiful, and that was exactly the way
she had been dressed the first time he had seen her at that village dance, when he had forced his way through the crowd and
enjoyed the petty triumph of carrying her off from a score of
rivals. Noun would remind him tenderly of that day—unaware, poor child, that Raymon's love did not go back that far,
and that what had been for her a day of pride had been for him
only a day of satisfied vanity. And the courage with which she
sacrificed her reputation to him, a courage that should have
made him love her more, actually displeased him. If it were
the wife of a peer of France running such risks, that would indeed be a priceless conquest—but a lady's maid? What is
courage in one is nothing but presumption in the other. In the
first case, a world of jealous rivals envies you; in the second, a
rabble of scandalized servants condemns you. The aristocrat
sacrifices to you her twenty previous lovers, the maid only the
husband she might have had.

Why are you surprised? Raymon was a worldly, fashionable man with refined tastes and poetic passions. For him, a
working-class girl was not a lady, and it was only Noun's unusual beauty, combined with the sentiments aroused by a day
of popular merrymaking, that had entranced him. None of
this was his fault. He had been brought up to take his destined place in society; all his thoughts had been directed to
high ends, all his faculties shaped for princely good fortune,
and it was only despite himself that the fire in his blood had
led him to such a bourgeois amour. He had done everything
possible to prolong his pleasure, but now it was over, and he
wondered what he should do next. Extravagantly generous
ideas had gone through his mind; on the days when he was
most in love with his mistress he had even thought of raising
her to his level and making her his wife. . . . Yes, really! He
had thought about it; but love, which makes all things possible, was growing weaker, fading away together with the risks

of the adventure and the zest of the intrigue. There would be no marriage, and I assure you that Raymon reasoned it out very carefully and with the best interests of his mistress at heart.

If he had really loved her, he could have sacrificed his future, his family, his reputation, and still been happy with her—thus making her happy, for love is as much a bond as marriage. But since his passion had cooled, what kind of future could he give her? Should he marry her only to show her day after day an unhappy face, an unfeeling heart, an ungratified soul? Should he marry her to make her hateful to his family, contemptible to his friends, ridiculous to his servants? To give her a social position in which she would feel out of place and die of humiliation? To overwhelm her with guilt by forcing her to become aware of the difficulties she had brought upon the man she loved?

No, you will certainly agree with him that it was impossible, that it would not have been a generous thing to do, that a man does not quarrel with society in that way, and that such heroic virtue is like that of Don Quixote breaking his lance against a windmill: it indicates a courage strong as steel but capable of being destroyed by a breath of wind, and an old-fashioned notion of chivalry admired in another age but despised in our own.

After having considered all these factors, M. de Ramière understood that it would be best to break his unhappy bonds. Noun's visits were becoming awkward. His mother, who had gone to Paris for the winter, would soon hear about this little scandal; she was already surprised at his frequent visits to their country house at Cercy and the many weeks he spent there, and though he had claimed he was occupied with an important piece of work that required him to be away from the distractions of the city, that excuse was beginning to wear thin. It hurt Raymon to lie to such a good mother and deprive her of his company, so—how shall I say it?—he left Cercy and did not return.

Noun wept, waited, and even, after a long time had gone by, dared to write him. Poor girl—that was the last straw! A letter from a lady's maid! And yet she had taken the good paper and the perfumed wax from Mme. Delmare's desk, and the style from her heart. . . . But her spelling! Are you aware that a syllable more or less either adds to or detracts from the sentiment? Unfortunately, the poor half-savage girl from Bourbon was even unaware that there were rules of grammar. She was sure that she wrote and spoke as well as her mistress, and when she saw that Raymon didn't return, she thought, "And yet, my letter was the kind that should have brought him back to me."

Raymon had lacked the courage to read the letter through to the end. It might have been a masterpiece of naive and charming passion; Saint-Bernardin's Virginia might not have written a more delightful one to Paul after she had left her native land. But M. de Ramière, afraid it might make him blush in shame, quickly threw it into the fire. But again, why are you surprised? His education had prejudiced him, and self-love is a part of love just as self-interest is a part of friendship.

M. de Ramière's absence had been noticed by the society he frequented, which says much for him in this world in which all men more or less resemble one another. It is possible to be intelligent and nevertheless enjoy society, just as one may despise it and still be a fool. Raymon liked it, and he was right to do so; he was popular and sought after, and all those people who generally wore masks of indifference or mockery looked at him attentively and with pleasure. Unhappy people may be misanthropic, but those who are liked are rarely ungrateful; or at least Raymon was not. He appreciated every sign of interest, he was proud of having many friends, and he enjoyed having everyone think well of him.

He had been an unqualified success in this society of absolutely inflexible prejudices; even his faults had found favor, and when he tried to understand the reason for the universal affection he enjoyed, he found it in himself: in his desire to obtain it, his joy at doing so, and the inexhaustible good will he felt for others.

He also owed it to his mother, whose superior intelligence, delightful conversation, and personal virtues made her an exceptional woman. It was to her that he owed those excellent principles that always brought him back to the right path and kept him, despite the impetuous impulses of a twenty-five-year-old man, from ever forfeiting public approval. That same public also treated him more indulgently than it did others because of his mother's skill in finding excuses for him even while she was criticizing him—in commanding indulgence for him while she seemed to be begging for it. She was one of those women who have lived through so many different eras that their minds have become as flexible as the fates to which they have adapted, who have been enriched by the experience of misfortune, who have escaped the scaffolds of '93, the vices of the Directory, the vanities of the Empire, and the schisms of the Restoration:* rare women, whose type is dying out. . . .

Raymon reappeared in society at a ball given by the Spanish ambassador.

"There's Monsieur de Ramière, if I'm not mistaken," said a pretty woman to her neighbor.

"He's like a comet that appears at irregular intervals," was the response. "It's been centuries since anyone has heard anything about that handsome young man."

The woman who said that was a middle-aged foreigner from Sicily.

Her companion blushed as she replied in turn, "He *is* very handsome, isn't he?"

"And quite charming, I assure you," said the Sicilian.

"You must be talking about the dark-eyed Raymon, hero of all our drawing rooms," said a good-looking colonel of the guard.

"He has a face that would tempt an artist's pencil," the young woman responded.

"And an ungovernable face as well, which may please you even more," said the colonel.

The young woman was his wife.

"Why do you say an ungovernable face?" asked the Sicilian woman.

"Because, madame, it is full of southern passions, worthy of the brilliant sun of Palermo."

Two or three young women leaned their flower-bedecked heads closer to hear what the colonel was saying.

"He was a lot of competition for the garrison this year," he continued. "The rest of us will have to pick a quarrel with him in order to get rid of him."

---

*scaffolds of '93: a reference to the mass guillotining during the Reign of Terror (1793–94); *the Directory*: the government that followed the coup d'etat which ended the Terror and which was notable for its corruption and intrigue (1794–95); *the Empire*: the period of Napoleon and his grandiose dreams of glory (as First Consul, 1795–1804; as Emperor, 1804–14); *the Restoration*: the return (with Louis XVIII) of the Bourbon monarchy after Napoleon's defeat; marked by bitter enmity between political moderates and ultraconservatives (1814–30).

"I don't care if he's another Lovelace,"* said a sharp-faced young woman. "I hate people everyone else loves."

The ultrasophisticated countess waited until the colonel had walked away, then tapped Mademoiselle de Nangy's fingers with her fan and said, "You shouldn't speak that way. You people here don't understand how to appreciate a man who wants to be liked."

"Do you think that all a man has to do is want it?" asked the young woman with the sardonic eyes.

"Mademoiselle," said the colonel, returning to ask her to dance, "be careful that the handsome Raymon doesn't hear you!"

Mlle. de Nangy began to laugh, but for the rest of the evening, no one in her group of pretty young women dared mention the name of M. de Ramière again.

*Lovelace: a fictional young nobleman who expends much energy plotting and carrying out the seduction of the virtuous heroine in *Clarissa*, the eighteenth-century epistolary novel by British author Samuel Richardson; the name is used as a synonym for a womanizer.

V

M. DE RAMIÈRE was neither bored nor repelled by what he saw as he wound his way through the elaborately dressed gathering.

What he felt, now that he had returned to his own world, was regret—even shame—for having allowed his misplaced affections to suggest so many mad ideas. Looking at the dazzling women, listening to their spirited and sophisticated conversation, hearing them being praised, he felt their almost royal dress and their elegant and witty speech as so many unspoken reproaches for having nearly betrayed his proper destiny. In addition to this vague unease, however, he also felt genuine remorse, because he always meant well and never intended to do anyone any harm; a woman's tears could break his heart, nearly impervious though it was.

Everyone agreed that the honors of the evening belonged to a young woman whose name no one knew, and who attracted everyone's attention because she had not previously appeared in society. Actually, the simplicity of her dress would itself have been enough to set her apart from the other women, all adorned with their diamonds and feathers and flowers. Her only jewelry consisted of the strands of pearls woven through her black hair; their pale, satiny color harmonized with her white crepe dress and her bare shoulders, and because the warm rooms had brought the faintest blush of pink to her face, she looked like a Bengal rose blooming in the snow. Small, delicate, slender, she had an ethereal beauty that flourished in the candlelight of a drawing room but would be extinguished by a ray of sunlight. Dancing, she was so light that a breath might have blown her away, but it was a lifeless, joyless lightness; seated, she curved forward, as if her upper body was too weak to support itself; speaking, her words were accompanied by a sad smile. Tales of fantasy were fashionable at that time, so the experts in the genre compared the young woman to an enchanting, magical apparition that would fade and disappear like a dream at the dawn's first light.

Meanwhile all the men wanted to dance with her.

"Hurry," said one of the more romantic of the dandies to a friend. "The cock will soon crow, and your partner's feet are barely touching the floor even now. In a little while you won't be able to feel her hand in yours!"

"Look at the contrast between Monsieur de Ramière's strong, dark features and those of that pale, delicate young woman," said one of the more "artistic" guests to her neighbor. "Doesn't the *strength* of the one bring out the *fragility* of the other?"

"She's the daughter of that old fool Carvajal, who was exiled as a Josephino* and died a ruined man on Bourbon Island," said a woman who knew everyone and served as a source of genealogical information at every social gathering. "I think this lovely exotic flower made a foolish marriage, but her aunt is in favor at Court."

Raymon had managed to get close to the beautiful stranger. Whenever he had been able to catch a glimpse of her he had been overcome by a strange emotion. He was sure he knew that wan, sad face—perhaps only from his dreams, but he had definitely seen her before, and he looked at her with the pleasure we all feel when we see a delightful vision we thought we had lost forever. But the object of his attention was disturbed by it; awkward and timid, like someone unused to society, she was embarrassed rather than pleased by her success, and Raymon left her to circle the room, looking for someone who could identify her.

When he finally learned that she was Mme. Delmare, he returned and asked her to dance. "You don't remember me," he said to her as soon as they were alone, "but I have not been able to forget you, madame. I saw you for only a second, and that through a haze, but in that second you seemed so good, so kind—"

Mme. Delmare started, then said quickly, "Oh, yes, monsieur, I do remember you! I recognized you, too."

Then she blushed, afraid she had said something improper, and looked around to see if anyone had heard her. Her diffi-

---

Josephino: name given to partisans of Napoleon's brother Joseph Bonaparte, whom Napoleon first named King of Naples (1806–1808) and then King of Spain (1808–13): many of his backers either chose to go or were sent into exile after Napoleon's defeat.

dence added to her charm, and Raymon found himself deeply moved by the sweet, slightly husky tone of her Creole voice—a voice that seemed made to pray or to bless.

"I was afraid I would never have an opportunity to thank you," he said. "I couldn't very well call on you, and I knew that you rarely went into society. I was also afraid that by approaching you I would be coming into contact with Monsieur Delmare, and our previous relations would make that unpleasant for both of us. I'm so happy for this chance to express my deepest, warmest gratitude!"

"I would like it more if Monsieur Delmare could share in your gratitude," she said. "If you knew him better, you would understand that he is as kind as he is brusque, and you would forgive him for having attacked you because you would know that his heart certainly bled more than your wound."

"Say no more about Monsieur Delmare, madame. I forgive him with all my heart. I was wrong to do what I did—he merely defended himself, and I must forget, not forgive. But you, madame, you who cared for me with such delicacy and generosity—I want to remember for the rest of my life your treatment of me, the purity of your expression, your angelic gentleness, your hands that poured balm on my wounds and that I wasn't able to kiss . . ."

As he spoke, Raymon was holding Mme. Delmare's hand so he could partner her in the contredance, and he pressed it lightly; all the young woman's blood rushed to her heart.

When he led her back to her seat, Mme. de Carvajal was not there, and many of the guests had already left the ball. Raymon sat down beside Mme. Delmare with that easy manner which comes from a fair amount of experience in affairs of the heart. We are awkward with women because of the violence of our desires, the headlong rush of our love; the man who is more practiced in such feelings is often more eager to please than to love. And yet that simple, unspoiled woman did move M. de Ramière more deeply than he had ever been moved before. . . . Perhaps he owed the emotion to the memory of the night he had spent in her house, but whatever the reason, it was at least true that the words from his mouth were not false to the feelings of his heart.

But it was equally true that the habits acquired with other women allowed him to speak with a power of persuasion that completely beguiled the inexperienced Indiana; she believed every word as if it had been invented for her alone.

In general—and most women know this—the more wittily a man speaks of love the less in love he truly is. Raymon was an exception; he expressed his passion skillfully and felt it fervently. It was not his passion, however, that made him eloquent, but his eloquence that made him passionate. When he was attracted to a woman, he became eloquent in order to woo her and fell in love with her while wooing. It was exactly what happens to lawyers and preachers, whose efforts make the sweat of their labors seem like the zealous tears of their convictions. Though he sometimes met women wise enough to mistrust his ardent declarations, there had been many follies committed in the name of love: he had run away with a young girl of good family; he had compromised women of very high rank; he had fought three scandalous duels; he had indiscreetly exposed his unruly heart and delirious senses to the throngs at a great social event and to a whole theater full of spectators. A man who can do all that without fear of being ridiculous or despised, and who succeeds in being neither the one nor the other, is beyond reach; he can dare anything and hope for everything, and even astute women with strong powers of resistance yielded to the illusion that Raymon was madly and uncontrollably in love whenever he spoke of being in love at all. A man who is a fool for love is a rare exception in society, and one that women appreciate.

I do not know how he arranged it, but when he escorted Mme. de Carvajal and Mme. Delmare to their carriage he managed to bring Indiana's tiny hand to his lips. Despite the fact that she was nineteen years old and came from a tropical climate—for nineteen years in Bourbon Island is the equivalent of twenty-five in our country—her fingers had never before felt a man's warm, furtive breath.

Ill and nervous as she was, the kiss made her cry out, and she had to be helped into the carriage. Raymon had never met a person with such a delicately balanced sensitivity. Noun, the Creole, was strong and healthy, and Parisian women do not faint when their hands are kissed.

"If I see her again," he thought as he walked away, "she'll make me lose my head."

By the next morning he had completely forgotten Noun; the only thing he remembered about her was that she was somehow connected to Mme. Delmare. All his thoughts and dreams were about the wan-faced Indiana, and whenever Raymon suspected he was falling in love, he looked for distractions—not to stifle his budding passion but to smother his reason, which would urge him to weigh the consequences. His temperament was a passionate one, and it was with passion that he pursued the object of his desire; he was no more able to extinguish the fires within him than he was able to rekindle them once he felt them begin to dim and disappear.

He managed that morning to learn that M. Delmare had gone to Brussels on a business trip and left his wife with Mme. de Carvajal, whom he did not much like, but who was Mme. Delmare's only relative. Delmare himself was nothing but a soldier risen from the ranks; his family was poor and obscure, and he must have been quite ashamed of them because he never stopped saying that he was *not* ashamed of them. But despite the fact that he was always blaming his wife for her scorn of his background, a scorn she had never felt, he was aware that he should not make her live on intimate terms with his uneducated relatives. Besides, although he did not care for Mme. de Carvajal, he had his reasons for treating her with great deference.

Mme. de Carvajal was descended from a noble Spanish family and was one of those women who could not bear to be of little importance in the world. When Napoleon had ruled Europe, she had burned incense to his glory, and later, with her husband and brother-in-law, she had embraced the party of the Josephinos; but her husband lost his life when that short-lived dynasty imposed by Napoleon fell, and her brother-in-law, Indiana's father, sought refuge in the French colonies. At that point Mme. de Carvajal, a clever, energetic woman, went to live in Paris, where thanks to some fortunate speculations on the stock market, she was able to rebuild her fortune on the ruins of her former splendor. In addition, by virtue of her shrewdness, capacity for intrigue, and piety, she had also achieved some measure of favor and influence at Court; and her salon, while not brilliant, was one of the most respected of those under the protection of the Civil List.

When Indiana, married to Colonel Delmare, arrived in France after the death of her father, Mme. de Carvajal was not enthusiastic about having to acknowledge such an undistinguished man as a member of her family; but when she saw M. Delmare prospering, thanks to his industriousness, common sense, and commercial flair, she decided that those qualities were worth a dowry, and for Indiana's sake, she therefore bought for them the small manor house of Lagny and the factory that was part of it.

At the end of two years, thanks to Delmare's specialized knowledge and the financial help of Sir Ralph Brown, who was his wife's cousin, the business had prospered and the colonel was beginning to pay off his debts. Since in Mme. de Carvajal's eyes money was the supreme good, this success made her look favorably on Indiana, whom she promised to make her heir. Totally indifferent to that, Indiana was considerate of and affectionate to her aunt out of gratitude, not self-interest; but the colonel's behavior was motivated at least as much by the latter as by the former, and he forced himself to endure attacks on some of his most deeply held ideas. A man of definite political principles who never listened to reason where the glory of his old emperor was concerned, and who defended his feelings with the obstinacy of a sixty-year-old child, it took all his patience and self-control to keep from exploding in Mme. de Carvajal's salon, where no one did anything but praise the Restoration. What poor Delmare suffered there at the hands of half a dozen old women is beyond description, and his irritation with them was at least partly responsible for the bad humor with which he often treated his wife.

Having explained all that, let us return to M. de Ramière. At the end of three days, after diligently pursuing every means of acquiring information about the family, he had learned all these facts and decided that the best way to see Indiana would be under the protective wing of Mme. de Carvajal. On the evening of the third day, he paid a call on her.

He found only four or five odd-looking elderly people playing the Spanish card game *reversi*, and two or three innocuous young men who were as insignificant as it is possible to be with sixteen quarterings of noble blood. Indiana was bent over her aunt's embroidery frame, patiently filling in a portion of the background of her work and apparently quite absorbed by the mechanical occupation—and perhaps also pleased to use it as an escape from the tedious chatter of her neighbors. Behind the veil of long black hair that fell over the flowers of her embroidery, she might even have been reliving the fleeting emotions of that moment in which something new had been introduced into her life. When the servant announced the arrival of several newcomers and made it necessary for her to rise, she did so mechanically, for she had paid no attention to the names; and she had barely lifted her eyes from her embroidery before the sound of a voice went through her like an electric shock, forcing her to lean on her worktable to keep from falling.

VI

RAYMON had not expected the drawing room to be so quiet—so sparsely populated by such silent guests—and he realized it would be impossible to say a word that could not be heard anywhere in the room. The card-playing dowagers seemed to be there for no other reason but to inhibit any impulse the younger people might have to speak freely among themselves, and Raymon imagined he could see on their stern faces the secret satisfaction of the old when they are able to take revenge against the young by keeping them from enjoying themselves. He had hoped to be able to talk to Indiana more easily and intimately than at the ball, but though it was just the opposite, the unforeseen difficulty only made his desire more intense, his glances more passionate, his conversation— seemingly general but in fact directed to Mme. Delmare alone —more scintillating. The poor child was completely unfamiliar with such tactics; she couldn't resist because she wasn't being asked to surrender, but she was forced to hear the pleas of an ardent heart, learn how much she was loved, and allow herself to be surrounded by all the dangers of seduction without being able to defend herself. As Raymon became more daring, she could only become more embarrassed.

Mme. de Carvajal, who had heard of M. de Ramière's reputation for wit and had some pretensions of her own in that area, was eager to cross swords with him, so she left her card game to engage him in a philosophical discussion about love, which she proceeded to comment on with a great deal of Spanish passion and German metaphysics. Raymon was delighted, because by responding on an intellectual level to the aunt he could say to the niece everything she would otherwise have refused to listen to. The young woman, totally helpless before such a spirited and skillful attack, couldn't even begin to participate in that thorny conversation—although her aunt, who was eager to have her shine in such company, tried very hard to make her testify to the truths of some of the more subtle points of the theory of love. Blushing, Indiana protested that she knew nothing about such things, and Raymon, ecstatic at the sight of her flushed cheeks and agitated breathing, swore to himself that he would teach her.

Indiana slept even less well that night than she usually did. As we have said, she had never been in love, and her heart was ripe for that emotion which none of the men she had yet met had been able to arouse. Brought up by an eccentric and violent father, she had never known the happiness of being loved. M. de Carvajal, a man consumed by his political passions and embittered by his disappointed ambitions, had been known as the most ruthless plantation owner and most disagreeable neighbor in the colonies, and his daughter had suffered cruelly from his fretful temper. But because she had constantly had under her eyes the painful picture of the evils of slavery, and because she herself had had to endure the difficulties of isolation and dependence, she had acquired a patience capable of withstanding every trial, an unlimited sweetness and kindness toward her inferiors—and a will of iron and an infinite capacity to resist everything that tried to oppress her. By marrying Delmare, she had simply changed her master; by going to live at Lagny, she had merely changed the location of her prison and the site of her solitude. She did not love her husband, perhaps for the very reason that she was told it was her duty to love him and because resisting such moral pressure had become a kind of second nature, a principle of conduct, a matter of conscience. No one had ever taught her any rule of behavior but that of blind obedience.

Growing up in the wilderness, neglected by her father, living among slaves whom she could help only by her pity and her tears, she had gotten into the habit of thinking, "Some day everything will be different, and I will be able to help others. Some day someone will love me, and I will give my whole heart to the man who will give me his. Meanwhile I will suffer in silence and save my love as a reward for the man who will rescue me." That emancipator, the messiah, had not come; she was still waiting for him. She had come to realize that there were more obstacles, even to her thoughts, under the clipped trees of Lagny than there had been under the wild palms of Bourbon, and these days when she found herself saying out of habit, "Some day everything will be different . . . some day a man will come . . ." she would force the longing back down into the depths of her heart and say instead, "Only death will bring that day!"

So she began to die. A strange illness was devouring her youth, leaving her weak and unable to sleep; when the doctors looked for an organic cause, they could find none because there was none. All her faculties were failing equally, all her organs degenerating slowly; her heartbeat was weak, her eyes were lusterless, her blood circulated only as a result of excitement or fever: another few weeks or months and the poor prisoner would surely die. But despite her discouraged resignation, her need remained the same, and her silent, wounded heart was still, against her will, calling out to some generous, youthful heart that might bring her own to life. So far, the person she had loved most was Noun, the cheerfully courageous companion of all her troubles, and the man who had seemed to like her most was her phlegmatic cousin Ralph. What food for her restless thoughts: a poor, ignorant young girl as neglected as herself, and an Englishman whose only passion was fox hunting!

Mme. Delmare's unhappiness was real, and the first time she felt the warm breath of a vibrant young spirit penetrate the glacial atmosphere in which she lived, the first time she heard a tender and caressing word, the first time she experienced trembling lips branding the flesh of her hand, she forgot the duties that had been imposed on her, the prudence that had been recommended to her, the future that had been predicted for her, and remembered only her hateful past, her long suffering, her tyrannical masters. It never occurred to her that the man in front of her might be a liar or a philanderer; she saw him as she wanted him to be, as she had dreamed of him; and Raymon could easily have deceived her if he had not been sincere.

But how could he not have been sincere with such a lovely and loving woman? Had any other woman ever shown him her heart so openly and innocently? Had it ever seemed possible with any other woman to imagine a secure and happy future? Had this woman—this slave who was waiting only for his sign to break her chains, only for his word to follow him—not been born to love him? Surely heaven must have created for Raymon alone this melancholy child from Bourbon, whom no one had ever loved and who would die without him.

Yet together with the feverish joy that had filled her heart, Mme. Delmare also experienced a feeling of terror. She thought of her quick-tempered, sharp-eyed, vindictive husband, and she was afraid—not for herself, because she was used to his threats, but for the man who was about to undertake a fight to the death with her tyrannical ruler. She was so ignorant of the world that she saw life as a tragic melodrama, and despite her timidity, she was more frightened of exposing her lover to danger than of destroying herself.

And that was the secret of her resistance and the reason for her virtue. The next day she resolved to avoid M. de Ramière. There was to be a ball that evening at the home of one of the leading bankers of Paris, and Mme. de Carvajal, like all women who have no special ties to anyone in particular, was very fond of society in general. She wanted Indiana to accompany her, but the young woman knew that Raymon would be there and decided not to go. Since Indiana was able to show resistance only by her behavior, not by her words, she decided to avoid her aunt's persecution by pretending to accept the invitation; she allowed herself to be dressed for the occasion, waited until she knew Mme. de Carvajal was ready, then changed into a robe, settled herself by the fire, and waited with firm resolve for the coming confrontation. When the old woman, as stiff and bedizened as a Van Dyck portrait, came to fetch her, Indiana said that she was ill and not strong enough to go out.

Her aunt urged her to make an effort.

"I'd be glad to go if I could, but you see that I can hardly stand," she replied. "I'd only be a nuisance to you, so please, dear aunt, go without me. I'll enjoy thinking about your pleasure."

"Go without you!" exclaimed Mme. de Carvajal, who hated the idea of having taken the trouble to dress for no reason and was horrified at the thought of spending an evening at home alone. "But what will I do there without you? I'm an old woman, and no one comes near me except to speak to you. My niece's beautiful eyes are my only attraction!"

"Your wit will take their place, my dear aunt," said Indiana.

Mme. de Carvajal allowed herself to be persuaded and finally left, after which Indiana hid her face in her hands and began to weep; she had made a great sacrifice and was sure that she had destroyed the whole wonderful future she had imagined the day before.

But Raymon would not allow that to happen. The first thing he saw at the ball was the old marchioness's towering aigrette. When he looked for Indiana's white gown and black hair in her immediate vicinity and didn't see her, he approached Mme. de Carvajal and heard her say in an undertone to another lady, "My niece is ill—or rather," she added quickly, to excuse her own presence at the ball, "she is indulging in a girlish whim. She wanted to be left alone with a book in front of the drawing room fire, just like the heroine in a sentimental romance."

"Can she be avoiding me?" Raymon wondered.

He left the ball immediately, hurried to the marchioness's house, went in without speaking to the gatekeeper, and asked the sleepy servant he found in the hallway for Mme. Delmare.

"Madame Delmare is ill."

"I know. Madame de Carvajal sent me to find out how she is."

"I will tell Madame you are here."

"That won't be necessary. Madame Delmare will see me."

And Raymon went into the drawing room, which had the same feel of silent desolation as the deserted hallway, without being announced. A single lamp, covered with a green taffeta shade, cast its feeble light over the large room. Indiana's back was to the door; entirely hidden in the depths of a large chair, she was mournfully watching the burning logs just as she had been doing the night Raymon had climbed the walls of Lagny, but she was even sadder now, because her vague unhappiness and undefined desires had for a brief moment been replaced by a fleeting joy, a now lost ray of happiness.

Raymon was wearing dancing shoes for the ball and was able to approach her soundlessly over the thick, soft carpet. He saw that she was weeping. By the time she looked up, he was at her feet, and he took her hands and held them firmly. I must confess that she was overjoyed at seeing her plans for resistance fail. Knowing that she loved with all the strength of her passion this man who was able to ignore and overcome every obstacle and who had just made her happy despite herself, she felt grateful to heaven for refusing her sacrifice, and instead of scolding Raymon, she was close to thanking him.

As for him, he knew already that he was loved. He had no need to see the radiance behind her tears to understand that he was the master and could dare anything. Without giving her any time to question him, without explaining his unexpected presence, without apologizing or trying to make himself less guilty than he was, he simply said, "Indiana, you're crying. Why? I must know."

She trembled at hearing him use her first name, but even that boldness pleased her.

"Why do you want to know? I shouldn't tell you," she replied.

"It doesn't matter, because I know why, Indiana. I know your whole history, your whole life, because everything that concerns you is important to me. I was determined to learn all about you, but I learned nothing that one moment in your presence hadn't already taught me, nothing I hadn't known from the second I was brought in and laid at your feet, smashed and bloody, and realized that your husband was angry at seeing you—so beautiful and so kind!—support me with your soft arms and revive me with your sweet breath. He was jealous, and I understand that! I would have been jealous in his place, too—or rather, in his place I would have killed myself, because to be your husband, madame, to possess you, hold you, caress you, and not deserve you or be loved by you, is to be the most miserable man on earth!"

"Oh, stop!" she cried, putting her hands over his mouth. "Don't say anything else or you will make me guilty, too! Why do you speak to me about him? Why do you want to teach me to say dreadful things about him? If he should hear you! But it's not I who have spoken ill of him, not I who have given you permission to commit such a crime! I don't hate him—I respect him, I love him!"

"Why don't you admit that you're terribly afraid of him, that the tyrant has broken your spirit and that fear has sat beside you ever since you became his prey! Indiana, you've been violated by the very touch of that boor whose iron hand has made you bow your head and who has squeezed every bit of life out of you! Poor child—so young and beautiful and to have suffered so much already! Oh, yes, you have, Indiana— you can't deceive me as you do the others, because I don't look at you as the others do. I know all the secrets of your life, and it's impossible to hide the truth from me.

"Let those who look at you only because you're beautiful say when they notice how pale and weak you are, 'She's ill.' So be it. But I, I who look at you with my heart, whose soul surrounds you with concern and love, I know better. I know what your illness is. I know that if fate had willed you to be mine—and oh, what misery to have come too late!—you wouldn't be ill. Indiana, I swear to you on my life that I would have loved you so much that you would have loved me, too, and blessed your chains. I would have carried you in my arms to keep your feet from hurting, and I would have warmed them with my breath. I would have held you next to my heart to ease your suffering, given my blood to make up for the blood you lack, spent the nights when you couldn't fall asleep soothing you with soft words and smiling at you to give you courage—weeping all the while to see you suffer. When sleep was finally ready to come, my lips would have gently brushed your silken eyelids so they would close more softly, and I would have knelt by your bedside and watched over you. I would have made the air breathe gently on you, forced your dreams to shower you with flowers. I would have silently kissed your hair and counted your heartbeats with ecstasy, and when you had awakened, Indiana, you would have found me at your feet, guarding you like a jealous master, serving you like a slave, watching for your first smile, seizing upon your first thought, your first look, your first kiss—"

"Enough, enough!" cried Indiana, breathless and trembling with emotion. "This is unbearable!"

And yet, if people died of happiness, Indiana would have died at that moment.

"Don't say these things to me," she said. "I can never be happy. Don't show me heaven on earth when I'm destined to die."

"To die!" Raymon exclaimed, pulling her into his arms. "You, die? Before having lived—before having loved? No, you will not die! I won't allow you to die, because my life is tied to yours from now on. You are the woman I have dreamed of, the purity I have worshiped, the will-o'-the-wisp that has always eluded me, the bright star that shone in the sky and told me, 'Continue to endure this miserable life, and heaven will send you one of its angels to keep you company.' From the beginning of time, Indiana, you were always destined to be mine, your soul was always promised to mine! Men and their rigid laws have disposed of you and deprived me of the companion God would have chosen for me if God did not sometimes forget his promises. But what do men and their laws matter if I love you even when you are in someone else's arms and if you can love me despite my wretched luck in having lost you! Indiana, I tell you that you belong to me, that you are the other half of my soul, which has been trying to rejoin its mate for a long time. When you were on Bourbon Island and dreamed of finding a friend, I was that friend. When you heard the word

husband and your heart thrilled with hope and fear, it was because I was supposed to be that husband. Don't you recognize
me? Doesn't it seem as if we must have met twenty years ago?
Didn't I know you, my angel, when you stopped my bleeding
with the voile you wore and put your hand on my dying heart
to bring it back to life? Ah, I remember that very well! When I
opened my eyes, I thought, 'There she is, just as she is in my
dreams, pale, melancholy, kind. She is my own good angel,
fated to fill my cup with undreamed-of rapture.' And the physical life that returned to me was your doing. We weren't
brought together in an ordinary way, or by some lucky chance,
or without rhyme or reason—no, it was death itself that
opened the doors to my new life. It was your husband, your
master, who obeyed his own destiny by carrying my bloody
body and throwing it at your feet, saying, 'This is for you.'
And now nothing can part us—"

"*He* can part us!" interrupted Indiana, who had been listening, enraptured, to her lover's words. "You don't know him.
He's a man who cannot be deceived, an unforgiving man, and
he will kill you, Raymon!"

Weeping, she hid her face against his chest while he embraced her passionately.

"Let him come!" he exclaimed. "Let him come this minute
and try to snatch this moment of happiness from me! I defy
him! Stay where you are, Indiana, against my heart, which is
your refuge and your protection. Love me, and I will be invul-
nerable. You know very well that that man can't kill me—I
was exposed to his blows when I was completely defenseless,
but thanks to you, my good angel who hovered over me with
your protective wings, I survived. So don't be afraid for me.
Believe me when I tell you that we will find a way to evade
him. I'm not even worried about you anymore, because I will
be nearby, and when this master of yours tries to persecute
you, I will protect you. If necessary, I will rescue you from his
ruthless rule. Do you want me to kill him? Tell me that you
love me, and then if you want me to kill him, I will—"

"Stop! Stop! Don't say such things! You frighten me! If you
must kill someone, kill me, because I've lived one full day of
life and I ask nothing more."

"Die if you wish, but let it be from happiness!" cried Raymon, kissing her on the lips.

But that was too violent a storm for such a fragile plant: she
paled, clutched at her heart, and fainted.

At first Raymon thought that his caresses would make warm blood flow back to her icy veins, but though he covered her hands with kisses and called her by the sweetest names, her hands remained glacial. This was not the deliberate swoon one sees so often in society women; Indiana had been seriously ill for a long time and sometimes suffered nervous convulsions that could last for hours. Finally, in desperation, Raymon had to call for help. He rang, and a maid appeared; but the vial she held slipped from her hand as she recognized Raymon and cried out in surprise.

Immediately recovering his self-possession, he whispered, "Be quiet, Noun! I knew you were here, and I came to see you. I didn't expect to find your mistress here, because I thought she was at the ball. I frightened her when I came in, and she fainted. I'm going now—don't say anything foolish."

And Raymon fled, leaving each of the two women with a secret that was destined to break the heart of the other.

VII

WHEN he woke up the next morning, Raymon found a second letter from Noun. Instead of tossing it away as contemptuously as the first, he opened it eagerly because there might be news of Mme. Delmare. Indeed there was, but how embarrassing for him this web of intrigue was going to be! Noun wrote that her condition would soon be impossible to hide, that Mme. Delmare had already noticed her hollowed cheeks and drawn expression, even if she didn't know the reason for them, and that though she, Noun, was afraid of the harsh colonel, she was even more afraid of how her gentle mistress would respond: she knew she'd be forgiven, but she'd die of shame at having to confess her sin. What would happen to her if Raymon didn't protect her from the humiliations she'd have to endure? He must promise to think about her situation, or she would fling herself at Mme. Delmare's feet and tell her everything.

This threat was a powerful incentive to action, and Raymon's first object became to separate Noun from her mistress.

"Be careful not to say anything without my permission," he wrote. "'Try to be at Lagny this evening. I will be there."

On his way to Lagny, he tried to decide what to do. Noun was too sensible to hope for the impossible; she had never dared say the word *marriage*, and that undemanding generosity was what made it possible for Raymon to tell himself that he had never deceived her and that she must have foreseen her probable fate—which in turn made him feel less guilty. The thought of having to give her money was not what bothered him. He was ready to give half his fortune to the poor girl and make her rich, ready to take care of her in every way that the most demanding sense of justice could require—but he was *not* ready to tell her that he still loved her, for he was incapable of telling a bald lie. His behavior at this moment of crisis may seem hypocritical and dishonorable, but his heart was just as sincere as it had always been. He had loved Noun with his senses, and he loved Mme. Delmare with all his heart and soul; so far, he had lied to neither one of them, and he did not want to begin now. But he felt that it was as impossible to deal Noun the fatal blow as it would be to deceive her. Raymon was very unhappy: he had to choose between barbaric brutality and unmanly cowardice, and he still had not made up his mind which it would be by the time he reached the gate to Lagny park.

Meanwhile Noun, who was probably not expecting such a prompt reply to her letter, had become a little more hopeful.

"He still loves me," she thought. "He's not going to abandon me. He's neglected me a little, but that's understandable. He's in Paris, going to balls and dinner parties and surrounded by women who must all be in love with him—it's natural for him to forget about his poor little Creole for a while. Who am I that he should give up so many fine ladies, all of them richer and more beautiful than me? Who knows," she added naively, "maybe even the queen of France is in love with him."

The thought of Raymon being seduced by all the luxuries of aristocratic society gave Noun an idea for making herself more attractive to him. She put on one of her mistress's gowns, lit a fire in Mme. Delmare's room, gathered the most exquisite flowers in the greenhouse and decorated the mantel with them, prepared a selection of fruit and fine wines—in short, brought into play all the elegant niceties of a lady's boudoir that she had never before even dreamed of. And when she looked at herself in the large mirror, she thought quite justly that she was prettier than the flowers with which she had adorned herself.

"He used to tell me," she said to herself, "that I didn't need any ornaments to make me beautiful, and that no woman at court, with all her diamonds, was as brilliant as one of my smiles. Still, he's now surrounded by all those women he used to despise, so I must try to be as charming and gay and lively as they are, and make him love me again, the way he used to."

Raymon left his horse at a charcoal burner's cottage in the woods and entered the park with a key. This time there was no risk of being taken for a thief: almost all the servants had gone with their masters; he had taken the gardener into his confidence; and he knew the grounds of Lagny as well as he did his own.

It was a cold night, and the trees were almost hidden by the thick haze that turned their dark trunks into wavering, insubstantial forms. Raymon had to wander up and down several paths before he found the summerhouse, where Noun, completely enveloped in a hooded cape, was waiting for him.

"We can't stay here, it's too cold," she told him. "Follow me, and be quiet."

Raymon found it repugnant to enter Mme. Delmare's house as her maid's lover, but he had to agree; Noun was walking ahead with light steps, and this was to be their last meeting.

She led him across the garden, quieted the dogs, noiselessly opened the doors, took his hand, and conducted him silently through the dark corridors until they finally entered a simply and elegantly furnished circular room that was permeated with the subtle scent of flowering orange branches and lit by opalescent wax candles burning in the candelabra. The floor was covered with petals of Bengal roses and the divan with violets, a subtle warmth soothed every pore, and the crystal glasses glittering on the table were no more brilliant than the glossy fruit nestling in the moss-lined baskets.

Dazzled by the sudden contrast between the darkness he had come from and the bright light inside, Raymon was at first bewildered, but he soon realized where he was. The exquisite taste and chaste simplicity of the furnishings; the books of travel and love on the mahogany shelves; the embroidery frame with its pretty piece of work that testified to hours of patient, dreary labor; the harp whose strings still seemed to vibrate with songs of wistful yearning; the engravings that illustrated the pastoral love of Paul and Virginia, the peaks of Bourbon Island, and the blue coastline of Saint-Paul; and especially the narrow bed half-hidden behind its muslin curtains, a modest, white, virginal bed with a bit of palm on top of its headboard, taken perhaps from her native land on the day she left there and serving as a kind of sacred symbol—everything spoke of Mme. Delmare. Raymon felt a sudden thrill at the thought that the woman hidden by her cloak, the woman who had brought him here, might be Indiana herself—an extravagant notion that seemed to be supported by the sight in the mirror of a powdered, elegantly dressed figure, a phantom woman entering a ballroom and removing her cloak to reveal her radiant, half-naked self under the gleaming lights. But the illusion lasted only a moment. Indiana would have been more seemly: her breasts would have been hidden by three layers of gauze, the camelias in her hair would not have been arranged in such seductive disorder, and though she might have worn satin slippers, her more modest gown would not have exposed the mysteries of her shapely legs.

Taller and more robust than her mistress, Noun was dressed in her finery but did not really inhabit it. She was graceful, but her grace lacked nobility; she was beautiful, but like a woman, not a fairy; she promised sensual delight, but not ultimate ecstasy.

After having examined her in the mirror without moving his head, Raymon turned around and looked only at those objects that could give him a purer reflection of Indiana: the musical instruments, the engravings, the narrow, chaste bed. He was intoxicated by the vague, lingering perfume of her presence in this sanctuary, and he tingled with desire as he anticipated the day when Indiana herself would welcome him to its delights—and meanwhile Noun stood behind him, her arms folded and her heart filled with joy at what she assumed to be his great pleasure at all her painstaking efforts to please him.

Finally breaking his silence, he said, "Thank you for these preparations, and especially for having brought me here. But I think I've enjoyed your thoughtful surprise long enough, and now we should leave. We don't belong in this room, and I must respect Madame Delmare even in her absence."

"How cruel you are!" said Noun, who had not understood his words but could feel his cold displeasure. "I did all this for you because I hoped it would please you, and instead you turn away from me."

"No, dear Noun, I will never turn away from you. I've come here to have a serious talk with you and to prove my real affection for you. I understand that you wanted to please me, and I'm grateful—but I found your youth and your natural charms more becoming than these borrowed clothes."

Again Noun only half understood him, and she wept as she said, "I'm so unhappy. I hate myself because I don't please you anymore. I should have realized that you wouldn't love a poor, uneducated girl like me for very long. I'm not blaming you for anything—I knew you wouldn't marry me, but if you had kept on loving me, I would have sacrificed everything without one regret, put up with everything without one complaint. . . . I'm ruined, I've lost my good name, I may be turned out, I'm going to give birth to someone who will be even more unfortunate than I am, and no one will pity me. The whole world will think it has the right to trample me underfoot! But if you still loved me, how happily I could accept all that!"

Noun kept saying this over and over, using different words, of course, but always meaning the same thing and being a hundred times more expressive than I can possibly be. How can we explain such an outpouring of eloquence in someone as uneducated and inexperienced as she was except as a response to genuine passion and profound suffering? Under those circumstances words take on a greater significance than at any other time, the simplest of them becoming sublime because of the emotion that evokes them and the tone in which they are spoken. By abandoning herself to her frenzied delirium, the humblest woman becomes more touching and more persuasive than her more cultured sister, who has been trained to express herself with moderation and restraint.

Raymon was flattered to find himself the object of such a generous-hearted sentiment, and for a moment, gratitude, compassion, perhaps even a bit of vanity, succeeded in rekindling a spark of love.

Noun was drowning in tears. She had torn the flowers from her hair, which now cascaded over her magnificent shoulders, and if Mme. Delmare had owed her charm only to her enslaved condition and her suffering, Noun's beauty would at that moment have been infinitely greater than hers; she was absolutely splendid in her grief and her love. Raymon, conquered, took her in his arms, made her sit next to him on the sofa, then moved the little table with its fruits and wines closer and poured a few drops of orange-flavored water into a vermeil cup.

More comforted by his thoughtfulness than by the drink itself, Noun dried her tears and threw herself at Raymon's feet, clinging passionately to his knees and crying, "Tell me that you still love me and I'll be cured, I'll be saved! Kiss me the way you used to kiss me, and I won't regret having ruined myself to give you a few days of happiness."

As she embraced him with her firm, dark arms, her long hair tumbled all over him, and her huge black eyes looked at him with that wild tropical lust which can triumph over the most determined spiritual, moral, or intellectual resistance. Raymon forgot everything—his resolutions, his new love, even where he was. He returned Noun's voluptuous caresses with equal ardor; their lips met as they drank from the same cup, and the wines they thus shared made them lose the last vestiges of reason.

Little by little a vague memory of Indiana began to float in and out of Raymon's drunken consciousness. The two mirrored panels that each reflected Noun's image into infinity seemed to be peopled by a thousand phantoms, and as he stared into the depths of that double image he thought he could see, in the final hazy and indistinct reflection of Noun, the slender, willowy form of Mme. Delmare.

Noun, unaccustomed to the strong liquor she had been drinking, was too muddled to understand the strange things her lover was saying, or she would have realized that he was thinking of another woman even in the heat of his most frenzied passion; she would have seen him kiss the scarf and the ribbons Indiana had worn, inhale the perfumes that reminded him of her, and crumple in his burning hands the voile that had covered her breasts. Noun took all those acts as homage to herself, whereas Raymon looked at her and saw nothing but Indiana's dress. When his kissed Noun's black hair, he imagined himself kissing Indiana's black hair; it was Indiana he saw in the fumes of the punch Noun ignited for him, Indiana he saw smiling at him from behind those white muslin curtains, Indiana he saw on the pure and spotless bed to which he drunkenly and lustfully led his touseled Creole.

When Raymon woke up, a dim light was entering the room through the slats of the shutters, and for a long time he lay where he was, immobile, bemused, puzzled at finding himself in that bed and wondering if it was all a dream. Everything had been put back into order. Early in the morning, Noun, who had gone to bed in that room a queen, had awakened a maid: she had removed the flowers and cleared away the remains of the food and drink; the furniture was back where it belonged; there was no sign of the night's orgy; and Indiana's room was once again a sanctuary of innocence and virtue.

Overwhelmed with shame, he got out of bed and wanted to leave, but he was locked in. The window was thirty feet from the ground, and he had to remain in the room with his remorse, like the mythical Ixion on his wheel.

He knelt down and faced the messy bed, blushing at its disorder. Wringing his hands, he cried out, "Oh, Indiana, what have I done? Could you ever forgive such outrageous behavior? And even if you could, I could never forgive myself! You must be strong enough to resist me, Indiana, because you're too sweet and trusting to understand that the man to whom you are ready to surrender the treasures of your innocence is nothing but a vile beast! Turn your back on me, crush me under your feet! I have defiled the refuge of your sacred modesty, gotten drunk on your wines like a lackey with your maid, sullied your gown with my foul breath and your undergarments with my infamous kisses on another woman's breast, poisoned the sleep of your lonely nights and cast over this bed, which even your husband respected, an aura of seduction and debauchery! What security will you now find behind these curtains whose mysteries I've dared to profane? What lascivious dreams, what harrowing, corrosive thoughts, will attack your mind and suck it dry? What fantasies of vice and wickedness will come to crawl over the virginal sheets? And your sleep, pure as a child's, what chaste goddess will want to protect it now? Have I not driven away the angel of purity that guarded your bed and left it open to the devil of lust, to whom I have sold your soul? And won't the uncontrollable fires that consume this lascivious Creole come to inhabit your body and goad it without pity? Oh, how unhappy, how guilty and unhappy I am, and how I wish I could wash away with my blood the shameful stain I have left on this bed!"

And Raymon watered the bed with his tears.

When Noun came in, wearing her apron and her bandanna, she saw him kneeling and thought he was praying. Not knowing that people in society do not pray, she waited quietly until he became aware of her presence.

When he did, he was both embarrassed and annoyed, but he had neither the courage to scold her nor the decency to give her a friendly word. Instead, he finally said, "Why did you lock me in? It's broad daylight now, and I can't leave without compromising you."

"Then you won't leave," Noun answered, her tone caressing. "No one will see you because the house is empty. The gardener never comes to this part of the building, and I'm the only one who has keys to it, so you're my prisoner and you'll have to stay here with me all day."

Raymon, who felt nothing but loathing for his mistress at this point, was in despair at these words, but he had no choice and resigned himself to remain in the room in which he had suffered so much, but which still held an unconquerable attraction for him.

When Noun left him to get breakfast for them, he examined the silent witnesses of Indiana's solitude in broad daylight. He opened her books and leafed through her albums, then closed them quickly, as if afraid of violating her privacy and committing still further outrages against her feminine secrets. Finally he began to pace up and down, and then he noticed, on the wooden panel opposite the bed, a large, richly framed painting covered with a double layer of cloth.

Thinking it might be a portrait of Indiana, Raymon, eager to see it, forgot all his scruples, climbed on a chair, removed the pins, and was amazed to find the full-length portrait of a handsome young man.

VIII

"IT seems to me that I know that man," he said to Noun, forcing himself to sound indifferent.

"Ah, it's not nice to pry into my mistress's secrets!" she replied, placing the breakfast tray on a table.

Raymon turned pale. "Secrets!" he said. "If that's a secret, then you were supposed to keep it, and you were doubly guilty in bringing me to this room."

"No, of course it's not a secret," said Noun, laughing. "Monsieur Delmare himself helped hang Sir Ralph's portrait there. Do you really think Madame Delmare could have any secrets from such a jealous husband?"

"Sir Ralph? Who is Sir Ralph?"

"Sir Rodolphe Brown, Madame's cousin and childhood friend—and mine, too, because he's such a good man!"

Surprised, Raymon examined the portrait uneasily.

We have said that Sir Ralph was a very handsome young man, always impeccably dressed, tall, with a fair complexion and a thick head of blond hair; he would probably not appeal to a romantic young girl, but any sensible woman would find him quite attractive. The impassive baronet had been painted in a hunting costume—looking very much as we saw him in the first chapter of this story—and surrounded by his dogs, the beautiful griffon Ophelia in the foreground because of her silvery gray fur and her elegant lines. Sir Ralph held a hunting horn in one hand and the reins of a magnificent dapple-gray English hunter in the other. It was all admirably drawn: in its precise rendition of every detail, its faithful reproduction of surface reality, its depiction of the minutiae of bourgeois life, it was a perfect example of a family painting—one to make nursemaids cry, dogs howl, and shopkeepers swoon with pleasure. The only thing in the world more insignificant than the portrait was the original.

Yet Raymon's response to it was violent anger.

"What?" he thought. "Does that virile young Englishman have the right to be admitted into Madame Delmare's most private room? Is his insipid face always here, coldly observing the most intimate acts of her life? Can he see her, guard her, follow her every movement, possess her at every moment of every hour? Can he watch her sleep at night and surprise the secrets of her dreams? Can he see her in the morning, when she gets out of bed all white and shivering, her dainty bare feet stepping lightly on the carpet? And when she dresses, carefully drawing the curtains so that not even the daylight can enter too boldly, when she thinks she is completely alone, completely safe, is that insolent face feasting on her charms? That man in his boots is observing everything?"

"Is the painting usually covered like this?" he asked the maid.

"When Madame Delmare isn't here," she replied, "always. But don't bother replacing it—she'll be back in a few days."

"In that case, Noun, you should tell her that there's a very impertinent expression on that man's face. If I were Monsieur Delmare, I wouldn't allow this painting to hang here unless I had cut the eyes out first! But that's just like the stupid jealousy of most husbands—they imagine all sorts of things and have no real understanding of anything!"

"But what do you have against poor Mr. Brown's face?" Noun asked as she made up her mistress's bed. "I never used to like him much because I always heard everyone tell Madame that he was selfish, but ever since he took such good care of you—"

"Oh, yes," said Raymon, interrupting her. "Now I remember—he was the one who helped me that day! But it was only because Madame Delmare asked him to."

"Yes, because she's so good, so kind," said poor Noun. "No one who has lived with her could help being good and kind, too."

She had no idea of how interested Raymon was in everything she had to say about Mme. Delmare.

Though they spent the day quietly, Noun was unable to find the courage to talk about what was most important to her; finally, however, as evening approached, she forced herself to ask Raymon what he meant to do.

Raymon meant mostly to rid himself of a dangerous witness, one who was also a woman he no longer loved. But he certainly meant to provide for her, so in a tremulous voice he proceeded to tell her about the generous arrangements he was prepared to make.

The poor girl was bitterly insulted; she began to tear her hair and would have beaten her head against the wall if Raymon hadn't held her back by force.

Using all the eloquence and powers of persuasion that nature had given him, he tried to explain that the financial support was not for her but for the child she was going to bring into the world. "It's *my* duty to give you this money as the child's inheritance," he told her, "and it would be wrong to let a false sense of pride keep you from doing *your* duty."

Noun quieted down and wiped her eyes.

"All right," she said, "I'll accept the money if you promise to keep on loving me, because though you may be doing your duty to the child that way, you won't be doing it to the mother. Your gift will keep him alive, but your coldness will kill me. Can't you take me on as a servant in your home? You can see that I'm not demanding—I'm not aiming for what another woman in my place might have been clever enough to get from you—all I want is to be your servant! Or ask your mother to take me on as a maid. I swear she'll be satisfied with me, and that way, even if you don't love me anymore, at least I'll be able to see you."

"What you're asking is impossible, my dear Noun. No one can take you on in your present condition, and I would never deceive my mother or take advantage of her confidence in me—I'd never stoop so low! Go to Lyons or Bordeaux, and I promise that you'll have everything you need until you can show yourself again. Then I'll get you a place with one of my acquaintances—even here in Paris, if you want . . . if you'd like to be near me. But under the same roof? Impossible!"

"'Impossible,'" Noun repeated sadly. "I see that you hate me, that you're humiliated by me. But no, I won't go away to die alone and ashamed, deserted in some faraway city where you can forget all about me. What do I care about keeping my reputation? It's your love I want to keep!"

"Noun, if you're afraid that I'm lying, I'll go with you. The same carriage will take us both wherever you want to go—anywhere except Paris or my mother's—and I'll give you all the care and attention that I know I owe you."

"Yes, for a day, and then you'll abandon me in a strange place, like a useless burden," she said, smiling bitterly. "No, monsieur, no, I'm staying here. To be with you I would have given up the person I loved most in the world before I met you, but I don't care enough about hiding my shame to give up both my love *and* my friendship. I'll kneel at Madame Delmare's feet and tell her everything. I know she'll forgive me, because she's a good person and she loves me. We were born on almost the same day—she's my foster sister—and we've never been separated. She won't want me to leave her. She'll cry with me, she'll love my poor child . . . Who knows? Since she isn't lucky enough to have one herself, maybe she'll even bring it up as her own! Oh, I was mad to think of leaving her—she's the only person in the world who will pity me!"

As Raymon began to realize that this decision presented him with an insoluble problem, they suddenly heard the rumbling of a carriage in the courtyard.

Noun, horrified, ran to the window. "It's Madame Delmare!" she cried. "You must leave immediately!"

They were in such a state that neither of them could find the key to the secret stairway. Noun took Raymon's arm and pulled him into the hallway, but before they reached the stairs they heard footsteps coming toward them. Mme. Delmare was close by: the candle carried by the servant who accompanied her was already casting its flickering light on their frightened faces. Noun had barely enough time to retrace her steps, and still pulling Raymon behind her, she led them both back into the bedroom.

A dressing room with a glass door offered temporary refuge, but there was no way to lock the door and Mme. Delmare might go in there right away; to avoid being seen immediately Raymon would have to hide behind the curtains of the sleeping alcove. Mme. Delmare was unlikely to go directly to bed, and by the time she did, Noun might have found a way to help him escape. . . .

Indiana entered the room briskly, flung her fur hat onto the bed, and kissed Noun with the familiarity of a sister. There was so little light that she never noticed how upset Noun looked.

"Were you expecting me?" she asked, approaching the fire. "How did you know I was coming?"

Without waiting for a reply, she continued, "Monsieur Delmare will be here tomorrow. I left Paris as soon as I received his letter, because there are reasons why I'd rather receive him here than there. I'll tell you. . . . But say something, Noun. You don't seem as glad to see me as you usually do."

"I'm unhappy," said Noun, kneeling to remove her mistress's shoes. "I have something to tell you, too, but later. Right now, come to the drawing room."

"Heavens, no! What an idea—it's freezing there!"

"No, there's a good fire."

"You must be imagining things! I just walked through there."

"But your supper is waiting for you."

"I don't want any supper. Besides, nothing is ready. Please get my boa—I left it in the carriage."

"In a minute."

"Why not right now? Go on, go on!"

She was playfully pushing Noun out as she spoke and the maid, seeing that she would have to keep her head and take some risks, left the room. As soon as she had, Indiana threw the bolt, took off her cloak, and tossed it onto the bed next to her hat. At that moment she was so close to Raymon that he actually took a step backward, and the bed, which evidently rested on well-oiled castors, made a slight noise as it moved. Indiana, thinking she herself had probably moved it, was surprised but not frightened, and she pushed the curtain open a bit more; then she saw, in the half-light cast by the fire, a man's head silhouetted against the wall.

Terrified, she shrieked and ran toward the mantel to pull the bell rope and call for help. Once again Raymon would rather have been taken for a thief than be discovered in such a situation, but if he didn't identify himself immediately, Indiana would call the servants and her reputation would be compromised. He decided to put his faith in her love for him. Rushing over to her, he tried to stop her screams and keep her away from the rope by saying softly—lest Noun, who was undoubtedly nearby, hear him—"It is I, Indiana. Please look at me and forgive me, Indiana! Forgive the unhappy man who lost his head, the poor man who couldn't bear to return you to your husband without having seen you one more time!"

And all the while he was holding Indiana in his arms—as much to melt her heart as to keep her from pulling the rope—Noun was feverishly knocking. Mme. Delmare finally freed herself from Raymon's embrace, ran to open the door, came back, collapsed into a chair.

Looking as if she were on the verge of death, Noun threw herself against the door to keep the servants, who were now running aimlessly back and forth in the hallway, from participating in the strange scene; even more pale than her mistress, her legs about to give way, supported only by the door, she waited to hear her fate.

Raymon felt that if he were skillful enough, he might yet be able to deceive both women at once.

"Madame," he said, kneeling in front of Indiana, "my presence must seem outrageous to you, but I'm here at your feet to beg your pardon. If you will give me a few moments alone with you, I'll explain—"

"Do not speak to me, monsieur, and leave this room immediately," said Mme. Delmare, interrupting him and recovering all her dignity. "Leave here in full view of everyone. Noun, open that door for Monsieur and let him pass. I want all the servants to see him and to understand that the shame of his disgraceful behavior is his alone."

Noun, believing her secret discovered, flung herself to her knees beside Raymon. Mme. Delmare looked at her in silent amazement.

Raymon tried to take Indiana's hand, but she pulled it away indignantly. Flushed with anger, she rose and pointed to the door.

"Leave, I say," she repeated. "Leave, because your behavior is detestable. Is this one of your habits, to hide yourself in a bedroom like a thief? To force your way into a family? Is this an example of the pure devotion you offered me? Is this the way you were going to protect me, respect me, defend me? So this is how you worship me! You see a woman who has nursed you with her own hands and defied her husband's anger to bring you back to life. You pretend to be grateful to her, you promise her a love worthy of her, and in return for her care, in return for her trustfulness, you try to surprise her in her sleep and satisfy your desires in the most contemptible way! You win over her maid, you almost manage to creep into her bed like an already successful lover, you have no hesitation about allowing her servants to believe in an intimacy that doesn't exist! Well, monsieur, you have certainly taken great pains to disenchant me very quickly! Leave, I tell you. I don't want you to remain in this house another second. . . . And you, you impossible girl who has so little respect for your mistress's honor, you deserve to be turned out! Get away from that door, I tell you!"

Dazed, stupefied, stricken, Noun stared at Raymon, begging for an explanation of this incredible mystery. Then, almost more dead than alive, she crawled to Indiana, clutched her arm.

and cried out angrily from behind clenched teeth, "Did you say that this man is in love with you?"

"Oh, I'm sure you must be aware of that," Mme. Delmare answered, pushing her away contemptuously. "Surely you must know why a man wants to hide behind a woman's bed curtains. Oh, Noun," she added, seeing the young girl's misery, "I would never have believed you capable of such shameful behavior! To sell the honor of someone who had so much faith in yours!"

Indiana was weeping, but with as much rage as pain. Raymon had never seen her so beautiful, but he hardly dared look at her: her air of affronted pride—of a woman insulted in the very core of her being—forced him to lower his eyes. And he was paralyzed by Noun's presence. If he had been alone with Mme. Delmare, he might have been able to soothe her, but Noun, her features distorted by fury and hate, was not only there but a terrifying sight.

A knock at the door startled all three of them. Noun dashed back to her post, ready once again to keep anyone from entering, but Mme. Delmare intercepted her with a commanding gesture and at the same time signaled Raymon to withdraw to a corner of the room. Then, with the sangfroid that made her so remarkable in moments of crisis, she wrapped herself in a shawl, opened the door herself, and asked the servant what he wanted.

"Mr. Rodolphe Brown has just arrived," he announced, "and he wishes to know if Madame will receive him."

"Tell Sir Ralph that I'm delighted he has come and will join him immediately. Make a fire in the drawing room and have them prepare some supper. Wait a minute! Bring me the key to the small park."

The servant left. Indiana remained standing at the half-open door, refusing to listen to Noun and imperiously ordering Raymon to remain silent.

When the servant returned after a few minutes, Mme. Delmare, still keeping the door between him and M. de Ramière, took the key, told him to see to it that supper was prepared immediately, and, as soon as he had gone, turned to Raymon.

"The arrival of my cousin, Sir Rodolphe Brown," she said, "has spared you the scandal I intended to bring down on your head. He is a man with a strong sense of honor and would immediately assume the duty of defending me, but since I would be very reluctant to risk the life of a man like that at the hands

of a man like you, I will allow you to leave quietly. Noun, wh
let you in, will know how to get you out. Now go!"

"We will meet again, madame," Raymon said, trying
sound confident, "and although I have done wrong, you ma
regret your severity with me."

"I hope, monsieur, that we will never meet again," sh
replied.

And still standing erect at the door, without deigning even
nod, she watched him leave with his unsteady and unhappy a
complice.

Raymon, alone with Noun in the darkness of the park, wa
expecting her to reproach him, but she said not one word. Sh
led him to the gate of the small park, and when he turned an
tried to take her hand, she had already disappeared. Wanting
know his fate, he called out to her softly, but there was no an
swer. Instead the gardener suddenly appeared out of nowher
and whispered, "You must leave, sir. Madame has arrived, an
you might be discovered."

Raymon left, the taste of ashes in his heart. Miserable at hav
ing offended Indiana, thinking only of how he might pacify he
he almost completely forgot about Noun; it was his nature to b
easily annoyed by minor difficulties but to be spurred by th
challenge of obstacles that seemed insurmountable.

That evening, when Mme. Delmare went to her room after
silent meal with Sir Ralph, Noun did not come, as she alway
did, to help her undress. She rang for her, but to no avail, an
deciding that the girl was deliberately disobeying her sum
mons, she locked her door and went to bed, where she spent
sleepless night. As soon as it was light, she went down into th
park, feeling a need for the cold air to penetrate her body an
give her some relief from the raging fever that was consumin
her.

At this time yesterday she had been happy, surrendering he
self to the novelty of an intoxicating love, and within twenty
four hours she had suffered a series of the most dreadfu
disappointments, deceptions, and disillusionments. First ther
had been the news of her husband's return several days soone
than she had expected. The four or five days she had thought
spend in Paris had seemed a promise of a lifetime of endless
happiness, a dream of love that was never to be interrupted b
any awakening; but she had had to abandon those hopes earl
in the morning, resume her yoke, and return home so her mas
ter would not meet Raymon at Mme. de Carvajal's, for Indian

was sure it would be impossible to fool her husband if he were to see her in Raymon's presence. And then to be so grossly insulted by this same Raymon—this Raymon whom she had adored as if he were a god! And as a final blow there was the discovery that her lifelong companion, the young Creole she loved so dearly, was unworthy of her confidence and her respect!

Indiana had cried all night; now she let herself sink to the ground, still white with the morning's frost, on the bank of the stream that flowed through the park. It was the end of March, and nature was beginning to awaken; though it was cold, the morning had its charms: a wispy mist still rested on the water like a floating scarf, and the birds were singing their first springtime songs of love. Indiana felt comforted, and her soul overflowed with religious feeling.

"God has wanted this to happen," she thought; "it has been a rude awakening, but it's for my own good. That man might have made me behave immorally, might have ruined me, but now that I see how vile he is, I will be on guard against the stormy, dangerous passion seething within him. . . . I will love my husband . . . I will *try* to love him! At the very least I will be obedient, make him happy by never contradicting him, avoid doing anything that might arouse his jealousy—because now I know how little one can depend on the false promises men make when they want to win us. I may even be happy, if God takes pity on my suffering and sends me an early death. . . ."

From behind the willows on the other side of the stream she could hear the sound of the mill wheel that started the machinery in her husband's factory. The water, rushing through the gates that had just been opened, was becoming turbulent, and as Indiana sadly watched the swift rush of the stream, she saw floating between the reeds something like a roll of cloth, which the current was trying to carry away. Standing up, she leaned over the water and clearly saw a woman's clothes—clothes she recognized only too well. Stunned, she remained rooted to the spot, but she did not have to move: the water was slowly leading to her, from the weeds in which it had been caught, a body.

She screamed, and the workmen from the factory came running; Mme. Delmare had fainted, and Noun's body was floating in the water at her feet.

PART TWO

IX

Two months have gone by, and nothing has changed at Lagny —that house I last showed you on a winter evening—except that now a springtime in full bloom surrounds the moss-covered slate roof and the gray-stone and red-brick walls. The family group is scattered, each enjoying the mild, perfumed evening air in his or her different way as the setting sun gilds the windows and the sounds of the factory mingle with those of the farm. M. Delmare is sitting on the front steps with his gun and shooting swallows on the wing. Mme. Delmare is sitting at her embroidery frame near the drawing room window and looking out from time to time to watch with a sad face the colonel's cruel sport. Ophelia is leaping about, barking with indignation at such a style of hunting, and Sir Ralph, sitting astride the stone coping, is smoking a cigar and observing the pleasure or displeasure of those around him with his usual impassivity.

"Indiana, put your embroidery away!" exclaimed the colonel, setting down his gun. "You work as if you were being paid by the hour."

"It's still light out," Mme. Delmare replied.

"Never mind that. Come to the window, I have something to tell you."

Indiana obeyed, and the colonel walked over to the window, which was almost on a level with the ground.

He said to her, in the kind of bantering tone an old and jealous husband sometimes uses, "Since you've been so good and worked so hard today, I have a nice surprise for you."

Indiana forced herself to smile; a more sensitive man than the colonel would have been driven to the brink of despair by such a smile.

"You'll be glad to know," he continued, "that I've invited one of your humble admirers to lunch tomorrow. I'm sure you want to know which one, because I know you have a pretty fine collection of them, don't you, you flirt!"

"Is it our dear old priest?" asked Indiana, whose melancholy was always increased by her husband's labored attempts at humor.

"Oh, no!"

"Then it must be the mayor of Chailly or the old notary from Fontainebleau."

"Ah, how tricky women are! You know very well that it's none of those. Ralph, tell Madame the name she has on the tip of her tongue but doesn't want to say."

"I wouldn't think you needed such a long preface to announce a visit from Monsieur de Ramière," said Sir Ralph tranquilly, tossing away his cigar. "I don't suppose she much cares."

Feeling herself begin to blush, Indiana pretended she had to look for something and left the window for a few minutes. When she returned, she had more or less regained her composure.

"You must be teasing me," she said, her whole body trembling.

"On the contrary, I'm quite serious. He'll be here at eleven o'clock tomorrow morning."

"The man who tried to steal your invention? The man you almost killed as a trespasser? I must say that you're both very forgiving to forget such grievances!"

"You set me the example yourself, my dear, by welcoming him so warmly when he called on you at your aunt's."

Indiana paled.

"I was not responsible for that visit, and I was so little flattered by it that if I were in your place, I wouldn't receive him."

"You women are all such cunning liars that you lie for the sheer pleasure of it! I heard that you danced every dance with him."

"Then you didn't hear the truth."

"It was your own aunt who told me! Besides, you don't have to defend yourself because I don't mind at all. Your aunt was trying to bring about a reconciliation between us—which Monsieur de Ramière wanted very much—and I have to admit that he's not only been very helpful to me, but so tactful and discreet about it that I almost didn't know he was doing anything. So, since I'm not the savage you think I am, and since I don't like being under any obligation to a stranger, I thought I would square our accounts."

"How?"

"By visiting him at Cercy this morning with Ralph and trying to make a friend of him. His mother was there—a charming woman!—and the house itself is elegant and luxurious without being ostentatious. There wasn't any trace of the self-importance you often find in those old aristocratic families. . . . When all's said and done, this Ramière's a good fellow, and I've invited him to have lunch with us and then visit the factory. I've had good reports about his brother, and it's true that he can't hurt my business by using my procedures, so I'd just as soon have that family profit from them as another. Besides, you can't keep such things hidden for very long, and if manufacturing methods continue to progress as they're doing, my secret will soon only be a stage secret anyway!"

"Well, my dear Delmare," said Sir Ralph, "you know I've always disapproved of your secrecy. If a man is a good citizen, then any discovery he makes belongs to his country, and if I—"

"There you go again with your ideas of philanthropy, Sir Ralph! You want me to think that your fortune isn't really yours and that if your country decides to lay claim to it tomorrow, you'll be quite ready to exchange it for a beggar's cup and a walking stick! Nonsense! Someone like you—a man who likes his luxuries as much as a sultan does his—shouldn't preach contempt for wealth!"

"What I say has nothing to do with philanthropy," Sir Ralph responded. "It's not philanthropy but intelligent self-interest that would lead us to do good to others simply to prevent them from doing harm to us. Everyone knows that I'm a selfish man, and I'm no longer ashamed of it, because after a careful analysis of every virtue, I've discovered that self-interest is the basis of them all. Love and devotion, which seem to be generous and disinterested passions, are probably the most self-centered ones that exist, and I assure you that patriotism is equally so. I don't think much of men, but since I fear them as much as I dislike them, I certainly wouldn't do anything to let them know that. So we are therefore *both* selfish men—the only difference is that I admit it and you deny it."

They began a discussion in which each of them egoistically tried to prove the egoism of the other, and Indiana took the opportunity to go to her room, where she would be free to think about what this unexpected turn of events might mean.

This is a good time to tell you not only what those thoughts were, but also to describe the consequences of Noun's death for the various people affected by it.

To the reader as well as to me, it seems clear that poor Noun—in one of those moments of violent emotional crisis when the most extreme resolutions seem the easiest to act upon—must have thrown herself into the river out of desperation; but since she probably hadn't returned to the house after leaving Raymon, and since no one had either seen her or had any idea of what she intended to do, suicide was never even suggested as an explanation for her mysterious death.

Two people must have been sure that her death had been a deliberate act: M. de Ramière and the gardener of Lagny. The former hid his grief by pretending to be ill; the latter kept silent out of fear and guilt. This man, whose greed had led him to connive at the lovers' meetings during the entire winter, was the only person who might have noticed the young Creole's unhappiness, but since he feared, with reason, the reproach of his masters and the contempt of his fellow servants, he said nothing about it. And when M. Delmare, having previously learned about the intrigue, became suspicious and asked him if anything else had happened during his absence, the gardener insisted defiantly that nothing had. Some people in the neighborhood—not a very populated one, by the way—had sometimes seen Noun walking along the road to Cercy late at night, but there hadn't seemed to be any communication between her and M. de Ramière after the end of January. Since she had died on March 28, this left bad luck as the only explanation for her death: walking through the park at night, she must have lost her bearings in the dense fog that had covered the area for several days, missed the bridge that crossed the narrow stream, and fallen from the steep banks into the rain-swollen water.

Sir Ralph, who was more observant than his conversation would seem to indicate, had deduced that M. de Ramière was somehow responsible, but he said nothing about his suspicions because he felt it would be useless and cruel to reproach a man who was already unfortunate enough to have such a source of remorse in his life. He even advised the colonel, who expressed his own doubts about the matter to him, that it was absolutely necessary, given the state of Mme. Delmare's health, to continue to conceal from her the possible reasons for her childhood friend's suicide. Thus poor Noun's destiny was to have her death treated with the same secrecy as her love affair;

there was a tacit understanding not to talk about it in front of Indiana, and soon no one talked about it at all.

But these precautions were useless, because Indiana had her own reasons for suspecting at least part of the truth: the bitter accusations she had heaped on Noun's head on that fateful evening seemed reason enough for the unhappy girl to have decided to take her life. That was why the horrible moment when she first discovered the dead body floating on the water was the final blow to her already troubled sleep and her already heavy heart; her illness, which had been progressing slowly, began to advance more rapidly, and this young and possibly healthy woman, hiding her suffering from her husband's unsubtle and unseeing eyes, refused to be cured and was allowing herself to die under the weight of her sorrow and discouragement.

"Oh, how unhappy I am!" she exclaimed as she entered her room after learning of Raymon's imminent visit. "A curse on this man who comes here only to bring despair and death! O God, why do you allow him to come between you and me, to give him the power to point at me and say, 'She's mine! I will make her lose her sanity, I will ruin her life, and if she resists me, I will blanket everything around her with guilt, regret, and terror!' O God, it isn't fair to persecute a poor woman like this!"

She began to weep bitterly, for the memory of Raymon brought with it the heartbreakingly vivid memory of Noun.

"Poor Noun! Poor friend and companion of my childhood and my native land!" she thought sadly. "Poor unfortunate girl! That man was our murderer, as fatal to you as to me! I can't tell you how unhappy I am without you—you who loved me, who guessed at my sorrows, who knew how to make them easier to bear by your innocent gaiety! Was it for this that I brought you from so far away? How did that man get you to betray me? He must have deceived you so completely that you didn't understand what you had done until you saw how angry I was! Oh, Noun, I was so angry that I was too harsh with you, so harsh that my cruelty drove you to your death! Poor girl, why didn't you wait a few hours, until my resentment had blown away like a feather in the wind? Why didn't you come to me and throw yourself into my arms and say, 'I was a fool, and he took advantage of my foolishness. I didn't know what I was doing, but you know how much I love and respect you.' I would have hugged you, we would have cried together, and

you would still be alive. But you're dead! So young, so beautiful, so full of life—and dead! Dead at nineteen, and such a terrible death!"

Though she was unaware of it, Indiana was not only weeping for her companion, but also for the illusions that had filled
three days of her life, the most beautiful days, the only ones
she had ever truly lived, for during those three days she had
loved with a passion Raymon couldn't have begun to imagine
even if he had been the most arrogant and presumptuous man
alive. And just as her love had been deep and blind, so had her
sense of betrayal been sharp and painful; the first love of a
heart like hers is always modest and chaste.

Nevertheless, Indiana's initial response had been due more
to shame and anger than the result of careful reflection, and I
have no doubt that Raymon would have been forgiven if he
had had a few more minutes in which to beg such a pardon.
But fate had frustrated both his love and his cunning, and Indiana now honestly believed that she would hate him forever.

X

As for Raymon, it was neither the blow to his ego nor a spirit of Don Juanism that made him pursue Indiana's love and forgiveness more zealously than ever, but a sense that they were probably unattainable—which inevitably made him feel that no other woman on earth was her equal or worth the effort to win. That was what he was like: his entire life was ruled by an insatiable craving for adventure and excitement. If he loved society, with its rigid rules and restrictions, it was because he enjoyed the challenge of resisting and outwitting them, and if he hated the usual kinds of "acceptable" dissipation, it was because he despised pleasures that were easily acquired and therefore not worth the having.

You mustn't think, however, that Noun's death had left him unmoved. On hearing the news, he felt such self-disgust that his first impulse had been to load his pistols and blow his brains out; only the thought of his mother stopped him. What would become of that aged, failing woman whose life had been so full of trouble and grief, who lived only for him, her treasure, her only hope? Should he break her heart and cut short the few remaining years of her life? No, certainly not. The best way to atone for his crime would be to devote himself to her totally, and here turned to his mother in Paris fully determined to make her forget how he had for all practical purposes left her alone during a large part of the winter.

In his own circle, Raymon exerted an incredible influence, for with all his faults and despite all his youthful escapades, he was nevertheless superior to most men in society. We have not explained the reasons for his reputation for wit and talent because they weren't relevant to the events we had to describe, but it is now time to inform you that this Raymon, whose frivolity and moral frailty you have witnessed and perhaps criticized, is the same Raymon who once exercised a powerful

influence over your thoughts, whatever they may be today.
You avidly devoured his political pamphlets, and when you
read his articles in the newspapers of the time, you were often
swayed by the irresistible charm of his style and the urbanely
courteous tone in which he made his points.

I am referring to a time long past—or rather, what is considered long past these days, when one counts not by centuries or
even by rulers, but by ministers. I am referring to the time of
Martignac*—to that time of uneasy quiet, more like an armi-
stice than a peace, which had somehow been inserted into the
midst of our political era; to those fifteen months of a reign
characterized by ideas that were to have such a peculiar influence on our principles and morals, and perhaps even be responsible for the strange results of our last revolution.

Certain young talents began to flourish in those days, and
since they were unfortunate enough to come of age in a time
of transition, they had to pay their tribute to the tendencies of
the time: conciliation, vacillation, compromise. As far as I
know, there has never been another period when the skillful
use of words hid so much ignorance or so completely distorted
reality. It was a time of constraints and restrictions, and it
would be hard to decide who made the most use of them, the
short-robed Jesuits or the long-robed lawyers. Political moderation became as much a part of social discourse as polite manners, and each fulfilled the same function: it masked antagonisms
and taught the antagonists to fight secretly and without scandal. In defense of those young men, however, we must admit
that they were often like light boats swept along in the wake of
great ships, not understanding where they were being led, but
proud and happy to be part of the flotilla and filling their new
sails.

Although by birth and fortune Raymon should have been
one of the partisans of absolute monarchy, he sacrificed his
position among that group in favor of the "modern" ideas of

*time of Martignac: period (1828–29) when King Charles X called on
this moderate statesman to be chief minister of France. By forming a
cabinet composed of both reactionaries and moderates, he tried—unsuc-
cessfully—to reconcile the conflicting demands of the old aristocracy
who believed in absolute monarchy and the new bourgeoisie who believed in a constitutional monarchy, which they hoped would preserve
some of the hard-won rights of the Revolution.

his time and became a fervent apostle of the Charter*; at least that was what he thought he was doing and what he exerted himself to prove. But outmoded theories are subject to interpretation, and the Charter of Louis XVIII was already like the Gospel of Jesus Christ: everyone felt free to interpret the text as he wished, and people paid no more attention to such interpretations than they did to sermons. It was a time of luxurious living and idle amusements, when civilization slept at the edge of a bottomless abyss and was interested only in enjoying its final pleasures.

Raymon had taken his stand on that wavering political line between abuse of power and abuse of freedom—a vague, shifting ground on which many men searched, though in vain, for shelter from the impending storm. He thought, as did other young and inexperienced people, that it was still possible to be a conscientious spokesman for that position, which was clearly an error at a time when people pretended to listen to the voice of reason but stifled it whenever and wherever it was heard. Since he had no political ambitions, he thought he was disinterested, but he was wrong. He enjoyed and profited from society as it was; it couldn't be changed without diminishing his pleasures and advantages, and when one realizes how perfectly content one is, one also soon recognizes the need for moderation and the advantages of maintaining the status quo. What man is so ungrateful as to reproach Providence with the unhappiness of others if that same Providence showers down on him nothing but smiles and benefits? It would have been impossible to persuade those young supporters of a constitutional monarchy that the constitution was already old and useless, a heavy, exhausting burden on society, when it weighed so lightly on them and brought with it only benefits! Who believes in a misery he himself does not experience?

Nothing is easier, and more frequently done, than to fool oneself when one is an intellectual skilled in all the subtleties of language, for language is a queen—a sovereign who prostitutes herself by taking on every role, honorable or ignoble, sometimes by openly making herself alluring, sometimes by stealthily concealing herself to the point of invisibility; she is a

*the Charter: a document, signed in 1814 by Louis XVIII on his ascension to the throne, that established a constitutional monarchy and represented an attempt to allow for the antagonistic political claims of the old aristocracy and the emerging middle class.

special pleader who has an answer for everything, who has always foreseen everything, who will take on a thousand different shapes to prove herself right. The most honest man is the one who is the best thinker and doer; the most powerful man, the one who is the best speaker and writer.

Rich enough not to have to write for money, Raymon wrote because he wanted to, and—or at least so he told himself, in perfect good faith—because he felt it was his duty. He had a rare ability to argue skillfully even against proven facts; this had made him an invaluable man to the ministry—whose aims he served much better by his impartial criticisms than others did with their blind loyalty—and even more invaluable to that fashionable society of golden youth which was quite willing to give up the more absurd features of their ancient privileges but still wanted to preserve the real advantages of their present position.

Actually, they were very talented, those men who were still trying to keep society from tottering over the brink of the precipice and who fought with great equanimity and self-possession against the catastrophe that was about to engulf them even though they were themselves suspended between two dangers. To succeed in creating for themselves convictions that every aspect of reality gave the lie to, and to make those convictions prevail among others who have no convictions at all, is proof of an extraordinarily impressive skill, one quite beyond the understanding of the ordinary uncultivated mind that has not studied the magic art of transformation. . . .

Raymon had therefore no sooner returned to that society which was both his world and his element than he was swept into its vital and exciting currents. His love affairs, which had absorbed him so intently, were temporarily erased from his mind by more important interests, which he approached with his usual boldness and intensity; and when he saw himself more sought after than ever by the most distinguished people in Paris, he knew that he loved life more than ever. Was he guilty in forgetting his secret remorse while reaping well-earned rewards for the services he rendered his country? Almost despite himself, he felt life flooding back into his throbbing heart, his active mind, his strong and vigorous body, and he was convinced that destiny itself was working to make him happy—though sometimes a restless ghost would visit his dreams, and then he would beg forgiveness for trying to protect himself from the terrors of the grave by clinging to the affections of the living.

But no sooner had he returned to his previous life than he also felt the old need to combine his political speculations, his ambitious dreams, and his visions of philosophical possibilities with his desire for love and adventure. I use the word *ambitious*, but it was not an ambition for honors or wealth, which he didn't need, but for reputation and popularity within his aristocratic society.

After the tragic ending of his double intrigue, he had at first despaired of ever seeing Mme. Delmare again. But even while he was still sounding the depths of his loss and brooding over the treasure that had escaped him, he found himself not only hoping but confidently expecting to recapture it. When he considered the obstacles blocking his way, he quickly realized that the most difficult ones would come from Indiana herself and that it would therefore be best to use her husband to disguise his attack. It was not an original idea, but it was a proven one; jealous husbands are particularly well suited for that kind of service.

Two weeks after Raymon had first thought of this, he was on the way to Lagny, where he was expected for lunch. You will not insist that I tell you all the details of the clever services he had performed for M. Delmare to make himself agreeable to that gentleman; I would rather, since I am describing the characters of this story, draw a quick sketch of the colonel.

Do you know what people in the provinces mean when they say someone is an honest man? They mean someone who doesn't encroach on his neighbor's field, who doesn't ask his creditors for one sou more than what they owe him, who tips his hat to everyone who greets him; someone who doesn't attack young women on the public roads, and who doesn't set anyone's barn on fire, who doesn't rob passersby from a dark corner of his property. As long as he religiously respects the lives and the money of his fellow citizens, nothing more is asked of him. He may beat his wife, mistreat his servants, ruin his children, and it is no one's business. Society condemns only those acts that do it harm; it is not concerned with private life.

And such was the morality of M. Delmare. He had never studied any social contract other than the one that says, "Every man is master in his own house." He considered all tender feelings to be female nonsense and sentimental silliness. He

was a man without wit, tact, or education—and was regarded
more highly than many who were more talented and amiable.
He had large shoulders and a strong wrist, was an expert with
the saber and the sword, and was very quick to take offense.
Since he often didn't understand a joke, he was constantly
worried that people were making fun of him; and since he was
also incapable of responding appropriately, he had only one
way to defend himself: to compel everyone to be silent by
threatening them. His favorite expressions involved giving
someone a beating or settling an affair of honor, and people always used the word *brave* before his name because military
courage is apparently a question of having broad shoulders and
a long mustache, of swearing crudely, and of reaching for a
sword at the slightest provocation.

God preserve me from thinking that military camps brutal-
ize all men, but I do believe that one must have a very strong
sense of innate decency to resist their unconsciously barbaric
habits of domination. If you have done your military service,
you are quite familiar with the kind of officer whose uniform
seems to be part of his flesh, and you will admit that there are
large numbers of them among the remains of the imperial
troops. Those men, united and urged on by a powerful hand,
accomplished military miracles and towered over the smoke of
the battlefields like giants, but when they returned to civilian
life, those same heroes were nothing more than unthinking,
vulgar, belligerent soldiers; we were lucky if they didn't behave in society as if they were in a conquered country!

It was not so much their fault as the fault of the times. They
were naive, and they believed in the flattery that had come
with victory; they allowed themselves to be persuaded that
they were great patriots because they had defended their country—some of them against their will, others for money or
glory. But *did* they defend it, those thousands of men who
blindly adopted the error of a single man and who, after having saved France, allowed it to be basely destroyed? And
though I agree that a soldier's loyalty to his officer is a grand
and noble sentiment, I call it loyalty, not patriotism. I congratulate those who conquered Spain, I do not thank them. As to
the honor of France, I cannot understand how that can be the
way to establish it among our neighbors, and I find it hard to
believe that the emperor's generals were greatly concerned
about it during that depressing stage of our glory. However, I

know that it is forbidden to speak about these things objectively, and I will be silent. History will be the judge.

M. Delmare had all the virtues and all the faults of these men. Childishly innocent about certain fine points of honor, he managed his affairs to his maximum benefit without disturbing himself about the good or bad effects of his actions on others. The law was his only conscience, his rights under the law his only moral guidelines. His honesty was narrow and rigid: he didn't borrow because he was afraid he might not be able to repay, and he didn't lend because he was afraid he would never be repaid. He never took anything and he never gave anything: he would rather die than pick up a piece of kindling from the king's forests, but he would kill you without a qualm for picking up a twig in his. He was useful only to himself, but harmful to no one. He paid no attention to anything happening around him lest he be forced to do someone a favor, but if he did feel himself honor bound to do so, no one could show more good will, zeal, and generosity. Being at the same time both as trusting as a child and as suspicious as a tyrant, he might believe a false oath and distrust a sincere promise. Just as it had in the army, form meant everything to him; his behavior was so ruled by public opinion that neither common sense nor reason counted for anything in his decisions, and when he had said, "That's the way things are done," he thought he had found the ultimate, indisputable argument.

His nature was the exact opposite of his wife's; his heart could not have been less capable of understanding her heart, his mind less suited to appreciating her mind. And yet her mute, stubborn opposition to him, born of her slavery, was certainly sometimes unjust and too severe. Mme. Delmare had too little faith in her husband's heart; she thought it cruel, but it was merely hard. When he lost his temper, the outbreak was more rough than angry, and his manners were more unpolished than impertinent. He was not evil by nature; he had his moments of compassion, which led him to repentance, and in his repentance he was almost sensitive. It was life in the camps that had made brutality one of his principles. With a less vulnerable, less gentle wife, he would have been as timid as a tame wolf, but this woman had been discouraged by her fate and did not even try to find ways to make it better.

XI

RAYMON'S courage almost failed him as he stepped down from his tilbury in the courtyard at Lagny: he was about to go back into that house which held so many terrible memories! His overpowering passion, reinforced by his logical arguments, made it possible for him to muffle his feelings of remorse but not to eliminate them completely, and at that moment they were as strong as his desire.

The first person to greet him was Sir Ralph, and seeing him dressed in his inevitable hunting costume, flanked by his dogs, as serious as a Scottish laird, Raymon imagined for a moment that the portrait he had seen in Mme. Delmare's bedroom had come to life. A few minutes later M. Delmare joined them, and they sat down to lunch without Indiana having made an appearance. Crossing the hallway, passing in front of the billiard room, recognizing the places he had previously seen under such different circumstances, had so upset Raymon that he could hardly remember why he was there.

"Isn't Madame Delmare coming down?" the colonel asked Lelièvre sharply.

"Madame didn't sleep well," Lelièvre replied, "and Mademoiselle Noun—I'm sorry, I keep saying that name!—Mademoiselle Fanny, I mean, said she was resting now."

"Then how come I just saw her at her window? Fanny is mistaken. Go tell Madame that lunch is served—or rather, won't you, Sir Ralph, please go upstairs and see if your cousin is really too ill to join us?"

When Raymon had heard the servant use Noun's name out of habit, he had felt a twinge of nervous regret; but at the colonel's request, he felt a surge of jealous rage.

"He's sending him to her bedroom!" he thought. "It's not enough that he hangs the man's portrait there, but now he's sending him there in person! This Englishman can do what the husband himself doesn't dare . . ."

M. Delmare, as if he had guessed what Raymon was thinking, said, "Don't be surprised at my request. Sir Ralph is the family doctor, he's a cousin, and he's a fine man we're all very fond of."

Ralph was gone for about ten minutes, during which time Raymon was distracted and ill at ease; he ate nothing and kept looking at the door.

Finally the Englishman reappeared. "Indiana is really not well," he said. "I prescribed a return to bed."

He then sat down at the table and proceeded to eat a hearty meal, as did the colonel.

"She must be doing this as an excuse for not seeing me," thought Raymon. "Neither of these two men believe she's ill—the husband is more angry than worried! Good, this is better than I had hoped for."

Her resistance revived his determination. Noun's image, which had seemed to be everywhere, faded, and was soon replaced by the willowy silhouette of Indiana. In the drawing room he sat down at her embroidery frame and casually—while making conversation and pretending to be thinking of something else—examined the skillful craftsmanship of the flowers she was working on, fingered the skeins of silks she must have handled, inhaled the perfume left on them by her tiny fingers. He had already seen this same piece of work in Indiana's bedroom; at that time she had barely begun it, and now it was covered with flowers that had been watered with daily tears and had blossomed beneath her feverish breaths. Raymon felt tears come to his own eyes, and when he raised them by some inexplicable sympathy to the same horizon that Indiana sadly contemplated every day, he could see in the distance the white walls of Cercy outlined against the dark hills.

The colonel's voice suddenly roused him.

"Well, my good neighbor," he said, "it's time to pay my debt to you and keep my promise. The factory is going full force and all the workers are at their places. Here's some paper and pencil so you can take notes."

Raymon followed the colonel, examined the factory with eager curiosity, made comments that proved he knew both chemistry and mechanics equally well, listened with unimaginable patience to M. Delmare's endless dissertations, agreed with some of his ideas and disagreed with others, and in every way acted as if he were passionately absorbed by everything he saw and heard, while in reality he was paying hardly any attention and his mind was filled with nothing but thoughts of Indiana.

As a matter of fact, he really did know something about every branch of science and was interested in every discovery or invention, and he was indeed helping his brother, who had put his entire fortune into a similar though much larger enterprise. It also seemed to him that the best way to exploit the opportunities of this meeting was to concentrate on M. Delmare's technical knowledge, which was his one area of superiority.

Sir Ralph, without much of a mind for business but with a good grasp of politics, interjected some astute comments about broader economic issues; the factory workers, eager to display their skill to an expert, outdid themselves in enterprise and productivity; and Raymon looked at everything, listened to everything, answered everything—and thought only of the love affair that was responsible for bringing him there.

When they had completely covered the internal workings, the discussion turned to the amount and force of the water power. They left the factory and climbed to the top of the lock, where they asked the man in charge of the gates to open them and report the various depths.

"Beg pardon, monsieur," said the man, speaking to M. Delmare, who was saying that the maximum depth was fifteen feet, "but we've seen it at seventeen feet this year."

"When was that? You're making a mistake," said the colonel.

"Excuse me, monsieur, but it was the night before you returned from Belgium—the night Mademoiselle Noun was found drowned. And the proof is that her body passed over that dike down there and didn't stop until it got to just where Monsieur is standing right now."

As he spoke, he pointed to where Raymon stood. The unhappy young man turned deathly pale as he looked at the water flowing at his feet and imagined he could see the livid face still reflected in it, the corpse still floating on it. He felt dizzy and would have fallen into the river if Sir Ralph had not grabbed his arm and pulled him away.

"You may be right," said the colonel, who had noticed nothing and whose thoughts were so far from Noun that he had no idea of Raymon's state of mind, "but that was unusual, and the average depth of the water is . . . But what the devil is the matter with you two?" he asked abruptly.

"Nothing," replied Sir Ralph. "I stepped on Monsieur's foot

as I turned around, and it must have been very painful. I'm so sorry."

Sir Ralph's answer was given in such a natural, matter-of-fact tone that Raymon was sure he actually thought he was telling the truth. They exchanged a few polite phrases, then the conversation took up where it had left off.

Raymon left Lagny a few hours later without having seen Indiana. That was better than he had hoped for, better than finding her untroubled and indifferent.

When he returned, however, it was the same thing. That second time the colonel was alone, and to win him over, Raymon marshaled his almost infinite resources to charm him. He flattered his host in a thousand clever ways, praising Napoleon, whom he did not like; deploring the indifference of the government, which had contemptuously abandoned the glorious remnants of the Grand Army and disrespectfully condemned them to a life of oblivion; propounding the precepts of the opposition as forcefully as his opinions allowed; choosing from among his various beliefs those that were most likely to be shared by M. Delmare; and finally, in order to win his confidence, even creating for himself a personality and character quite unlike his own and becoming a bon vivant, a jovial companion, an insouciant good-for-nothing.

"If my wife were ever to become interested in that man . . ." the colonel thought as he watched him drive away. Then he began to snicker at the very idea, for he had decided that Raymon was nothing more than a frivolous "charmer."

Mme. de Ramière was staying at Cercy at that time. Raymon spoke to her about Mme. Delmare's grace and intelligence, and without specifically asking his mother to pay her a visit, he was clever enough to lead her to think of doing so and believe it was her own idea.

"She is the only one of my neighbors I don't know, and since I've just recently arrived here, it's for me to make the first call. I will go with you to Lagny next week."

The day finally came.

"She can't avoid me now," thought Raymon.

He was right. When Indiana saw an unknown elderly woman get out of the carriage, she herself came to the entryway to greet her. But as soon as she recognized Raymon as the man with her, she understood that he must somehow have persuaded his mother to make this visit, and she felt such contempt for that kind of deception that she was able to act with dignity and composure. She received Mme. de Ramière kindly and respectfully, but her coldness to Raymon was so glacial that he felt he couldn't endure it. He was not used to such disdain; a mere glance was usually enough to win over even those whose minds were set against him, and his pride was hurt. He decided to behave as if he were indifferent to what he chose to consider a woman's whims and excused himself to join M. Delmare in the park, leaving the two women alone.

Little by little Indiana, won over by the charm that a woman of superior intelligence and a high-minded, generous spirit knows how to exert even in her most superficial relations, lost some of her reserve and became affectionate and almost vivacious with Mme. de Ramière. Because she had never known her own mother, and because Mme. de Carvajal, despite her presents and her praise, was far from maternal, her heart responded to this woman's warmth and sympathy.

When Raymon rejoined his mother just as she was getting into her carriage, he saw Indiana kiss Mme. de Ramière's hand. Poor Indiana needed to attach herself to someone; she grasped eagerly at anything that offered a possibility of interest or affection to fill the unrelieved loneliness of her empty life—and besides, she told herself, surely Raymon's mother would save her from the trap her son was trying to set.

"I will throw myself into that good woman's arms and tell her everything if I have to," she was already thinking. "I will beg her to save me from her son, and her prudence will protect both of us."

Raymon's ideas were very different.

"My wonderful mother!" he thought as he returned with her to Cercy. "Her charm and goodness work miracles! I already owe her everything—my education, my success in the world, my position in society. The only thing lacking was the joy of owing to her the heart of a woman like Indiana."

Clearly, Raymon loved his mother because he needed her and because of what she did for him; that is why all children love their mothers.

Later that week Raymon received an invitation to spend three days at Bellerive—Sir Rodolphe Brown's magnificent country house located between Cercy and Lagny—where the baronet had invited the best shots in the neighborhood to join a hunting party to thin out some of the game that was devouring his gardens and woods. Raymon did not like Sir Ralph, and he did not like to hunt; but he knew that Indiana acted as her cousin's hostess during such great occasions, and the hope of meeting her there made him decide to accept the invitation.

Sir Ralph, however, was not expecting her to come this time because she had excused herself on the grounds of ill health. But he had not reckoned on M. Delmare. Although he resented any effort his wife made to amuse herself, he was even more irritated when she refused to accept whatever amusements he decided to allow her, so he complained bitterly. "Do you want the whole countryside to think I keep you under lock and key? You make it look as if I were a jealous husband, which is a ridiculous role that I won't accept. And besides, how can you be so impolite to your cousin? Is it right to refuse to help him when it's thanks to him that we have the factory and are so prosperous? He needs you, and you hesitate? I don't understand you or your notions! You like all the people I don't like, and those I do like are unfortunate enough to displease you!"

"I don't think such a reproach applies in this case," replied Mme. Delmare. "I love my cousin like a brother, and we were already old friends when you first met him."

"Yes, yes, you always have an answer. But I know very well that you don't find the poor man romantic enough! You think he's cold and self-centered because he doesn't read novels or cry at the death of a dog. Besides, I'm not only talking about him. How did you receive Monsieur de Ramière, whom I find a very agreeable young man? When Madame de Carvajal introduces him to you, you're very cordial, but when I want you to be nice to him, you decide you can't stand him and go to bed whenever he calls! Do you want it to look as if I don't know how to behave? You must put a stop to all this and begin living like everyone else!"

Given his plans, Raymon felt it inadvisable to show too much eagerness—a pretense of indifference is a successful ploy with almost every woman who thinks she is loved—and by the time he arrived at Sir Ralph's the hunt was already in progress. Since he didn't expect Indiana to arrive before dinner, Raymon decided to use the time to prepare his plan of action.

This would be his best opportunity to justify his behavior. He had two full days ahead of him and decided to apportion his time carefully: he would spend what remained of the present day breaking through her defenses, the next day persuading her, the day after that being happy. He even looked at his watch and calculated almost to the hour when he would know if he had failed or succeeded.

XII

HE had been in the drawing room for almost two hours before he heard Mme. Delmare's soft, slightly husky voice in the next room. As a result of having spent so much time thinking about how he would seduce her, he had become as passionately involved in the subject as an author with his theme or a lawyer with his case, and when he saw Indiana he felt like an actor who is so steeped in his role that when he finds himself in the presence of the principal character of the play, he can no longer distinguish his theatrical emotions from his real ones.

She was so changed that a feeling of true concern managed to penetrate even the many layers of Raymon's feverish projects. Sorrow and illness had left their mark on her; she was barely pretty anymore, and he actually felt that his conquest would satisfy his pride more than his pleasure. But of course he also felt that it was nothing less than his duty to restore her to health and happiness.

Seeing her so pale and sad, he was sure she would be incapable of putting up a very strong defense. How could such a fragile shell contain a moral will that was determined enough to have any great powers of resistance?

He decided he would first try to frighten her by telling her how ill and depressed she looked, then entice her by holding out the possibility of a better life and urging her to reach out for it.

"Indiana," he said, his secret assurance hidden beneath an air of profound melancholy, "what's happened to you since I last saw you? I never dreamed that this moment which I've worked so hard to bring about would be so painful for me!"

This was not what Indiana had expected to hear. She had been sure Raymon would be awkward, timid, overcome by guilt—but instead of accusing himself, swearing he was sorry, pleading for pardon, all his sadness and pity was for *her*! She must be in a terrible state indeed to inspire compassion on the part of a man who should have begged for hers!

A sophisticated Frenchwoman would not have lost her head in such a delicate situation, but Indiana had no experience of the world; she was neither subtle enough nor insincere enough, and she was completely incapable of maintaining her moral advantage. His words reminded her of all she had suffered, and tears began to glisten on the edge of her eyelids.

"It's true, I'm not well," she said weakly as she sat down, exhausted, on the chair Raymon offered her. "Indeed, I think I'm quite ill, and to *you*, monsieur, I feel I have every right to complain."

Raymon hadn't hoped to be able to broach the subject so quickly, and—as the saying goes—he grabbed the bull by the horns. Taking one of her cold, dry hands in his, he said, "Don't say that, Indiana! Don't tell me that I'm responsible for your troubles, or I won't know whether to laugh with pleasure or cry with grief!"

"Pleasure!" she repeated, her large, sad, blue eyes full of amazement.

"I should have said hope, because if I'm responsible for causing your unhappiness, then I may also be able to cure it. Oh, won't you say just one word," he added, kneeling beside her on a cushion that had fallen from the sofa. "One word asking for my blood . . . my life . . . !"

"That's enough!" said Indiana bitterly, removing her hand from his. "You've broken your promises once before, and there's no way to repair the damage you did!"

"But I want to! I will!" he exclaimed, reaching for her hand again.

"It's too late," she said. "Can you give me back Noun, my sister, my only friend?"

Raymon's blood turned to ice, and there was no need to simulate emotion: some feelings are so genuine and powerful that no further artifice is necessary.

"She knows everything," he thought, "and she has judged me."

Nothing could be more humiliating to him than to be reproached for his crime by the woman who had been his innocent accomplice, nothing more bitter than to see Noun being wept for by her rival.

"Yes, monsieur," said Indiana, raising her tear-washed face, "you are responsible—" But she stopped when she saw how pale Raymon had become; he must have looked quite frightening, because in truth he had never felt such pain in all his life.

And as soon as she noticed it, her kind heart, and the tenderness he inspired in her despite everything, made him once again her master.

"Forgive me!" she said, dismayed. "I can see that I hurt you, but I've suffered so much myself! Sit down, and let us talk about something else."

Her quick and generous response touched Raymon even more profoundly; he began to sob, and he covered Indiana's hand with tears and kisses as he brought it to his lips. It was the first time he had been able to cry since Noun's death, and it was thanks to Indiana that he felt some relief from that terrible weight.

"Oh, if you can weep for her like this, you who never even knew her, if you can feel so badly about the pain you have caused me, I daren't reproach you for it anymore. Let us weep for her together, monsieur, so that she may see us from her place in heaven and forgive us!"

Raymon broke out in a cold sweat. Although her words *you who never even knew her* had removed a great weight from his mind, that appeal to his victim from Indiana's innocent lips struck him with superstitious terror. Finding it hard to breathe, he got up and walked nervously over to a window, sitting down next to it and taking in great gulps of fresh air. Indiana remained where she was, silent, deeply moved, secretly happy to see Raymon weep like a child and lose his self-control like a woman.

"He is a good man," she said softly to herself. "He loves me, and his heart is warm and generous. He did wrong, but he has paid for his sin with his remorse. I should have forgiven him sooner."

Mistaking the anguish of a guilty man for the repentance of a loving one, she looked at him with tenderness; her confidence in him was returning.

"You mustn't weep anymore," she said, walking over to him. "I'm the one who killed her, the one responsible for her death, the one who will have to live with that burden all my life. I gave way to my fury and suspicion, and that hurt and humiliated her. All my bitterness against you was let loose on her! You were the one who had offended me, yet it was my poor friend that I punished. . . . I was very hard on her!"

"And on me," said Raymon, instantly forgetting all the past so he could concentrate on the present.

Indiana blushed.

"Perhaps I shouldn't have held you responsible for the terrible loss I suffered on that awful night," she said, "but I can't forget how imprudent and presumptuous you were. Your thoughtlessness, your lack of delicacy, your complete indifference to my well-being . . . I thought you loved me, and you didn't even respect me!"

Raymon's strength, determination, love, and expectations all returned. The sinister impressions that had made his blood run cold vanished like a nightmare, and he was again young, vital, full of desire, passion, and hopes for the future.

"I'm guilty if you hate me," he said vehemently, throwing himself at her feet. "But if you love me, I'm not and never have been. Tell me, Indiana, do you love me?"

"Do you deserve it?" she asked.

"If, to deserve it, I have to idolize you——" Raymon began.

"Listen to me," she interrupted, giving him her hands and fixing her tear-filled but glowing eyes on him. "Listen carefully. Do you know what it means to love a woman like me? No, you do not. You thought you would merely be gratifying a momentary caprice. You judged my heart by the blasé hearts of all the other women over whom you have ruled, and you don't realize that I've never yet loved anyone and that I will not give my pure and untouched heart in exchange for a withered and dissipated one, my unstinting love for a measured one, my entire life for the sensation of a day!"

"Madame, I love you passionately, intensely. My heart is also young and ardent, and although it's not worthy of yours, no man's heart ever will be. I know how you must be loved—and I didn't just learn it now. Don't I know your life? Didn't I describe it to you the first time we spoke, at that ball? Wasn't I able to read the whole history of your heart in your first look? What do you think I fell in love with? Your beauty? Oh, that's certainly enough to drive even an older and more measured man wild, but as for me—I love that delicate and charming envelope because inside is a pure and heavenly soul, because a celestial flame burns within it, because I see you as not only a woman but an angel."

"I know you are a skillful flatterer, but don't hope to win me by appealing to my vanity. I need affection, not praise. I must be loved totally, unconditionally, exclusively, hopelessly. You must be ready to sacrifice everything to me, fortune, reputation, duty, occupation, principles, family—*everything*, monsieur—because that is how I will love, and you must do the same. I'm sure you see that you can't love me like that!"

This was not Raymon's first experience with a woman who took love seriously—though fortunately for society such cases are rare—and he knew that promises made in the name of love did not have to be honored—again fortunately for society. In his experience, the women who had required those solemn oaths were often the first to break them, so he wasn't the least frightened by Indiana's requirements; as a matter of fact, he was so bewitched by the irresistible charm of this woman who was so frail yet so passionate, so physically weak yet so morally strong, that no thought of either the experiences of the past or the possibilities of the future ever crossed his mind. She was so beautiful, so alive, so impressive as she dictated her laws to him, that he remained at her feet as if mesmerized.

"I swear," he told her, "to be yours body and soul. I give you the rights to my life, my blood, my will. Take and dispose of everything—my fortune, my honor, my conscience, my thoughts, my whole being—as you see fit."

"Careful, be quiet," Indiana said, interrupting him. "My cousin is coming."

Indeed, at that moment the stolid Sir Ralph came into the room and expressed great surprise and pleasure at seeing his cousin there so unexpectedly. He asked permission to kiss her as a sign of his gratitude, then slowly and methodically lowered his head and kissed her on the lips, as was the custom among children in the country they had grown up in.

Raymon was furious, and as soon as Ralph had left them to give the servants some orders, he turned to Indiana with a desire to remove all traces of that impertinent kiss.

But she refused to allow it, telling him quietly, "Remember, you have much to atone for if you want me to believe in you."

Raymon did not understand the delicacy of her rebuff; he saw it only as a rebuff and was angry with Sir Ralph because of it. In a little while, he noticed that her cousin used the familiar *tu* when he spoke to her privately, and Raymon angrily concluded that Sir Ralph's usual formality was nothing but the prudent behavior of a favored lover; but when Indiana looked at him a few moments later and he saw the youthful innocence of her gaze, he blushed for his insulting suspicions.

Raymon was at his best that evening. There were many

guests, and everyone wanted to hear what he had to say; there was no getting away from the fame his talents had won him, and if Indiana had been vain, she would have had her first taste of happiness in listening to him speak. Instead, her simple, inexperienced mind was made uneasy by Raymon's obvious superiority. She was frightened by and fought against the almost magical power he was able to exert over those around him, thanks to a kind of magnetic charm that surely comes from either heaven or hell. Such people's rule is incomplete and ephemeral, but so incontestable that no mediocre mind can resist it and so fleeting that no trace of it survives them; after they die, people are amazed by the sensation they had caused during their lifetime.

There were, of course, moments when Indiana was fascinated by so much brilliance, but they didn't last long because she would almost immediately recognize that what she was thirsting for was happiness, not glory. She asked herself fearfully if such a man, for whom life held so many different possibilities, so many absorbing interests, would be able to devote himself to her heart and soul, to sacrifice all his ambitions to her. Watching him as he warmly defended his positions—about purely speculative doctrines and about interests that had nothing to do with their love—with such skill and ability, with so much passion and yet so much composure, she was overwhelmed by the feeling that she played only a small part in his life while he was everything in hers, and terrified by the thought that she was nothing more than a passing fancy to him while he was the dream of a whole lifetime for her.

When he offered her his arm as they left the drawing room, he whispered a few words of love to her, but she responded sadly, "How intelligent you are!"

He understood the reprimand and spent all of the next day at her side. The other guests, absorbed by their hunting, left them completely alone.

Raymon was eloquent, but Indiana had such a need to believe him that half his eloquence would have been more than enough. Women of France, you do not know what a Creole woman is like; you are not the kind to be dupes or victims, and you would not have been so easily convinced!

XIII

WHEN Sir Ralph returned from hunting and took Indiana's pulse, as he did every day, Raymon, who was watching him closely, noticed an almost imperceptible glimmer of surprise and pleasure flash over his generally impassive face. By some inexplicable impulse, the two men's eyes met, and Sir Ralph's light ones locked like an owl's on Raymon's dark ones and forced them to look away. . . . For the rest of the day the baronet watched Mme. Delmare with a keen attentiveness that might have been described as interest or solicitude if his face had been capable of reflecting any such clearly defined emotion, and Raymon tried to decide if he seemed fearful or hopeful—but without success: Ralph was impenetrable.

Suddenly, as Raymon was standing with some people a little behind Indiana's chair, he heard Ralph say to her in a low voice, "It would be good for you, cousin, to go riding tomorrow."

"But you know I have no horse just now," she replied.

"We'll find one for you. Would you like to hunt with us?"

Indiana gave several different reasons for refusing the invitation, and Raymon understood that she would prefer to remain with him; but he also understood that her cousin would go to great lengths to keep her from doing so. Leaving the group he was talking to, he approached her and added his urgings to Sir Ralph's. He resented this meddlesome chaperon and was determined to thwart his efforts.

"If you agree to follow the hunt, madame," he said to Indiana, "you will give me the courage to follow your example. I don't enjoy hunting, but to have the privilege of serving as your equerry—"

"In that case I will go," she said impetuously.

Her eyes met Raymon's for only a moment, but swift as the exchange was, Sir Ralph caught it on the wing—and for the rest of the evening Raymon could neither look at nor speak to Indiana without Sir Ralph's eyes or ears being aware of it. A feeling of dislike, almost of jealousy, filled Raymon's heart. What right did this cousin, this family friend, have to behave like a headmaster in charge of the woman with whom *he* was in love? He swore that he would make Sir Ralph regret having assumed such a role and looked for a way to irritate him without compromising Indiana, but it proved impossible; Sir Ralph was a perfect host, acting always with a dignity and a courtesy that left no opening for cutting wit or critical attack.

Quite early the next morning, Raymon had a surprise visit from his stony-faced host, whose manner was even stiffer than usual. Raymon's impatient heart beat faster with the hope of some provocation he might respond to, but it was only a question of a saddle horse that Raymon had brought to Bellerive and said he wanted to sell. Five minutes later the bargain had been concluded. There was no arguing about the price; Sir Ralph took some gold coins from his pocket, counted them out on the mantel with a quite extraordinary sangfroid, and didn't deign to reply to Raymon when the latter politely protested that there was no need to be so scrupulously exact.

As Ralph was leaving, he turned around and said, "Monsieur, the horse belongs to me as of this morning."

Raymon thought he understood that this was a way to keep him from joining the hunt, and he said dryly that he had no intention of hunting on foot.

"Monsieur," Sir Ralph replied somewhat pompously, "I am too well aware of the laws of hospitality to allow anything like that."

And he left.

When Raymon went down into the courtyard, he saw Indiana in her riding habit, playing gaily with Ophelia, who was chewing up her mistress's batiste handkerchief. Her cheeks were once again a faint, rosy pink, and her eyes once again shone with a long absent brilliance; black curls peeped out from her little hat, and the tight-fitting jacket buttoned all the way to the top emphasized her slim, graceful figure: she had become pretty again. In my opinion, the principal charm of Creoles is the extreme delicacy of their features and proportions, which enables them to retain the sweet appeal of children for a long time; Indiana, in this laughing and playful mood, looked like a fourteen-year-old.

Raymon, struck by her charming appearance, felt a thrill of

triumph and paid her the least trite compliment he could devise.

"You were worried about my health," she said to him softly, "but can't you see that now I want to live?"

He could reply only by a look full of gratitude and joy, for Sir Ralph was leading a horse over to his cousin.

Raymon recognized the one he had just sold.

Indiana had seen him putting the horse through its paces in the courtyard the day before and exclaimed in surprise: "What? Is Monsieur de Ramière good enough to lend me his horse?"

"Didn't you admire how handsome and gentle the horse was yesterday?" Sir Ralph asked her. "Well, today he's yours, and I'm only sorry, my dear, that I couldn't offer him to you sooner."

"You're becoming a humorist, cousin," said Indiana, "but I don't understand the joke. Whom shall I thank——Monsieur de Ramière, who allows me to borrow his horse, or you, who may have asked him to do so?"

"You must thank your cousin, who bought this horse for you and is giving him to you as a gift," said M. Delmare.

"Is that true, my dear Ralph?" asked Indiana, stroking the beautiful animal with the delight of a young girl receiving her first piece of jewelry.

"Hadn't we agreed that I would give you a horse in exchange for the piece of embroidery you are working for me? Go on, mount him. Don't be afraid—I've studied his disposition, and I've even ridden him myself this morning."

Indiana threw her arms around Sir Ralph's neck and from there launched herself onto Raymon's horse, fearlessly making him execute spirited half-turns to the left and right.

This domestic scene took place in a corner of the courtyard, and as Raymon observed the display of their simple and trusting mutual affection, he felt himself becoming enraged at the thought that he, who was passionately in love with Indiana, would have less than a full day in which to be alone with her.

"How happy I am!" she said, calling him to her side as they rode down the avenue leading to the park. "It's as if my dear Ralph knew exactly what gift would give me the most pleasure. . . . And you, Raymon, aren't you pleased that the horse which has carried you is now mine? Oh, how I will love and cherish him! What do you call him? I want to use the name you gave him."

"If anyone here is happy, it must be your cousin, who can give you gifts and receive your kisses," Raymon replied.

She laughed. "Are you really jealous of such a friendship? Of such great big childish kisses?"

"Jealous? Yes, perhaps I am, Indiana. I don't really know. What I *do* know is that when this pink-cheeked young cousin puts his lips to yours, when he holds you in his arms to help you mount the horse that he *gives* you and that I *sell* you, I suffer. No, madame, I am *not* happy to see you the owner of the horse I loved. I quite understand that one might be happy to offer it to you, but to be the merchant who makes it possible for someone else to make a gesture that gives you pleasure is an exquisitely painful humiliation for me. If I thought Sir Ralph capable of deliberately planning an act of such subtle cunning, I would seek satisfaction."

"Oh, I can't believe you are so jealous! How can you envy our ordinary domestic intimacy, you who are for me someone outside ordinary life, someone who will create a world of magical enchantment for me, a world that *only* you can create? I'm already disappointed in you, Raymon—I think you're only angry at my poor cousin because your pride is hurt. You seem to care more about the ordinary courtesy that I show him in public than about the unique affection I might have for someone else in secret."

"Forgive me, Indiana, forgive me! I'm wrong. You're an angel of goodness, and I don't deserve you—but I must admit that it's very painful to see that man assume such rights over you."

"*Assume* rights, Raymon? Don't you know that we're bound to him with sacred bonds of gratitude? Don't you know that his mother was my mother's sister, that we were born in the same valley, that during his adolescence he protected my childhood, was my only teacher, my only friend, the only one I could depend on, that he's followed me wherever I've gone, leaving the country I left to come live where I now live—in a word, that he's the only person in the world who loves me and cares about what happens to me?"

"Everything you tell me, Indiana, pours salt in the wound! You say this Englishman loves you? Do you know how *I* love you?"

"There's no comparison. If I had to choose between two rivals who loved me in the same way, I would have to give preference to the one who had felt that attachment first, but I assure you, Raymon, that I will never ask you to love me as Ralph does."

"Tell me about him, please, since it's impossible to penetrate his stony mask."

"Must I be the one to describe my cousin?" she asked with a smile. "I confess that I'm reluctant, because I love him so much that I would like to flatter him, for I'm afraid you won't appreciate him as he really is. Come, then, help me—what do *you* think he's like?"

"All right, but you must forgive me if what I say hurts you. . . . His face indicates someone who is a total nonentity, yet when he condescends to say anything, his conversation shows him to be educated and sensible. But he speaks so ponderously and so monotonously that one can die of boredom listening to him—no one can profit from his knowledge because he communicates it so tiresomely and dispassionately. And then his thoughts are essentially ordinary and commonplace, so that the formal purity of his diction doesn't matter. I think that he's retained every idea he was ever taught, but that he is too apathetic and his intelligence too mediocre to have developed any of his own. He is exactly the kind of man the world sees as a serious-minded person, but three quarters of his reputation is due to his solemnity, and the rest to his essential indifference."

"There's some truth in what you say, but also some prejudice," said Indiana. "I've known Ralph since the day I was born, and I haven't been able to come to such definite conclusions as you've reached so quickly. . . . It's true that his greatest fault is that he often sees the world through others' eyes, but that isn't the fault of his mind but of his education. You think that he would have been completely commonplace without education, but I think that without it he would have been much less so.

"I have to tell you something about his life in order for you to understand his personality. He was unlucky enough to have a brilliant brother who was openly preferred by his parents and had all the qualities he himself lacked: this brother learned easily, was gifted in all the arts, had a sparkling wit and a face that was more expressive than Ralph's even if less conventionally handsome. He was also affectionate, eager, lively—in a word, he was lovable. Ralph, on the other hand, loved solitude, learned slowly, did not make much of what he did know, was awkward, undemonstrative, and melancholy. When his parents saw how different he was from his older brother they treated him badly and—even worse!—humiliated him—which only made him a gloomy, daydreaming child whose every faculty was paralyzed by an unconquerable timidity.

"They managed to instill in him such deep feelings of self-hatred and self-contempt that he became discouraged with life, and when he was fifteen years old he began to show signs of melancholia, which is a purely physical illness under the cloudy sky of England, but entirely psychological under the life-giving one of Bourbon. He has often told me about the day he left his house fully determined to drown himself. While he was sitting on the beach and collecting his thoughts before carrying out his plan, he saw my Negro nurse coming toward him, carrying me in her arms. I was five years old then, they say I was pretty, and I had always liked my quiet cousin—something no one else did. Of course, he had always been kind and attentive to me, too, and that was unusual in my father's house. . . . Both of us were unhappy, so we had understood each other from the start. He would teach me his father's language, and I would babble to him in mine—and that mixture of Spanish and English was probably an expression of Ralph's personality. When I threw my arms around his neck that day, I saw that he was crying, and without understanding why, I also began to cry. At that, he hugged me and, as he told me later, swore to himself that he would stay alive for me because I was a child who was neglected if not hated, and I could be helped by his friendship. That way his life would at least be useful. I became the first and only person in his unhappy existence to whom he felt any connection. From that day on, we were almost never apart, and we spent our days happy and free in the solitude of the mountains.

"But these stories of our childhood may be boring you. If you'd rather gallop off and join the hunt . . ."

"Idiot!" said Raymon, grabbing the bridle of her horse.

"Then I'll go on," she resumed. "When Edmond Brown, Ralph's older brother, died at the age of twenty, their mother let herself die of grief and their father was inconsolable. Ralph would have been glad to relieve some of his sorrow, but his first halting attempts were greeted so coldly that his natural timidity was intensified. He was so afraid of having his sympathy rebuffed as either inadequate or unwanted that he would spend long, silent hours next to that grieving old man without daring to speak to him or show him any sign of affection—which then led his father to accuse him of being unfeeling! Edmond's death left poor Ralph even more unhappy and misunderstood than before, and I was his only consolation."

"Despite everything you say, I can't feel sorry for him," Raymon interrupted, "and there's one thing I don't understand at all. Why didn't the two of you marry?"

"For a very good reason," she replied. "When I was old enough to be married, Ralph, who is ten years older than I—which is an enormous difference in our climate, where girls become women so quickly—was already married."

"Sir Ralph is a widower? I never heard anyone speak about a wife."

"Never mention her to him. She was young, rich, and beautiful, but she had loved Edmond and was engaged to marry him, so when for various reasons, including family interests, she had to marry Ralph instead, she didn't even try to hide her distaste for him. He had to go to England with her, and when he returned to Bourbon a year after his wife's death, I was already married to Monsieur Delmare and about to leave for Europe. Ralph tried to live alone, but solitude made his illness worse. Although he's never spoken to me about his wife, I have good reason to believe that he was even more unhappy in his marriage than he had been in his father's house and that his painful memories just added to his natural melancholy. When his condition worsened, he sold his coffee plantation and came to settle in France.

"The way in which he introduced himself to my husband was nothing if not original, and it would have made me laugh if it hadn't also been such a touching proof of his warm feelings for me. 'Monsieur,' he said, 'I love your wife. I was the one who brought her up, and I think of her as my sister, or more accurately, my daughter. She is my only remaining relative and the only one in the world for whom I have any affection. I hope you will not mind if I settle near you, so the three of us can spend our lives together. People say that you are a jealous man where your wife is concerned, but also that you are a man of honor. When I give you my word that I have never loved her as a man loves a woman and never will love her in that way, you will be able to see me come and go with as little concern as if I were really your brother-in-law. Do you agree, monsieur?'

"Monsieur Delmare, who is proud of his reputation for military rectitude, was impressed by such a frank and open declaration and responded to it with a kind of ostentatious confidence

Nevertheless, it took several months of careful watching before that confidence became real, not just something to which he had boastfully given lip service. Now it is as unshakable as Ralph's constancy itself."

"Indiana, are you sure that Sir Ralph isn't deceiving himself a little when he swears he was never in love with you?" Raymon asked.

"I was twelve years old when he left Bourbon to go to England with his wife. I was sixteen when he returned to find me married, and he was more pleased than unhappy. Now he is an old man."

"At twenty-nine?"

"Don't laugh. He looks young, but his heart is worn out with suffering and he loves nothing anymore because he doesn't want to suffer anymore."

"Not even you?"

"Not even me. His friendship is only a matter of habit. In the old days, when he protected me and took charge of my education, it was a generous, giving friendship, and then I loved him the way he now loves me—because I needed him. Today I try as hard as I can to repay my debt to him, and I spend my life trying to make *his* life as pleasant and interesting as I can. When I was a child, I loved him instinctively rather than by choice, and now that he's an adult, he too loves me less with his heart than with his instincts—he loves me because he needs me, because I'm the only one who loves him. As a matter of fact, ever since Monsieur Delmare began to show some liking for him, Ralph loves him almost as much as he loves me. He was enormously courageous in protecting me against my father's tyranny, but he's much more tepid and cautious in defending me against my husband's. As long as I'm near him, he doesn't reproach himself for allowing me to suffer, nor does he care if I'm unhappy, provided that I'm alive. He chooses not to give me any support that would make my life easier, because standing up to Monsieur Delmare and risking his anger would make his own life less pleasant. Having been told over and over that his heart is dry and unfeeling, he's convinced himself that it's true, whereas in reality his distrust of himself has kept him from using it and it's dried up from inactivity. He's a man who might have developed if he had ever received affection from anyone, but he never has, so he has shriveled up instead. Now he believes that happiness means a peaceful existence, and pleasure a comfortable one. He doesn't concern himself about other people's troubles. I must use the word—Ralph is selfish."

"So much the better," said Raymon. "I'm not afraid of him anymore, and if you like, I'll even love him."

"Oh, yes, Raymon, love him," she answered, "because he will appreciate it! And as for us, let's not try to understand why people love us, but only how they love us. The person who can be loved—for whatever reason—is so lucky!"

Grasping her delicate, slender waist, Raymon replied, "You say that because you are lonely and sad, Indiana, but as for me I want you to know why I love you as well as how I love you—and especially why."

"Because you want to make me happy?" she asked, looking at him with a sad intensity.

"Because I want to give you my life," said Raymon, brushing his lips over her floating hair.

A nearby blast of the horn warned them to be careful; it was Sir Ralph, who may or may not have seen them.

XIV

RAYMON was amazed at the change that came over Indiana as soon as the hounds were let loose. Her eyes sparkled, her cheeks flushed, and her nostrils flared with either fear or pleasure as she spurred her horse and abruptly galloped after Ralph. Raymon had no idea that Indiana shared Ralph's passion for hunting, nor did he know that this frail, timid woman was capable of a more than masculine courage, a kind of frenzied bravery that sometimes manifests itself in the weakest people and is occasionally mistaken for nervous hysteria. Women rarely have the physical courage with which to confront pain or danger, but those same challenges often enable them to rise to heights of moral exaltation. Every fiber of Indiana's being responded to the tumult, the animation, all the thrilling activities of the hunt, which with its strategies, calculations, sorties, unpredictable outcomes, and exhaustion is a miniature version of war. Her dreary life of stultifying boredom created a need for this kind of excitement, and when the opportunity came, she would throw off her lethargy and expend in one day all the energy that she had been unable to use in a year.

Raymon found it frightening to see her race off like that, fearlessly abandoning herself to the unfamiliar horse, spurring him through the thickets, avoiding with astonishing skill the branches that snapped back at her face as she rode through them, unhesitatingly jumping ditches, confidently risking herself on the muddy and slippery ground, unconcerned about the danger of breaking her bones, and on fire to be the first to pick up the steaming trail of the boar. So much strength of purpose almost disgusted him. Men, especially lovers, have a simpleminded fatuousness that makes them prefer to protect weak women rather than admire strong ones, and, if the truth be told, Raymon recoiled from the thought of the daring and determination such an intrepid spirit might show in a love affair. There was no resignation in a heart like that; it was not the heart of a woman like poor Noun, who preferred to drown herself rather than fight against her misfortunes.

"If she's going to be as carried away by her love as by her amusements," he thought, "if she's going to cling to me as fiercely and obstinately as she clings to the idea of that boar, then neither society's restrictions nor the law's restraints will be able to control her, and I will have to give up my own destiny, sacrifice my own future—"

Raymon's reflections were cut short by sudden cries of alarm and distress. He recognized Indiana's voice and anxiously urged his horse forward, only to be joined almost immediately by Ralph, who asked him if he had also heard the shouts.

At that moment a few frightened beaters rode up to them, confusedly trying to explain that the boar had charged Mme. Delmare and thrown her to the ground. Then some of the hunters appeared, even more upset, calling to Sir Ralph and telling him to come quickly because the injured person needed his medical skill.

"It's useless," said the last of these to arrive. "There's no hope—nothing you can do will be of any help now."

At those horrible words Raymon looked at Sir Ralph. His face was pale and gloomy, but he neither cried out nor foamed at the mouth nor wrung his hands. He merely took his hunting knife and with a truly English phlegm prepared to cut his throat. Raymon wrenched his weapon away and led him in the direction from which the cries had come.

Ralph thought he was awakening from a dream when he saw Indiana rush over to him and urgently lead him to the colonel, who lay on the ground and gave no sign of life. Ralph saw instantly that he wasn't dead and bled him immediately, but he had broken a leg and had to be carried back to the house.

As for Mme. Delmare, what had probably happened was that in all the commotion of the accident, people had mistakenly substituted her name for her husband's—or, even more likely, that Ralph and Raymon had heard the name that interested them most.

She had not been hurt at all, but her shock and concern had made her almost too weak to walk. Raymon had to support her, and he was reassured about her womanly heart when he saw how deeply moved she was by the injury to a husband who had much to be forgiven before he could be pitied.

Sir Ralph had already recovered his usual imperturbability, and only his extraordinary pallor indicated how strongly he had been affected; he had nearly lost one of the two people he loved.

Raymon, who was the only one to have remained composed and therefore the only one able to understand what he had seen in that moment of tension and confusion, had been able to judge for himself how Ralph's affection for his cousin was hardly the same as his feeling for her husband. His observation completely contradicted Indiana's opinion on the subject and remained in Raymon's mind long after the other witnesses of the incident had forgotten what they had seen.

And he never told Indiana about the suicide attempt he had witnessed. There was something ungenerous about this silence, something more than a little mean-spirited and selfish, but perhaps you will forgive it on the grounds that it was due to a lover's jealousy.

It was six weeks before the colonel could be taken back, with much difficulty, to Lagny, and six months more before he could walk again, because before the broken bone had completely mended, he suffered an attack of acute rheumatism in the injured leg that resulted in excruciating pain and complete immobility. His wife was endlessly gentle and considerate in her care of him; she never left his bedside, and she endured without a single complaint his bad temper and his bitter moods, his military brusqueness and his invalid's impatience.

Despite that grim and depressing existence, her health returned and flourished, and her whole being was bathed in happiness. Raymon loved her, really loved her. He came every day, allowing no difficulty to stand in the way of seeing her; he was not discouraged by the husband's ailments, the cousin's coldness, or the restrictions that governed their meetings. A single one of his glances would fill Indiana's heart with joy for an entire day, and she no longer complained about life: her soul was overflowing, her youth was being employed, and her moral and spiritual nature was being nourished.

Gradually the colonel, who was naive enough to believe that his neighbor kept coming because he was interested in the state of his health, began to feel something like friendship for Raymon. Madame de Ramière also visited occasionally, sanctioning the relationship by her presence, and she and Indiana developed a warm and enthusiastic friendship. In the end, the wife's lover did indeed become the husband's friend.

Because they met so regularly, Raymon and Ralph were inevitably thrown together and forced into a kind of intimacy. They called each other "my dear friend" and shook hands every morning and evening; if either had a small favor to ask of the other, the usual phrase was something like "I'm counting on your friendship"; and when they spoke of each other, they said, "He's my friend."

Yet despite the fact that both men were as frank and outspoken in the world as it was possible to be, they didn't care for each other at all. They had diametrically opposed opinions about everything and shared neither likes nor dislikes about anything, and though both of them loved Indiana, it was in such different ways that that love divided them instead of bringing them together. Each felt a perverse pleasure in contradicting the other, but because their attacks were cloaked as generalizations, it was impossible for either to respond to the other's sharp and occasionally insulting remarks as if they were personal affronts.

Their major and most frequent arguments would begin with politics and end with morality. As they sat in the evening around M. Delmare's armchair, the slightest pretext or most trivial issue could set them off. They were careful to maintain the superficial courtesy that was imposed on Ralph by his philosophy and on Raymon by the social customs and manners of his world, but they would nevertheless occasionally say some very harsh things to each other—hidden, of course, by a veil of hints and allusions. This amused the colonel no end, because he was by nature aggressive and quarrelsome, and since he himself could no longer fight battles, he was reduced to enjoying other people's arguments instead.

I myself believe that a man's political opinion is determined by the kind of man he is. Tell me how you feel and think, and I will tell you your political opinions. Sooner or later our characters make themselves felt, and they are more important than the ranks or fortunes due to accidents of birth or the superficial beliefs and prejudices of education. You may find that a very sweeping statement, but how could I think well of a person who supports a theory or system that no one with any generosity of spirit could possibly accept? Show me a man who supports the death penalty, and no matter how enlightened or conscientious he might be in other areas, there could never be any sympathetic connection between him and me. If such a man should wish to teach me things I do not know, he would never succeed, because I am constitutionally incapable of having any confidence in him.

Ralph and Raymon differed about everything, although before they met each other, their opinions had not always been very clearly defined. But from the moment they recognized each other as opponents, each one immediately took a position completely opposed to the other's and maintained it firmly, absolutely, uncompromisingly. In all cases Raymon was the champion of society as it was, and Ralph attacked its structure at every point.

There was a very simple reason for that: Raymon was happy and had always been treated perfectly well by everyone, while Ralph was a disappointed man who had known nothing but life's evils and sorrows; one therefore found everything good and to his liking, and the other found fault with everything. Men and events had favored Raymon and mistreated Ralph, and like children, both of them generalized from those personal experiences and set themselves up as ultimate judges of all the great social questions—though neither of them was the slightest bit competent to do so.

Ralph constantly held forth about his dream republic, in which there would be no abuses, prejudices, or injustice—a dream based solely on his hope of a new race of men. Raymon, on the other hand, supported with equal fervor a hereditary monarchy—preferring, he said, to endure abuses, prejudices, and injustice rather than to see scaffolds erected and innocent blood shed.

The colonel was almost always on Ralph's side at the beginning of these discussions because he hated the Bourbons and his opinions were based on his emotional animosity. Raymon, however, would soon bring him over to his own side by seeming to prove that the monarchy was much closer in principle to the Empire than to the Republic. Ralph was direct and unsubtle, incapable of clever persuasion, an inept debater; his candor was so unpolished, his logic so dull, his principles so absolute, his attacks against everyone so unsparing, his truths so harsh, that he could convince no one.

"*Parbleu!*" he would answer the colonel when the latter complained about England's intervention. "What does a reasonable, sensible man like you have against a whole country that fought against you fairly?"

"Fairly?" Delmare would repeat, grinding his teeth and brandishing his crutch.

"We should leave these political questions to be resolved by the countries concerned," Sir Ralph would resume, "since we have adopted a form of government that doesn't allow us to decide what is in our own best interest. If a country is responsible for the errors of its legislature, what country is guiltier than yours?"

"And that's why I say shame on France, monsieur!" the colonel would exclaim. "Shame on her for abandoning Napoleon and submitting to a king imposed by foreign bayonets!"

"*I* do not say 'shame on France,' monsieur," Ralph would counter, "but 'pity poor France'! I pity her for having been so weak and exhausted when she was purged of her tyrant that she had to accept your tattered shreds of a constitutional Charter—a sad remnant of a liberty you are just beginning to respect now that you have cast it aside and must conquer it all over again."

At which point Raymon would pick up the gauntlet Sir Ralph had thrown down. A defender of the Charter, he also wanted to be a defender of liberty, and he proved to Ralph with great skill that the former was the expression of the latter and that if he destroyed the Charter, he would also be destroying his idol. In vain did the baronet try to reply to Raymon's illogical arguments; the latter was somehow able to demonstrate with admirable clarity that a more broadly based suffrage would inevitably lead to the excesses of 1793 and that the nation was not yet ready for liberty, which is not the same as license. And when Sir Ralph would then maintain that it was absurd to limit a constitution to a certain number of articles because what was sufficient at the beginning would become insufficient later on, and tried to support his argument by an analogy with the situation of an invalid whose needs increased every day, Raymon would reply to such clumsily expressed commonplaces that the Charter was not a rigid, inflexible mold, but a malleable form that would expand with the country's needs and be elastic enough to respond to the nation's demands—though in reality, of course, it would satisfy only those of the crown.

Delmare had not budged an inch since 1815. He was as obstinately entrenched in his positions and prejudices as the emigrés of Coblentz, the eternal objects of his caustic scorn. A childish old man, he had understood nothing about the great drama of Napoleon's downfall. He saw it only as the result of the fortunes of war, when in reality it represented the triumph of the power of public opinion. He kept talking about treason, about the selling-out of the country—as if an entire nation could betray a single man or as if France had let herself be sold by a few generals! He would accuse the Bourbons of tyranny and forget how in the good old days of the Empire there had not been enough hands to till the country's soil or bread to feed her families. He would complain about the current state of the police under Franchet and praise what it had been under Fouché. It was still the day after Waterloo for him.

It was curious to hear the sentimental idiocies of both Delmare and M. de Ramière, each of whom was an unrealistic altruist—the former under Napoleon's sword, the latter under Saint Louis's scepter; M. Delmare planted at the foot of the pyramids, Raymon seated under the monarchy shaded by the oak of Vincennes. Their opposing utopias ended by becoming reconciled to each other as Raymon enmeshed the colonel with his chivalric phrases, demanded ten concessions for every one he made, and little by little accustomed the colonel to think of twenty-five years of victory spiraling up to and culminating under the monarchy's white flag. If Ralph's blunt directness had not constantly interrupted the flow of Raymon's flowery rhetoric, the latter would certainly have won the old soldier over to the throne of 1815, but Ralph's awkwardness rubbed Delmare the wrong way, and the brusqueness with which he proclaimed his principles served only to anchor Delmare more firmly to his imperialism, which meant that all of Raymon's efforts were wasted: Ralph trampled his bouquets of eloquence underfoot, and the colonel returned to his tricolor with more enthusiasm than ever, swearing that some fine day he would shake the dust off it, spit on the lilies, and restore the Duc de Reichstadt to the throne of his fathers. Beginning by reconquering the world, he inevitably ended by bemoaning France's shame, the rheumatism that kept him glued to his chair, and the Bourbons' ingratitude to the old soldiers who had been burned by the desert sun and frozen on the ice floes of the Moscow River.

"My poor friend," Ralph would say, "be fair! You complain that the Restoration didn't pay Napoleon's soldiers for the services they had rendered to the Empire and that it reimbursed its emigrés. But tell the truth—if Napoleon could return tomorrow, as powerful as ever, would you like it if he ignored you and instead rewarded those in favor of the crown? It's everyone for himself and his own. Those financial questions

involve private interests, and the country finds such issue
unimportant now that you are all useless but must still be sup
ported despite your uselessness and even despite the fact tha
you're the ones who complain the loudest! When we finall
get a Republic, it will certainly brush off every one of your de
mands, and a good thing too!"

The colonel was as enraged by these general and perfectl
obvious observations as if they had been personal insults, an
Ralph, who with all his common sense could not conceive tha
a man he respected might be so petty, continued to offend hir
with his tactless ways.

Before Raymon's arrival on the scene, there had been an un
spoken agreement between the two men to avoid any subjec
that might wound either of their susceptibilities or lead to an
painful confrontations, but Raymon introduced into their soli
tude all the subtleties of language and all the petty treacherie
of conventional society. He taught them that people can allov
themselves to say anything to each other, can even taunt or re
proach each other, under the pretext of conducting an objec
tive discussion. This habit, tolerated in all the drawing room
of society, was possible there because the strong passions o
the Hundred Days had finally become attenuated, nothing
more than mere weak statements of delicately nuanced shade
of belief; but the colonel had preserved all the original vehe
mence of his convictions, while Ralph made the serious erro
of thinking he could be brought to listen to reason. Instead, M
Delmare became more and more angry with him and turne
increasingly to Raymon, whose graceful turns of phrase en
abled him to defend his position and still allow the colonel t
preserve his self-esteem.

It is very dangerous to introduce politics into the family cir
cle. If happy families still exist today, I strongly advise then
not to subscribe to any newspaper or read one word of any
government budget, but to withdraw to their country homes
take shelter there as if in an oasis, and draw an impregnabl
line between themselves and the rest of the world, because i
they allow any sound of our disputes to penetrate their retreat
that will be the end of their peace and harmony. It is hard t
imagine how much bad temper and bitterness can be created
by differences of political opinion among close relatives, who
often use those differences as a convenient excuse for bringing
up the deficiencies of one another's moral character, menta
ability, and emotional sensitivity.

None of them would dare call another a cheat, an imbecile, an opportunist, or a clown, but the same ideas can be expressed by saying "Jesuit," "royalist," "revolutionary," or "middle-of-the-roader." They are different words but the same insults, and all the more painful because everyone is allowed to pursue the argument endlessly, without mercy and without restraint—which signals the end of mutual tolerance for everyone's failings, the end of all charitable feelings, the end of a generous and delicate reserve about one another's lives. Nothing is any longer ignored or passed over in silence; everything is considered to be a political statement, and under that guise, everyone's hate and spite is given free rein. Oh, you happy people who live in the countryside—if there still is a countryside in France—keep away from politics and sit by the fireplace reading fairy tales aloud to one another! But the contamination is so widespread that hardly anyplace is solitary and isolated enough to protect the man who wants to find a refuge from the storms of our civil disorders.

The little château in Brie had defended itself against such a fatal invasion for years, but it too finally lost its indifference to the outside world, its active domestic life, its long, silent, meditative evenings. Loud arguments aroused its sleeping echoes, and bitter, threatening words frightened the faded cherubs who had smiled through the dust from the ancient hangings for a hundred years. The strong emotions of contemporary life had penetrated the old house, and all the outmoded splendors, all the outdated remnants of an earlier age of frivolous pleasures, watched with dismay the entrance of the present day, with all its doubts and declamations, as represented by the three men who daily shut themselves up in there and did nothing but quarrel from morning to night.

XV

DESPITE this atmosphere of continuous dissension, Indiana, youthfully confident, saw a joyous future before her. This wa her first experience of happiness, and her vivid imaginatio and warm heart allowed her to supplement its deficiencie with pure, keen, ingeniously contrived pleasures that enriche the precarious blessings destiny allowed her; after all, Raymo loved her. And in truth, he was not lying when he told her tha she was the only love of his life: he had never before loved s purely or for so long. When he was with her, he thought o nothing else; politics and his social world were erased from hi mind, and he enjoyed being part of her domestic life and bein treated like one of the family. He admired her patience an willpower, was astonished by the contrast between her intel lect and her character, and was especially amazed by how after having so solemnly laid down the conditions of their rela tionship, she proved so undemanding, so satisfied with her fev stolen moments of joy, so blindly hopeful and trusting. Tha was because she had never loved before, and this new an selfless passion included a multitude of delicate and noble sen timents that gave it a power Raymon could not begin to under stand.

At first he had been bothered by the eternal presence of th husband or cousin because he had intended to manage thi love affair like all his previous ones, but Indiana soon force him to rise to her level. Her resignation in the face of constan surveillance, the pleasure with which she stole an occasiona glance at him, the silent eloquence of her eyes, her sublim smile when a sudden comment would show her that they thought the same way—all these became subtle pleasures tha Raymon, thanks to his discriminating mind and fine education learned to recognize and appreciate.

How different this chaste creature who could not even seen

to imagine the consummation of her love was from all the other women he knew, who were interested only in achieving it as quickly as possible while denying their purpose as strenuously as possible! When Raymon unexpectedly found himself alone with Indiana, she neither blushed nor turned away in embarrassment; on the contrary, her clear, untroubled eyes were always fixed on him with delight, and her rosy lips were always parted in that same angelic smile—like that of a little girl who has known only a mother's kisses. Seeing her so confiding, so passionate, so pure, living a life so completely centered in her heart that she didn't even know how tortured her lover's heart was when he sat at her feet, Raymon did not dare be a man lest he seem unequal to her vision of him, and it became a matter of pride for him to match her virtue.

As ignorant as if she were a real Creole, Indiana had never before thought about any of the important issues now being discussed in her home every day. She had been brought up by Sir Ralph, who had a poor opinion of woman's intellectual capacity and reasoning ability and had therefore taught her only what he felt would be of immediate and practical use, with the result that she had only a slight familiarity with a very abridged version of world history and was bored to death by any serious discussion. But when she heard Raymon hold forth on all those dry topics with his winning wit and lyrical language, she would listen intently, try to understand, then timidly ask the kind of naive questions a sophisticated ten-year-old brought up in a more worldly society would easily have been able to answer. Raymon enjoyed instructing such a virgin intellect, especially one that seemed bound to adopt his principles, but despite the power he exercised over her untrained mind, his plausible but fallacious arguments would sometimes meet with surprising resistance.

Indiana disapproved of a civilization built on a foundation of abstract principles and proposed in its stead one based on the straightforward ideas and simple rules of good sense and common humanity, and her arguments had a childlike simplicity and directness that sometimes embarrassed Raymon and always charmed him. In all seriousness, he set himself the task of gradually winning her over to his beliefs and policies. It would have satisfied his pride to be able to persuade someone so morally scrupulous and naturally intelligent to agree with him, but he found it rather difficult to achieve his aim: her unhappy memories made it much easier for her to respond to Ralph's more generous theories, his unyielding hatred for society's vices, and his eager impatience for a world in which other laws and another kind of morality would prevail.

But then Raymon would suddenly discredit his adversary by claiming that such hatred for the present day was due to selfishness, and he would paint with glowing colors the portrait of his own sentiments: his devotion to the royal family, which he presented as loyalty maintained in the face of much danger, and his respect for the persecuted faith of his forebears—those religious beliefs that he clung to out of some instinctive need and made no effort to explain logically. And then there was the happiness of loving his fellow man and of knowing himself joined to his contemporaries by all the ties of honor and disinterested good will, and the pleasure of serving his country by resisting dangerous innovations and by being ready to preserve domestic harmony by shedding, if necessary, the last drop of his own blood to spare the lowest of his countrymen from losing one drop of his! He would describe these benevolent ideals with such skillful artistry that Indiana's love and respect for him led her to love and respect whatever he did. And as it seemed to be taken as a proven fact that Ralph was selfish, everyone smiled when *he* expressed a generous idea, convinced that at such times his heart and his mind must be in opposition. Surely it was better to believe Raymon, whose heart and mind were both so well disposed, so fraternal, so all embracing. . . .

Yet there were moments when Raymon would almost forget his love and think of nothing but his antipathy, moments when he was with Indiana but could see only Sir Ralph, who dared in his cold, ungracious, commonsensical way to oppose him— him, a man of such superior talents, a man who had bested some of the mightiest opponents in his world! He would occasionally feel humiliated at finding himself fighting such an insignificant adversary, and then he would bear down on him with the full weight of all his resources, leaving the poor man—who was in any case slow in marshaling his ideas and even slower in expressing them—crushed by the consciousness of his own ineptitude.

At such times it would seem to Indiana that Raymon had completely forgotten her, and she trembled with fear and anxiety at the thought that all those noble and high-principled feelings might be only a pompous scaffolding of words, the self-conscious fluency of the lawyer who listens to himself with pleasure as he sets forth the sentimental drama that is

upposed to take his audience's heart by storm. She was espe-
ially disturbed when she would meet his eyes and seem to
ee that he was not so much pleased at having been under-
tood by her as triumphantly self-satisfied at knowing he had
resented such a good case. Then she would think of Ralph,
he selfish one, and wonder fearfully if they had done him an
njustice; but Ralph had no idea of how to prolong this uncer-
ainty or turn it to his advantage, and Raymon was always
lever enough to dissipate it.

There was thus in this domestic scene only one person
whose existence was truly troubled, whose happiness was truly
poiled, and that existence and that happiness belonged to
Ralph: the man who had been born to misfortune; who had
ever known any brilliant prospects or intense, fulfilling joys;
who had never complained about his great, secret unhappiness
nd who was therefore pitied for it by no one; the man whose
ruly miserable fate was neither poetic nor dramatic nor adven-
urous, but ordinary, bourgeois, and commonplace; whose life
ad never been eased by any friendship or charmed by any
ove but who endured silently and heroically because the pull
f life and the need to hope were strong; a lonely person who
ad had a mother and father like everyone else, a brother, a
wife, a son, a friend, and who had gathered from all those rela-
ionships little pleasure and none of it lasting; a stranger to life
who passed through it in melancholy indifference, not even
eing romantic enough to enjoy the bittersweet pleasure of
nowing how great his misfortune was.

Despite his strong character, he sometimes felt shackled by
is own standards of behavior. He hated Raymon and could
ave driven him from Lagny with one word; he didn't say that
word because he had one governing rule of life—just one, but
tronger than Raymon's thousands. It was neither the church
or monarchy nor society nor reputation nor law that dictated
is sacrifices and was responsible for his steadfast courage,
ut his conscience.

Because he had lived so much by himself, he had never got-
en into the habit of relying on other people, but on the other
and, this same isolation had taught him to know himself. He
ad made a friend of his own heart, and after a lifetime of ex-
mining himself and trying to understand why people acted so
njustly to him, he had come to the conclusion that it was
hrough no fault or vice of his and that he hadn't deserved it.
Iaving so little self-esteem, and convinced that he was an in-

sipid and ordinary person, this no longer irritated him. He understood that people were indifferent to him and had learned
how to respond to that indifference, though he knew in his
heart that he was capable of feeling every emotion he was incapable of inspiring; and while he was ready to forgive everyone else's faults, he had determined to forgive none of his
own. It was this completely internal life, with its entirely private feelings, that made him seem so selfish—and it may well
be that self-respect is very like selfishness and is often confused with it.

Nevertheless, just as it sometimes happens that when we
want to do our best we may end up doing less well than usual,
so it happened that Sir Ralph did Indiana great and irreparable
harm because of his over-scrupulous conscience and his dread
of someday having to reproach himself. His mistake was in deciding not to tell her the truth about Noun's death. If he had,
she might have considered more carefully the dangers to
which her love for Raymon exposed her, but we will see later
why Sir Ralph did not dare enlighten his cousin and what reasons he had for remaining silent about such an important point.
In any event, when he did decide to speak, it was already too
late; Raymon was firmly entrenched in his position.

M. Delmare had not yet completely recovered when he received news of an unexpected event that was to be of great importance in the future life of the couple: a Belgian business
firm, upon which all the prosperity of his factory depended,
had suddenly gone bankrupt, and the colonel had to leave for
Antwerp immediately.

Seeing him so weak and still in pain, his wife wanted to go
with him; M. Delmare, however, threatened by total ruin and
resolved to honor all his obligations, was afraid that if she did,
it would look as if he were running away, so he decided to
leave her at Lagny as a guaranty that he would return. He even
refused to allow Sir Ralph to accompany him, begging him instead to remain with Mme. Delmare and prevent any nervous
or insistent creditors from annoying her.

In the midst of all these concerns Indiana was disturbed
only by the possibility of having to leave Lagny and be separated from Raymon, but he assured her that the colonel would
have to go to Paris before anything definitive could happen.
Besides, he swore that he would find some excuse to follow
her no matter where she went, and the poor trusting woman
was almost happy to endure a misfortune that would allow her

test Raymon's love. As for him, ever since he had heard the
news his mind had been absorbed by a vague, constant, nag-
ing thought: for the first time in six months, he was finally
going to be alone with Indiana. She had never seemed to avoid
such a situation, and though he was in no hurry to complete his
triumph over a love whose naive innocence was so strangely
new to him, he was nevertheless beginning to feel that it was a
point of honor to bring it to some conclusion. Of course he
was sincerity itself in repudiating any malicious suggestions
about the nature of his relations with Mme. Delmare, and he
assured everyone that there was nothing between them but an
untroubled and pleasant friendship; actually, he would not
have admitted for anything in the world, not even to his best
friend, that he had been passionately in love for six months
and had not yet enjoyed the fruits of that love.

He was more than a little disappointed when he realized that
Sir Ralph was determined to watch over Indiana as carefully
as M. Delmare would have, and that he would arrive at Lagny
in the morning and not return to Bellerive until night—even
insisting, with an intolerable, exaggerated courtesy, that since
both he and Raymon had to take the same road for part of the
way to their respective homes, they should leave together.
Raymon found such coercion extremely distasteful, and Indiana felt that it was not only offensively insulting but indicated
a desire on Ralph's part to assume complete control over her
behavior.

Raymon was afraid to ask her for a private meeting because
whenever he had tentatively suggested it in the past, Indiana
had reminded him of certain promises he had made and sworn
to keep. But meanwhile the colonel had already been gone a
week and might return at any time; he had to take advantage of
this opportunity. It would be disgraceful to allow Sir Ralph the
victory.

One morning he slipped the following letter into Indiana's
hand:

> *Indiana, don't you love me as much as I love you? Oh,*
> *my angel, you don't seem to see how unhappy I am—un-*
> *happy for you and your future, not mine, because wherever*
> *you go, I will go too, to live and die beside you. But I can't*
> *bear the idea that you may have to live in poverty, you who*
> *are so fragile, so weak! How will you endure the priva-*
> *tions? Your cousin is rich and generous, and your husband*

may accept from him what he would certainly refuse from me. Ralph will be the one to make your life easier, and I won't be able to do a thing for you!

So you see, my dear friend, that I have much to make me depressed and gloomy. You are heroic, you make light of everything, you refuse to allow me to feel sorry for you. But, oh, how I need to hear your words and see your gentle glances in order to keep my courage up—and how unkind fate has been to me! Instead of bringing me the liberty to spend time freely at your side, these days have brought me nothing but restrictions that are even more insupportable than before. Say the word, Indiana, so that we may have an hour alone, so that I may water your white hands with my tears, tell you how much I am suffering, hear you say something that will console and reassure me.

And, Indiana, I have a childish fancy, a lover's fancy, to be in your room. Ah, don't be afraid, my gentle Creole! I've sworn not only to respect you but to fear you, and that is exactly why I would like to go to your room. I want to kneel in the same place where you were so angry with me, and where, despite all my audacity, I hadn't the courage even to look at you. Now I would like to spend an hour of quiet, contemplative content there, and I would ask only one favor of you—I would beg you to put your hand on my heart and purify it of its crime, to calm if it is beating too quickly, and to restore its confidence if you finally feel it worthy of you. Oh, how I burn to prove to you that I __am__ worthy now, that I know and understand you now, that I revere you with as pure and holy a love as any young girl feels for the Madonna! I want to be sure that you are no longer afraid of me and that you respect me as much as I adore you. I would like to live for an hour, my head resting on your heart, as the angels do in heaven. Oh, Indiana, will you allow me this? One hour—the first, perhaps the last!

It is time to forgive me, Indiana, to let me once again enjoy the confidence that I was so cruelly deprived of and that I have redeemed at so high a cost. Aren't you satisfied with me? Tell me, haven't I spent six months behind your chair, contenting myself with only the sight of your white neck through the curls of your black hair as it fell over the embroidery, and the scent of your perfume as it was faintly wafted to me on the breeze from the window? Doesn't such submission deserve the reward of a kiss? A sisterly kiss on

*the forehead, if that is what you wish. I swear that I will re-
main faithful to our agreements and ask for nothing—but
can you be cruel enough to grant me nothing? Can it be
that you are afraid of yourself?*

Indiana went to her room to read the letter, and she immediately replied to it, slipping the response into Raymon's hands
together with the all-too-familiar key to the park gate.

*Afraid of you, Raymon? Oh, no, not anymore! I know
that you love me because of how happy it makes me feel to
believe it. So come, for I'm not afraid of myself, either. If I
loved you less, I might be less sure, but I love you with a
love you cannot begin to imagine. . . . Leave here early, so
Ralph won't suspect anything, and return at midnight. You
know the park and the house, so here is the key to the small
gate, which you should lock behind you.*

Such sublimely innocent trust made Raymon blush. Counting on the dark, the opportunity, the danger, he had worked to
inspire her confidence with the intention of abusing it, and if
Indiana had shown any fear or suspicion, she would have been
lost; but relying on his good faith, she had put herself into his
hands, and he swore that she would have no reason to regret it.
Besides, the important thing was to spend the night in her
room in order not to seem a fool in his own eyes and in order
to foil Ralph's precautions, so he could laugh at him in secret.
He needed that satisfaction.

XVI

BUT that evening Ralph was truly unbearable, even more dull, leaden, and tedious than usual. There was no point to anything he said, and worst of all, as the evening progressed, he showed no sign of being ready to leave. Indiana began to feel uneasy, looking first at the clock, which had just struck eleven, then at the door, which was creaking in the wind, and finally at the vacuous face of her cousin, sitting opposite her in front of the fire, peacefully looking at the flames and totally oblivious of how inconvenient his presence was.

That frozen mask, however, was hiding a deeply troubling anxiety. Because Ralph observed everything carefully and dispassionately, nothing escaped him. He had not been fooled by Raymon's pretense of an early departure, and he was quite aware of Indiana's nervous impatience. He suffered from it more than she did herself, and he wavered uncertainly between the desire to warn her and the fear of giving way to feelings he had forbidden himself to express. Finally his concern for his cousin's well-being carried the day, and taking his courage in hand, he broke the silence.

"I was just remembering," he said suddenly, following his silent line of thought, "that a year ago today the two of us were sitting here in front of this fireplace, just as we are now. It was about the same time of day, and the weather was as cold and dreary as it is tonight. You were ill and depressed—which almost makes me believe in premonitions."

"What is he leading up to?" Indiana wondered, looking at her cousin with a mixture of surprise and misgiving.

"Do you remember that you felt even worse than usual that evening?" he continued. "I remember what you said as clearly as if your words were still hanging in the air. 'You'll say that I'm mad,' you said, 'but I'm sure that some catastrophe is hovering over us. Someone is in great danger—most probably me.' Then you added, 'I tell you, Ralph, there is about to be a great change in my life, and I'm afraid.' Those were your exact words, Indiana."

"I'm no longer ill," she replied, suddenly as pale as she had been at that earlier time Sir Ralph was talking about, "and I no longer believe in those foolish fears."

"But *I* believe in them, Indiana, because I think you were a true prophet that night. There *was* a catastrophe hovering over us—an evil influence was threatening this peaceful home."

"I don't understand you!"

"You will soon, my poor friend. That was the night Raymon de Ramière was brought here. Do you remember the condition he was in?"

Ralph, not daring to look at his cousin, waited a few moments for her reply; when there was none, he continued. "I was told to bring him back to life, and I did, as much to please you as to do what common humanity required me to do. But I tell you, Indiana, that I did a terrible thing when I saved that man's life! I'm the one responsible for all the harm—"

"I don't know what harm you mean," Indiana interrupted curtly.

She was deeply hurt by the explanation she already anticipated.

"I mean the death of that poor unfortunate Noun," said Ralph. "If not for him, she would still be alive. If not for his fatal love, that beautiful, honest girl who loved you so much would still be with you. . . ."

Indiana did not understand; she simply thought—and with great anger—that her cousin had chosen a particularly cruel way to attack her affection for M. de Ramière. She rose and said, "That is quite enough."

Ralph paid no attention. "What has always astonished me," he went on, "is that you've never guessed his real motive for climbing over the wall."

The slightest shadow of a doubt entered Indiana's heart; her legs would no longer support her, and she sat down again.

Ralph had just buried his knife in her breast and opened a gaping wound. As soon as he became aware of the effect of his words, he was horrified; all he could think about was the harm he had done to the person he loved most in the world, and he felt as if his heart would break. He would have wept bitter tears if he had been able to weep, but the poor man had never had that gift any more than he had any other that might allow

him to translate the feelings of his heart; and the seeming coldness with which he had spoken made him sound like an execu-
tioner to Indiana.

"This is the first time," she said bitterly, "that you've allowed your dislike of Monsieur de Ramière to lead you to behave in a way unworthy of you, but I see no reason why your
vengefulness should also include staining the memory of
someone I loved, someone who should be sacred to us because
of her tragic end. I will not ask you any questions, Sir Ralph—
I don't know what you mean, and I won't listen to anything
else you may have to say."

She stood up and left Sir Ralph alone, almost paralyzed with
self-loathing.

He had been perfectly aware that he could tell Indiana the
truth only at a great cost to himself; his conscience, however,
had told him he had to speak, no matter what the result would
mean to him personally, so he had—and as awkwardly and
tactlessly as only he could possibly have done! What he had
not understood was how much of a shock such a belated revelation would be.

He left the house in a state of desperation, tramping through
the woods in an aimless frenzy.

It was midnight, and Raymon was at the park gate; but even
as he opened it, he felt his exaltation subside. What was going
to happen at this rendezvous? He had made virtuous resolutions, but were a chaste conversation and a sisterly kiss to be
his only rewards for the anguish and suffering he was enduring
at this moment? If you remember the circumstances of his last
furtive nocturnal walk along those paths, you will acknowledge that it took a certain amount of moral courage to go in
pursuit of pleasure along such a route and amid such memories.

By late October the weather in the suburbs of Paris becomes
damp and foggy, especially at night and especially near rivers
and streams. By chance, the fog was as dense this night as it
had been the previous spring, and Raymon walked uncertainly
among the mist-shrouded trees; as he passed in front of the
summerhouse that contained during the winter a fine collection of geraniums, as he glanced at the door, and his heart beat
faster in spite of himself at the fanciful notion that he might
see a cloaked woman emerge from it. . . . Smiling at such superstitious weakness, he continued along his way, but he had

begun to feel cold, and the closer he came to the stream, the more difficult he found it to breathe.

He had to cross the water to reach the garden, and the only possible passage in that area was over a little wooden bridge that joined the two banks; the fog was even thicker at the water's edge, and Raymon had to cling to the ramp to keep from blundering into the reeds. The moon was just rising, and as it tried to pierce the vapors, its wavering light made the plants that were being agitated by the wind and the current seem to move mysteriously. The breeze that rustled through the leaves and ruffled the surface of the water sounded almost like a human moan, like half-formed human words. Raymon heard a faint noise beside him, and a sudden movement disturbed the reeds: a curlew was flying away at his approach. The cry of that water bird is just like the wail of an abandoned child, and when it is heard in the rush-filled hollows, it is easy to imagine that one is hearing someone's last drowning gasps. You may think Raymon weak and cowardly because his teeth began to chatter and he almost fell, but he soon conquered his ridiculous fears and began to cross the bridge.

Midway across, a shape, barely distinguishable as human, suddenly appeared in front of him at the other ramp, as if waiting for him. Raymon was bewildered, his ideas were in a turmoil, and he was so confused that he was incapable of reasoning; he retraced his steps and hid among the trees, staring fixedly at the shadowy apparition that seemed to remain suspended in the air, as vague and indistinct as the water's mist and the moon's flickering light. Just as he was beginning to believe that he was mistaken, that in his preoccupation he had taken the outline of a tree or a shrub for a human shape, he distinctly saw it move and come toward him.

If he had been able to, he would have fled as fearfully as the child who passes a cemetery at night and thinks he hears mysterious footsteps behind him; but he was in a state of paralysis, and he had to cling for support to the trunk of the willow tree behind which he was hidden. Then Sir Ralph, enveloped in a light-colored cloak that made him look from even a few yards away like a ghost, passed right in front of him and was soon hidden from sight on the path from which Raymon had just come.

"Blundering spy!" Raymon thought as he saw the other looking for his tracks. "I've evaded your cowardly vigilance, and while you look for me down here, I'll be enjoying myself up there."

This time he crossed the bridge as swiftly as a bird and as confidently as a lover. He was no longer afraid. Noun had never existed; his real life was about to begin; Indiana was awaiting for him at the house while Ralph was standing sentinel to keep him from getting in!

"That's right, be alert," said Raymon joyously, seeing Ralph searching for him in the opposite direction. "Guard me carefully, good Rodolphe Brown. Protect my happiness, my meddling friend, and if the dogs are awake or the servants worried, why, calm them down, keep them quiet, tell them, 'Don't worry, I'm keeping watch, sleep in peace.'"

No more scruples, no more remorse, no more virtue for Raymon. He had paid a high price for the coming hour. The blood that had been frozen in his veins now rushed to his head with an almost delirious energy. The fearful terrors of death, the gloomy visions of the tomb—those were then; now it was time for the mad impetuosities of love, the vivid joys of life. Raymon felt young and bold, the way we do when an ugly dream that has held us in its spell is dissipated by the radiant sunbeam that awakens and revivifies us.

"Poor Ralph," he thought as he climbed the secret stairway with a light step, "you're the one responsible for this!"

PART THREE

XVII

FTER leaving Ralph, Indiana had locked herself in her room, early overpowered by a dizzying whirlwind of stormy oughts. This was not the first time that vague suspicions had st a sinister light on the fragile foundation of her happiness. I. Delmare had occasionally let slip some crude pleasantries, eant as compliments, in which he congratulated Raymon on s amorous adventures in such a way that even those who new nothing about any of the incidents would understand hat was meant. And there was the gardener: every time Indi- a spoke to him, Noun's name came up, no matter how irrele- antly, and each time her name was followed by M. de amière's, as if both were inevitably and obsessively associ- ed in the man's mind. Indiana had been struck by his strange d seemingly pointless remarks; the least comment could row him into a state of confusion, almost as if he were bur- ened by some weighty, guilty secret that his every effort to de only made more obvious.

On other occasions, Raymon's own agitation had given rise doubts that she had never tried to clarify, but which she uld never completely ignore. One particular instance would ertainly have enlightened her if she had not deliberately osed her mind to any possibility of mistrust. When Noun had een pulled from the water, she had been wearing a very ex- ensive ring, which Indiana had first noticed shortly before her eath and which Noun claimed to have found. Since then Indi- a had always worn it as a token of her sorrow, and she had ften noticed that Raymon turned pale whenever he kissed her and. Once he had begged her never to speak of Noun because e felt responsible for her death, and when she tried to ease his onscience of that painful thought by taking all the blame on erself, he had said, "No, my poor Indiana, don't accuse your- elf—you have no idea of how guilty I am."

Those words, spoken in such a somber and bitter tone, ha
frightened Indiana. She hadn't dared insist on an explanatio
and even now, when she was beginning to think about al
those separate incidents, she still lacked the courage to piec
them together.

She opened her window, and when she looked out at th
pale moon fitfully illuminating the peaceful night from behin
the silvery mist on the horizon, when she reminded herself tha
Raymon was going to come and was perhaps already in th
park, when she thought of all the happiness she had been an
ticipating from this stolen hour of love and mystery, sh
cursed Ralph, who with a few words had forever destroyed he
trust and put an end to her tranquility. She even felt that sh
hated him—that unhappy man who had been a father to he
that man who had sacrificed his future for her, because hi
only joy, his only future, lay in Indiana's friendship, and h
had resigned himself to losing it in order to save her.

Indiana could no more read into the depths of his heart tha
she had been able to penetrate Raymon's. She was unjust, bu
as a result of ignorance, not ingratitude. Her passion was to
strong to allow her to respond to the blow that had been deliv
ered with anything but equal violence, and for a moment sh
blamed everything on Ralph, preferring to accuse him rathe
than to suspect Raymon.

And there was no time to think clearly or come to any con
clusions: Raymon was on his way. It might even be Raymo
whom she had been watching for the past few minutes near th
little bridge. . . . How she would have despised Ralph if sh
had been able to guess that the vague form appearing and dis
appearing into the fog was his, and that like a sentry at the gat
of the Elysée Palace, he was standing guard to try to prevent
guilty man from entering!

All of a sudden she had one of those strange, irrational idea
that only a troubled, unsettled mind can imagine. She woul
risk her whole future on a bizarre but subtle test, one that Ray
mon could not possibly be prepared for. When she heard hi
footsteps on the secret stairway, she had barely finished he
mysterious preparations, and she ran to unlock her door an
return to her chair, so nervous that she was on the point o
fainting; but as in all the crises of her life, she kept her ability
to think clearly and judge accurately.

Raymon was still breathless and pale when he pushed ope
the door, impatient to return to the clarity of the real world. In-

ana, wrapped in a fur-lined cloak, had her back to him, and
some strange coincidence she had chosen to wear the same
ap Noun had borrowed the last time she had gone to meet
aymon in the park. Do you remember that at that time he had
d the totally improbable notion that the woman enveloped in
e cloak was Mme. Delmare? Now, seeing by the light of the
ckering lamp the same apparition sitting listlessly in a chair,
exactly the same room in which so many memories awaited
m—the same guilt-filled room he had never entered since
at most miserable night of his life—he took a step backward
d remained in the doorway, frightened by the motionless
gure and trembling lest she turn to him the livid face of a
owned woman.

Indiana had no idea of the effect she was producing on Ray-
on. She had wrapped a typical island bandanna around her
ad and tied it carelessly in true Creole fashion, just as Noun
d always done. Raymon almost stumbled in his panic at see-
g his superstitious fears realized, but as soon as he recog-
zed the woman he had come to seduce he forgot the one he
d already seduced, and approached her. She looked serious
d thoughtful as she examined him—more carefully then ten-
rly—and she made no gesture to draw him to her side.

Surprised by such a welcome, Raymon could attribute it
ly to a young girl's modest, delicate reserve, some maidenly
ruple. He knelt at her feet and asked, "Are you afraid of me,
y beloved?"

As he spoke, he noticed that she was holding something out
him, drawing it to his attention with an almost playful pre-
nse of gravity. Looking more closely, he saw a mass of black
ir, of all different lengths, which Indiana was smoothing out
her hands.

"Do you recognize this?" she asked, her limpid eyes fixed
him with an oddly penetrating gleam.

Raymon hesitated, looked at her bandanna, and thought he
nderstood. "Naughty child!" he said, taking the hair in his
nd. "Why did you cut it? It was so beautiful, and I loved it
much!"

"You asked me yesterday if I would sacrifice it for you,"
e said with the shadow of a smile.

"Oh, Indiana, you know that this will make you more beau-
ul than ever to me!" Raymon exclaimed. "Give me that hair!
won't miss seeing what I admired every day on your head,

because now no one can stop me from kissing it every day
Give it to me—I'll keep it forever!"

But as he held the abundant mass of hair, some of it lon
enough to reach the floor, he thought it felt dry and coarse
nothing like the silken strands his fingers had sometime
brushed against. This was lifeless and heavy, as if it had bee
cut a long time ago and had lost all its warm, fragrant, vita
force. He shuddered, then inspected it more closely, searchin
for the blue highlights that made Indiana's hair shine like th
blue-black wing of a crow; he saw only the black of an African
the texture of an Indian, the heaviness of death.

Indiana's clear, probing eyes never left Raymon's, whic
then happened to fasten on a half-open ebony box from whic
several strands of the same hair were still protruding.

"It isn't yours!" he said, untying the bandanna that con
cealed Indiana's hair.

It was all there, untouched, tumbling over her shoulders i
all its luxuriant glory.

She pushed him away with a gesture and asked, still point
ing to the hair, "You don't recognize this? You never admire
it? Never caressed it? Has it lost all its fragrance in the dam
night air? Don't you have a single thought, a single tear, fo
the one who wore this ring?"

Raymon, overwhelmed by so many painful emotions, sanl
into a chair and allowed Noun's hair to fall from his unstead
hand. He was a high-strung man, quick to respond to stimuli
easily upset; a tremor passed through his whole body, and h
fell to the floor in a faint.

When he came to, Indiana was kneeling beside him, cover
ing him with tears and begging his pardon; but Raymon n
longer loved her.

"You have hurt me deeply," he told her, "so deeply that yo
can't possibly cure the wound. You'll never be able to restor
my confidence in your heart, because you've just shown m
how vengeful and cruel it can be. Poor Noun! Poor, unfortu
nate girl! It's not you I wronged, but her. She's the one wh
had the right to avenge herself, and she didn't. She killed her
self to leave me free, sacrificed her own life for my peace o
mind. *You* would not have done as much, madame! Give m
her hair, it's mine—it belongs to me because it's all I have lef
of the only woman who ever really loved me! Oh, poor Noun
you deserved a better love than mine! And you, madame, *yo*
dare reproach me with her death? *You* whom I loved so muc

that I forgot her—yes, forgot her to the point where I defied even the frightful tortures of guilt? *You,* whose promise of a single kiss led me to cross that river, walk over that bridge, all alone except for the terror at my side and the hellish visions of my crime pursuing me from behind? *You,* who discovered how madly and passionately I love you and then buried your long nails in my heart just to find the last drop of blood? Ah, I was as stupid as I was wrong to reject a love that was as self-sacrificing as hers for one as ferocious as yours!"

Indiana was silent. Pale and motionless, her hair disheveled and her eyes staring into space, she actually moved Raymon to pity, and he took her hand.

"And with all of that," he said, "and despite my better judgment, I know that my love for you is so strong that I can forget both the past and the present—the crime that destroyed my life and the crime that you have just committed. Love me, and I will forgive you."

Her anguish reawakened both Raymon's desire and his vanity. Seeing her so humble, so appalled at the thought of losing his love, so willing to accept whatever he decided about their future to atone for what she had done, he remembered his reasons for triumphing over Ralph's vigilance and understood all the advantages of his position. For a few minutes he pretended to be thinking, so melancholy and abstracted that he barely responded to Indiana's tears and caresses; he waited until she had sobbed her heart out, until she had begun to realize how empty her life would be without him, until she had worn herself out with all her harrowing, desperate sensations—and then, when he saw her at his feet, weak, exhausted, waiting for the word that would finally kill her, he took her in his arms and crushed her against him in a violent, passionate rage. More dead than alive, she yielded like a weak child, making no effort to resist his kisses.

But suddenly, as if awakening from a dream, she tore herself away from his burning caresses and ran to the other end of the room, where Sir Ralph's portrait hung on the panel; there—panting, wild-eyed, gripped by some overpowering emotion—she pressed herself against the painting of that grave man with the untroubled face as if to put herself under his protection.

Raymon thought she had been so deeply moved while in his arms that she was afraid of her feelings; he was sure that she was his. He ran to her, authoritatively forced her from her re-

treat, and told her that he had come with the intention of keeping his promises but that her cruelty had canceled them.

"I am no longer your slave or your ally," he said, "but only
the man who loves you madly and holds you in his arms—you
who are wicked, capricious, and cruel, but also beautiful, foolish, and adorable. If you had spoken to me gently and shown
that you trusted me, I would have been able to control myself,
and if you had been as calm and generous-spirited as you were
yesterday, I would have been as meek and mild as I have always been. But you've aroused all my passions and turned all
my ideas upside down—you've made me unhappy, cowardly,
ill, furious, and desperate, one after the other, and now you
must make me happy, or I will no longer be able to have any
faith in you, no longer be able to love or bless you. Forgive me
if I frighten you, Indiana, but it's your fault—you've made me
suffer so much that I can no longer be reasonable!"

Indiana trembled. She had so little experience that she
thought it impossible to resist him, and she was ready to do out
of fear what she wouldn't have done for love. Struggling fee-
bly in Raymon's arms, she managed to say forlornly, "Would
you really be capable of using force against me?"

Raymon stopped, struck by the moral resistance that per-
sisted even after the physical resistance had ended, and he
pushed her away, exclaiming, "Never! I would rather die than
have you come to me any way except of your own free will!"

He fell to his knees, and everything that a mind can supply
in place of a heart, everything that imagination can do to
clothe physical desire with poetry, he put into a fervent and
daring plea. And when he saw that she was still not ready to
surrender, he accepted his defeat and began to reproach her
with not loving him, half-ashamed and half-amused to find
himself saying anything so incredibly vulgar and trite, and almost embarrassed at having a relationship with a woman so
naive that the words didn't make her smile.

Instead the reproach went to Indiana's heart more directly
than all his flowery flatteries.

Until she suddenly remembered.

"Raymon," she said, "the one who loved you so much . .
the one we were talking about before . . . I suppose she did
everything you wanted?"

"Everything!" replied Raymon, impatient at the unwelcome
intrusion of Noun. "And instead of constantly reminding me of

her, you would do better to make me forget how much she loved me!"

"Listen," said Indiana, thoughtfully and seriously. "I still have some things to ask you, so be patient a little longer. Perhaps you weren't as guilty as I thought, and it would make me very happy to be able to forgive you for what I considered a terrible insult. Tell me—when I found you here, had you come to see her or me?"

Raymon hesitated; then, realizing that she would soon learn the truth anyway—indeed, might already know it—he replied, "I came to see her."

"Well," she said sadly, "I prefer that. I would rather suffer from an infidelity than from an insult. Now, Raymon, please continue to be honest with me. How long had you been in my room before I came in? Remember that Ralph knows everything, and that if I ask him—"

"There is no need for Sir Ralph's denunciations, madame. I had been here since the night before."

"And you had spent the night in this room? All right, you needn't say anything. Your silence is my answer."

Neither spoke for a few moments, then Indiana rose and was about to say something when a sudden sharp rap at the door made her blood freeze. Neither she nor Raymon dared move or even breathe.

A sheet of paper, a page from a notebook, slid under the door. Written in pencil, almost illegibly, were the words:

Your husband is here.

        Ralph

XVIII

"It's a lie, and a stupid one at that!" said Raymon as soon as the last echos of Ralph's footsteps had faded away. "Someone should teach Sir Ralph a lesson, and I—"

"I forbid you to even think of such a thing," said Indiana, in a cold, determined tone that allowed no discussion. "Ralph has never lied. My husband is here, and we are lost. This would have terrified me earlier, but now I don't seem to care!"

"Very well, then, since we're doomed to die," said Raymon in a state of exaltation, "be mine! Forgive me for everything, and let your last words in our final moment be of love, my last breath be a sigh of happiness."

"Such a moment of courage might have been the most wonderful moment of my life," she said, "but you've spoiled it for me."

They heard the sound of wheels in the yard, followed by the loud clamor of an impatient, heavy hand ringing the bell at the gate.

"I recognize his ring," said Indiana, who had been listening attentively. "Ralph was telling the truth, but you still have time to escape if you leave immediately!"

"I won't leave!" cried Raymon. "I suspect we've been betrayed, and I won't allow you to be the only victim. I insist on remaining here to protect you!"

"There's been no betrayal. Listen, you can hear the servants moving about. They'll be opening the gate in a few minutes. . . . You must go! The moon isn't completely out, and the shrubbery will hide you. Not another word—just go!"

Raymon had to obey her, and she went with him to the foot of the stairs so she could look carefully at the clumps of bushes in the garden. Everything was quiet; no one was about. She remained on that last step for a long time, listening fearfully to the sound of his receding footsteps on the gravel and completely forgetting the imminent approach of her husband; his rage meant nothing to her as long as Raymon was safely out of his reach!

As for him, he crossed the stream and then the park swiftly and silently. When he arrived at the little door, his excitement made him awkward, and he had some trouble opening it; but as soon as he was outside, Sir Ralph appeared in front of him and said, as coolly as if they were meeting at a ball, "Please give me the key. If anyone looks for it, it will cause less of a stir for it to be found with me."

Raymon would have preferred the worst insult to such contemptuous generosity. He replied, "I'm not the man to forget a sincere favor, but I *am* a man who will avenge an insult and punish a betrayal."

Without any change in either his tone or his expression, Ralph said, "I do not want your gratitude, and your threats leave me quite unmoved. But this is neither the time nor the place for conversation. Here's your path, and try to have some consideration for Madame Delmare's reputation."

Then he disappeared.

Completely disoriented after a night of such agitation, Raymon was at that moment almost unnerved enough to believe in magic; by the time he reached home, it was nearly daybreak and he immediately went to bed with a fever.

In the morning, Indiana presided over the breakfast table and served her husband and cousin with untroubled dignity. She had not yet a chance to think about her situation, and it was instinct alone that was responsible for her self-possession and presence of mind. In fact, the colonel was gloomy and preoccupied, but only because of his business affairs; there was not a single jealous or suspicious thought in his mind.

By evening, Raymon felt strong enough to consider his love, and he found that it had diminished considerably. He enjoyed the challenge of real difficulties, but he hated annoyances—and he could foresee innumerable occasions for annoyance now that Indiana had the right to reproach him. . . . Finally he remembered that honor required him to find out what had happened to her, and he sent his servant to see what he could discover by prowling around Lagny.

The messenger returned with the following letter, which Mme. Delmare herself had given him.

Last night I hoped I would lose either my mind or my life; unfortunately, I have kept both. I won't complain, be-

*cause I deserve my unhappiness. I chose to live such a
stormy life, and it would be cowardly to retreat from it
now. I don't know if you are guilty, and I don't want to
know—so shall we agree never to return to the subject? Let
this be the last mention of it, because it hurts both of us too
much.*

*You said one thing that gave me a cruel satisfaction. Oh,
poor Noun, you who are now in heaven, forgive me! You
who no longer suffer, you who no longer love him—you
may even be able to feel sorry for me! Raymon, you told me
that you sacrificed that poor, unfortunate girl for me because you loved me more than you loved her. Oh, don't
deny it! You said it, and I need to believe it so much that I
do believe it. And yet everything you did and said last
night—all your arguments, all your wild behavior—should
make me doubt it. I forgave you then because of your emotional state, but by now you've been able to think calmly
and go back to being your true self—so tell me, will you
give up your wish to love me in that way? I, who love you
with all my heart, had hoped to arouse in you a love as
pure as mine. I hadn't really thought about the future. I
hadn't looked very far ahead, and I didn't concern myself
about whether or not I might someday, won over by your
devotion, sacrifice to you my scruples and my repugnance.
But today I know that it can never happen—I see in such a
future only a frightening parallel between Noun and me,
and oh, I can't bear the thought of not being loved more
than she was! If I believed that . . . And yet she was more
beautiful than I—much more! Why did you prefer me? It
must have been because you loved me in a different way, a
better way. . . . That's what I wanted to say to you. Will you
give up the idea of being my lover in the same way you
were hers? If you do, I can still respect you, still believe in
your remorse, your sincerity, your love. If not, forget me,
because you will never see me again. That might kill me,
but I would rather die than sink so low as to be nothing
more than your mistress.*

Indiana's pride offended Raymon; he wouldn't have thought
it possible for a woman who had thrown herself into his arms
to resist him—and to give such logical reasons for her resistance. He was unsure of how to reply to her letter.

"She doesn't love me," he thought. "She has a cold heart and she's arrogant."

That was when he completely stopped loving her. She had shaken his self-esteem, deprived him of a hoped-for triumph, disappointed his dreams of pleasure: he now felt about her exactly the way he had felt about Noun. Poor Indiana—she who had so wanted to mean more than that to him! He misunderstood the quality of her passionate love; he scorned her unconditional trust. He had never understood her, so how could he have continued to love her?

Spitefully—this time not out of pride but out of a desire for revenge—he swore to triumph over her. It was no longer a question of consummating a passion but of punishing an insult, no more a matter of possessing a woman but of conquering her. He vowed that he would be her master, even if only for a day, and that he would then abandon her just for the pleasure of seeing her at his feet.

Under the impetus of such feelings, he wrote her the following letter:

> You want me to promise. . . . What are you thinking of, you foolish girl? I will promise anything you want because I cannot help but obey you, but if I don't keep my promises, I won't be guilty before either you or God. If you loved me, Indiana, you wouldn't torture me like this, you wouldn't make me risk breaking my word, you wouldn't blush at the thought of being my mistress. Instead, you think being in my arms would shame and disgrace you . . .

But he felt his bitterness coming through too clearly, so he tore up the sheet and, after giving himself some time to think, began again:

> You say that you almost went out of your mind that night; well, I did. Completely. I was wrong—no, I was mad! Try to forget those insane hours. Now that I'm calm again and have thought it over, I can say that I'm still worthy of you. May God bless you, my heavenly angel, for having saved me from myself and reminded me of how I ought to love you. Give me your orders, Indiana, for you know I'm your slave! I would give my life for an hour in your arms, but I can suffer for a whole lifetime to have one of your smiles. I will be your friend and your brother—nothing

*more. If I suffer, you will never know about it. If my blood
takes fire when I'm near you, if I can't breathe, if I feel
faint when I brush your hand with mine, if one of your
sweet sisterly kisses sets my skin aflame—why, I will order
my blood to cool, my head to be steady, my lips to respect
you. I will be gentle, submissive, and miserable if that will
make you happy, and I will do all that, Indiana, if only I
can hear you say once more that you love me. Oh, say it,
Indiana! Give me back your confidence and my joy, and tell
me when we can see each other again. I have no idea of
what might have happened later that night—why don't you
tell me about it? Why have you let me suffer since this
morning? Carle said that he saw the three of you walking
together in the park and that the colonel seemed sick or unhappy, but not angry. That means Ralph did not betray us
after all! What a strange man he is! But can we depend on
his discretion—and how will I dare show myself at Lagny
now that our fate is in his hands? But I will dare it anyway.
If I have to beg him, I will swallow my pride, conquer my
dislike, do anything and everything rather than lose you.
One word from you, and I will carry a burden of remorse
for the rest of my life, because I would commit any crime
for you. I would even abandon my mother for you. Oh, if
you only realized how much I love you, Indiana!*

The pen fell from Raymon's hands; he was terribly tired,
practically asleep, but he forced himself to reread the letter to
make sure that his drowsiness had not distorted his ideas. He
was so physically exhausted, however, that it was impossible
to make any sense of what he had written, so he rang for his
servant, told him to take the letter to Lagny before daybreak,
then fell into that deep and precious sleep known only to those
who are completely satisfied with themselves.

Indiana never went to bed at all. She wasn't even aware of
being tired, and she spent the entire night writing. When she
received Raymon's letter she answered it immediately:

*Thank you, Raymon, thank you! You've given me back
my strength and my life itself. Now I can do anything, endure anything, and all because you love me and are not
frightened by whatever may happen. Yes, we will see each
other again; yes, we will dare everything and defy everyone. Ralph can do whatever he wants about our secret—*

*I'm not afraid of anything, not even my husband, because
you love me.*

*Do you want to know about our business affairs? I forgot
to mention them yesterday, yet they've taken a turn that af-
fects my fortune. We are ruined. We will have to sell Lagny,
perhaps even go to live in the colonies. But what do I care
about that? I can't even make myself think about it. I know
that we'll always be together because that's what you
promised me, Raymon, and I'm depending on that promise
just as you may depend on my courage. Nothing will
frighten me, nothing will stop me—my place is at your side,
and only death can tear me from it.*

"What typically female exaggeration!" thought Raymon,
rumpling the note. "All women have to stimulate themselves
with the prospect of romantic, dangerous schemes, just like in-
valids who need sharp, spicy seasonings to whet their ap-
petites! But I've done what I wanted to do. I've recovered my
influence and reestablished my power over her, and as for the
rest of her nonsense—well, we shall see what all those threats
come down to! Silly, false creatures—they're always ready to
undertake the impossible, and their generosity is so exaggerated and ostentatious that it inevitably leads to scandal! No
one reading this letter could possibly imagine that she counts
out her kisses and rations her caresses like a miser!"

He went to Lagny that same day. Ralph wasn't there, and
the colonel received him warmly and spoke to him freely. He
led him into the park so they would be less likely to be disturbed, and told him that he was a ruined man and that the factory would be put up for sale the following day. Raymon
offered to help, but Delmare refused.

"No, my friend," he said. "It was hard enough for me to
know that I owed my success to Ralph's generosity, and I
couldn't wait to repay him. When I sell this property, I'll be
able to clear all my debts at one time, and though I won't have
any money left after that, I still have courage, energy, and experience. The future lies before me. I've already built a fortune
from nothing once, and I can do it again. I must, because of
my wife—she's young and I don't want to leave her impover-
ished. I'll start my new business in Bourbon because she still
has some property there, and in a few years—ten at most—I
hope we'll be able to meet again."

Raymon clasped the colonel's hand, smiling inwardly to

hear the colonel talk so confidently about the future—about ten years!—when his bald head and worn-out body showed all the signs of an existence barely clinging to life. Still, he pretended to share his hopes.

"I'm delighted to see that you're not discouraged by your reverses," he said. "Such self-confidence proves you a true man, a man of intrepid character and strong will. But does Madame Delmare share your courage? Aren't you afraid she will be reluctant to agree to leave France?"

"That would be a shame," he replied, "but wives are made to obey, not to rule. I haven't yet told Indiana exactly what I intend to do. Except for you, my friend, I can't imagine what she might regret leaving—and yet, if only out of a spirit of contradiction, I foresee tears, attacks of nerves . . . Devil take all women! However, that doesn't matter, and I count on you, my dear Raymon, to make my particular woman listen to reason. She has confidence in you, so please use your influence to keep her from crying. I hate tears!"

Raymon promised to return the next day and tell Mme. Delmare about her husband's decision.

"You'll be doing me a great favor," said the colonel. "I'll take Ralph to the farm, so you'll be able to talk to her alone."

"Well, that works out to my advantage!" Raymon thought as he left Lagny.

XIX

. DELMARE'S plans were exactly what Raymon might
ve wished for: since he could see that this love affair was all
t over for him and would soon bring him nothing but irritat-
g obligations and demands, he was quite content to have
ents arrange themselves in such a way that he would be
ared the inevitable tedium that is part of a dying relation-
ip. All that remained was to reap the benefits of Indiana's
nal moments of exaltation and trust to his usual good luck
at he would be spared her tears and reproaches.

He therefore returned to Lagny the next day with every in-
ntion of leading poor Indiana's fervor to its logical conclu-
on.

"Do you know what your husband wants me to do, Indi-
a?" he asked her when they met. "I must say that it's cer-
inly a strange commission! He expects me to beg you to
turn to Bourbon with him, to leave me, to break my heart
d destroy my life. I wouldn't say he's chosen the right man
plead his cause, would you?"

Her gravity was so imposing that a grudging respect began
replace his artificial gaiety.

"Why are you telling me this?" she asked. "Are you afraid
at I'll let him change my mind? That I'll obey him? You
edn't worry, Raymon, I've made my decision. I've spent
o nights looking at it from every point of view, and I realize
hat I will be exposing myself to, what I will have to defy,
hat I will have to sacrifice, what I will have to disregard and
nore—and I assure you that I'm quite ready to do and endure
hatever is necessary because I know that you will guide me
d support me through it all."

Raymon came very close to being frightened by the firm re-
lve she showed in making such mad promises, but then he de-
ded that his earlier opinion was correct: Indiana didn't really

love him but was only applying to her own situation the exagge ated responses she had read about in novels. To match the pa sion of his romantic mistress he began to improvise dramati eloquent speeches that succeeded in perpetuating her error, b any impartial observer would have seen quite clearly that th love scene was in reality a contest between theatrical illusion a genuine emotion, and that Raymon's bombastic grandiloquenc was nothing but a cold, cruel parody of Indiana's simply e pressed real feelings: one was mind, the other heart.

Despite what Raymon persuaded himself he believed abo Indiana's sincerity, he nevertheless felt that it would be th better part of wisdom to undermine her plans to resist her hu band and to convince her instead to pretend that she was wi ing—or at least not unwilling—to leave with him until sh could express her rebellion openly. He told her that it wou be best to postpone her announcement until they had actual left Lagny; that way she would avoid a scandal in front of th servants and prevent Ralph's dangerous intervention in the affairs.

But Ralph did not leave his unfortunate friends. First he ha offered his entire fortune, his Bellerive château, his incom from England, and the money he would make by selling hi plantations in the colonies; but the colonel, who no longer fe as friendly to Ralph as he had and was reluctant to owe hir anything, would not change his mind. If Ralph had been a persuasive as Raymon, he might have been able to sway M Delmare; but the poor baronet thought that once he had clearl explained his ideas and expressed his feelings, he had said an done everything he could, and he was never able to believ that any further speech or action on his part could make any one change his mind. So he rented Bellerive and followed M and Mme. Delmare to Paris, where they were waiting until was time to leave for Bourbon.

Lagny, its factory, and all its appurtenances were put up fc sale. The winter was a depressing one for Indiana. Raymo was, of course, in Paris; he saw her every day, he was attentiv and affectionate—but he never stayed with her for more tha an hour. He would arrive at the end of dinner, and as soon a the colonel went out to take care of some business, Raymo would also leave to attend some social function. As you know society was Raymon's element, his reality; its noise and bustl and animated multitudes were the breath of life to him, th arena in which he could display all his wit and intelligence an superiority. In an intimate relationship he was amiable, but in society he became brilliant; and then he was no longer a member of this group or another, a friend of this person or that, but the man of intellect who belongs to everyone alike and for whom society is like a country.

And then, as we have said, Raymon had his principles. When he saw how the colonel liked and respected him, how he thought of him as the personification of truth and honor, how he wanted him to act as an intermediary between himself and Indiana, he resolved to justify that confidence, deserve that respect, reconcile husband and wife, and resist any claims on the part of the latter that might jeopardize the tranquility of the former. He became once again a moral, virtuous, philosophical person.

You will see how long that lasted.

Indiana, who understood nothing about this conversion, suffered horribly at seeing herself so neglected, yet at least she was still spared the need to acknowledge the complete destruction of all her hopes. It was easy to deceive her; she asked nothing better than to be deceived, because her real life was so bitter and desolate! Her husband had become almost impossible to live with; in public he pretended to a manly, courageous, stoic indifference to his misfortune, but in the privacy of his home he was nothing more than an irritable, demanding, silly child. Indiana was his scapegoat, and we must admit that much of it was her fault. If she had affectionately but firmly protested or complained, Delmare, who was only crude and rough, would have been ashamed to be considered mean-spirited or unkind. Anyone prepared to descend to his intellectual level and discuss things within the framework of his limited ideas could easily have softened his heart and controlled his behavior, but there was something proud and unyielding in Indiana's silent submission to him; it was the silent submission of the slave who feels his hatred is a virtue and his misfortune a sign of merit. Her haughty resignation was a little like the stiff dignity of a king who would rather accept chains and imprisonment than abdicate his throne and deprive himself of a meaningless title. An ordinary woman would have been able to dominate such a vulgar man: she would have seemed to agree with whatever he said, but felt free to think otherwise; she would have pretended to share his prejudices but secretly rebelled against them; she would have caressed him but betrayed him. Indiana saw many women acting like that, but she felt so superior to them that she would have blushed to imitate them. Since her behavior was virtuous, chaste, and respectful to her master, she felt it completely unnecessary to flatter him by her words, and she didn't want his affection because she had none for him. She would have found it much more shameful to pretend to love this husband she disliked than to actually give that love to the man who inspired it in her. Deceit was the major crime in her eyes: she was ready to proclaim her love for Raymon twenty times a day, and only the fear of doing him harm prevented her.

Her cold obedience irritated the colonel much more than open defiance would have; he might have lost some measure of self-respect if he had not been the absolute master in his own home, but he suffered much more from the consciousness of being a master only in such a hateful, ridiculous way. He wanted to convince, and instead he commanded; to sway, and he ruled. Sometimes he would give orders that were badly expressed or harmful to his own best interests; Indiana made sure that they were carried out without question, without discussion, with the perfect indifference of a horse that pulls the plow in whatever direction he is told. When Delmare saw the results of his misunderstood words or ill-conceived instructions, he would be furious; but when Indiana pointed out to him with a glacial calm that she had only seen to it that his orders were obeyed exactly as he had given them, all that rage had to be directed against himself—which was cruel punishment for a violent man whose self-esteem was so uncertain.

Had he lived in Smyrna or Cairo, he would have killed his wife at such times—and yet he loved with all his heart that weak woman who lived with him in utter subjection and religiously kept the secret of his ill treatment hidden from the world. He loved her, or perhaps he felt sorry for her; I'm not sure which. He would have liked her to love him, for he was proud of her education and her breeding, and he would have felt better in his own eyes if she had at least condescended to discuss his ideas and his principles. Sometimes he would enter her bedroom in the morning with the intention of quarreling with her, and when he found her still asleep, he was afraid to awaken her. He would stand there silently looking at her, intimidated by her delicate health, her pallor, the sad resignation and calm melancholy so apparent even in her immobility. He would be flooded with feelings of guilt, self-reproach, anger and fear, and he would blush at the thought of the influence such a frail figure had exerted over his destiny—over him, a man of iron, accustomed to command, to see whole squadrons of mettlesome horses and martial men set into motion by a single word from his lips!

And such a child-woman had made such a man unhappy! Because of her he was forced to look into himself, to examine his decisions and modify many of them and reverse others—and all that without once hearing her say, "You're wrong, I think you should do this instead of that." Not once had she begged him; not once had she tried to claim the right to be his equal or his companion. This insignificant woman, whom he could have crushed in his hand if he had wanted to, was lying there, perhaps dreaming of someone else right under his eyes and defying him even in her sleep. He was tempted to strangle her, to drag her around the room by the hair, to trample her underfoot and force her to beg for mercy and forgiveness; but she was so pretty, so dainty and fragile, that he would instead feel sorry for her, like a child who is moved to pity the bird he had meant to kill. And this man of bronze would weep like a woman and leave the room so she would not have the satisfaction of seeing his tears.

To tell the truth, I don't know which of them was more unhappy, he or she. She was cruel because she was virtuous, just as he was kind because he was weak; she had too much patience, and he had none; she had the defects of her good qualities, and he the good qualities of his defects.

A swarm of friends and acquaintances milled around these two ill-matched people and tried to bring them together, some of them because they had nothing else to do, others because it made them feel important, and still others because of misguided affection. Some took the wife's side, others the husband's. They quarreled among themselves because of M. and Mme. Delmare, although those two did not quarrel with each other at all; Indiana's submission to her husband was so complete that the colonel could never, under any circumstances, find anything to quarrel about. And then there were those who knew nothing about the matter but wanted to make themselves necessary to the couple: some would advise Mme. Delmare to submit to her husband, unaware that she was only too submissive, while others would advise M. Delmare to be a rigid disciplinarian and not allow his wife to usurp his authority. This last group—dull, thick-headed people who feel themselves so unimportant that they are always afraid others will pay no attention to them, and who mistakenly reverse cause and effect—belongs to a species that you will find everywhere you go, all tangled up in other people's affairs and noisily making sure that they are noticed.

M. and Mme. Delmare had made many acquaintances in Melun and Fontainebleau; they met them all again in Paris, and it was those people in particular who were most avid in spreading ill-natured gossip about them. I am sure you know that small-town wit is the nastiest in the world and that good people are always misunderstood and superior minds always despised in such places. When it is a question of coming to the aid of a fool or a boor you will see them running. If you have an argument with anyone, they will come to watch as if they were at the theater, making bets on the results and practically falling over you in their eagerness to see and hear everything. They will cover the loser with contempt and curse him, because the weakest one is always the one who is wrong. If you attack prejudice, small-mindedness, or viciousness, you are insulting them personally and attacking them in what they hold most dear; you are a dangerous traitor. People whose names you do not even know will bring you to court to exact reparations for what they consider your damaging allusions to them.

What can I say? If you meet one of these people, be careful not to step on his shadow—not even at sunset, when a man's shadow is thirty feet long—because all that space belongs to the inhabitant of a small town and you have no right to set foot on it. If you breathe the same air that he breathes, you are endangering his health; if you drink from his fountain, you are making it go dry; if you give your trade to the local businesses, you are driving up the prices he himself must pay; if you offer him tobacco, you are ruining his lungs; if you think his daughter is pretty, you are about to seduce her, if you praise his wife's domestic skills you are being ironic because you really despise her for her ignorance; if you should by some miracle find a reason to compliment him in his own home, he will misunderstand what you say and tell everyone that you insulted him. Take your household goods and move with them into the darkest part of the forest or the most desolate spot on the moors, because only in such places will the small-town man leave you in peace!

Even the sturdy walls surrounding Paris did not save the poor Delmares from being pursued by the small town. The wealthy families of Fontainebleau and Melun came to Paris for the winter and brought with them the blessings of their provincial ways. Partisans of both Delmare and his wife formed coteries around each of them and did everything humanly possible to make their situation even worse than it was. They succeeded; the couple's unhappiness increased, and their misunderstandings and mutual obstinacy did not lessen.

Ralph was sensible enough not to get involved. Indiana had originally suspected him of provoking her husband's anger with her, or at the very least, of wanting to end Raymon's intimacy with her, but she soon recognized the injustice of her suspicions. Delmare's complete ease with Raymon was incontrovertible proof of her cousin's silence. She wanted to thank Ralph, but whenever they were alone and she began to say anything about it, he pretended not to understand her allusions and adamantly refused to acknowledge her overtures. It was such a delicate subject that she didn't have the courage to force the issue; instead, she tried to make him understand her gratitude by a multitude of delicate, subtle, affectionate attentions—but Ralph pretended not to be aware of them, and Indiana's pride was wounded by what she considered such arrogant generosity. Fearing to seem like a guilty wife begging pardon of a stern witness, she once again became cold and distant with poor Ralph. It seemed to her that his behavior was another sign of his selfishness; it showed that he still loved her, but no longer respected her—that he wanted her companionship only because he needed distractions, didn't want to lose the comforts she was responsible for creating in his home, and chose not to deprive himself of the benefits she never tired of showering on him. She imagined that he was not the least bit concerned about whether she had behaved badly toward either her husband or herself.

"What a perfect demonstration of his contempt for women," she thought. "He sees them as nothing more than domestic animals, good for running a house, preparing meals, and serving tea. He won't do them the honor of having a real discussion with them, and he doesn't even care about their faults provided that they don't affect him personally by interfering with his comfort or disturbing his habits. Ralph doesn't need my heart. As long as my hands can make his pudding and play the harp, what does he care about my love for another man, my secret sorrows, my frustration under the yoke that is crushing me? I am his servant, and that is all he wants from me."

XX

INDIANA no longer complained to Raymon; his excuses were so unconvincing that she was afraid she might begin to find him unforgivable, and since the one thing she dreaded even more than being deceived was being abandoned, she could no longer *not* believe in him or in the future he had promised her. The life she led with her husband and Ralph had become unbearable, and if she hadn't hoped to soon be free of the domination of those two men, she too would have drowned herself. She thought of it often, telling herself that if Raymon treated her as he had Noun, she would have no other way to avoid an unbearable future but to join Noun, and the somber, ever present thought comforted her.

It was almost time for them to leave. Completely unaware of what his wife was planning, the colonel went about every day settling his affairs and paying his creditors one after another; Indiana, sure of her courage, watched all his preparations in perfect tranquility and was busy with her own preparations—trying, for example, to make an ally of her aunt, Mme. de Carvajal, by telling her how much she hated to leave France. The old marchioness, who had great hopes of using her niece's beauty as a drawing card for her salon, told the colonel that it was his duty to leave his wife in France, that it would be barbarous to expose her to the fatigue and danger of such a crossing so soon after she had begun to regain her health, that—in a word—it was for him to rebuild his fortune and for Indiana to remain and take care of her old aunt.

At first M. Delmare ignored these pronouncements, taking them as the meanderings of an old woman in her dotage, but he was forced to pay more attention to them when Mme. de Carvajal made it quite clear that Indiana's inheritance was at stake. Delmare loved money with the powerful passion of a man who has worked very hard all his life to accumulate it, but he was also in his own way a proud man, so he stood his ground and insisted that his wife would follow him at any cost. The marchioness, who believed that money must be the supreme god of every sensible man, remained unconvinced that this was his last word on the subject and continued to encourage her niece's resistance, promising to cover such behavior in the eyes of the world by the cloak of her own respectability. Only a coarse nature corrupted by intrigue and ambition, and a hypocritical heart warped by devotion to external show, could have pretended to be so oblivious to the real reasons for Indiana's rebellion. Although her passion for Raymon was unknown to everyone but her husband, she had not yet created an open scandal, so the secret was mentioned only in whispers—but more than a dozen people had whispered it in confidence to Mme. de Carvajal! The old fool was flattered by it; she wanted her niece to be the latest fashion in society, someone whose name was on every tongue, and an affair with Raymon was a good beginning.

And yet Mme. de Carvajal was not a depraved woman of the Regency period; the Restoration had imposed a veneer of virtue, and since the court demanded proper *behavior,* the marchioness hated nothing more than the kind of scandal that brings ruin in its wake. Under Mme. du Barry, her principles would have been less rigid; now, under the Dauphine, she was stiff-necked and unbending. But only for what showed on the outside. Her contempt and disapproval were reserved for glaringly public sins, and she always waited to see how an intrigue would work out before condemning it. Infidelities that remained discreet were easily forgiven by her, but she reverted to a sterner Spanish judgment for those that could be glimpsed through the shutters: there was no guilt unless the act became known to casual bystanders or the general public. By these standards, Indiana, with her chaste, modest, and completely private love, was a precious catch to exhibit and exploit; such a woman might fascinate the leading lights of that hypocritical society and resist the dangers of its most subtle ruses. A pure soul and a passionate heart presented some interesting possibilities. . . . Poor Indiana! Her fatal destiny carried her so far beyond all her expectations and led her into such depths of misery that she was at least spared her aunt's dreadful protection.

Raymon was not at all worried about what would become of Indiana. His love for her had already reached its last unpleasant stage: boredom. To bore the person one loves is to sink as low as possible in the eyes of that beloved, but luckily, Indiana had no idea that this had happened and was allowed a last few days of illusion.

Returning home from a ball early one morning, Raymon found Indiana in his room. She had come at midnight and had been waiting for him for five long hours, without a fire at the most frigid time of the year and enduring both the cold and her anxiety with the same cheerless but unswerving patience that had been the pattern of her whole life.

She raised her head when he came in, and Raymon, speechless with astonishment, could see no sign of either anger or reproach.

"I've been waiting for you," she said gently. "You haven't come to see me for three days, and since things have happened that you should know about without any further delay, I came here last night to tell you about them."

"How incredibly reckless!" said Raymon, carefully locking the door behind him. "And my servants know you're here because they just told me so!"

"I didn't try to hide my presence," she replied icily. "And I think you used the wrong word."

"Yes, I said 'reckless,' but I should have said 'mad.'"

"I would have said 'courageous.' But never mind that. Listen to what I have to say. Monsieur Delmare wants to leave for Bordeaux in three days, going from there to the colonies. You agreed to protect me against his violence if he should resort to it, and he most certainly will, because I told him about my plans last night and he locked me into my room. I got out through a window— see, my hands are bloody. They may be looking for me at this very moment, but Ralph is at Bellerive, so he won't be able to tell them where I am. I've decided to go into hiding until Monsieur Delmare has accepted my decision and is ready to leave without me. Have you thought about where I can stay? It's been so long since I've seen you alone that I have no idea what your plans are, but when I once said that I doubted your determination to go ahead with this, you told me that you couldn't imagine a love that wasn't based on confidence. You reminded me that you had never doubted me, and you proved to me that I wasn't being fair to you. I was afraid that if I didn't dismiss my childish fears, and if I demanded all the thousand little proofs of love demanded by women involved in ordinary affairs, I would prove unworthy of you, so I resigned myself to your brief visits, our awkward meetings, your eagerness to avoid any intimate conversation, and I remained confident in you. Let heaven be my witness that I turned aside my anxiety and fear as if they were criminal thoughts! Now I want to be rewarded for my faith. The time has come for you to tell me if you accept my sacrifices."

The crisis was so immediate that Raymon could no longer pre-

nd. Desperate, furious at being so hopelessly caught in his own
ap, he lost his head and allowed his rage to escape in a stream
coarse, brutal curses.

"You're mad!" he cried, flinging himself into a chair. "Where
d you get your idea of love? Tell me, in what romance written
r chambermaids did you learn about the world?"

He stopped, realizing that he had been much too rough with
er and that he had to find other ways of saying the same thing
that she would leave without feeling insulted.

But she sat there as steadily as if she had come prepared to
ear anything.

"Go on," she said, crossing her hands over her heart to steady
, "I'm listening. I assume you have more to say to me?"

Raymon thought this was his signal to go through yet another
ve scene.

He sprang up from the chair and cried out, "I will never accept
ich a sacrifice! Never! When I told you I would be strong
nough to do it, Indiana, I was flattering myself—or rather, I was
ialigning myself, because only a coward would allow the
oman he loves to be dishonored. You know so little about life
iat you don't realize the consequences of such a plan, and I was
afraid of losing you that I wasn't able to think about it ratio-
ally."

"You seem to be able to think rationally now," she said, refus-
ig to allow him to hold the hand he had tried to take.

"Indiana," he began again, "don't you see that you would be
iving me the dishonorable role while saving the heroic one for
ourself, and that you're condemning me only because I want to
ontinue to remain worthy of your love? Oh, you poor, naive,
mple-hearted woman, would you be able to love me if I were to
icrifice your life to my pleasure, your reputation to my selfish
esires?"

"You contradict yourself," said Indiana. "If I can make you
appy by being with you, why do you care about what people
ill think? Is that more important to you than I am?"

"Oh, it's not for myself that I care, Indiana!"

"For whom, then? For me? I knew you would have these scru-
les, so I made it easier for you. I didn't wait for you to tear me
way from my home—I didn't even consult you before leaving it
rever. I took that final, irrevocable step myself, and you have
othing to reproach yourself with. I'm already dishonored, Ray-
10n. While I was waiting for you, I counted on that clock the
ours that marked my disgrace, and now, though I am as unsul-
ed this morning as I was yesterday, in the eyes of the world I've

lost my reputation. Yesterday women still felt sorry for me, b
today they will feel only contempt. I thought about all that befo
I left."

"Abominable feminine foresight!" Raymon thought.

Then, trying to dissuade her just as he would a bailiff come
claim his furniture, he said in a cajoling, paternal tone, "You ex
aggerate the importance of what you've done. No, my dear, or
silly action doesn't mean that everything is lost. I can keep m
servants from talking about this—"

"And mine, who are certainly searching for me at this ver
moment? And my husband—do you think that he will quietl
keep this secret? Do you think that he will want to take me bac
after I've spent an entire night under your roof? Do you advis
me to return to him, throw myself at his feet, and beg him, as
sign that he forgives me, to kindly replace the chain that ha
crushed my life and wasted my youth? Do you accept so easil
and without the slightest regret that the woman you love s
dearly should return to be ruled by another man when you are th
master of that woman's fate, when you can keep her in your arm
for the rest of your life, when she is here in your power and of
fering to remain there forever? Aren't you afraid, or at least re
luctant, to return her to the ruthless master who may be waitin
for her only to kill her?"

An idea suddenly flashed across Raymon's mind. This was th
time to subdue her womanly pride—if not now, it might b
never. She had just offered him all the sacrifices that he had n
desire to accept, and she stood there fearlessly certain that sh
ran no risks other than those she had just enumerated; but Ray
mon had thought of a way in which he could either rid himself c
such demanding devotion or at least take advantage of it. He wa
too good a friend of Delmare, he owed him too much considera
tion, to steal his wife; he would content himself with seducin
her.

"You're right, my Indiana," he cried enthusiastically. "You re
store me to my true self and rekindle the rapture that the though
of your danger and the fear of doing you harm had cooled! For
give me for my childish fear and try to understand how much o
it was due to my true, tender love for you. But your soft voic
makes by blood tingle, and your fervent words make my vein
take fire! Forgive me, oh, forgive me for having been able t
think of anything else but this sacred moment when you finall
belong to me. Let me forget all the dangers that threaten us an
get down on my knees to thank you for the happiness you brin
me. Let me abandon myself completely to this hour of bliss that

end at your feet and that could not be paid for even with my
e's blood! Let your stupid husband, that beast who locks you
and falls asleep in the middle of his vulgar violence, let him
me and try to snatch you from my arms—you, my treasure,
y very life! From now on you belong not to him but to me—
u are my beloved, my companion, my mistress . . ."

As he spoke, he gradually worked himself into a state of exal-
ion, as he usually did when pleading his case. The situation
s romantic, powerful, and full of possible danger. As a true
scendant of a race of valiant knights, Raymon loved danger.
ery sound he heard in the street could mean that the husband
s coming to claim his wife and his rival's blood, and to enjoy
voluptuous pleasures of love in such a context was a pleasure
ymon found worthy of him. For fifteen minutes he was pas-
onately in love with Indiana, lavishing upon her all the seduc-
words of his blazing eloquence. His language was powerful
d his emotion sincere, because for the moment this man who
ought of love as a social pastime truly believed in the game he
s playing. And to her shame, Indiana was idiotic enough to
ke those lying words for truth! She gave herself up to them
th delight, she was ecstatic, she glowed with hope and joy; she
rgave everything, and she almost agreed to everything.

But Raymon ruined it all by going too quickly. If he had had
ough artistry to be patient and keep Indiana there for another
enty-four hours, she might have been his. But day was break-
g, bright and golden; the room was flooded with sunlight, and
e street noises were getting louder with each passing moment.
hen Raymon looked at the clock, he saw that it was already
ven.

"It's time to put an end to this," he thought. "Delmare may
me at any minute, and I must convince her to go home before
at happens."

He became more urgent and less tender. His lips betrayed an
patient desire that was more domineering than delicate, and
s kisses were brusque and almost angry. Indiana was fright-
ed. A good angel spread its wings over that wavering, troubled
ul; she came to herself and rebuffed his cold, selfish, vicious
ack.

"Let me be," she said. "I don't want to do out of weakness
hat I am prepared to do out of love or gratitude. You can't pos-
bly need any proof of my affection—my being here is proof
ough, and I bring with me our future. But for now I must have
clear conscience so that I may be strong, steady, and calm in
e face of the powerful obstacles that still separate us."

"What are you talking about?" said Raymon, too furious at h
resistance to listen to her.

His frustration and anger made him completely lose his hea
and he pushed her away roughly, paced the room with his hea
beating rapidly and his head feeling ready to explode, the
dashed over to the pitcher and drank a large glass of water, whi
managed to calm his hysteria and cool his love.

He looked at her ironically and said, "Enough, madame, i
time for you to leave."

A ray of light suddenly seemed to illuminate Raymon's so
laying it bare for her to see.

"You're right," she said, walking toward the door.

"Don't forget your cloak and scarf," he said, stopping her.

"Of course," she replied. "Those signs of my presence mig
compromise you."

"You're being childish," he said in a coaxing tone as
helped her adjust her cloak with pretended concern. "You kno
very well that I love you, but you enjoy torturing me and yo
drive me mad. Wait here while I call a cab. I would escort yo
home if I could, but that would ruin you."

"You don't think I'm already ruined?" she asked bitterly.

"No, my dear," replied Raymon, who wanted nothing mo
than to persuade her to leave him in peace. "Since no one ha
come here to ask about you, they obviously haven't missed yo
yet. True, I would have been the last person to be suspected o
anything, but still, it would be only natural to inquire about yo
at the homes of all your acquaintances. And besides, you can g
to your aunt and put yourself under her protection—as a matt
of fact, that's what I advise you to do. She'll say that you spe
the night with her, and that will settle everything."

Indiana wasn't listening; in a state close to stupor, she wa
watching the enormous red sun rise over the horizon of bu
nished rooftops. When Raymon tried to rouse her, she looked
him without any recognition. There was a greenish tinge on he
cheeks, and her dry lips seemed paralyzed.

Raymon was frightened. He remembered the other one's su
cide and dreaded having to seem a criminal twice over in h
own eyes; but he was too mentally exhausted to make another e
fort to deceive her, and not knowing what else to do, he sat he
down gently in his armchair and went upstairs to his mother
room.

XXI

HE found her awake. She had developed the habit of rising early when she had been an *emigrée* and worked hard all day long, and she kept it even after she had recovered her wealth.

When Raymon—pale, agitated, and still in full dress from the previous evening's ball—entered her room, she realized immediately that he was in one of the frequent crises that characterized his stormy life. He had always gone to her for refuge and help during those periods, and they always ended without leaving the slightest trace of grief or regret anywhere except in her maternal heart, for her son's life had flourished and expanded at the expense of her own, now weary and worn. Raymon's character—both impetuous and cold, emotional and unfeeling—was a direct result of her inexhaustible love and unconditional acceptance; he would have been a better man if his mother had not been so good a woman, but she had accustomed him to accept and profit from all her sacrifices, and taught him to desire and promote his own well-being as zealously as she worked for it herself. Because she thought her role in life was to preserve him from unhappiness and to sacrifice her own interests to his, he had grown to feel that the whole world was created for him and that his mother had only to say the word for it to be his. Her generous spirit was responsible for his selfish heart.

She paled, this poor mother, sat up in bed, and looked at him anxiously, as if to say, "What's wrong? What can I do for you?"

Taking the dry, transparent hand she held out to him, he said, "Mother, I'm terribly unhappy—you must help me, save me from all my difficulties! As you know, I love Madame Delmare . . ."

"I did not know it," said Mme. de Ramière, her tone one of affectionate reproof.

"Oh, yes, you did, my dear mother, don't try to deny it," said Raymon, who felt he had no time to lose. "You knew it but your exquisite sense of delicacy kept you from being the first to mention it. . . . Well, Mother, that woman is driving me insane—I feel as if I'm losing my mind."

"Tell me about it," said Mme. de Ramière, as keen and animated as a young woman, thanks to her all-encompassing maternal love.

"I will—I'll tell you everything, especially since this time I haven't done anything wrong. For the last few months I've been trying to restrain her, get her to control her feverish imagination and remember her obligations, but my prudence only intensifies her insatiable thirst for adventure and danger. In that way she's like all the other women of her country—and she's in my room at this very moment, against my will, and I have no idea of how to make her leave!"

"The poor unhappy child!" said Mme. de Ramière, hurriedly getting dressed. "So timid, so sweet! I will go to her, talk to her—that is what you want me to do, isn't it?"

"Oh, yes," said Raymon, whose own heart was softened by his mother's tender concern. "Speak to her kindly and make her see reason. She will have to pay attention to the voice of virtue if it comes from your lips, and your affection may even help her recover some self-control. Poor woman, how she's suffering!"

Upset by the morning's various emotions, he sank into a chair and began to weep. His mother wept with him and refused to go downstairs until she had made him take a few tranquilizing drops of ether.

Indiana, however, was not weeping, and when she saw Mme. de Ramière, she rose to greet her with such dignified composure that Raymon's mother was surprised and even embarrassed—as if she had been inconsiderate and lacking in respect by coming unannounced to see her in Raymon's bedroom. But then she allowed herself to follow the instincts of her heart; with deep and genuine emotion she opened her arms to Indiana, and the poor woman unhesitatingly rushed into them, sobbing bitterly. The two of them held each other and wept for a long time.

When Mme. de Ramière began to speak, Indiana stopped her.

"Don't say anything, madame," she said, drying her tears. "There are no words that wouldn't hurt me. You've proved your affection by being here, by embracing me, and that's eased my heart as much as it can be eased. Now I'm going to leave, and you don't have to persuade me to do what I already know I must."

"I came to comfort you, not to send you away," said Mme. de Ramière.

"No one can comfort me," Indiana replied. "If you love me, that will help a little—but please don't say anything. Adieu, madame. You believe in God—pray for me."

"I won't allow you to leave here alone!" Mme. de Ramière exclaimed. "I will go with you. I will speak to your husband, explain what you've done, defend you, protect you!"

"You're a kind and generous woman," said Indiana, embracing her once more, "but that's impossible. You were the only one not to know Raymon's secret. By evening everyone will be talking about this, and it will be awkward for you. Let me be the only one to suffer from the scandal—it won't be for long."

"What do you mean? Would you take your own life? Commit such a sin? My dear child, surely you believe in God, don't you?"

"And therefore I leave for Bourbon in three days."

"Let me hold you in my arms again, dear child! Let me bless you. . . . God will reward your courage."

"I hope so," said Indiana, looking out at the sky.

Mme. de Ramière, who was reluctant to allow Indiana to make such a long journey on foot when she was so physically weak and emotionally distraught, at least wanted to send for a carriage, but Indiana refused; she was determined to return alone and without fanfare.

"I'm quite strong enough," she said. "One word from Raymon was enough to give me all the strength I need."

She wrapped herself in her cloak, lowered her black lace veil, and was led to a little-used door by Mme. de Ramière. Once outside, her first steps were so unsteady that she was afraid her legs would refuse to carry her, and she expected to feel at any moment her husband's rough hands forcing her to the ground and dragging her along in the gutter. Soon, however, the everyday street sounds, the indifferent passersby, and the penetrating chill of the morning air restored both her strength and her composure; but it was an unnatural strength and an ominous composure—like the calm that sometimes occurs at sea and frightens the experienced sailor more than the tempest's turbulence. She walked along the riverbank from the Institut to the Chambre des Deputés, then, lost in thought—a thought devoid of any ideas—forgot to cross the bridge to the other side of the river and continued to put one foot in front of the other without any notion of where she was going.

Unaware of what she was doing, she had come very close to the water, which was depositing at her feet drifting pieces of ice that made a dry, cold, crackling sound on the stones that edged the river. The water seemed to mesmerize her. One can get used to the most frightening ideas by acknowledging them, and they may even become quite acceptable: the thought of Noun's suicide had for a long time soothed Indiana's troubled hours, and little by little the idea of suicide had begun to seem a seductive temptation. Only the thought of her religion had kept her from giving in to the temptation, but just then her mind was incapable of any thought at all; she barely remembered that there was a God or that there had been a Raymon, and she continued to walk ever closer to the river, drawn to it as if it could mitigate her suffering.

The biting cold of the water soaking her shoes brought her abruptly back to consciousness, rousing her from a state very like sleepwalking; looking about to see where she was, she became aware of Paris around her and the Seine swirling at her feet, its oily surface giving back the reflection of white houses and blue-gray sky. Her perceptions of the moving water and the motionless ground became confused, and it seemed to her that the water was immobile and the ground heaving. In that moment of vertigo, she leaned forward, fascinated by what she took to be a solid mass—but she was distracted by a barking dog leaping all over her, and those few seconds of delay were enough to prevent her from accomplishing her purpose. A man, guided by the sound of the dog, ran over to her, grabbed her by the waist, pulled her back, and laid her down on the ruins of some boat that had been abandoned on the bank; she looked straight at him without any sign of recognition. Removing his cloak, he wrapped it around her, took her hands and rubbed them in his to warm them, called her by name; but she was too weak to make any effort. She hadn't eaten for the past forty-eight hours.

Nevertheless, when some warmth and feeling had returned to her benumbed arms and legs, she saw that it was Ralph who was kneeling beside her, holding her hands and waiting for her to regain consciousness.

"Did you meet Noun?" she asked him. Then she added, still under the influence of her obsession, "I saw her walking along that path"—she pointed to the river—"and I wanted to follow her. But she was going too fast, and I'm too weak to walk. It was like a nightmare."

Ralph looked at her, and he too felt as if his head were bursting and his brain on fire.

"Let's go," he said.

"Yes, let's go," she agreed. "But first see if you can find my feet. I think I lost them on the stones."

Becoming aware that her feet were wet and frozen, without feeling, Ralph carried her to a nearby house, where some kind-hearted woman brought her back to her senses while he sent a message to M. Delmare that his wife had been found. The colonel had not yet returned home to receive the message; he was still out searching, in a frenzy of anxiety and rage. Ralph, knowing more about the matter than he did, had gone directly to M. de Ramière's, where he found only Raymon, who had just gotten into bed and treated him very superciliously. Then he had thought of Noun, and he began to walk along the river in one direction while his servant went in the other. Ophelia had immediately picked up her mistress's scent and led Sir Ralph to the place where he had found her.

A little later, when Indiana was able to think about all that had happened, she tried to remember those moments of delirium, but no trace of them was left in her mind; she was completely unable to explain to her cousin the reasons for her behavior. His heart understood them anyway; there was no need for him to question her. He simply took her hand and said to her, gently but very seriously, "Cousin, I want you to promise me something—the last proof of friendship I shall ever ask of you."

"What is it?" she replied. "To do something for you is the only pleasure I have left."

"Then swear to me that you will never again think of suicide without first talking to me. In turn, I give you my word of honor that I won't try to stop you—but I do want to know about it when you come to such a decision. Surely you realize that I care as little about life as you do, and that I've often had the same idea myself."

"Why do you speak to me about suicide?" she asked him. "I never wanted to take my own life—I'm afraid of God. Though if it weren't for that . . ."

"A little while ago, Indiana, when I caught hold of you, when poor Ophelia"—and he patted the dog—"had her teeth around a piece of your dress, you had forgotten all about God, and about the whole world and poor Ralph as well."

Indiana was on the verge of tears as she took his hand and said sadly, "Why did you stop me? I would be with God now, and it wouldn't have been a sin because I didn't know what I was doing."

"I was aware of that, but I thought it would be better to die after giving it some thought. We'll speak about this again if you wish."

Indiana shuddered. Their cab stopped in front of the house, where she would have to confront her husband. She was too weak to climb the stairs, and Ralph carried her to her room. Their staff had been reduced to only two servants—a maid, who had gone out to gossip about Mme. Delmare's disappearance with the other servants in the neighborhood, and Lelièvre, who as a last desperate measure had been sent to the morgue to inspect all the bodies that had been brought there that morning. Ralph was therefore the one who stayed with Indiana to take care of her. When she heard the loud peal of the doorbell announcing the colonel's return, she was in a state of mental and physical prostration, and the sound sent a tremor of fear and hate through her body.

Clutching her cousin's arm, she said desperately, "Listen to me, Ralph, and if you have any affection for me at all, spare me the sight of that man in my present state. I can't bear for him to feel sorry for me—I'd rather face his anger than his compassion! Don't open the door, or if you do, send him away. Tell him that I haven't been found . . ."

Her lips quivered, but she held Ralph with a convulsive strength.

The poor baronet, pulled in opposite directions by his divided loyalties, didn't know what to do. Delmare was ringing the bell with a fury that would soon break it, and his wife was almost dying in her armchair.

Finally he said, "You're only thinking about how angry he is, not about how miserable and worried he must be. You think he hates you, but if you had seen how unhappy he was this morning!"

Indiana dejectedly let go of his arm, and Ralph went to open the door.

"She's here, is she?" cried the colonel as he came bursting

in. "By God, I've done enough running after her! I'm much obliged to her for all the trouble she's given me! I'd better not see her, because I'd kill her if I did!"

"Remember that she can hear you," Ralph said, speaking softly, "and she's in no condition to stand any painful excitement. Try to keep your temper."

"Damn! Damn! Damn!" shouted the colonel. "I've had enough painful excitement myself this morning! It's just as well that I have nerves of steel. Which of us, please tell me, is the most offended, the most exhausted, the one with the most right to be sick? Where did you finally find her? What was she doing? It's her fault that I insulted that crazy old Carvajal woman when she kept confusing me with her answers that didn't answer anything and telling me that this whole escapade was my fault! *Morbleu!* I've had more than I can stand!"

Shouting in his harsh, gruff voice, Delmare worked himself into a frenzy and finally flung himself into one of the chairs in the anteroom, where he sat wiping the sweat that was streaming down his face despite the glacial temperature and describing his difficulties, anxieties, and sufferings—all interspersed with many oaths and curses. He asked a thousand questions and luckily didn't wait for any response, because poor Ralph, who couldn't lie and was unable to think of anything to say that would pacify the colonel, merely sat silently and impassively on the edge of a table, as if he had absolutely no interest in the sufferings of those two people—though in truth he was even more unhappy about their unhappiness than they were themselves.

Indiana, hearing her husband's outburst, found herself stronger than she had expected. She preferred his rage, which she felt justified her actions, to a generous magnanimity that would have made her regret them. Wiping away the last trace of her tears and gathering all her strength—quite willing to use it up in a single day because she cared so little about resuming her burdensome life—she went out to meet him, and when her husband confronted her with his hard, imperious manner, he found himself once again embarrassed by her superior moral character. He tried to match her aloof dignity, but it was, as always, impossible.

"Will you deign to tell me, madame, where you spent the morning and perhaps the night?"

That *perhaps* indicated to Indiana that her absence had not been noticed for a long time, and this increased her courage.

"No, monsieur, I do not intend to tell you that."

Delmare looked as if he would explode with rage and astonishment. "You really hope to hide the truth from me?" he asked, his voice despite himself unsteady.

"I don't care about that," she replied coldly. "If I refuse to answer you, it's only because of the principle involved. You must understand that you have no right to ask me that question."

"I have no right! Who is the master here, you or I? Which of us wears a skirt and should be at her sewing? Do you want my beard? That would be very becoming, wouldn't it, you silly woman!"

"I know that I am the slave and you the master. The laws of this country have made you my master. You can tie me up, pin my hands behind my back, control my actions. You have all the rights of the one who is stronger, and society confirms those rights—but you have no rights over my will, monsieur, and you cannot command it. Only God can change or rule it. Try to find a law, a prison, an instrument of torture that will give you power over me—you might as well try to order the air and lay hands on space!"

"Be quiet, you foolish, impertinent creature. You sound like a novel, and those high-flown phrases are boring."

"You can make me keep quiet, but you can't keep me from thinking."

"That idiotic pride is like the pride of a worm! You take advantage of my pity for you! But you'll soon see that I can break your high and mighty will without too much trouble."

"I don't advise you to try it. You would lose your quiet, peaceful life, and it wouldn't do your dignity much good either."

"You think so?" he said, crushing her hand between his thumb and forefinger.

"I do," she said, without the slightest change in her expression.

Almost instantly Ralph was holding the colonel's arm in his iron grasp and bending it like a reed, saying in the mildest, most unaggressive tone possible, "Please do not touch one hair of this woman's head."

Delmare wanted to hurl himself at Ralph, but he felt that he was in the wrong, and there was nothing in the world he feared so much as having to feel ashamed of himself. He simply pushed Ralph away and contented himself with saying, "Mind your own business."

Then, turning to his wife again and keeping his arms stiffly at his sides to resist the temptation to strike her, he said, "So, madame, you openly rebel against me? You refuse to return to Bourbon with me? You want us to separate? Very well, I also—"

"That is not what I want. I wanted it yesterday—that was my will—but not today. You shut me in my room by force. I left by the window to prove to you that your ability to control a woman's actions if you don't also control her will is an absurd use of power. I spent a few hours away from your domination, breathing the air of liberty, to show you that you're not *morally* my master and that I answer to no one on earth but myself. As I walked along, I decided that I owed it to my conscience and my own sense of duty to return and place myself under your control. I did that of my own free will. My cousin didn't *bring me back,* he *accompanied* me. If I hadn't wanted to go with him, I assure you that he wouldn't have been able to make me follow him. So, monsieur, don't waste your time fighting against my convictions, because you'll never be able to change them—you lost your right even to *try* to change them when you attempted to do so by force. Continue with your preparations to leave. I'm ready to help you and to go with you, not because you want me to, but because I *choose* to. Although you may punish me for it, I will never obey anyone but myself."

"I pity your irrational, preposterous mind," said the colonel, shrugging his shoulders.

And he went to his own room to continue putting his papers in order, actually quite satisfied with his wife's decision because he knew there would be no further problems: he respected her word as much as he despised her ideas.

XXII

AFTER he had received Sir Ralph so brusquely and replied to his inquiries so curtly, Raymon was exhausted and fell into a sound sleep. When he awakened, he was flooded with a sense of well-being, for he was sure that the worst of the crisis was finally over. He had known for a long time that he would eventually have to defend his freedom against Indiana's love and its exaggerated romantic requirements, and he had been trying to find the courage to protect himself from those impossible claims. Now that he had finally taken that difficult step and said no, he would never have to say it again: everything had gone better than he had dared hope, and Indiana had neither wept too much nor argued too insistently; she had understood from his first word, and her pride had immediately made her reasonable.

Raymon was quite content with his guardian angel—for he did indeed have one, his very own in whom he had implicit faith and on whom he had always depended to arrange everything so that other people would be hurt rather than himself. So far, this angel had treated him so well that there was no possible doubt of its existence, and to try to foresee the results of his faults and worry about their consequences would have seemed like ingratitude toward the good God who watched over him.

When he got out of bed, he was still a bit weary from his earlier imaginative efforts. Then his mother returned from Mme. de Carvajal, where she had gone to inquire about Mme Delmare, and he learned that the marchioness was much more disturbed by Mme. de Ramière's questions, despite the subtlety with which she had tried to phrase them, than she was about Indiana. The only aspect of Indiana's flight that troubled her aunt was the scandal it would cause, and when she complained bitterly about that same niece whom she had been

raising to the skies the day before, Mme. de Ramière under-
tood quite clearly that poor Indiana had alienated her relative
orever and lost the only support to which she might have had
natural claim.

To anyone who could have seen into the depths of the mar-
hioness's soul, that might have seemed a small loss indeed,
ut Mme. de Carvajal, whose youthful adventures had been
loaked in prudence or lost sight of during the turbulence of
arious revolutions, had the reputation, even with Mme. de
.amière, of being virtue personified. Raymon's mother wept,
nd tried to find excuses for Indiana, but Mme. de Carvajal
old her caustically that she was not objective enough to be a
ood judge.

"But what will happen to the poor young woman? Who will
rotect her if her husband mistreats her?" asked Mme. de
.amière.

"Whatever happens to her will be the will of God," the mar-
hioness replied. "As for me, I want nothing more to do with
er, and I never want to see her again."

Being both kind-hearted and truly anxious, Mme. de Ramière
vas determined to get news of Mme. Delmare and had herself
riven to the street on which she lived; once there, she sent her
ootman to question the porter, asking him also to try to see Sir
.alph if he were home. She waited in her carriage, and Sir
.alph soon came down and joined her there.

Mme. de Ramière was probably the only person who judged
.alph accurately: it took only a few words for each of them to
auge the sincere and disinterested concern of the other. Ralph
escribed what had happened during the morning and asked no
uestions about what might have happened during the night,
ut Mme. de Ramière thought it her duty to tell him what she
new, especially since she hoped to make him an ally in her
esire to put an end to the impossible liaison. Ralph, who felt
nore at ease with her than with anybody else, made no effort
o hide his profound shock.

"Do you mean to say, madame, that she spent the night in
our house?" he asked, trying to repress the shudder that went
hrough his entire body.

"A lonely and unhappy night, no doubt. Raymon certainly
new nothing about her plans and didn't come home until six
'clock in the morning, and at seven o'clock he came to my
oom and asked me to go down and try to calm the poor un-
appy child."

"She meant to leave her husband! She was ready to lose her reputation!" said Ralph, his eyes staring vacantly into space, and his heart unable to think of anything else. "How she must love him, this man who is so unworthy of her!"

He had forgotten that he was speaking to Raymon's mother.

"I've suspected something like this for a long time," he continued. "Why couldn't I have foreseen the exact day on which she would destroy her life forever? I would have killed her first!"

Such language coming from Ralph, whom she had thought of as a reasonable, tolerant man, surprised Mme. de Ramière; she was sorry she had trusted to appearances.

"My God, do you judge her so harshly too?" she cried in dismay. "Will you abandon her, like her aunt? Are you all so incapable of being merciful and forgiving? After having suffered so bitterly for her one mistake, won't she have even a single friend to help her?"

"You needn't worry about that as far as I'm concerned, madame," Ralph replied. "I've known about this situation for the past six months, and I said nothing to anyone. I surprised their first kiss, and I didn't force Monsieur de Ramière off his horse. I saw the love letters they left for each other in the woods, and I didn't slash them with my whip. I met Monsieur de Ramière on the bridge he had to cross to see her, and though it was dark and we were alone and I'm much stronger than he is, I didn't throw him into the river—and after I let him go and then discovered that he had managed to steal into her room anyway, I didn't knock down the door and hurl him out the window but quietly warned them about the husband's arrival and allowed him to live in order to protect her honor. So you see, madame, that I'm quite capable of being merciful and forgiving.

"This morning I had that man within my grasp, and I knew that he was the cause of all our troubles. If I had no right to accuse him without any proof, I certainly had the right to quarrel with him because of his arrogant, jeering manner. Well, instead of that, I endured his insults, his ridicule, and his contempt because I knew that his death would have meant the death of Indiana. I let him turn over on the other side and go back to sleep, while Indiana, mad and more dead than alive, was walking along the edge of the Seine and getting ready to join his other victim. You see, madame, how patient I am with those I hate and how indulgent to those I love."

Mme. de Ramière, seated opposite Ralph in her carriage, looked at him and was frightened. He was so different from the way she had always seen him that she thought he might somehow have become unbalanced. His allusion to Noun's death only confirmed her suspicion, for she knew nothing about that episode and supposed that the words Ralph had let slip out had no connection with the rest of what he had been saying.

His state of mind was in fact extraordinarily tumultuous—a condition that occurs at least once in the lives of the most rational and imperturbable of men and carries them to the very edge of sanity, where just one more step would bring them to the other side. Though his rage, like that of all men with undemonstrative, contained natures, was barely visible, it was deep, like that of all men with noble souls; and the working of this stupendously powerful combination made him quite terrifying.

She took his hand and said gently, "My dear Sir Ralph, you must be suffering very much to say such things, for you are hurting me deeply without even realizing it. You forget that the man of whom you are speaking is my son and that the wrongs he has committed—if he has in truth done so—must break my heart even more than yours."

Ralph immediately recovered himself and, kissing Mme. de Ramière's hand with a cordial warmth whose existence was as rarely witnessed as his fury, said, "Forgive me, madame. You're right—I *am* suffering very much, and I've forgotten the respect I owe you. If you can forget the bitterness I've just allowed myself to show, I assure you that it will never be revealed again."

Despite this reassurance, Mme. de Ramière was still uneasy at the profound hatred and enmity Ralph had shown he harbored for her son and began to try to find excuses for him.

Ralph stopped her. "I understand your fears, madame," he said, "but you needn't worry. Monsieur de Ramière and I are not likely to meet again in the near future. As for my cousin, you did right to tell me what happened, and I swear that she will have at least one friend left even if the whole world should abandon her!"

When Mme. de Ramière returned home, it was late afternoon, and she found Raymon voluptuously warming his cashmere-slippered feet in front of the fire and drinking tea to dispel the last traces of the morning's agitation. He was still a little depressed by those emotions he had artificially induced

in himself, but that despondency was being replaced by a
kinds of pleasant visions: he finally felt free again, and he wa
contentedly imagining all the priceless gratifications of tha
precious condition which he always protected so carelessly.

"Why am I so quickly bored by this invaluable freedom?
he thought. "When I'm caught in a woman's trap, I can hardl
wait to break out and recover my peace of mind, and the co
of that is usually very high. Well, I swear I won't sacrifice m
independence so quickly again! The problems I had with thos
two Creoles will be a warning to me, and from now on, I wi
have nothing to do with anyone but sophisticated, frivolou
Parisians—women who understand the world. Perhaps
should even get married and put an end to all this . . ."

He was still absorbed in these comfortably bourgeois idea
when his mother came in, worn out both physically and emo
tionally.

"She's better," she told him. "Everything went as well a
possible, and I hope she will grow less disturbed in time."

"Who?" asked Raymon, suddenly awakened from hi
dreams of castles in Spain.

The next day, however, he decided that there was still on
more thing he had to do: win back that woman's respect, if no
her love. He had no intention of allowing her to think that sh
had been the one to decide to leave him; he wanted to per
suade her that she had been convinced to do so by his superic
good sense and generosity of spirit. Even after having rejecte
her, he still wanted to dominate her, and this is the letter h
wrote:

> My friend, I'm not asking you to forgive me for whatever
> cruel or impertinent comments I might have made in the
> delirium of my passion. When someone is feverish and inco-
> herent, it isn't possible for him to think clearly and express
> himself properly. I'm not a god, and it's not my fault if I
> can't control the churning of my blood, the whirling of my
> brain, the madness that overcomes me whenever I am near
> you. It's I who might have the right to complain of the fero-
> cious indifference with which you pitilessly condemned me
> to frightful torments, but I understand that it wasn't your
> fault either. You were too perfect to act as we do—we ordi-
> nary mortals who are subject to the common human pas-
> sions and slaves to our carnal appetites. As I told you very
> often, Indiana, you're not a woman, and when I can think of

*you calmly, I know that you're an angel and I adore you as
if you were enshrined in my heart like a divinity. Unfortunately, when I was near you the "old Adam" often tried to
assert his rights! The sweet breath from your lips used to set
mine afire, and when I leaned over you and my hair would
brush against yours, I would be transported into a state of
voluptuous bliss so overwhelming that no words can describe it! At such times I would forget that you were an ema-
nation from heaven, a symbol of future eternal happiness,
an angel sent by God to guide my steps in this life and give
me a foretaste of the joys of another. Oh, why, you pure
spirit, did you appear to me in the bewitching shape of a
woman? Why, you angel of light, did you come to me
clothed in the seductive attractions of hell? I used to think
that I held happiness in my arms, and it was only virtue.*

*Forgive me for these unseemly regrets, my friend. I wasn't
worthy of you. If you had agreed to come down to my level,
we might both have been happier, but as it was, my inferior-
ity made you suffer, and your very virtues became crimes
against me.*

*Now that you forgive me—and I know that you do, be-
cause perfection includes the quality of mercy—I must tell
you how much I thank you and bless you. "Thank you"?
Oh, no, that cannot be the word, because my heart is more
shattered than yours by the courage that tears you from my
arms. But I do admire you, and through my tears, I even
congratulate you. Yes, I do, my Indiana, because you have
found the strength to go through with this heroic sacrifice
that breaks my heart, ruins my life, destroys my future. And
still I love you enough to endure it all without complaint,
for my honor is unimportant and yours means everything. I
would sacrifice my honor to you a thousand times over,
while yours is more precious than all the happiness you
might have given me. Oh, no, I could never have bought
that happiness at such a price! I would have tried to dull
the pangs of remorse in the ecstasy of exquisite sensations,
in the transports of heavenly gratification at being in your
arms—but it would have been impossible. Guilt would have
searched me out even there, poisoning every day of my life,
and the world's contempt would have been directed more
at me than at you. O God! To see you shamed and brought
low by me, forfeiting the respect of everyone around you
and being insulted even as you were in my arms—and not*

*to be able to do anything about it! For you do understand
that even if I had—oh, so willingly!—spilt the last drop of
blood in my veins, I might have been able to avenge you,
but never to justify you. My every effort to defend you
would have been another accusation against you, and even
my death would have been seen as an incontrovertible
proof of your crime. Poor Indiana, I would have been responsible for ruining you, and how miserable I would have
been!*

*So go, my beloved, go where you will be able to reap the
rewards of virtue and piety. God will reward us for making
such a sacrifice, for God is good. He will reunite us in a
happier life, and perhaps even—but no, even to think of
that is a sin, though I cannot stop myself from doing it!
Adieu, Indiana, adieu! Our love is a crime, and my heart is
broken. Where will I get the strength to say good-bye?*

Raymon himself brought this letter to Indiana, but she shut
herself up in her room and refused to see him. He slipped it to
the maid without being seen, greeted the husband cordially
and left the house, feeling more light-hearted than usual as he
walked down and away from the final steps. The weather
seemed nicer, the women more beautiful, the shops more attractive: it was one of the best days of Raymon's life.

Indiana put the letter, still unsealed, into a box that she
didn't plan to open until she reached the colonies.

She wanted to visit her aunt and say good-bye, but Sir
Ralph's objection to such a visit was obstinately unyielding.
He had seen Mme. de Carvajal, and he knew that she would
show Indiana nothing but contempt and scorn; her hypocritical
severity infuriated him, and he couldn't bear the idea of Indiana being exposed to it.

The next day, just as Delmare and his wife were about to get
into the coach, Sir Ralph said to them with his usual self-possession, "My friends, I have often tried to make you see that I
wanted to go with you, but you never seemed to understand—
or at least to answer—me. Will you allow me to accompany
you?"

"To Bordeaux?"

"To Bourbon."

"You mustn't even think of doing that," replied M. Delmare. "You can't possibly transfer your entire establishment
from place to place to follow a household whose situation is so

unsettled and whose future so uncertain. It would be a shameful abuse of your friendship to accept such a sacrifice of your life and your social position. You're young, rich, free—you should remarry and have a family."

"That is not the issue," Ralph replied coldly. "Since I don't know how to say things indirectly, let me tell you frankly what I think. It has seemed to me that during the past six months your friendship for me has cooled, perhaps because I've offended you in some way that I'm too insensitive to see. If I'm wrong, a few words will be enough to reassure me—just tell me that I may go with you. If I *have* done something that deserves such harsh treatment, you must tell me what it is, and not leave me to suffer because I had no opportunity to make amends for my faults."

The colonel was so moved by this simple and generous overture that he forgot all the wounded susceptibilities that had alienated him from his friend. He held out his hand and swore that his friendship was deeper than ever and that he had rejected his offer only because he thought it was the right thing to do.

Indiana remained silent.

Ralph tried to get her to speak. "And you, Indiana," he said, his voice choked with emotion, "are you still my friend?"

That word evoked all the memories that bound their hearts: her filial affection for him, her childhood, their years of shared habits and intimacies. Both weeping, they threw themselves into each other's arms, and Ralph all but fainted; under that robust physical shell and behind the placid, reserved facade were constantly seething emotions.

White-faced and silent, he sat down to keep from falling; then, after a few seconds, he took the colonel's hand in one of his, Indiana's in the other, and said to them both, "We may be parting forever, so please tell me the truth. You refuse my offer to go with you on my account, not on yours?"

"I swear on my honor that by refusing your request I'm sacrificing my happiness to yours," said Delmare

"And you know that I would never want to leave you," said Indiana.

"God forbid that I should doubt your sincerity at such a moment as this!" said Ralph. "I believe you, and I'm happy."

And he disappeared.

Six weeks later the brig *Coraly* sailed from the port of Bordeaux. Ralph had written to his friends that he would join

them there a few days before their departure, but since he
wrote in his usual laconic style, it was impossible to tell if he
planned to go with them or merely say a final good-bye. They
waited for him until the last moment, but he still hadn't appeared when the captain gave his signal to weigh anchor. As
the last houses disappeared behind the tree-lined shore, the
usual dull pain gnawing at Indiana's heart was made worse by
certain gloomy forebodings. She trembled at the thought that
she was to be left alone in the world with the husband she
hated—that she would have to live and die with him without a
single friend or relative to comfort or protect her against his
violent, domineering will.

Then she turned around and saw on the bridge behind her
Ralph's untroubled, benevolent face smiling into hers.

"So you haven't abandoned me after all?" she said, throwing herself into his arms as the tears flowed down her face.

"Never!" he replied, holding her tightly.

XXIII

A letter from Mme. Delmare to M. de Ramière

Bourbon, June 3, 18—

I had resolved not to cause you any annoyance by reminding you of my existence, but when I arrived here and
read the letter you sent me the night before I left Paris, I realized that I owe you a reply. In my terrible suffering I went
too far. I thought you were contemptible, and I owe you an
apology—not as a lover but as a man.

Forgive me, Raymon, for considering you a monster in
that most awful moment of my life, but a single word, a single look, had destroyed every bit of trust and confidence I
had ever known. I understand that I can never again be
happy, but I hope that I will not sink so low as to despise
you: that would be the final blow.

Yes, I did think you were a coward and, worse yet, an
egoist—the most despicable thing in the world. You filled
me with such horror that I thought even Bourbon Island
wasn't far enough away from you, and my rage gave me the
strength to drain my cup to the lees.

But after I had read your letter I felt better. I'm not sorry
for you, but I no longer loathe you, and I have no desire to
destroy your life by making you feel guilty for having ruined mine. Be happy, be carefree, forget me. I'm still alive,
and I may live for a long time.

And I realize that it wasn't you who were guilty but I
who was mad. Your heart wasn't cold—it was closed. You
didn't lie to me—I deceived myself. You neither broke your
promises nor were unfeeling—you just didn't love me.

O my God, you didn't love me! How on earth must you
be loved in order to love in return? But I shan't stoop to
complain. I'm not writing to poison your present with hateful memories of the past, or to play on your sympathy and

ask you to share sorrows that I'm quite strong enough to bear on my own. On the contrary, now that I know you better and understand the role you're best suited to play, I'm writing to absolve and forgive you for everything.

I won't amuse myself by countering the charges in your letter; it would be too easy. Nor will I reply to your observations about my obligations and duties. Believe me, Raymon, I was very aware of them, and I wouldn't have been so ready to disregard them if I hadn't loved you so much. You needn't tell me that my sin would have cost me everyone's respect, for I understood that quite clearly. I knew that I would have been branded deeply, indelibly, and painfully; that I would have been denounced by everyone, covered with shame, and left with no one to pity or comfort me. What I did not know was that I couldn't depend on you to open your arms and help me forget the scorn, the misery, the desertion of all my friends. I couldn't even imagine that you might refuse my sacrifice after having allowed me to make it. I hadn't thought that was possible. I went to your house expecting your sense of duty and your principles to lead you to rebuff me, but I was sure that once you had realized the inevitable consequences of what I had done, you would feel bound to help me endure them. In all truth, I would never have believed that you would allow me to face the results of such a dangerous resolution alone—that you would allow me to bear the entire brunt of my act instead of sheltering me in your heart and defending me with your love.

How I would have defied those accusations from a world that would have been so distant and so incapable of hurting me! How your affection would have made me strong enough to brave its hatred! How weak my remorse would have been, and how easily extinguished by your love! I would have been so engrossed in you that I would have forgotten myself, so proud of your love that I couldn't have been ashamed of mine. One word from you, one kiss, one glance, would have been enough to absolve me, and there would have been no room in such a life for even the memory of men and their laws. All that because I was mad—or because, according to you, I had learned about life from having read too many silly, childish, romantic novels meant for chambermaids, novels that capture the imagination by describing heroic deeds and impossible raptures. That was

*quite true, Raymon, and that's what horrifies me most—
that you were right!*

*What I don't understand as clearly is why the situation
wasn't equally impossible for both of us. Why was I, a weak
woman, able to find enough strength in my feelings for you
to put myself into such a false situation while you, a valiant
man, couldn't find enough courage in yours even to follow
me? Yet you had shared those dreams of the future, agreed
with all those illusions, encouraged me to believe in that
impossible dream. You had listened to my childish plans
and trivial hopes, smiled at me with pleasure, looked at me
with affection, and spoken to me of love and gratitude. You
were as blind, unthinking, and melodramatic as I was. How
is it that your sanity returned only at the moment of danger? I had thought danger inspired one's spirit, strength-
ened one's resolve, roused one's courage—and there you
were, all atremble at the moment of crisis! Do you men
have no courage except the physical courage that can confront death? Are you incapable of the moral courage that
can accept unhappiness? You who explain everything so
well, will you please explain that to me?*

*Perhaps it's because your dream wasn't the same as
mine: for me, courage came from love. You had imagined
that you loved me, but you woke up from that fancy the day
I came to you confidently looking for the protection of that
love. You must have been living with some strange delu-
sions if you hadn't foreseen all the obstacles you would
have to face when it was time for action! You never said a
word about them until it was already too late!*

*But why should I reproach you for this now? Are people
responsible for the impulses of their hearts? Was it possible
for you to choose to love me always? I suppose not. My
misfortune was that I couldn't make you like me for a
longer time and with more genuine feeling. I've tried to understand why that was so. The reason certainly can't be
found in my own heart, but there must be a reason. Perhaps
I loved you too much. Perhaps my tenderness was tiresome
and irritating. You're a man—you like your independence
and your pleasures, and I was a burden to you. I did sometimes try to limit your freedom—but oh, such a minor offense to justify such a cruel desertion!*

*Well, enjoy that freedom which has been bought at the
expense of my whole life; I will trouble it no more. Why*

didn't you teach me that lesson sooner? It would have been less painful for me, and perhaps for you too.

Be happy. That is the last wish my broken heart will ever make. Don't tell me to think of God; leave that to the priests, whose duty it is to soften the hard hearts of the guilty. As for me, I am more religious than you. I don't serve the same God, but I serve mine better and with a purer heart. Your God is the god of men—the king, the founder and upholder of your kind; mine is the God of the universe, the creator, the support and hope of all His creatures. Yours made everything only for men; mine made every species to work for the good of every other. You think you are the masters of the world; I think you are only its tyrants. You think that God protects you and authorizes you to rule the earth; I think that He may allow it for a little while but that the day will come when He will scatter you to the winds with a breath. No, Raymon, you don't believe in God at all; or rather, as Ralph said to you one day at Lagny, you don't believe in anything. Your education, and your need for a supreme and unquestioned authority that can oppose the brute force of the people, have led you to adopt unquestioningly the beliefs of your ancestors; but a true belief in the existence of God has never actually penetrated your heart, and you have most likely never prayed to Him. As for me, I have only one belief, and it's probably the only one that you don't have: I believe in God. I reject the religion you have invented, and I think that for all you pretend otherwise, your morality and your principles are nothing but the interests of your social group, which you have erected into laws and pretend to have received from God Himself, just as your priests have instituted religious rituals and ceremonies in order to build up their power and wealth and make themselves felt by every nation. But all that is a lie, and impious as well. I who pray to Him, I who understand Him, I know very well that there is nothing in common between Him and you, and that by clinging to Him with all my might I also separate myself from you, whose every act overthrows His work and defiles His gifts. It ill becomes you to invoke His name to crush the resistance of a weak woman and stifle the wailing of a broken heart. God does not want anyone to oppress or destroy any of His creations. If He condescended to intervene in our petty affairs, He would subdue the strong and strengthen the weak; He

*would pass His powerful hand over our unequal heads and
make them as level as the surface of the sea; He would say
to the slave, "Throw off your chains and run to the mountains, where I have prepared water, flowers, and sunshine
for you"; He would say to the kings, "Toss your purple
robes to the beggars so they may sit on them, and go sleep
in the valleys, where I have prepared carpets of moss and
heather for you"; He would say to the powerful ones,
"Bend your knees and take on the burdens of your weaker
brothers, for you will need them in the future and I will give
them strength and courage." Yes, those are my dreams—all
of another life and another world, a place where the laws
of the brutal will not have bowed the heads of the peaceful,
where at the very least it will not be a crime to resist or to
flee, where man will be able to escape man as the gazelle
escapes the panther, where he will not be caught in the
chains of law and made to kneel at the foot of his enemy,
and where the voice of prejudice will not be heard insulting
his suffering and telling him that he is a vile coward for not
wanting to get down on his knees and crawl.*

*No, don't speak to me about God—not you, Raymon!
Don't send me into exile and reduce me to silence in His
name, because it's not His will but men's power to which I
submit. If I listened to my inner voice, which God has given
me, and to the noble instinct of a strong and bold nature,
which is probably the only true kind of conscience, I would
flee to the desert and learn how to live without help, protection, or love; I would live by and for myself in the heart of
our beautiful mountains and forget the tyrants, the unjust,
the ungrateful. But unfortunately man cannot live without
his fellowman, and even Ralph cannot live alone.*

*Good-bye forever, Raymon! May you be happy without
me! I forgive you for all the harm you've done me. Talk to
your mother about me occasionally; she is the best woman
I have ever known. And please understand that I feel neither hatred nor desire for revenge; my anguish is worthy of
the love I had for you.*

Indiana

The unfortunate woman was boasting. That deep, resigned
unhappiness she claimed to feel was only what she thought
self-respect required of her in any communication with Ray-

mon; when she was alone she yielded without any restraint t
her stormy, all-consuming emotions, and sometimes her eye
would even glimmer with some nameless hope. Despite all th
hard lessons of experience and the ever present memories o
Raymon's cold indifference to everything that didn't con
tribute directly to his own pleasure or well-being, her faith i
him was probably never completely extinguished. If she ha
really faced the basic, unadorned truth, she would have bee
incapable of enduring the prospect of her empty, hopeless ex
istence.

Woman is foolish by nature. Although her subtle percep
tions give her an unquestioned superiority to us men in som
respects, heaven seems to have balanced that advantage b
also giving her a blind vanity and an idiotic gullibility. Th
only requirement for dominating those sensitive creature
seems to be the ability to apply praise and approval with a cer
tain amount of skill. Men who are incapable of achieving eve
the most limited ascendancy over other men can sometime
succeed in acquiring unlimited power over women; flattery i
the yoke that bends those fervent but frivolous heads so low
and heaven help the man who would like to be frank and ope
in his love, for he will share the fate of Ralph!

If you were to tell me that Indiana is an exception, as i
proved by her unswerving, stoical patience in enduring he
marital yoke, I would ask you to look at the other side of th
coin and see how representative of other women—miserabl
weak and stupidly blind—she was in her relations with Ray
mon. Have you ever known a woman who was not as easy t
deceive as ready to be deceived; who was not able to keep
secret hope locked in her heart for ten years only to sacrifice i
carelessly in a single moment of frenzy; who could not be
foolish and weak in the arms of one man and strong and in
domitable in those of another?

XXIV

MME. DELMARE'S home life, however, had become more peaceful. Many of her difficulties had disappeared along with all her false friends, whose malicious zeal and poisonous meddling had exacerbated her problems, while Sir Ralph, who lived with them and added unobtrusively to their comforts in many silent ways, was very good at smoothing the rough edges of a shared life. Besides, Indiana was very often alone. Her house was in the mountains above the town: M. Delmare, preoccupied by his commercial dealings with France and India, had a warehouse near the port and went down there every morning and stayed away all day; Ralph spent his time studying natural history or supervising the work of the plantation; and Indiana was thus left free to revert to the indolence of Creole life and pass the most scorching hours of the afternoon in her cane chair and the long hours of dusk in the solitude of the mountains.

Bourbon is a large, oval-shaped cone, with a circumference at the base of about a hundred and thirty miles and mountains that rise to a height of about ten thousand feet; beyond the sharp cliffs, narrow valleys, and tall forests of this imposing mass of land is an unbroken horizon girdled by the blue sea and visible from almost everywhere. Thanks to an opening between two high peaks directly opposite the house, Indiana could see from her bedroom windows the white sails of boats on the Indian Ocean, and she spent many silent hours staring at that magical sight; but instead of uplifting her, the magnificent view only made her melancholy thoughts even more bleak and hopeless, bitter and grim, and she would often lower the raffia shade that covered her window and hide from the daylight itself in order to shed her secret, scalding tears.

But when the evening breezes began to blow, wafting to her nostrils the odor of the fertile rice-fields, she would leave Del-

mare and Ralph to linger on the veranda with their cigars and
their aromatic drinks made from the wild orchid, and go for a
walk to the top of some accessible peak. There, on the extinct
crater of a dead volcano, she would watch the setting sun
merge its dying light with the red gases of the atmosphere,
sending a fine cloud of gold or ruby dust motes to float over
the murmuring stalks of the sugarcane and the color-drenched
walls of the cliffs.

Occasionally she went down into the gorges of the Saint-
Gilles River, but only rarely, because the sight of the sea both
troubled and fascinated her. She was obsessed by the thought
that some other land—a magical land, beyond the waves and
through the far-off haze—was on the verge of revealing itself.
Sometimes the coastal clouds would assume strange shapes;
once she saw a great white surge of water in the distance, and it
looked like the facade of the Louvre; another time two square
sails suddenly emerged from the fog and reminded her of Notre
Dame in Paris when dense vapor would rise from the Seine,
hide the foundations of the towers, and make them look as if
they were suspended in the sky; at still other times the flocks of
fleecy pink clouds, constantly changing shape, seemed to be
images of all the architectural styles and caprices of a great me-
tropolis. The poor woman's mind was clouded by these illusions of the past; she would begin to quiver with joy at the sight
of that imaginary Paris, forget that in reality it was connected
with the unhappiest period of her life, and even sometimes believe—when she would once again be standing high above the
coast and staring at the receding line of gorges that separated
her from the ocean—that she had been launched into space and
was flying through the air toward that magnificent city of her
imagination. At such times she would cling to the rock against
which she was leaning, and anyone seeing her burning eyes,
her rapid breathing, and the appalling expression of joy on her
face might have thought her quite mad.

Yet those were her only hours of pleasure, her only moments of well-being; those times were the best part of her day,
all she could look forward to. If her husband had decided to
forbid those solitary outings, I don't know what her fancy
would have found in their stead, because she was a woman
who had to be able to construct a set of dreams in order to live;
her nature was to yearn for something that was not memory,
anticipation, hope, or regret, but desire itself, in all its vora-
cious intensity.

And that was how the poor woman lived under that tropical sky, week after week and month after month—loving and embracing a shadow, cherishing an illusion.

Ralph, on the other hand, found himself drawn instead to the dark, secluded inner places of the island never reached by the sea breeze: the ocean reminded him of France, and the very idea of that country of dreadful memories was hateful to him. He could not forget that he had been so unhappy there that he almost lost his courage—he who was so used to unhappiness and had always supported it so patiently! He did everything he could to forget that period, for though he was completely disgusted with life, he wanted to live as long as he felt needed. He was very careful never to say a word about the time he had spent there. He would have given anything to remove all traces of that ghastly experience from Indiana's heart as well, but he had so little self-confidence, so little faith in his ability to say the right thing, that he avoided her instead of trying to distract her; and this excessive reserve, which was a result of his extreme sensitivity, served only to reinforce the perception of him as cold, selfish, and unfeeling. He would go far off to suffer alone, and anyone watching his obsessive forays into the woods and up to the mountaintops in pursuit of birds and insects would have taken him for a sportsman and a naturalist entirely absorbed by his innocent passion and completely indifferent to the emotional currents swirling around him. But hunting and studying were only physical activities behind which he could continue to mask his bitter reveries.

The slopes of this conical island are seamed by many deep ravines carrying pure, turbulent streams of water down to the sea. One of these gorges, Bernica, is a particularly picturesque spot: a narrow, deep valley hidden between two perpendicular walls of rock, the surfaces of which are studded with clumps of shrubs and tufts of fern. A stream flows through the channel formed between the two walls, and at its farthest end it plunges to awesome depths and creates a small basin surrounded by reeds and shrouded in mist. Around the banks of this lake and along the shores of the tiny rivulet fed by its overflow grow banana, litchi, and orange trees, their dark green leaves carpeting the inner walls of the gorge. This was Ralph's refuge, both from the heat and from human society, and all his walks led to this one spot, where the cool, monotonous plash of the waterfall would lull his melancholy to sleep. When his heart was overflowing with his secret agony—so long left unspoken, so

cruelly unnoticed—this is where he would go to expend all his
youthful unused energy and superabundant strength in unseen
tears and unheard laments.

In order for you to understand Ralph's character, I have to
explain that at least half his life had been spent hidden in the
depths of this ravine. It was where he had gone when he was a
very young child to steel himself against the injustices he suffered at the hands of his family; it was where he had gone to
teach himself to bear the destiny that had arbitrarily been imposed upon him; it was where he had gone to learn to make
stoicism his second nature. It was also where he had gone as
an adolescent, carrying the tiny Indiana on his shoulders, and
where he had settled her on the grass alongside the stream
while he fished or tried to climb the cliff to look for bird nests.

His only companions in that solitude had been the gulls, pe-
trels, coots, and terns that had chosen to rear their wild prog-
eny in the nooks and crannies of those inaccessible walls and
who never stopped their gliding, wheeling, circling, and hovering. In the evenings they would gather in nervous groups and
fill the gorge with the echoes of their raucous, savage noise.
Ralph had enjoyed watching their majestic flight and listening
to their mournful sounds, and he had taught his little pupil
their names and habits. He had shown her the beautiful Madagascar teal, with its orange breast and emerald-green back, and
taught her to admire the flight of the red-winged tropic bird,
which sometimes accidentally finds itself on these shores but
which usually flies in several hours the more than two hundred
leagues from the island of Mauritius to the island of Rodriguez, where it always returns to sleep under the velvety
leaves of the tree that hides its nest; he had pointed out the petrel, that bird synonymous with storms, which also soars with
its tapering wings over these cliffs, and the frigate-bird, the
granite-colored queen of the sea, with its forked tail and sharp
beak—that creature whose country is the air, whose nature is
constant movement, and whose cry of distress is heard above
everything else. All those untamed natives of the place had become so accustomed to the two children playing around their
nests that they showed almost no fear of them, no matter how
close they came to their homes, and when Ralph managed to
reach the ledge on which they had established their nests, they
would fly up in a black eddy and mockingly swirl around a
few feet over his head. Indiana would laugh at their twists and
turns, then carefully carry home in her straw hat the eggs

Ralph had managed to steal for her, often at the cost of having to fight off powerful attacks from the wings of the huge amphibious creatures.

These memories would come rushing back to Ralph, but with great bitterness, because times had changed, and the child who had always been his companion was no longer his friend—or at least not in the same open-hearted, unreserved way as before. Though she returned his affection, his devotion, his concern, there was something that prevented her from having complete confidence in him, a memory that was at the center of both their emotional lives. Ralph knew that he could do nothing about it; once, at a time of great danger, he had dared to try, and his courage had done him no good. Now it would be barbaric to refer to it again, and Ralph had decided that he would rather forgive Raymon, the man he respected less than anyone else in the world, than add to Indiana's unhappiness by condemning him, regardless of how just such a condemnation would be.

So he said nothing, and even avoided Indiana. They lived under the same roof, but he had arranged his life so that he would hardly see her except at mealtimes—yet he watched over her like a mysterious providence. He would leave the house only when the heat was at its height and she remained in her hammock, but in the evening, when she had gone to take her walk, he would manage to find some reason for leaving Delmare on the veranda so he might wait for her at the foot of her favorite cliff. He would stay there for hours, sometimes watching her through the moon-silvered branches, but always respecting the space that separated them and never daring to cut short her sad imaginings by even a moment. When she came down again into the valley, she would always find him sitting on one of the several large, flat rocks beside a little stream that ran alongside the path to the house; and as soon as he saw Indiana's white dress appear on the bank, he would silently rise, offer her his arm, and escort her back home without ever saying a word unless she herself, sadder and more depressed than usual, spoke first. Then, after he had left her, he would go to his room and not retire himself until he was sure everyone else had gone to sleep. If he heard Delmare raise his voice, he would rush to find him and use the first excuse that came to mind to either distract him or pacify him, never once allowing him to suspect that that had been his purpose.

The tropical house, which one might almost describe as di-

aphanous compared to those of our own climate and which
therefore made privacy an impossibility, forced the colonel to
be a little more restrained in expressing his temper. The in
escapable presence of Ralph, who would appear at the slight
est sound to stand between him and his wife, made him try to
moderate his rages, for he was too proud to enjoy being put in
the wrong by that silent, severe critic; but even if he waited
until bedtime in an effort to free himself from his judge before
giving vent to the bad temper resulting from the irritations of
the day's business, it was useless: that almost supernatural
presence waited with him, and at his first harsh word, the first
tone loud enough to be heard through the thin walls, there
would come from Ralph's room, as if by chance, the sound of
furniture being moved or someone pacing sleeplessly, and that
would be enough to make Delmare realize that Indiana's discreet, patient protector was awake and on the alert.

PART FOUR

XXV

THE ministry of the eighth of August,* which was responsible for so many major changes in France, was a serious threat to Raymon's personal security as well. Monsieur de Ramière was not a man to be misled by what seemed to others a day of victory. Politics had been the mainspring of his intellectual life, the basis of all his ideas and all his dreams of the future, and he had hoped that the king, by making skillful concessions when and where necessary, would be able to maintain the equilibrium that assured the continued existence of the nobility; but when the Prince of Polignac became minister, those hopes were destroyed. Raymon was quite astute about the new kind of society he lived in, and understood the consequences of such an appointment very well; he knew that what seemed such a triumph to others in his party was not only illusory but dangerous, for his own future was tied to that of the monarchy, and the future of both hung by a thread, with his fortune and perhaps even his life at risk.

He found himself in a delicate and embarrassing position. Honor required him to disregard all personal risks and devote himself to the well-being of the royal family, whose interests had up to then been so closely identified with his own. In that respect, he could not be false to his conscience or to the respect he owed his forefathers, but the king's turn toward absolutism shocked his prudence, his common sense, and—so he told himself—his deepest convictions. It put into question his whole existence, and worse yet, it made him look ridiculous—

---

*ministry of the eighth of August: date on which in 1829 the moderate Martignac was replaced as minister by the ultraconservative, ultraroyalist, ultra-Catholic Prince de Polignac, who believed in absolute monarchy and immediately began to dismantle the Charter by changing the electoral laws and abrogating freedom of the press—reactionary measures that led to the Revolution of 1830.

him, the renowned spokesman for the crown who had so ofte
promised, in the name of that crown, that the oaths which ha
been sworn would be faithfully honored and that there woul
be justice for all! Now, everything the government was doin
gave the lie to the imprudent assertions of the young man wh
had worked so hard to steer a middle course, and all thos
lazily indifferent spirits who two days earlier had asked noth
ing better than to cling to the constitutional monarchy wer
now rushing to join the opposition and denounce Raymon an
his coterie as hypocrites and rascals—or, even more galling, a
fools and incompetents.

After having been considered such a brilliant player of th
political game, Raymon found it humiliating to be treated as
simple-minded dupe. Secretly he began to feel nothing bu
contempt and scorn for that royalty which was bringing sham
on itself and him with it, and he would have liked to find som
honorable way to separate himself from it before the fina
struggle. For a while he made incredible efforts to consolidat
his standing with both sides. The opposition group, whic
needed recruits at that time, was not very particular about ad
mitting new adherents, and since it asked very little in the wa
of credentials, many joined. Of course, the leaders did not dis
dain support from those with either noble or well-know
names either, and every day their newspapers were filled wit
a kind of subtle flattery meant to detach the most illustriou
jewels from the worn-out crown. Raymon was not fooled b
those declarations of esteem, but he was sure that those wh
made them would be useful and did not by any means rebuf
them. As for the supporters of the throne, as their situation be
came more desperate, they became more intolerant, drivin
even their strongest and most useful defenders from their rank
without the slightest consideration for their feelings. They
soon began to make Raymon feel the weight of their distrus
and dissatisfaction, and since he believed that his entire exis
tence depended on his reputation, he very opportunely suffered
an acute attack of rheumatism which forced him to temporarily
give up all activity and retire to the country with his mother.

Surrounded by the frenzied activity of an entire society in
the process of dissolution, Raymon—living as he did in an iso
lation forced on him as much by his inability to choose politi
cal sides as by his illness—felt cast aside, almost like a corpse
for everyone else, even the most obscure and the least compe
tent, was involved in the struggle under one or the other of the

warlike banners waving from every corner. His intense pain, his fever, his solitude, and his boredom all combined to make his thoughts take a different turn. He asked himself, probably for the first time in his life, if society was worth all the trouble he had taken to please it, and his judgment was colored by the recognition of how society had proven itself so indifferent to him, so forgetful of his talents and his fame. Then he consoled himself for having been so gullible by assuring himself that he had used society only for his own personal gratification, which he had indeed found there, but thanks only to his own efforts: nothing confirms us in our egoism so much as this kind of reflection. Raymon's conclusion was that man in the contemporary world needed both public social triumphs and private domestic pleasures.

His mother, who had been tireless in nursing him, fell dangerously ill herself, and it should have been his turn to forget his own sufferings and take care of her; but he was not strong enough. Warm-hearted, passionate people are capable of great physical efforts in times of need; tepid, disengaged people can't call on such supernatural reserves of strength, and although Raymon was what was known in society as a "good son," he succumbed to his exhaustion. Lying on his bed of pain, with no one to keep him company except paid servants and an occasional friend in a hurry to return to the excitement of social life, he began to think of Indiana with sincere regret, for she would have been very useful to him at such a time. He remembered the devoted, unstinting care she had given her peevish old husband and imagined the gentle attentions she would have known how to lavish on her lover.

"If I had accepted her sacrifice, she would have been dishonored," he thought, "but what difference would that make to me now? Even though I've been abandoned by a frivolous, selfish world, I wouldn't be alone because the woman who would have been scorned by that same world would be enveloping me with love. She would have sympathized with my sorrows and done everything possible to relieve them. Why did I ever send that woman away? She loved me so much that her efforts to make me happy would have consoled her for all the insults heaped upon her by others."

He resolved to get married when his health improved, and he reviewed all the names and faces that had attracted him in the drawing rooms of the two different groups he had moved in. Ravishing images flitted through his mind: strands of hair

enlaced with flowers, snow-white shoulders swathed in swans
down, swelling breasts subtly hidden by sheer muslin or
smooth satin—all these seductive phantoms fluttered their
gauzy wings before his feverishly heavy eyes. But he had seen
those beauties only in the ballroom, and when he woke from
his hazy dreams he wondered if their rosy lips could smile in
anything but coquetry, if their white hands could soothe
painful sores, if their scintillating wit could stoop to the humble task of consoling and distracting a terribly bored invalid.
Raymon was able to think more clearly than most men and
therefore distrusted the flirtatiousness of women more than
they did, just as he understood and hated selfishness more than
most men because he knew how little his own happiness could
benefit from it. In addition, he found it as hard to choose a
wife as to choose a political party, and for the same reasons.
He belonged to a proud aristocratic family that wouldn't toler-
ate any alliance with someone of lower rank, yet the only secure fortunes were to be found among the middle class. It
seemed clear that those were the people destined to rise on the
ruins of the others and that the son-in-law of a manufacturer or
a speculator would have the best chance of staying afloat in all
the turbulence, but Raymon thought it best to wait and see
what happened before making a decision that would determine
the course of his whole future life.

Such reflections made it quite obvious to him that love was
not a very important factor in a marriage of convenience and
that the chance of finding a partner worthy of his love and able
to contribute to his happiness was very slight. Meanwhile his
illness might last a long time, and the hope of better days to
come does not lessen the sharp pangs of present pain. He
thought again of his blind stupidity in refusing to run away
with Indiana and cursed himself for having so misunderstood
his true interests.

In the midst of all this he received her letter from Bourbon
and was profoundly impressed by the quality of her serious,
unwavering sentiments in a situation that might well have
crushed her spirit.

"I misjudged her," he thought. "She really did love me, and
she still does. For me, she would have been capable of the
kind of heroic gesture I never imagined a woman could make,
and even now, a single word would probably draw her like a
magnet from one end of the world to the other. If it wouldn't
take six or eight months for that to happen, I'd like to try!"

He fell asleep thinking about it, but was soon awakened by ominous sounds from the room next to his. He got up with difficulty, put on a dressing gown, and made his way to his mother's room. She was much worse.

In the morning, having no illusions about how much time she had left, she gathered her strength to talk to her son about his future.

"You are losing your best friend," she told him. "May God replace her with someone worthy of you. But be careful, Raymon, not to risk the tranquility of your whole life for the sake of ambition. Unfortunately, I've known only one woman whom I would have wanted to call daughter, but heaven has disposed of her otherwise. Nevertheless, listen to me, my son. Monsieur Delmare is old and worn out. Who knows how that long trip affected his strength? Respect the honor of his wife as long as he lives, but if, as I believe, he will soon follow me to the grave, remember that there is still one woman in the world who loves you almost as much as your mother has loved you."

That evening Mme. de Ramière died in the arms of her son. Raymon's grief was bitter and real. His mother had been truly necessary to him; without her, he had no moral touchstone for his life, and his sense of loss was too profound for any false emotions or selfish calculations. Weeping bitter tears over her bloodless forehead and lifeless eyes, he denounced heaven, cursed his fate, and even wept for Indiana; and after reproaching God for treating him as if he were like anyone else and taking away everything he loved, he first demanded reparations and then doubted His existence, preferring to deny Him rather than submit to His decrees. Losing everything real in his life, he also lost all his illusions, and he returned to his bed of feverish suffering as shattered by what had happened as if he were a deposed king or a fallen angel.

When he had more or less recovered, he thought about the condition of his country. Things were getting worse; people were even threatening to refuse to pay their taxes. Amazed by his party's foolish and unjustified optimism, he decided it would be best to still remain on the sidelines, and he continued to live in seclusion at Cercy with only the melancholy memories of his mother and Indiana.

The more he considered the idea he had so casually thought of and then dismissed, the more he came to believe that Indiana was not permanently lost to him if he would take the trouble to call her back. He saw many disadvantages in the plan, but many more advantages. His mother had suggested he wait for Indiana to be widowed and then marry her, but that was inconvenient. Delmare might live another twenty years, and besides, Raymon had no intention of giving up the possibility of making a brilliant marriage. His fertile, optimistic imagination came up with a better plan. With just a little effort he could exert a limitless influence over his Indiana, and he was sure that he was adept enough to make that sublimely ardent woman into a submissive and devoted mistress.

He would be able to protect her from the contempt of public opinion, conceal her behind the impenetrable wall of his private life, guard her like a hidden treasure, and enjoy her pure and generous affection whenever he felt the need to temporarily withdraw from society and enjoy some quiet hours. There would be no difficulty in avoiding the husband's wrath, because he certainly wouldn't travel halfway across the world to look for his wife when all his business interests made it absolutely essential that he remain where he was. And Indiana herself, after having lived under the severe restrictions of her marital yoke, would hardly demand too much in the way of amusements or liberty. Her only ambition was to be loved, and Raymon knew that he would love her, if only out of gratitude, as soon as she had proved useful to him—and he remembered how uncomplainingly gentle she had been during those long days of his coldness and neglect! He promised himself that he would guard his freedom so adroitly that she would find it impossible to complain, and he flattered himself that he would be able to make her forget her deepest convictions and accept anything, even his eventual marriage—basing that hope on the many known examples of intimate liaisons impervious to every law of society, thanks to the prudence and skill with which both parties had managed to avoid openly flouting convention.

"Besides," he said, continuing to reason with himself, "she will have made the ultimate, irrevocable sacrifice. She will have crossed the world for me, leaving behind every means of existence and every possibility of pardon. Society doesn't forgive small-minded, ordinary lapses, but it's often astonished and disarmed by any bold or exceptional behavior, so it may feel sorry—perhaps even admire—this woman who will have done for me what no other woman would have dared to do. It may fault her, but it won't laugh at her, and no one will fault *me* for protecting such a woman after she has given such extraordinary proof of her love. On the contrary, some people may actually praise me for my courage—or at the very least, defend me—and my reputation will be the subject of endless discussion. Sometimes society wants to be defied and admires those who go off the beaten track. These days one must know how to direct public opinion . . ."

Under the influence of such thoughts he wrote Indiana exactly the kind of letter one might expect from the pen of such a subtle and experienced man. It exuded love, grief, and above all, truth. Poor truth! Is it really such a flexible reed, to yield to every breeze and change with every breath?

Raymon was astute enough not to come right out and explain the object of his letter in so many words. He pretended to believe that Indiana's return was a joy beyond hoping for, but this time he said very little about her duties. He told her about his mother's last words, and he described in graphic detail his state of despair at her loss, the boredom of his solitary existence, and the danger of his political position. He drew a somber picture of the revolution looming over the horizon of France, and though he claimed to be grateful that he was facing its dangers alone, he let it be understood that the moment had come for her to prove the unswerving loyalty and reckless devotion of which she had boasted. Raymon cursed his fate, claiming that his virtue had cost him dear, that his burden was very heavy, that he had held his happiness in his hand and been strong enough to let it go, dooming himself to eternal loneliness.

"Don't tell me again," he added, "that you once loved me, because then I become so weak and discouraged that I curse my strength and hate my sense of duty. Tell me that you are happy and have forgotten me, so I will have the courage not to go to you and break the chains that separate us."

In a word, he said that he was unhappy. For Indiana, that was the same as saying that he was waiting for her.

XXVI

DURING the three months it took that letter to arrive at Bourbon, Indiana's situation had become almost intolerable because of a domestic incident that had major consequences for her. She had fallen into the habit of writing a daily summary of her sorrows and sufferings; this journal was addressed to Raymon, and though she had no intention of ever sending it to him, she used it as a way to talk to him, sometimes lovingly, sometimes bitterly, about the miseries of her life and her unalterable feelings for him. These papers fell into Delmare's hands—or rather, he broke open the box in which Indiana kept them, together with Raymon's old letters to her, and devoured them in a frenzy of fury and jealousy. At the height of his rage, his heart racing and his fists clenched, he lost his self-control and went outside to wait for her. If she had returned from her walk a few minutes later, the unhappy man might have had enough time to come to his senses, but their evil star so arranged things that she appeared almost immediately. Without a word, he grabbed her by the hair, threw her to the ground, and stomped on her forehead with the heel of his boot.

No sooner had he imprinted the bloody mark of his brutality on that weak creature than he was filled with horror at what he had done. Shocked, he fled to his room, locked the door, and loaded his pistol in order to blow his brains out; but just as he was about to pull the trigger, he looked out the window and saw that Indiana had gotten to her feet and was calmly wiping away the blood that covered her face. Since he thought he had killed her, his first reaction at seeing her alive was joy, but then his anger flared up again.

He screamed out to her: "It's only a scratch, and what you really deserve is to die a thousand times over! And I won't kill myself, because if I do, you'll throw yourself into your lover's arms and celebrate my death! I refuse to make you both happy—I want to live to make you suffer, to see you slowly pine away out of boredom, to punish you as the contemptible creature you are, the vile wretch who's made a fool out of me!"

As Delmare was trying to control his rage, Ralph approached the veranda and found Indiana in a state of complete disarray, still stunned by the horrible scene that had just been played out. While it was happening, she hadn't shown the least sign of fear, uttered the slightest cry, or lifted a finger to beg pardon or ask for mercy; it was almost as if she was so tired of life that she had deliberately not called for help so Delmare would have enough time to finish murdering her. Ralph had been just a few steps away when the assault had taken place, and he hadn't heard a thing.

"Indiana, who has hurt you like this?" he cried out, aghast.

"Do you have to ask?" she replied with a bitter smile. "Who else but your *friend* would want to or has the *right* to?"

Ralph threw down his walking stick; his bare hands were all he needed to strangle Delmare. With two great strides he reached the door and forced it open with his fist—only to find Delmare, his face swollen and purple, lying on the floor and gasping for breath in a kind of convulsive fit.

Ralph picked up the papers scattered on the floor, and as soon as he recognized Raymon's handwriting and saw the broken box, he understood what had happened. Carefully collecting all the incriminating letters, he ran with them to Indiana, urged her to burn them immediately—Delmare had probably not taken the time to read them all—then go to her room and stay there while he called the slaves and asked for their help with the colonel.

But she refused to either burn the papers or hide her injury, saying haughtily, "No, I absolutely refuse! That man had no hesitation about telling Madame de Carvajal that I had run away from home, and he could hardly wait to inform everyone else about what he called my disgrace. Now I want people to look at my face and see the sign of his own disgrace, put there by his own efforts. It would be a strange kind of justice that would tell me to keep his crimes secret even though he was so quick to assume he had the right to brand me for what he considered mine!"

A little later, when Ralph saw that the colonel was well enough to listen to him, he told him what he thought of his behavior in no uncertain terms and with a stern, vigorous energy

no one would have imagined him capable of displaying. Delmare, who was by no means an evil man, began to cry like a
baby—but only as an emotional response to his immediate
feelings and without any real understanding of the sequence of
causes and effects that had led to the situation. Rushing to the
opposite extreme, he wanted to see his wife immediately and
beg her pardon, but Ralph objected and tried to make him understand that such an inadequate response would only undermine his authority without mitigating his fault. Ralph knew
very well that there are wrongs one cannot forgive and miseries one can never forget.

From that time on, Indiana hated the very sight of her husband. Everything he did to try to make up for the wrong he
had done succeeded only in making her lose even the little respect she had still felt for him. He had, in fact, made an enormous error. The man who feels that he cannot be coldly
implacable in his vengeance should never allow himself to feel
provoked or resentful, because there are only two possible positions: that of the Christian who forgives, or that of the
worldly man who retaliates; there is no middle ground. But
Delmare, like everyone else, was motivated by a certain self-
interest; he felt himself growing old, and his wife's care was
becoming more and more necessary to him with each passing
day. He was terrified of being left alone, and if, as a response
to his wounded pride, he would sometimes revert to his military habits and treat her roughly, a few moments' thought
would soon bring him around to the more characteristic weakness and vacillation common to all old men afraid of being deserted. Too weakened by age and anxieties to hope to become
a father, his habits had remained those of an old bachelor, and
he had taken on a wife as he might have taken on a house-
keeper. He forgave her for not loving him because he was concerned for his own comfort, not because he felt any particular
affection for her, and if he was unhappy to find that he did not
hold first place in her heart, it was because he was afraid it
meant that he would be less well attended to in his old age.

It was equally true that when Indiana, victimized by the
laws of society, marshaled all her mental arguments for hating
and despising those laws, there was a strong component of
self-interest in *her* intellectual position as well. But perhaps
this all-consuming craving for happiness, this hatred of injustice, this lifelong thirst for liberty are the constituent element
of what the English call "egoism," by which they mean a love

of self that is seen as one of mankind's rights, not as one of its sins. It seems to me that the person who suffers the most from a social institution that other people profit from has the obligation, if he has any spirit at all, to struggle against such an arbitrarily distributed burden; and I also think that the more noble his spirit, the more it must suffer from the festering wounds of such unjust restraints. If such a person had expected to be happy because he was virtuous, life's bitter experiences and disappointments must have caused him many desperate doubts and painful perplexities!

All of Indiana's thoughts, actions, and problems were part of the terrible ongoing struggle between nature and civilization. If she had thought she might hide among the island's uninhabited mountains, she would certainly have fled to them on the very day she had been attacked, but Bourbon was too small to allow her to evade any search parties, so she resolved to put the sea—and the fact that no one would know her exact destination—between her and her tyrannical master. Having made this decision, she felt easier in her mind and seemed almost carefree and gay, which so surprised and charmed Delmare that he told himself what all coarse and brutal men tell themselves: that it's a good idea to make women understand that they are subject to the power of the strongest.

Meanwhile Indiana thought of nothing but flight, solitude, and independence, revolving in her poor befuddled brain innumerable impractical projects based on romantic dreams of establishing herself somewhere in the empty wilds of India or Africa. At night, for as long as she could see them, she would watch the birds begin their return flight to Rodriguez, and that deserted island seemed to hold the promise of solitude—the most important requirement of a broken heart; but the same reasons that kept her from escaping to the interior of Bourbon were equally valid for the small neighboring islands, and she had to give up that idea as well.

Tradesmen from Madagascar would often come to the house to do business with her husband, and though they were dull, vulgar men with no subtlety or skill in any area of life other than their commercial affairs, their stories nevertheless captured Indiana's imagination. She enjoyed asking them questions about the marvels of their island, and everything they said in praise of its prodigious natural abundance intensified her desire to hide there. Its size, and the fact that the Europeans lived in only a small portion of the island, led her to hope that no one would ever be able to find her, and she looked no further; that was to be her refuge, and she occupied her idle mind with dreams of a future she planned to create by and for herself alone. She could already imagine her isolated hut sheltered by a virgin forest and bordering a nameless river, and in her mind she had already placed herself under the protection of tribes that had never been spoiled by any knowledge of our laws or prejudices. In her ignorance she hoped to find there all the virtues that have disappeared from our own hemisphere and to live in peace, undisturbed by any set of social restrictions; that weak woman who was unable to bear the anger of one man had no doubt that she could defy an entire uncivilized society and was certain that she would be immune both to the dangers of isolation and to the life-threatening illnesses of the climate!

Absorbed in her improbable and extravagant projects, she managed to forget her real and present problems. She created for herself another world, one that consoled her for the one in which she was condemned to live, and she began to be less pre-occupied with Raymon, who soon became a completely unim-portant factor in her solitary, preoccupied existence. While busy building her fanciful future, she let go some part of the past, and as her heart became freer and bolder, she imagined that she was harvesting in advance the fruits of her reclusive life.

Then Raymon's letter arrived, and that entire dreamlike edi-fice came tumbling down. She felt—or had thought she felt—that she no longer loved him, but I prefer to think that she had never loved him at all, at least not with the full strength of her soul. A one-sided, misdirected love is as different from a shared love as error is from truth, and even if our feverish feel-ings fool us into thinking that we are experiencing love in all its power, we will learn later, when we taste the delights of true love, how completely wrong we were.

But Raymon's description of his situation reawakened Indi-ana's generosity, which was such an essential, undeniable part of her nature. Thinking he was alone and unhappy, she felt obliged to forget the past and not try to foresee the future. Be-fore, she had wanted to leave her husband because she hated and resented him; now she was sorry that she didn't respect him so that she might make a real sacrifice for Raymon's sake: she was afraid that merely escaping from a hot-tempered mas-ter at the risk of her life and then braving the miseries of a four-month crossing was not enough of one. She would have given her life without thinking it a high enough price to pay for one of Raymon's smiles. Women are like that.

The only problem was leaving the island. It would be hard to evade Delmare's distrust and Ralph's solicitude, but even that was not the major obstacle. How could she avoid the publicity resulting from the law that required every passenger to publish an announcement in the newspapers about his impending departure?

Among the few ships anchored in the dangerous roads of Bourbon was the *Eugène,* soon to leave for Europe. Indiana tried to find an occasion for speaking to its captain without her husband's knowledge, but every time she said she wanted to take a walk along the port, he would go through the motions of putting Sir Ralph in charge of her and then follow them with his eyes as long as he could. Nevertheless, by patiently gathering every bit of relevant information, Indiana learned that the captain of the ship bound for France would often visit a relative living in the village of Saline in the interior of the island and then return to the ship to sleep. From that moment on, she almost never left the rock that served as her observation post, averting suspicion by using many different paths to get there and—after having watched the mountain roads in vain for the appearance of the person she wanted to see—returning home late at night just as carefully.

She had only two days left, because the offshore winds had already started to blow; it would soon become impossible to remain anchored in the roadstead, and Captain Random was surely eager to set sail.

Finally, running the risk of being seen and losing her last chance, but praying to the God of the weak and the oppressed, she went right down to the Saline road itself and less than an hour later saw Captain Random coming down the path. Like all sailors, he was rough-mannered and cynical regardless of his mood, and Indiana was terrified at the mere sight of him. Nevertheless, she took her courage in hand and walked steadily and resolutely to meet him.

"Monsieur," she said, "I'm about to put my reputation and my life into your hands. I want to leave the colony and return to France. If you betray this secret instead of putting me under your protection, I will have to throw myself into the sea."

The captain replied with an oath that the sea would refuse to accept such a pretty victim, and that since she had come to him of her own free will, he would swear to carry her to the end of the world.

"Do you really agree, monsieur?" Indiana asked anxiously. "In that case, please let me pay you in advance for my passage."

And she handed him a small casket containing the jewels Mme. de Carvajal had given her a long time ago, the only fortune she had left.

But the sailor had other ideas, and what he said when he returned the casket made her blush.

"I'm a very unfortunate woman, monsieur," she said, trying to hold back the angry tears glistening behind her long lashes. "Because of what I asked you to do, you think you have the right to insult me—but if you only knew how miserable my life is here, you would pity me rather than despise me."

Captain Random was touched by her dignity: people who do no violence to their natural delicacy sometimes find it healthy and intact in an emergency. He thought about Colonel Delmare's unpleasant face and about the sensation his attack on his wife had caused in the colony, and even as he was looking lustfully at that frail, pretty creature, he was struck by her air of innocence and sincerity—and particularly by the white brand on her forehead, which was emphasized by the deep flush that covered her face. Besides, he had had some commercial dealings with Delmare that had left a bad taste in his mouth; the man was tight-fisted and inflexible in business matters.

"By God," he cried, "I despise a man who can kick such a pretty woman in the face! Delmare's a pirate, and I won't be sorry to play him such a trick. But be careful, madame, and remember that I'm risking my good name. You'll have to get out quietly, when there is no moon, and fly off like some poor petrel from a dark reef . . ."

"I know that you'll be breaking the law by doing this for me, monsieur," she replied, "and you may even have to pay a fine. That's why I'm offering you this casket and its contents, which is worth at least double the price of my passage."

The captain took the casket with a smile.

"Now isn't the time to settle our accounts," he said, "but I'm quite willing to take charge of your little fortune. Under the circumstances, you probably won't have much luggage, so hide among the rocks at the Latanier cove on the night we leave. I'll send two strong rowers to pick you up, and you'll be on board between one and two o'clock in the morning."

XXVII

THE day of her departure passed like a dream; she had been afraid it would be a long and difficult one, but it went by in a second. As she locked herself into her room, prepared the few clothes she intended to take with her, concealed them, one at a time, under the dress she was wearing, then walked down—a separate trip for each item thus hidden—to the Latanier cover, where she put them into a bark basket that she then buried in the sand, the silent countryside and the peaceful house were counterpoints to her inner turmoil.

Each time she went down to the beach she noticed the sea becoming rougher, the wind stronger. For safety's sake, the *Eugène* had already left the roadstead, and Indiana could see in the distance her white sails billowing in the breeze as she tacked about to keep her position, looking for all the world like a fiery racehorse impatiently pawing the ground as it waited for the starting signal; watching it, her eager heart beat more quickly. But each time she returned to the interior of the island, she would find the usual soft air, bright sunlight, singing birds, and buzzing insects—all the ordinary daily activity going on as if nothing were different, as if everything was oblivious to her intensely troubled state—and then she would find it difficult to believe in the reality of what she was about to do, and wonder if her approaching departure might not be only a dream.

Toward evening, the wind fell, and the *Eugène* came closer to the shore again. Indiana, sitting on her usual cliff at sunset, heard the echo of a cannon bouncing off the rocks—the signal that the ship would leave the next day at sunrise.

After dinner M. Delmare said he wasn't feeling well, and his wife thought that all was lost—that he would keep the house awake all night and that her plan was doomed to failure. Besides, she felt that he was suffering and needed her; this was no time to leave him. She asked herself who would pity and take care of that old man after she had abandoned him and was horrified at the realization that she had been about to commit what she herself thought of as a crime; she began to regret what she had planned to do, and was certain that the voice of her own conscience would condemn her even more strongly than the voice of society. If Delmare had demanded her services with his usual harshness, if he had been overbearing and capricious in his suffering, his oppressed slave would have thought it natural to resist him, but for the first time in his life he bore his pain patiently and was affectionate to his wife and grateful for her care.

At ten o'clock he announced that he was feeling much better, insisted that she go to her own room, and told everyone not to pay any further attention to him. Ralph agreed that every symptom of illness had disappeared and that a good night's rest was the only thing he needed. At eleven o'clock, all was calm. Weeping bitterly because she was going to commit a great sin, one for which only God could forgive her, Indiana knelt and prayed, then quietly entered her husband's room and saw that he was sleeping soundly, his face untroubled, his breathing regular. As she was about to leave, she noticed in the shadows someone asleep in a chair; it was Ralph, who without saying anything had come to watch over her husband lest he suffer another attack while he slept.

"Poor Ralph," she thought. "His behavior is such a reproach to me!"

She wanted to wake him up, confess everything, beg him to save her from herself—then she thought of Raymon.

"Another sacrifice for him," she told herself, "and this one the hardest of all—my own sense of duty!"

Love is woman's virtue. Love is what glorifies her sins in her own eyes and gives her the courage to endure the pangs of remorse. The more difficult it is for her to commit the sin, the more praise she feels she will deserve from the man she loves. That same excessive zeal is what puts the dagger into the hands of the religious fanatic.

Taking off the gold chain that had come to her from her mother and that she always wore, she gently put it around Ralph's neck as a pledge of eternal friendship, then lowered her lamp once again over her husband's face to make sure that he was still all right.

He must have been dreaming, for she heard him say weakly,
"Beware of that man, he'll destroy your life. . . ."

Quaking with fear, Indiana fled to her room, where she
stood wringing her hands in great confusion, no longer sure of
what she should do. Suddenly it occurred to her that she was
acting not for her own sake but for Raymon's, that she was
going to him not in pursuit of her own happiness but to bring
him happiness, and she knew that she would be willing to suffer even an eternity of damnation if she could make her lover's
life a happier one. She rushed out of the house and walked
quickly down to the Latanier cove, not daring to turn around
and look at what she was leaving behind.

As soon as she got there, she dug up her bark basket and sat
down on it to wait. Shivering and silent, she listened to the
whistling wind, the sloshing waves breaking at her feet, the
shrilly moaning seabirds among the great clumps of seaweed
clinging to the sides of the cliffs; but none of those sounds was
as loud as her own beating heart, which vibrated in her ears
like the tolling of a funeral bell.

She waited for a long time, and when she looked at her
watch she saw that it was past the hour that had been arranged.
The sea was rough and the coastline very difficult to navigate
even at the best of times, and she began to despair of ever seeing the men who were supposed to row her to the ship. When
she finally noticed the black outline of a pirogue dancing on
the gleaming waves as it tried to reach the shore, the swell was
so strong and the sea so high that the frail craft kept disappear-
ing from sight, as if burying itself repeatedly in the dark folds
of a silvery shroud. Getting to her feet, she replied to the rowers' signal several times, but each time the wind carried her
voice away before it could reach the sailors. Finally they were
close enough to hear her; they waited for a wave, and as soon
as they felt it lift their boat they redoubled their already strenu-
ous efforts and were at last cast onto the beach with the help of
the breaking waves.

Saint-Paul is built on sand from the sea and rocks from the
peaks, the latter being carried down a long distance by the powerful force of the Galets River and eventually settling at the
bottom of the sea, where they form ever changing mountains of
water-rounded stones that are then constantly destroyed,
shifted, and re-formed by the whims of the waves. Even the
most skillful pilot can never know for sure where these obstacles may be or how to avoid them, and since large ships in the

harbor of Saint-Denis are often cut loose from their mooring
because of the strong currents and then wrecked on the treach
erous coast, they must put to sea as quickly as possible when
ever the offshore wind begins to make the receding waves to
turbulent for safety; and that is what the *Eugène* had done.

The two rowers had no hesitation about blaming Indiana fo
the dangers to which they were exposing themselves, and
was with a torrent of dreadful oaths that they carried her an
her fate through the wild waves and howling winds. First the
complained that the ship should have raised anchor two hou
ago, but because of her, the captain had refused to give th
order; then, apropos of that, they added some further viciou
and insulting comments, which the unhappy fugitive had t
swallow in silent shame. When one of them reminded th
other that they had orders to be polite to the "captain's mis
tress" or risk being punished, the second replied, "Never min
that! I'm more worried about the sharks than about the captain
If we ever see Captain Random again, he's not going to be an
more dangerous than them!"

"Speaking of sharks," said the first, "I don't know if they'v
already got our scent, but I see something behind us tha
doesn't have the face of a Christian!"

"Fool! Can't you tell the difference between a dog and
shark? Hey there, my four-legged passenger! Did we forget t
take you? Well, I'll be damned if you're going to eat th
crew's biscuits! Our orders were to take a young lady—ther
was nothing about a dog."

As he was preparing to hit the animal with his oar, Indian
turned around and recognized the beautiful Ophelia, who ha
picked up her scent on the rocks and was swimming after her
Just as the sailor was about to strike, a wave carried the strug
gling animal away from the boat, and her mistress could hea
her whimpering with frustration and weariness. Indian
begged the oarsmen to take her up, and they pretended t
agree; but when the faithful animal got close enough, they
dashed out her brains, laughing raucously as they did it, and
Indiana saw the dead body of the poor, reasonless creature
who had loved her more than Raymon had. . . .

Just then a huge wave overwhelmed the pirogue, forcing i
down as if into the bottom of a cataract, and the sailors' up
roarious laughter changed to frightened curses. Fortunately
thanks to its lightness and buoyancy, the boat soon righted it
self like a diver, climbed to the top of the wave, then repeated

oth its plunge and its recovery. As they got farther from the
ore, however, the sea became calmer, and soon the boat was
imming swiftly and safely toward the ship, at which point
e men recovered their good humor and decided that it would
e the better part of wisdom to make amends for their coarse
ehavior. Indiana found their wheedling flattery more insult-
g than their complaints.

"Come on, young lady," said one of them, "don't be afraid.
ou're safe now, and the captain will probably give us some
f his best wine for fishing up such a pretty package."

The other one pretended to feel sorry that the waves had wet
e young lady's clothes, but she shouldn't worry—the captain
as there and ready to take very good care of her. Indiana lis-
ened to them in frozen silence as she realized the full horror
f her situation; she could think of no way to escape the hu-
iliations to which she would from now on be subjected but to
row herself into the sea, and two or three times she was actu-
lly on the point of launching herself into the waves. Only
hen she remembered that all her suffering was for Raymon's
ake, and that for his sake she would have to live even it meant
earing every disgrace, did she recover her sublime courage.

She brought her hand to her heavy heart and felt the hilt of
he dagger she had hidden there that morning out of a kind of
nstinctive sense of what the future might hold; knowing that
he had the weapon restored her confidence. It was a short,
harp stiletto that her father used to carry, one that had once
elonged to a member of the aristocratic Spanish family of
Medina-Sidonia, whose name, together with the date of 1300,
as incised into the blade; it had surely avenged more than
ne insult, punished more than one insolent offender, been
tained with much noble blood. With that knife Indiana felt
erself become a Spaniard again, and she boarded the ship
earlessly, telling herself that a woman could face any danger
s long as she had the means to take her own life rather than
ubmit to dishonor. The only vengeance she took on the two
ailors for their vile behavior was to reward them munificently
or their efforts, after which she went to her cabin and anx-
ously waited for the ship to set sail.

Dawn finally came, and the sea was full of pirogues bring-
ng the other passengers. Indiana peeped out from a porthole to
ook at them as they boarded, terrified lest she see her husband
ome to reclaim her, but at last she heard the cannon that sig-
aled their departure fade into an ever diminishing echo on her

island prison. The ship began to move, leaving a frothy foam
in its wake, and the sun climbed in the sky and cast its joyful
rose-colored rays on the white mountain peaks as they sank
lower and lower on the horizon.

When they were several miles out at sea, Captain Random,
in order to protect himself from any charges of complicity,
pretended to discover Mme. Delmare's presence on board his
ship. He acted surprised, questioned the sailors, seemed to lose
his temper and then quiet down again, and ended by writing up
a report of the discovery of a *stowaway*.

Forgive me if I say no more about this crossing. I will only
tell you that Captain Random, despite his lack of education and
polish, had enough natural good sense to quickly grasp Indiana's character; after a few attempts to take advantage of her de-
fenselessness, he began to be touched by it and instead became
her friend and protector. But neither his loyal devotion nor her
own dignity was able to spare Indiana the sly stares, mocking
comments, insulting innuendos, or lewd jokes that she had to
endure from the crew, and it was those—not the weariness,
boredom, dangers, discomforts, and seasickness, all of which
she ignored—that were the unfortunate woman's true torments.

XXVIII

THREE days after Raymon had sent off his letter to Bourbon, he had completely forgotten both it and its purpose, for he had paid a visit to a new neighbor. Lagny, left by M. Delmare to be sold for the benefit of his creditors, had been bought by a M. Hubert, a rich industrialist who was—unlike many rich industrialists—a clever and even an estimable man; and the new owner was already quite comfortably installed in the house that held so many memories for Raymon. At first, as he walked through the garden where Noun's footsteps still seemed to be imprinted on the gravel and through the large rooms that still seemed to echo with the sound of Indiana's soft voice, he rather self-indulgently enjoyed giving free rein to his emotions, but the new residents soon changed the current of his thoughts.

In the large drawing room, where Indiana used to sit at her embroidery, a tall, slim young woman—looking both innocent and knowing, amiable and self-possessed—now sat in front of an easel, making a watercolor copy of the bizarre wall decorations. It was a charming bit of work, displaying a subtle perception and a talent for understated irony, and it was an unmistakable demonstration of the artist's mocking nature. She had amused herself by exaggerating the pretentious gentility of the paintings: using the original colors of the now faded frescoes, she had managed to make quite clear the mannered graces of the aristocracy, the strange resemblance of the shepherd's hut to the noblewoman's boudoir, and the obsequious servility of everyone's attitudes and poses—all of which demonstrated a perfect understanding of how those artificially stiff figures symbolized the false and superficial nature of the age of Louis XIV. Along the side of that work of historical mimicry, she had written the word *pastiche*.

Unhurriedly raising her head, she examined Raymon with

large, knowing eyes—attractive but treacherous, and sparkling with a kind of caustic amusement; for some reason she reminded him of Shakespeare's Mistress Page. As they spoke about the influence of society on art, her manner was neither timid nor bold, neither too formally conventional nor too awkwardly self-conscious.

"Don't you agree, monsieur, that you can see the moral values of the time in those brush strokes?" she asked him, pointing to the Boucher-like rustic cupids covering the paneling. "It's clear that those sheep don't walk or sleep or chew their cud the way sheep do today. And that falsely pretty landscape all manicured and orderly, those improbable clumps of rose bushes with their thousands of petals right in the middle of the forest where nothing grows today but some eglantine, those tame birds that belong to a nonexistent species, those rose-colored gowns that no sun ever faded—don't all those things indicate a poetic vision of useless but happy lives, a dream of idle pleasures and indolent luxury? And yet I imagine those ridiculous fairy tales are just as valid as our own gloomy, complicated political theories! I wish I had been alive then," she added with a smile. "Frivolous woman that I am, I would have been much better equipped to paint fans and create masterpieces of embroidery than to discuss current affairs and understand the political debates of our legislators!"

M. Hubert left the two young people alone, and eventually their conversation drifted to the subject of Mme. Delmare.

"I know that you were very close to the people who lived in this house before, and it's very generous of you to come see the new faces here," said the young woman. "They say Madame Delmare was a remarkable person," she added, giving him a penetrating look, "and I imagine it will be hard for us to compete with the memories you must have of her here in this house."

"She was a fine woman, and her husband was a very worthy man," Raymon replied indifferently.

"I think she must have been something more than a fine woman," said the girl, pursuing the subject. "If I remember correctly, she had a special kind of charm, one that should be described more imaginatively and enthusiastically than by the word *fine*. I saw her about two years ago at a ball given by the Spanish ambassador. Do you remember how radiant she looked that night?"

Raymon winced at the memory of that evening when he had

poken to Indiana for the first time, and then he also remem-
ered that he had noticed the distinguished-looking young
voman with the fine eyes to whom he was talking at this very
noment; he hadn't even been curious about who she was.

It was only when he was saying good-bye to M. Hubert and
ongratulating him on his charming daughter that he learned
ier name.

"I'm not lucky enough to be her real father," said the indus-
rialist, "but I've done the next best thing by adopting her.
Don't you know the story?"

"I've been sick for several months, and all I know about you
s the good you've already done in the neighborhood," Ray-
non replied.

"There are some people," said M. Hubert with a smile, "who
congratulate me for having done a fine thing by adopting
Mademoiselle de Nangy. But you, monsieur, are capable of un-
lerstanding such things and will be able to judge if I did any-
hing more than what any honorable man would have done.
Ten years ago, a widower without children, I found that my
lard work had enabled me to amass a considerable sum of
money, and I was eager to invest it. Some nationalized property
n Burgundy—the Nangy château and its lands—was for sale,
ind it suited me perfectly. After I had owned it for some time, I
earned that the former owner and his seven-year-old grand-
laughter were living a life of poverty in some hovel. Of course,
he old gentleman had been indemnified for his property, but he
lad used the money to pay off debts he had incurred as an emi-
gré. I wanted to help, and I offered him a home in my house,
out even in his destitute state, he was still every bit the haughty
aristocrat. He refused to enter his ancestors' residence as a
charity case, stubbornly rejected any help from me, and died
shortly after we met.

"That was when I took the child, who was already proud
and quite reluctant to be dependent on me. But at that age prejudices aren't very deeply rooted, and resolutions don't last very
long. She soon got used to treating me as if I were her father,
and I brought her up as if she were my own daughter. I've been
more than repaid by the happiness she's brought my old age,
and to make sure that happiness continues, I've adopted Mademoiselle de Nangy. Now all I want is to find her a husband
who's worthy of her and who'll be able to manage the fortune
she'll inherit from me."

Encouraged by Raymon's interest and almost unaware of

what he was doing, this excellent man began, in true bourgeois
fashion, to make Raymon privy at this first meeting to all his
business affairs. It wasn't long before Raymon, an attentive
listener, realized that M. Hubert's wealth, resting on a solid
foundation and administered with great care, was considerable,
and that someone younger and with more elegant tastes than
that worthy gentleman could make it shine forth in all its
splendid brilliance. He felt that he was just the man for that
agreeable task, and he thanked his lucky stars for so arranging
things that his seemingly irreconcilable desires could be reconciled—thanks to several improbable chances—by a woman
who had a rank equal to his and a quite plebeian fortune as
well. It was too good an opportunity to miss, and he determined not to, especially since in addition to everything else the
heiress was charming. Raymon had no trouble resigning himself to his fate.

As for Indiana, he was unwilling to think about her and deliberately refused to face the occasional twinge of anxiety
caused by the thought of his letter. He tried to convince himself that poor Indiana wouldn't understand his meaning or
have the courage to respond to it even if she did, and he eventually succeeded in absolving himself of all blame, for he
would have been appalled to realize that he was selfish. Raymon was not one of those ingenuous villains who come forward on the stage and openly acknowledge their vices to
themselves as well as to others. Vice never sees its own ugli-
ness—if it did, it would be frightened by its own image.
Shakespeare's Iago, who *behaves* in a way that's true to his
nature, *sounds* false because he is forced by our dramatic con-
ventions to unmask himself, to himself be the one to lay bare
the secrets of his complex and crooked heart. In reality, man
seldom tramples his conscience underfoot so casually: he turns
it this way and that, pushes and pulls at it, twists it out of
shape, and when he has distorted it, made it flabby and shape-
less, worn it out, he then keeps it at his side like an indulgent
master whom he pretends to fear, consult, and obey but who in
reality gives in to his every whim or desire.

So Raymon returned often to Lagny, and M. Hubert was
glad to see him, because as you remember, Raymon knew how
to make himself liked. Before long, there was nothing the rich
bourgeois wanted more than to call Raymon his son-in-law—
except for his adopted daughter to choose him of her own free

will; he therefore allowed them complete freedom to be together so they might get to know and judge each other.

Laure de Nangy was in no hurry to make Raymon a happy man, and she kept him poised midway between fear and hope. Less generous than Indiana, but much more skillful in doling out balanced quantities of distance and warmth, pride and submissiveness, she was exactly the woman to bring Raymon to his knees, for she was as much superior to him in cunning as he was to Indiana. It hadn't taken her long to realize that her admirer lusted after her fortune at least as much as he desired her, nor was it a great surprise; she was too reasonable and practical to expect anything else, too knowledgeable of the world to have hoped for true love when two million was involved. She had decided on her course of behavior calmly and deliberately, and she did not think less of Raymon because he was as calculating and unsentimental as any of his contemporaries; she merely understood him too well to love him. It was a matter of pride with her to be as cold and contriving as her time; she would have lost her self-respect if she had believed in the silly illusions of an ignorant schoolgirl, and she would have blushed at being the kind of person who could be hoodwinked just as she would have blushed at being the kind of person who behaves foolishly. In short, she was as determined to avoid the entanglements of love as Indiana had been eager to surrender to them.

Mlle. de Nangy was therefore quite prepared to accept marriage as a social necessity, but it gave her a perverse pleasure to use the freedom she still enjoyed to make her suitor submit to her authority before he was able to deprive her of it. There were no youthful dreams, no sweet anticipation, no false but beckoning future for this young woman doomed to endure all the miseries of wealth; for her, life was a cold-blooded calculation, and happiness a childish illusion that had to be guarded against as if it were a ridiculous weakness.

While Raymon was working to establish his fortune, Indiana was approaching the shores of France. Imagine her alarm when she landed at Bordeaux and saw the revolutionary tricolor waving from the walls! The city was in an uproar; the prefect had almost been killed the night before, the people were rising in every quarter, the soldiers seemed to be preparing for a bloody conflict, and no one knew how the revolution had fared in Paris.

"I'm too late!" Indiana thought, thunderstruck at the possibility.

Almost hysterical, she left her few clothes and the little money that remained to her on the ship and began to run through the city in a frenzy. She tried to find transportation to Paris, but all the public conveyances were overflowing with people either fleeing or hurrying to share in the plunder of the conquered, and it was evening before she finally got a seat. Just as she climbed into the coach, an improvised patrol of National Guards came to stop the passengers from leaving and demanded to see their papers. Indiana had none. While she was trying to argue against the ludicrous suspicions of the winning party, all around her people were saying that the monarchy had fallen, the king had fled, the ministers and their minions had been murdered. When she heard those snippets of information, proclaimed with much laughter and stamping of feet and shouts of joy, she felt as if she had been dealt a deadly blow, although actually only one aspect of that whole revolution concerned her, only one man in all of France mattered to her. She fainted, and when she regained consciousness, she was in a hospital and several days had gone by.

Two months later she was discharged—without money, without clothes, without any personal effects, weak and dazed and worn out from the inflammatory brain fever that had several times brought her to the brink of death. When she found herself in the street, barely able to stand and with nowhere to turn for help, when she tried to think of her situation and realized that she was lost and alone in that large city, when she considered that Raymon's fate must have long since been decided and that there was no one who could put an end to her terrible uncertainty, she was overwhelmed by an almost paralyzing sense of horror at her total isolation. Her senses numbed by the despairing apathy that is the result of hopeless misery, she dragged her weary, feverish body down to the harbor and sat on a stone in the sun, trying to control her convulsive trembling and staring unseeingly at the water lapping at her feet. She remained there for several hours, lacking both the energy and the desire to move, then finally remembered that she had left her money and all her belongings on the *Eugène* and that it might still be possible to get them back; but night had fallen and she was afraid to ask any questions of the nearby sailors who were laughing and joking as they got ready to leave their work.

As a matter of fact, because she wanted to avoid attracting

heir attention, she left the pier and hid herself in an abandoned wreck of a house behind the wide Quinconces esplanade, spending the cold October night cowering in a corner, thinking bitter thoughts and quaking at every alarming sound. Finally day broke, and her hunger was sharp and implacable. She decided to beg for charity, but though her clothes were raggedy, they were still clearly better than was appropriate for a beggar; people stared at her curiously, suspiciously, with a look that said she couldn't put anything over on *them*—and gave her nothing. Once again she went down to the piers, and this time she asked about the *Eugène*. The first boatman she spoke to told her the ship was still in the roadstead outside Bordeaux, and she hired him to take her there.

She found Random eating breakfast.

"Well, my beautiful passenger, are you back from Paris already? You've come at just the right time, because I'm sailing tomorrow. Are you going back to Bourbon with me?"

He told Mme. Delmare that he had looked for her everywhere so that he could return her things. But Indiana hadn't been carrying any identification—not one piece of paper with her name on it!—when she had been taken to the hospital, so both the hospital and the police had had to list her on their books as "unidentified person" and the captain had been unable to trace her.

Despite her weakness and exhaustion, Indiana left for Paris the next day. When she learned what had happened politically, she should have been less worried, but anxiety is unreasonable and love is full of many childish fears.

As soon as she arrived, she rushed to Raymon's house and questioned the porter.

"Monsieur is very well," he said. "He's at Lagny."

"At Lagny? You mean Cercy, don't you?"

"No, madame, at Lagny, which he now owns."

"Dear Raymon," Indiana thought. "He bought that property for me so I would have someplace to go where I'll be out of reach of all the malicious gossip. He knew I'd come to him!"

Mad with joy at the prospect of the new life that was awaiting her, she decided to give herself the night and part of the next day to rest, and with a light heart she rented a room; it had been a long time since she had had a peaceful night's sleep! Her dreams were—deceptively—happy, yet she didn't mind waking up because when she did, she found hope at her

bedside. Because she knew how important all the little niceties
of dress were to Raymon, she put on the pretty new gown that
she had been able to order the day before and which was deliv-
ered just as she got out of bed. But when she started to arrange
her hair, she noticed that her long, splendid tresses had been
cut during her illness: she had been so preoccupied with her
major problems that she had actually been unaware of such a
minor one. . . .

Nevertheless, when she had combed her short black hair so
that it curled around her pale face, perched on her head a small
English hat—called at that time a "three-percenter" in acknowledgment of the fact that the rich were suffering from
lower interest rates and that the size of women's hats was
equally diminished—and attached a bouquet of the kind of
flowers whose scent Raymon loved, she was hopeful that he
would still find her attractive despite the fact that her illness
had erased every trace of tropical sun and left her as pale and
fragile as she had been when they first met.

In the afternoon she hired a carriage and arrived at a little
village near Fontainebleau at about nine o'clock at night.
There she ordered the driver to unharness the horses and wait
for her until the next day, then hurried through the woods on a
path that brought her to the grounds of Lagny in fifteen minutes. She tried to open the small gate that led into the park, but
it was locked from the inside. Since she wanted to enter without alerting the servants so she could surprise Raymon, she
walked alongside the old wall that enclosed the park and
looked for one of its many breaks; fortunately, she found one
that allowed her to climb over without too much difficulty.

Setting foot on ground that belonged to Raymon and was
soon to be her refuge, her sanctuary, her fortress, her very
country, she felt her heart leap with joy. Lightly and triumphantly, she sped along the winding paths she knew so well
and soon reached the English garden, dark and deserted from
where she stood. The plantings were all the same, but the fateful bridge she had dreaded seeing had disappeared, and even
the course of the stream had been altered; whatever might
have brought back memories of Noun's death had been
changed.

"He wanted to spare me any cruel reminders of what happened," she thought, "but he was wrong—I would have been
able to live with them. After all, wasn't it for my sake that he
did what makes him feel so guilty? But we're both sinners

now, because I've also committed a crime. By leaving my husband, I may have caused his death. Raymon can hold me in his arms, and each of us will be the lost innocence and virtue of the other."

There were planks where the new bridge was to be built and Indiana stepped nimbly across them and over the lawn. Her heart was beating so wildly that she had to stop, and she looked up at the windows of her old bedroom. How marvelous—a light was shining through the blue curtains! Of course Raymon was there—what other room could he have chosen?

The door to the secret stairway was open. "He must be expecting me at any moment, so he'll be happy but not terribly surprised."

At the top of the stairs she stopped again to catch her breath: she had more strength to face sorrow than joy. Bending down and looking through the keyhole, she saw that Raymon was alone, reading. Yes, it was really Raymon, looking strong and vigorous; his troubles hadn't aged him, and the political storms he had passed through hadn't caused him to lose a single hair of his head. There he sat, handsome and untroubled, his chin resting on the white hand that was barely visible through the black hair that tumbled over it.

Indiana pushed the door, which opened immediately.

"You were waiting for me," she cried, throwing herself at him and resting her weary head on his chest. "You counted the months and the days, and you knew I should have been here by now—but you also knew that all you had to do was ask me to come. You asked, and here I am, here I am! Oh, I am going to die!"

Her head was whirling, and she remained where she was for some time, gasping for breath, unable to speak or even to think. And then she opened her eyes, recognized Raymon as if she were coming out of a dream, cried out with happiness, and began to kiss him in a frenzy of mad exhilaration.

Raymon was speechless, so dazed he couldn't move.

"For heaven's sake, say something!" she exclaimed. "It's your Indiana, your slave, the woman you called back from exile and who's traveled thousands of miles just to love you and be your servant. It's your companion, the woman you chose and who risked everything, left everything, defied everything, just to bring you this moment of joy! Say that you're happy, say that you're pleased with her! I want my reward—just one word, one kiss, and I'll have been paid a hundred times over!"

But Raymon remained silent, his admirable presence of mind for once abandoning him. That astonishing woman kneeling at his feet filled him with guilt and terror; he hid his face in his hands and wanted to die.

"Oh, my God, my God, you're not speaking to me, you're not holding me, you're not kissing me!" Indiana cried, clinging to Raymon's knees and pressing them to her breast. "Is it because you can't? I know that happiness can hurt, that it can even kill! Oh, my God, you're suffering, you can't breathe, the shock of seeing me was too much for you! Try to just look at me and see how I've suffered, too, how pale I am, how I've aged. But it was all for you, and you'll only love me the more for it . . . Say something, Raymon, just one word. . . ."

"I would like to weep," he said, his voice sounding stifled.

"And so would I," she said, covering his hands with kisses. "Oh, yes, it would do you good. Weep at my breast, and my kisses will wipe away your tears. I've come to make you happy, to be whatever you want me to be—your friend, your servant, your mistress. Before, I was very cruel, very selfish, very foolish. I made you suffer because I couldn't understand that what I wanted was beyond your power to give. But I've thought about it, and I've decided that since you're ready to defy public opinion, I have no right to refuse to make whatever sacrifice is necessary. I'm yours to do with what you will—dispose of me, of my life's blood, of my life itself. I'm yours, body and soul. I've traveled thousands of miles to tell you this and to surrender myself to you. Take me, I'm your slave and you are my master."

I do not know what terrible idea passed through Raymon's mind when he heard that. He removed his hand from his face and looked at Indiana with diabolical cunning, then smiled a wicked and frightful smile as his eyes gleamed in appreciation of her beauty.

"The first thing we must do is hide you," he said, getting to his feet.

"Why do you have to hide me?" Indiana asked. "Aren't you free to welcome and protect me? I have no one in the whole world but you—without you I would be forced to beg on the streets. Why, even the world can't say that you're wrong to love me, because I'm the one who has done wrong! But where are you going?" she cried as she saw him move toward the door.

She was frightened, like a child who cannot bear to be left alone for a second, and she crawled after him on her knees.

He had planned to double-lock the door, but it was too late. It opened before he could reach it, and Laure de Nangy entered.

More angry than surprised, she allowed not the slightest exclamation to escape her as she stooped to focus her narrowed eyes on the half-conscious woman on the floor; then she drew herself erect and said with a cold, contemptuous smile, "Madame Delmare, you have succeeded in placing three people in a very awkward situation, but I do thank you for giving me the least ridiculous role. I shall play it by asking you to leave."

Indignation gave Indiana the strength to get to her feet, rise to her full height, and ask Raymon forcefully. "Who is this woman, and what right does she have to give me orders in your home?"

"You are in *my* home, madame," said Laure.

"Say something, monsieur!" said Indiana, shaking Raymon's arm in rage. "Is she your mistress or your wife?"

"My wife," Raymon replied in a daze.

"I forgive you for not knowing," said Mme. de Ramière with a cruel smile. "If you had remained where you belonged, you would have received an announcement." Then, with feigned friendliness, she turned to Raymon and said, "Oh, Raymon, I pity you. But you're still quite young, and I'm sure you'll learn that one must be a little more prudent in these matters. . . . I'll leave you alone to put an end to this ridiculous scene. If you didn't look so utterly miserable, I'd find the whole thing quite amusing."

With those words she left, feeling quite content with herself for having behaved with such impeccable dignity, and secretly triumphant at having such a club to hold over her husband—one that would assure his subordinate position in their relationship.

Indiana was alone in a closed carriage rapidly returning to Paris before she came back to her senses.

XXIX

WHEN the carriage stopped at the city gate, a man whom Indiana recognized as part of Raymon's household staff came to the door and asked where "Madame" wanted to be taken. She gave him the name and address of the rooming house she had stopped at the night before, and when she got to her room she collapsed in a chair and remained there until morning, not thinking of going to bed or of doing anything else except dying, but too hurt and apathetic to make the effort to kill herself. She was sure it was impossible to survive such pain and certain that death would come without her having to do anything about it, so she remained as she was all that day, without eating anything and without replying to the few offers of service made by the people in the house.

I know of nothing more horrible than a furnished room in a Parisian rooming house, especially when that house is on a dark, narrow street and the dim, dank light that enters it seems to crawl lethargically through the dirty windows and over the sooty ceilings. And the furniture! There is something repugnant about all that furniture which has nothing to do with your past, is unfamiliar with your habits, and evokes no fond memories as your eyes turn restlessly from one piece to another. All those objects that don't belong to anyone because they have belonged to everyone; that room where no one has left the slightest trace of his presence except for the occasional card bearing an unfamiliar name found tucked into the mirror frame; that mercenary resting place for so many travelers and lonely strangers which never gave a moment's true hospitality to any of them and which witnessed but was indifferent to and forgetful of so many human tragedies; that incessant jangling clamor from the street which doesn't even permit you to sleep and forget for a while the misery or weariness that has brought you there—all that is quite enough to disgust and exasperate anyone, especially someone as emotionally devastated as Indiana.

You poor provincial—you who have left your fields, your sky, your gardens, your house, and your family to shut yourself up in what is nothing more than a prison for your spirit and your soul—take a good look at Paris, that lovely Paris you had imagined such a miracle of beauty! Look at it, rain-swept and black with mud, noisy, a seething torrent of poisonous slime oozing all the way to the horizon! *That* is the reality, not the anticipated marvels—the endless spree of glittering, perfumed, splendid, intoxicating pleasures; the extraordinary surprises among the treasures of sight, sound, and taste, all vying with each other to entice your senses while you hesitate which to choose first and regret the impossibility of enjoying every intellectual and sensual pleasure simultaneously! And look, there is the Parisian—not the pleasant, charming, hospitable Parisian that had been described to you, but someone always rushing somewhere, always in a hurry, always worried and preoccupied! Exhausted, overwhelmed, and disappointed long before you've experienced very much of the intricate maze and its turbulent population, you retreat in dismay to one of those cheerful rooming houses, where the only servant of what is often a huge establishment hurriedly settles you in, then leaves you alone to die in peace if you are unable to overcome your fatigue and depression enough to take care of the thousand necessities of life.

But to be a woman and to find yourself in such a place—rejected by everyone; thousands of miles from anyone who cares about you; without money, which is worse than being without water in the middle of the desert; lacking one untarnished memory from your past life or one conceivable hope for the future with which to distract your thoughts from the intolerable present—*that* is to experience the ultimate degree of helpless misery! And thus did Indiana, totally crushed, submit passively and without a struggle to her fate—to her hunger pangs, her raging fever, her aching broken heart. She never complained, she never wept, she never made an effort to die an hour sooner so she might suffer an hour less.

The morning of the second day they found her on the floor, stiff with cold, her teeth clenched, her lips blue, her eyes dull, but still alive. When the landlady checked the desk drawers and saw how little was in them, she wondered if the hospital wouldn't be a better place for the unknown woman, who clearly couldn't pay the expenses of a long and costly illness; but since she thought of herself as a woman with a "warm and overflowing heart," she had the servant put Indiana to bed and sent for the doctor to find out if the patient was likely to live for more than a couple of days.

The doctor who showed up was not the one who had been sent for. When Indiana opened her eyes, she found him sitting by her bed, and I don't have to tell you who it was.

"It's you, it's you, my good angel!" she cried, throwing herself at him with all the force she could command. "But you're too late. All I can do is die blessing you!"

"You're not going to die, my dear," Ralph replied, deeply moved, "and you may still be content. The laws that were an obstacle to your happiness will never keep you from the object of your affection again. I would have liked to release you from that man's powerful spell because I neither like nor respect him, but I can't, and I'm tired of seeing you suffer. Until now your life has been miserable, and I've decided it can't possibly be worse. Besides, even if everything I'm afraid of, even if all my gloomy premonitions come true and your happiness lasts only a little while, you will at least have enjoyed it for that time and won't have to die without at least a taste of it. Fate seems to have placed you in a position where you are alone in the world and have no resource but me, which means that I have certain obligations and must be a father and a guardian to you—so I've come to tell you that I withdraw my objections to Monsieur de Ramière and you're free to share your life with him. Delmare is dead."

Tears rolled slowly down Ralph's cheeks as he spoke, but Indiana, abruptly sitting up in bed, merely wrung her hands in despair and cried: "My husband is dead, I killed him, and you talk to me about happiness and the future as if they were still possible for someone who hates and despises herself! But God is just, and I'm properly punished! Monsieur de Ramière is married!"

Completely exhausted, she collapsed into her cousin's arms, and it was several hours before they were able to talk again.

"Since you don't know what really happened, you're right to have a troubled conscience, but set your mind at rest," Ralph then told her, speaking solemnly but gently and sadly. "Delmare was almost dead when you left him. He never woke up from his final sleep, never knew that you had gone, never cursed you or cried out for you. I had been sleeping soundly next to his bed, and when I woke up early in the morning he was feverish, his face was purple, and he was breathing heavily. It was an attack of apoplexy. I ran to your room and was surprised not to see you, but I had no time to wonder why and wasn't seriously worried until after Delmare was gone. There was nothing I could do for him. Everything happened very quickly, and he died in my arms an hour later without ever recovering consciousness. At the very end, however, he made an effort—he felt for my hand, thinking it was yours because his own were already stiff and numb, tried to hold it tightly, and died, stammering out your name."

"I heard his last words," said Indiana soberly. "As I was saying good-bye to him forever, he spoke to me in his sleep. "Beware of that man, he'll destroy your life,' he told me. Those words are here," she said, putting one hand on her heart and the other on her head.

"When I was able to stop thinking about him and take my eyes off his body," Ralph continued, "I began to think about you, Indiana. I realized that you were finally free, and that if you wept for your master at all, it would be only out of the goodness of your heart or because of some religious feeling. I seemed to be the only one who would lose anything by his death. I was his friend, and if he wasn't always very sociable, at least he had no other friends and I had no rival for his affection. . . . I was afraid a sudden shock would be too much for you, so I waited at the door for you to return from your morning walk. I waited a long time. I won't try to describe how I felt or the efforts I made to find you after I discovered Ophelia's bloody and battered body washed up on the beach by the waves. I began to search for yours because I was sure that you had killed yourself, and for three days I thought there was nothing left in the whole world for me to love . . . But there's no point in talking about my grief—you must have known how I would react when you abandoned me.

"Then I heard a rumor that you had run away. A ship that had passed alongside the *Eugène* in the Mozambique Channel came into port, and one of the passengers had seen and recognized you. Within three days the whole island knew that you had left.

"I'll spare you the outrageous gossip that resulted from the coincidence of your husband's death and your flight having taken place on the same night. They drew some equally charitable conclusions about me, but I ignored them. I still had one more duty to perform—I had to find out how you were, and help you if you needed help. I left very soon after you did, but we had a bad crossing, and it took a long time to get here. I arrived just a week ago. My plan was to see Monsieur de Ramière immediately and ask about you, but luckily I ran into his servant Carle, who had just brought you here. I asked him only one question—where

you were living—and I came here convinced that I wouldn't find
you alone."

"Alone! Alone, humiliated, abandoned!" cried Indiana. "But
let's not talk about him—I don't ever want to talk about him
again! I don't want to love him anymore because I despise him.
You mustn't tell me that I did love him once, because it reminds
me of my sin and my shame, and that's a heavy burden for my
last moments. Oh, please be my comforting angel, you who
come to me in every crisis of my miserable life to offer me a
friendly hand. Carry out your last mission for me with pity and
sympathy. Speak to me affectionately and forgivingly so that I
can die in peace and with the hope of being pardoned by the
judge who waits for me up above."

She wanted to die, but grief rivets rather than weakens the
chains that bind us to life, and she wasn't so much dangerously
ill as languid and apathetic, almost to the point of imbecility.

Ralph did his best to distract her. He took her to Touraine
where she would be far from everything that could remind her of
Raymon, provided her with every comfort, devoted every waking minute of his life to making some of hers endurable; and
when he failed, when he had done everything his imagination
and affection could think of without succeeding in bringing a single gleam of pleasure to her cheerless, careworn face, he would
blame himself bitterly for the inadequacy of his words and the
futility of his tender feelings.

One day he found her more hopelessly depressed than usual.
Not daring to speak, he sat down beside her, silent and helpless.

Indiana turned to him, gently took his hand, and said, "Poor
Ralph, I'm causing you a lot of pain! You have the patience of a
saint to put up with the selfish, cowardly way I bear my unhappiness, and I assure you that the most demanding of women
couldn't ask more of a friendship than what yours has already
done for me! Now you should leave me. Let me be alone with
the misery that's gnawing away at my heart—don't contaminate
your good and pure life by contact with my corrupt and polluted
one! Go where you may find the happiness you can never find
near me."

"I do give up all hope of being able to cure you, Indiana, but
I'll never leave you, not even if you tell me that my presence an-
noys you. You still need material help, and if you don't want me
to be your friend, I can at least be your servant. But listen to me,
because I have a suggestion that I didn't want to make until I had
tried everything else, but which I know will work."

"I know only one remedy for unhappiness," she replied, "and that's forgetfulness. I've had enough experience to learn that rational argument is useless, so let's hope that time itself will cure me. If willpower were enough, my gratitude to you would already have made me as lighthearted and happy as I was when we were children. Believe me, my friend, I don't enjoy inflaming my wound and watching my trouble flourish and grow. Don't I know that you feel all my suffering as if it were your own? Believe me when I say that I'd like to forget everything, to be well again—but I'm only a weak woman, Ralph, and you must be patient and not think that I'm ungrateful."

She began to weep.

Ralph took her hand and said, "Listen to me, my dear Indiana. None of this is your fault, and I'm not blaming you for anything. We can't just decide to forget—it's not in our power. But though I can endure my own troubles patiently, I can't bear seeing you suffer. Besides, why should we struggle, weak creatures that we are, against our hard fate? It's quite enough to bear it. The God whom we both worship didn't condemn man to suffer without also giving him the instinct to avoid that suffering, and I've always thought that what makes man superior to the beasts is his ability to understand the remedy for his ills. That remedy is suicide, and that's what I'm suggesting and even advising."

Indiana was silent for a moment, then replied, "I've often thought about it. Once I was even very tempted by the idea, but I was stopped by my religious scruples. Since then solitude has given me the opportunity to develop my ideas, and the constant unhappiness that seemed to cling to me also taught me, little by little, a religion that was different from the religion taught by men. Before you came to rescue me, I had decided to allow myself to die of hunger, but you begged me to live and I had no right to refuse to make that sacrifice for you. And what stops me now is the thought of your future. What will you do, my poor Ralph, all alone in the world, without friends or family or love? Just now I hurt too much to be of any use to you, but I may get better. I swear I will do everything I can to regain my strength and become carefree and cheerful so that I can devote my life to you—this life that you've fought so hard to wrest from misfortune! Please be patient a little longer, Ralph."

"No, my friend, no, I don't want such a sacrifice from you, and I'll never accept it," Ralph replied. "In what way is my life more precious than yours? Why should you condemn yourself to a hateful future so that I may have a pleasant one? Do you think it could be truly pleasant if you weren't sharing my pleasure? No, I'm not quite as selfish as that! Believe me, it's best not to try to be impossibly heroic. It's arrogant and presumptuous to think one can be false to one's true self-interest. Let's look at our situation calmly and dispassionately, and spend our remaining days as if they were common property that neither one of us can dispose of at the expense of the other.

"For a long time now—perhaps since I was born—I have found life a heavy, tiresome burden, and I no longer feel strong enough to bear it without becoming bitter and irreligious. Let's go back to God together, Indiana. He who has exiled us on this world of trials and tribulations, this 'vale of tears,' will surely not refuse to open His arms to us when we appear before Him, weary and careworn, and beg for His mercy and indulgence. I believe in God, Indiana, and I was the one who first taught you to believe in Him. So trust me—an honest and frank heart cannot lie to anyone who questions it sincerely. I know for certain that we've both suffered enough here on earth to be cleansed of our sins. The baptism of unhappiness has surely purified our souls sufficiently to allow us to return them to God, who gave them to us."

Ralph and Indiana thought about this for several days, finally agreeing that they would die together. The only thing that remained to be decided was the kind of suicide they would choose.

"It's a serious matter," said Ralph, "but I've given it much thought, and this is my suggestion. Since what we want to do shouldn't be an impulsive response to some temporary crisis but a deliberate decision made only after careful consideration, we must look into our hearts as seriously as a Catholic receiving one of the sacraments of his church. For us, the whole world is the temple in which we worship God, and it's in the solitude of majestic, virgin nature, free of all human contamination, that we can best sense his power. We should therefore return to the wilderness, where we will be able to pray. I know that here, in this country swarming with men and their vices, in the heart of this civilization that denies or belittles God, I would be distracted and disturbed. I would be too sad, and I would like to die cheerfully, with a serene mind and with my eyes fixed on heaven.

"Where can we find such a place? I'll tell you where the idea of suicide appeared to me in its noblest aspect. It was at the edge of a precipice in Bourbon, where that splendid, diaphanous, rainbow-crowned waterfall begins its plunge into the Bernica ravine. That's where we spent the sweetest hours of our childhood, where I wept over the most bitter events of my life, where I learned to pray and to hope—and that's where, on a beautiful tropical night, I would like to plunge into those pure waters and go down into that deep, green whirlpool, that cool, flower-filled tomb.

"If you don't have any other preference, do me the favor of allowing us to make our double sacrifice in that place which witnessed the games of our childhood and the sorrows of our youth."

"I agree," said Indiana, putting her hand into Ralph's to seal their pact. "I've always been drawn to the banks of rivers or streams, partly because of a natural inclination and partly because of poor Noun. It will be sweet to die the way she did—it would be almost like an atonement for her death, which I was responsible for."

"And then," said Ralph, continuing, "a long ocean voyage, this time when we feel very differently from the way we felt during our others, is the best possible preparation for detaching ourselves from earthly ties and purifying ourselves before we kneel at the feet of the Supreme Being. Isolated from the world, ready to leave life joyfully at any moment, we'll be able to watch with wonder as the storms bring all the sea's elements to magnificent, tempestuous life. Come, Indiana, let's leave—let's shake the dust of this terrible country from our feet. To die here, under Raymon's eyes, would look like a petty, cowardly revenge. Let's leave his punishment to God, and let's even pray to Him to treat that cold and sterile heart with His infinite mercy."

They left. The schooner *Nahandove*, as swift and light as a bird, carried them back to the country they had twice abandoned, and no crossing had ever been so rapid or pleasant. It was as if a favorable wind had been charged with leading to a safe harbor those two unhappy beings who had been buffeted about for such a long time among the rocks and shoals of life. During those three months Indiana docilely obeyed Ralph's instructions and reaped the benefit of his good advice; the bracing, healthy sea air restored her physical strength and brought serenity to her weary heart. The certainty that she would soon be finished with her troubles had the same effect on her as a doctor's assurances have on a credulous patient, and she was able to forget her past life and open her soul to profound religious emotions. All her thoughts and impressions became impregnated with a mysterious charm, a heavenly perfume, and she discovered so much glorious splendor in the sea and the sky that it was almost as if she had never seen them before. Her face became peaceful again, and her gentle, melancholy blue eyes seemed to have glimpsed a ray of the divine essence.

A no less extraordinary change occurred in Ralph, both inwardly and in the way he looked; the same causes produced almost the same effects. His heart, which had been hardened against sorrow for such a long time, softened in the revitalizing warmth of hope. Heaven came down into his bitter and wounded heart as well. His words began to match his feelings, and for the first time Indiana understood his real nature. In the course of this holy intimacy, the painful shyness of the one and the unjust prejudices of the other disappeared: with every passing day Ralph shed a bit of awkwardness and Indiana an incorrect judgment. At the same time, in the face of Ralph's unsuspected virtues and sublime honesty, the painful memory of Raymon dulled, faded, and soon vanished completely; the more she honored the former, the less worthy did she find the latter, until finally, by dint of comparing the two men, every trace of her blind and fatal passion was erased.

XXX

THREE days after they had disembarked from the *Nahandove*, two of the passengers from that schooner went into the mountains of Bourbon Island. They had spent those three days in town resting—which you may find strange, given their purpose in coming to the colony in the first place, but which must have seemed reasonable to them—and on the evening when they were finally ready to leave, they had some *faham* tea on the veranda, dressed as carefully as if they were planning to attend some important social event, then set off on the mountain road and arrived after about an hour's walk at the Bernica ravine.

As fate would have it, that tropical island had seldom known a lovelier night. The moon, which was just rising over the black sea as they arrived, was beginning to cast a cool sheen on the dark waves; but it had not yet penetrated the gorge, and the surface of the lake reflected nothing but a few twinkling stars. The lemon trees growing on the higher slopes of the mountain remained dark, their brittle, shiny leaves still waiting to be sprinkled by the moon's glinting diamonds, and the softly rustling ebony and tamarind trees were also still in the shadows; only the topmost leaves of the tallest palm trees, a hundred feet above their slender trunks, were already shimmering with a pale, silvery-green light.

The seabirds were quiet in their cliffside crevices, and only some blue pigeons, hidden somewhere on the other side of the mountain, could be heard singing their far-off plaintive, lonesome song. Handsome beetles, looking like vivid, living jewels, rustled softly in the branches of the coffee trees or buzzed as they skimmed along the surface of the lake, and the plashing waterfall seemed to be carrying on a mysterious conversation with the echoes from its surrounding shores.

Following a steep and winding path, the two solitary walkers arrived at the top of the gorge, where the torrent begins its de-

scent to the bottom of the precipice as a column of a diaphanou
white mist, and there they found a small platform that was pe
fect for their purpose. Some vines hanging from the trunks c
the raffia palms formed a natural cradle suspended over the wa
terfall, so Sir Ralph, with his usual admirable composure, cu
away some of the branches that might have hindered their leap
then took his cousin's hand and had her sit down on a moss-cov
ered rock from which, during the day, there was a magnifice
view of all that wild splendor. Just then, however, everythin
was obscured by the darkness of the night and the vapors fro
the cascade, and the depth of the gorge seemed awesomely in
measurable.

"My dear Indiana," said Ralph, "we must be very careful i
carrying out our plans. It's so dark that if you choose a plac
from which to jump simply because you see no obstacles ther
you'll probably be dashed against the rocks, and that will mean
very slow and painful death. But if you hurl yourself in the dire
tion of that white line which marks the course of the waterfal
the water itself will carry you down to the lake and it will be im
possible to miss your aim. . . . Or, if you prefer, we can wait ar
other hour, and the moon will be high enough to give us light."

"I'd like to wait, especially since we ought to devote these la
moments to thoughts of God," replied Indiana.

"You're right, my friend," said Ralph. "Our final hour shoul
be one of meditation and prayer. I don't say that we should mak
our peace with the Eternal because that would be to forget th
distance that separates us from His almighty power, but I d
think that we should make peace with those who caused our su
fering and let the northwest wind carry our words of reconcilia
tion to those who are thousands of miles away from us."

Indiana was neither surprised nor upset by the suggestio
During the past few months, as she became aware of the chang
that had taken place in Ralph, her own thoughts had becom
more and more exalted. She no longer saw him as a dull, lifele
pedagogue but as a good angel who would free her from h
earthly torments, and she followed unprotestingly where he led.

"I agree," she said, "and I'm happy to say that it won't be di
ficult for me to forgive anyone. I have no feelings of hate or r
gret or love or resentment, and as a matter of fact, at this mome
I can hardly remember either my own sorrows or the ingratitud
of those around me. O God, you who can see into my heart—yo
know that it is pure and untroubled, and that all my thoughts
love and hope are turned toward you."

Then Ralph sat down at Indiana's feet and began to pray in a strong voice that could be heard even above the roar of the waterfall. It was probably the first time in his life that he gave voice to everything that he felt. He was about to die, and his soul was pure, clear, limpid; it was no longer in bondage to society but belonged only to God. His ardor was no longer a crime, and his spirit was free to soar. The veil that had hidden so many virtues, so much greatness of soul, so much strength and power, fell away, and the man's mind, at its first release, leaped immediately to the level of his heart.

Just as a bright flame burns through and dissipates the dark clouds of smoke surrounding it, so did the sacred fire that had burned unrecognized in the depths of his being finally send forth its brilliant light. As soon as his stiff self-consciousness was free of its earthly fears and constraints, the words to express his thoughts came easily, and the commonplace man who had never in all his life expressed anything but banalities became in his last hour more eloquent and persuasive than Raymon had ever been.

Don't expect me to repeat the strange things he confided to the echoes of that vast solitude; he himself, if he were here, would be unable to repeat them. There are some moments in life when we are in a state of exaltation or ecstasy, when our thoughts become more subtle, more spiritual if you will. Those rare moments raise us so high, carry us so far out of ourselves, that when we return to earth we have no memory of the incredible things we said or thought during the time of our intellectual intoxication. Who can understand the mysterious visions of the anchorite? Who can describe the visions of the poet before he has become tranquil enough to record them? Who can tell us about the marvels revealed to the just man at the instant heaven opens to receive him? Ralph—that man outwardly so ordinary, yet so exceptional because he truly believed in God and consulted his conscience every day—was settling his accounts with eternity, and it was time to be truly himself, to bare his soul, to throw off the disguise men had forced him to assume. As he cast off the hairshirt of unhappiness that had clung to his bones, he seemed as sublimely radiant as if he were already living in that place of heavenly rewards.

It never occurred to Indiana to be surprised, or to wonder if it could really be Ralph who was saying such things. The Ralph she had known was no more, and the Ralph she was listening to seemed to be the friend she had dreamed of, and who was now made flesh and blood for her at the brink of the grave. She felt her own pure soul rise with his; a profound religious sympath[y] carried her to the same emotional height, and tears of joy fe[ll] from her eyes onto Ralph's hair.

Then the moon rose over the top of the tallest palm tree, an[d] its rays, penetrating between the branches of the lianes, bathe[d] Indiana in a pale, misty light, In her white gown and with he[r] hair falling over her shoulders, she looked like the ghost of som[e] maiden lost in the wilderness.

Sir Ralph knelt at her feet and said, "Now, Indiana, you mu[st] forgive me for all the harm I've done you so that I can forgiv[e] myself for it."

"My poor Ralph," she replied, "what do I have to forgive yo[u] for? On the contrary, shouldn't I bless you until my last breat[h] just as I've had to bless you in all the unhappy days of my life?"

"I don't know for precisely what I can be blamed," he an[s]-wered, "but I'm sure that during my long, difficult battle wi[th] my destiny I must have often done, without meaning to, things [I] shouldn't have done."

"What battle do you mean?" asked Indiana.

"That's what I must explain to you before I can die—the se[-]cret of my life. You asked me about it on the ship that brought u[s] here, and I promised to tell you about it at Bernica, when th[e] moon would be shining down upon us for the last time."

"Then the time has come," she said, "and I'm listening."

"You'll have to be patient, Indiana, because it's a long story."

"I thought I knew your story, since we've almost always bee[n] together."

"You don't know it at all, not a single hour or day of it," sai[d] Ralph sadly. "When could I have told it to you? Heaven ha[s] willed that the only right time for me to speak to you about [it] should be this last moment of both our lives. But just as it woul[d] have been criminally wrong before, so it is legitimate and jus[t] today, and it will give me great satisfaction to tell it now, whe[n] I'm sure that no one can reproach me for doing so, and when [I] know that you will listen with your usual gentle patience. So be[ar] with me to the end the burden of my unhappiness, and if m[y] words weary or annoy you, listen to the waterfall singing th[e] hymn of the dead over me.

"I was born to love—but none of you wanted to believe it, an[d] that misunderstanding was crucial in forming my character. It'[s] true that nature was strangely inconsistent in giving me a war[m] heart, but also a face that was like a stone mask and a tongue tha[t] was heavy and slow. She refused me what she bestowed freel[y] on even the most loutish of my fellowmen—the ability to express feelings through words or looks. That lack is what made me self-centered. People judged my inner character by my outer covering, and like a sterile fruit, I withered under the rough husk I couldn't slough off. As a newborn babe I was rejected by the heart I needed most—my mother pushed me away from her breast with disgust because my infant's face couldn't return her smile. When I was hardly old enough to know the difference between an idea and a wish, I had already been branded with the hateful word 'egoist.'

"Then they decided that because I was unable to express my affection for anyone in words, I didn't love anyone, and therefore no one would love me. They made me miserable—and then said I wasn't sensitive enough to feel such an emotion. They all but banished me from my father's house and sent me to live on the cliffs like a lonely shorebird. You know what my childhood was like, Indiana. I spent long days in the wilderness, and no worried mother ever came to look for me, no friendly voice ever echoed through the silent ravines to remind me that it was growing dark and I should be home in bed. I grew up alone, and I lived alone—but God doesn't want me to be unhappy to the end of my days because I shan't die alone.

"And heaven did send me a gift, a consolation, a hope. You came into my life as if you had been created for me. Poor child—abandoned like me, thrown into the world without anyone to love or protect you, you seemed meant for me, or at least so I thought. Was I too presumptuous? For ten years you were completely mine. I didn't have to share you, I had no rivals, I felt no qualms about the future. And I hadn't yet learned about jealousy.

"That period, Indiana, was the least grim of my life. You were my sister, my daughter, my companion, my pupil, my whole society. Because you needed me, I became something more than a wild animal, and for your sake I came out of the depression into which I had been thrown by my family's contempt for me. I was useful to you, so I began to think better of myself. And—I must tell you everything, Indiana—after having accepted for your sake the burden of life, I did dream of a reward. I began to think—you must forgive these words, for even today I myself tremble at the sound of them—I began to think that someday you would be my wife. Although you were a child, I thought of you as my fiancée. In my imagination you were already a charming young woman, and I was impatient to see you grow up.

"My brother, who had been given my share of family affection, enjoyed quiet activities and cultivated a garden—which at that time you could see from here during the day, but which subsequent owners of the property have turned into a rice field—and taking care of his flowers was his greatest pleasure. Every morning he would go out to check on their progress and be surprised—because he was still only a child—that they hadn't grown overnight as much as he hoped. Well, Indiana, you were *my* greatest pleasure, the focus of all my attention, my only joy and my only treasure. You were my young plant, which I cultivated and was eager to see bloom, and I checked you every morning to see the results of another day that had gone by, because I was already a young man and you were still a child. I was fifteen years old and feeling passions you didn't even know the name of, and you were often surprised at how sad I looked as I played your childish games without any enthusiasm or joy. You couldn't begin to imagine that a fruit or a bird was no longer the same treasure for me as for you, and I began to seem cold and strange to you. Nevertheless, you loved me as I was, because despite my melancholy, every minute of my life was devoted to you, and everything I suffered made you even dearer to my heart because I had the insane hope that you would someday be able to change those sufferings to joys.

"Oh, Indiana, forgive me for that sacrilegious hope which kept me alive for ten years, but if it was a sin for that accursed boy to dream of you—a beautiful, simple child of the mountains—then God alone is guilty for having made that bold dream his only nourishment. How else could that bruised, misunderstood heart facing new trials every day and finding no refuge or peace anywhere, have survived? From whom could he who was your lover almost as soon as he was your father have hoped to have an affectionate look or smile if not from you?

"And you needn't be offended at the idea that you grew up under the wing of a poor bird consumed by love. There was never anything impure or shameful in my adoration, never a thought that might have endangered the purity of your soul, never a word that might have brushed the bloom of innocence from your dewy cheeks. My kisses were like a father's, and when your lips playfully met mine, they never felt the devouring fire of a man's desire. No, it wasn't the little blue-eyed toddler with whom I was in love—when you hugged and kissed me in your adorable way, you were only my child, or at most, my little sister—but my dream of a fifteen-year-old girl, which I projected into the future with all the ardor of my own fifteen years.

"When I read you *Paul and Virginia,* you hardly understood it, but you cried anyway. You thought it was about a brother and sister, but I knew it was a description of two tormented lovers, for whom I trembled with sympathy. You enjoyed the book, and I found it heartbreaking. You used to love to hear me read the descriptions of the faithful dog, the beautiful coconut palms, the songs of the negro Dominique, but I—when I was alone, I used to reread the conversations between Paul and his beloved, and think about the easily roused suspicions of the one and the secret sufferings of the other. Oh, how I understood them—how I recognized those adolescent anxieties, that search for an explanation of the mysteries of life in one's own heart, that enthusiastic grasp at the first available object of love! But do me the justice, Indiana, of acknowledging that I was never guilty of trying to shorten by even a single day the peaceful development of your childhood and that I never said a word to indicate that tears and torments were also a part of life. I left you, at the age of ten, as happy and secure in your ignorance as you had been when your nurse first put you into my arms on that day I had wanted to die.

"I would often come to sit here on this cliff, alone, and I would writhe in agony as I heard all around me the sounds of springtime and love, as I saw the sunbirds teasing and chasing one another and the insects wrapped in their voluptuous embraces, as I breathed the fevered scent given off by the palm trees and wafted on the gentle summer breezes. I was delirious then, frantic, mad. I would beg the flowers, the birds, the sound of the water, for love. I raged to experience that unknown happiness, the mere thought of which made me wild. But then I would see you down there on the path, gay and laughing and looking very tiny from up here, running to meet me and climbing the rocks so awkwardly that with your white dress and your dark hair you might have been a penguin from the Antarctic. And my blood would cool, my lips would stop burning, and at the sight of the seven-year-old Indiana I would forget the fifteen-year-old I had been dreaming of. I would open my arms to you with a pleasure that was purity itself, your kisses would cool my forehead, and I was once again a happy father.

"How many wonderfully free and joyous days we spent at the bottom of this ravine! How many times I bathed your feet in the pure water of the lake or watched you sleep among the reeds under the shade of a palm tree! Sometimes that would make my torments start up again. It hurt me to see you so tiny, and I wondered if I could survive my sufferings until you were old enough to understand and respond to my feelings. Without waking you, I would run your silken hair gently through my fingers and kiss it passionately, then take from my pouch the curls I had cut from your head in previous years, compare the color, and be thrilled to see that they were getting darker every spring. Then I would look at the four or five notches I had made on a nearby date tree to mark how you were growing. Oh, Indiana, those marks are still there—I saw them the last time I came up here to suffer! But unfortunately, although you became as beautiful a woman as you had been a child, although you did grow taller and your hair did become as black as ebony, none of it was for me. It was someone else who made your heart beat faster for the first time.

"Do you remember how we used to run, nimble as a couple of turtledoves, through the thickets of wild rose bushes? Do you also remember how we sometimes got lost in the woods around us? Once we tried to get to the top of the cloud-covered Salazes, but we hadn't realized that the higher we went, the less fruit there would be, or that the streams would be less fordable, the wind more penetrating, the cold more unbearable.

"When you saw that we had left the vegetation behind us, you wanted to turn back—but then we passed through the fern belt and found lots of strawberry plants, and you were so busy filling your basket with berries that you forgot about wanting to leave. It was hard to continue, however, because we were walking on volcanic rocks that were pocked with a kind of brown mold and sprinkled with plants that looked like clumps of wool. The sight of those poor, wind-battered weeds made us think of how good God was, to have given them the kind of warm covering they needed to survive the violent storms up there. Then the fog became so thick that we couldn't see where we were going and had to turn back. I carried you in my arms, carefully crawling down the steep slope. At nightfall we were just entering the first woods in the third level of vegetation. I picked some pomegranates for you, and I quenched my thirst with the cool water from the stalks of the lianes. That reminded us of the adventure of our favorite heroes when they were lost in the forest of the Red River, except that unlike them, we had no loving mothers or worried servants or faithful dogs to care about us. But I didn't mind—I was happy, I was proud, I was the one who was completely responsible for you—and I thought I was luckier than Paul.

"Yes, my love for you was a pure, deep, true passion even

then. Noun, when she was ten years old, was a full head taller than you. A Creole in the true sense of the term, she was already fully developed—a young woman in every way, her liquid eyes shining with a special significance. Well, I didn't love Noun—or rather, I loved her only because she was your playmate. It never occurred to me to wonder if she was beautiful or if she would someday be still more beautiful. To me, she was even more of a child than you, because it was you I loved, you I counted on. You were my chosen one, the companion of my life, the dream of my youth.

"But what I hadn't counted on was life itself and what the future would bring. My brother's death meant that I had to marry his fiancée. I won't describe that period of my life—though it wasn't the worst. I was married to a woman who hated me and whom I couldn't possibly love, I was a father and I lost my son, I was widowed and I learned that you had married!

"As I said, I won't talk about those days of exile in England, that hideously painful period of my life. If I hurt anyone, it wasn't you, and if anyone hurt me, I have no intention of complaining about it. But that was when I became more 'self-centered,' more 'selfish,' more 'egoistic'—in other words, more closed and suspicious—than ever. Because those I knew had no faith in me, I had gotten used to relying only on myself and depending on no one, so I had only the testimony of my own heart to support me during those ordeals. People made a crime of the fact that I couldn't love a woman who had married me only because she had been forced to, and who always treated me with contempt! They also said that one of the signs of my selfishness was that I didn't seem to love children. Raymon made some mocking comments about that on several occasions, saying that the qualities necessary to raise children were very different from those fostered by my rigidly methodical life as a bachelor. I suppose he didn't know that I had been a father, or that I was the one who had educated you. And none of you seemed to realize that the memory of my son was as sharp and poignant after all those long years as it had been the first day after his death, or that my heart broke every time I saw a blond head that reminded me of his. When a man is unhappy, people want to think it's his own fault, because otherwise they would have to pity him.

"But what no one will ever be able to understand is the rage and despair I felt when I—a poor child of the wilderness for whom no one had ever spared a sympathetic glance—was torn from Bourbon and set down in society, when I was forced to fill

someone else's place in a world that had already rejected me,
when I was supposed to understand that I had duties to perform
and obligations to fulfill to people who had never recognized
theirs to me! Not one of my relatives had ever tried to defend or
protect me, yet there they were, all of them, expecting me to
defend and protect *their* interests. They weren't even willing to
let me live alone in peace and quiet, something even the lowest
of outcasts is allowed to do! There was only one good thing in
my life—the hope that someday you would belong to me forever—and they took that away by saying you weren't rich
enough for me! What a bitter mockery that was! Not rich
enough for me, who had been fed by the mountains, repudiated
by his family, not been allowed to learn how to use wealth—
and who now found himself obliged to make other people's
wealth grow and prosper!

"Nevertheless, I submitted. I had no right to pray that my poor
little happiness be spared. I was disliked enough as it was—to resist would have made me hated. My mother, who was inconsolable at her other son's death, said she too would die if I didn't
submit to my destiny. My father, who accused me of not being
any comfort to him—as if it were my fault that he had never
loved me!—was ready to curse me if I didn't follow his orders. I
accepted my fate, but even you, who have been so unhappy
yourself, would never be able to understand what I suffered. Persecuted, oppressed, mistreated as I was—I tell you that if I didn't
return evil for evil, I can't possibly be as cold and unfeeling as
they say . . .

"When I returned here and saw the man to whom you had
been married—forgive me, Indiana, but that's when I really *was*
selfish. I suppose that love must always be selfish to some extent
because even mine was, and when I realized that you had been
given a master rather than a true husband by that sham marriage,
I felt an indescribable thrill of joy. You were surprised that I
seemed to like him, but it was because I didn't see him as my
rival. I knew very well that that old man could neither feel nor inspire love and that your heart would remain untouched and virginal. I was grateful for your cold indifference to him, and if he
had remained in Bourbon, I might have become a very guilty
man. But you both left me, and I couldn't live without you.
When I saw you again, as beautiful and pensive as I had long ago
dreamed you would be, I tried to conquer the love that was now
stronger than ever—but it was unconquerable, and I realized that
not seeing you was worse than seeing you. I needed to be with

you, to live under the same roof, to breathe the same air, to drink
in the sound of your voice at every hour of the day—and you
know the obstacles I had to overcome, the suspicions I had to
subdue, to accomplish that. I understood what I was undertaking.
I couldn't be with you without giving your husband a solemn
pledge—holding nothing back with either my words or my
heart—never to forget by word or deed that I was your brother
and nothing more. I've never broken a promise in my life, and
you know better than anyone else, Indiana, how I kept that one.

"I also understood that it would be difficult if not impossible
to play that role if I allowed even the slightest trace of any intimate or deep feeling to seep through my disguise. My passion
was so strong that I didn't dare play with danger. I realized I
would have to build a triple wall of ice around myself so that you
wouldn't be interested in me or sorry for me, because the least
sign of concern or compassion would have been my undoing. I
told myself that if you ever pitied me, it would mean that I'd already been guilty, and I made up my mind to bear silently all
your accusations of unfeeling selfishness—which thank heaven
you didn't spare me! I was more successful than I had planned to
be. You treated me with a kind of contemptuous pity, as if I were
a eunuch, and you behaved as if I had neither a heart nor a body.
But even if you had trampled me underfoot I wouldn't have had
the right to be angry or vengeful because that would have betrayed my feelings and shown you that I was a man.

"My complaint is against mankind in general, not you, Indiana. You were always kind and compassionate. You tolerated me
in the contemptible disguise I had assumed in order to be near
you, you never made me blush for my role, you took the place of
everything else in life for me. Sometimes I even allowed myself
to think that if you could accept me as the despicable person I
had made myself into so that you wouldn't be aware of the real
me, you might perhaps love that real me if you ever got to know
it. Who but you wouldn't have rejected me? Who but you would
have held out a hand to that senseless, speechless cretin? Everyone turned away in disgust from that 'egoist'—except the one
person in the world generous enough not to be wearied by such a
profitless relationship and magnanimous enough to spare some
of its own sacred life-giving fire for the frozen, shrunken spirit of
that miserable wretch! Only someone with a heart that had too
much of what I had too little of could have done that. In the
whole world there was only one Indiana capable of loving a
Ralph.

"Next to you, the person who showed me the most kindness was Delmare. You accused me of preferring him to you, of sacrificing your well-being to my own by refusing to interfere in your domestic quarrels. Blind, unjust woman! You never saw that I did as much as I could for you, and you certainly never understood that I couldn't take your part without betraying myself. What would have happened to you if Delmare had made me leave? Who would have protected you, patiently, silently, but with the steady perseverance of undying love? Not Raymon. And besides—out of gratitude, I suppose—I was fond of him in a way. Yes, I was fond of that crude, rough creature who might have deprived me of my only remaining joy and didn't, that poor man who was unhappy because you didn't love him and with whom I therefore felt a secret bond of sympathy. And I also liked him because I was never for a moment jealous of him. . . .

"And now I've come to the worst period of my life, that time when your love, which I had dreamed of so desperately, was given to someone else. That was when I finally felt the full force of an emotion I had repressed for so many years. That was when hate poisoned my heart and jealousy drained my strength. Until then my imagination had kept you pure, and even in my boldest dreams I had never lifted the veil of respect I had wrapped around you. But when I realized someone else was drawing you into his destiny, tearing you away from me, drinking long and deep of the ecstasy I hadn't even dared dream of, I went mad. I would have liked to see that detestable man at the bottom of this cliff, so I could hurl rocks down on him and smash his skull!

"Yet you were suffering so much that I forgot my own pain in seeing yours. I couldn't kill him because you would have wept for him. There were even times—God forgive me!—when I was ready to sink so low as to betray Delmare on behalf of my enemy. Yes, Indiana, I was so beside myself with grief when I saw you in such agony that I was sorry I had tried to tell you the truth about that man, and I would have willingly died if I could have bequeathed my heart to him! Oh, that evil, lecherous man! May God forgive him for the harm he has done to me, but I hope He punishes him for what he did to you! That's why I hate him—because I can forget what my own life has been, but I can't bear to think of what he made of yours. *He's* the one society should have branded at his birth, the one who should have been scorned and rejected as hard and cold and perverse, but instead he was lifted high and crowned with laurels! Oh, I know that that's the way the world is, and I shouldn't have been surprised or angry because I understand that when people admire the person who destroys the peace and happiness of others, they're only acting in accord with their own nature.

"Forgive me, Indiana, forgive me! It's probably cruel to say these things to you, but this is the first and the last time, so let me curse that worthless wretch who's driven you to the edge of the grave. You needed such a terrible lesson to open your eyes. You were deaf to the voice that cried out to you from Noun's grave and Delmare's deathbed: 'Beware of that man, he'll destroy your life.' Your evil genius led you to ignore the warning, and now you are the dishonored one condemned by society while he is accepted everywhere and forgiven everything. He did many evil things, and no one paid any attention to them. He killed Noun, and you forgot about it. He destroyed you, and you forgave him. And all because he knew how to look and sound like what he wasn't—because his magnetic eyes and clever words were able to fool every mind and heart. If nature had given him my impassive face and my dull mind, he would have been a perfectly good man.

"Yes, let God punish him—his behavior toward you was barbaric! Or perhaps God should forgive him after all, because he was probably more stupid than vicious! He didn't understand you or appreciate the happiness you would have brought him. Oh, you loved him so much, and he might have made your life so beautiful! In his place I wouldn't have pretended to be moral or virtuous—I would have snatched you from society and fled with you to the heart of the most remote mountain so I could have you all to myself, and the only thing I would have been afraid of was that you might not be enough of an outcast to allow me to take the place of the whole world for you! I would have been jealous, yes, but not the way he was—I wouldn't have wanted you to feel any consideration or respect for anyone else because it would have detracted from my love, and I would have suffered at the sight of another man giving you the smallest bit of pleasure or the most momentary gratification. That man would have been stealing what was mine, because your happiness would have been my concern, my responsibility, my life, my honor! Oh, how rich and content I would have been with this wild ravine for my only home, these mountain trees for my only wealth, if heaven had given them to me with your love! Let me weep, Indiana, for the first time in my life. God has not wanted me to die without knowing how comforting it can be."

Ralph was crying like a child. It was indeed the first time that stoical soul had ever given way to self-pity, and even then, there was more grief for Indiana's fate than for his own.

"Don't weep for me," he said, seeing her face also bathed in tears, "and don't feel sorry for me. Your pity wipes out the past, and the present isn't bitter anymore. You no longer love him, so I have no more reason to suffer."

"If I had known the real you, Ralph, I would never have loved him. It was your virtue that was responsible for my destruction."

Not responding to this, Ralph continued with a sad smile. "And then I have other reasons to be content, too. Without being aware of it, you told me something during those long hours on the ship when we were exchanging confidences. I realized that Raymon hadn't been quite as fortunate as he had boastfully claimed, and that made me feel a little better. At least I didn't have to blame myself for not having watched over you with sufficient care, for I had been arrogant enough to want to protect you against his seductiveness. I hadn't had enough faith in your own moral strength, so you must forgive me for that as well as for my other crimes, Indiana."

"You ask *me* to forgive *you*?" said Indiana. "When I'm the one who has made your whole life miserable? When I'm the one who has repaid such pure and generous love with such incredible blindness and callous ingratitude? I'm the one who should get down on my knees and beg *you* to forgive *me*!"

"Then my love doesn't disgust you or make you angry, Indiana? Oh, thank you, God! That means I can die happy! Listen to me, Indiana, you must stop blaming yourself for my suffering. At this moment I don't envy Raymon a single one of his pleasures, and if he had the heart of a real man, he would envy me, because now I'm the one who's your brother, your husband, your lover—and for all eternity! From the day you promised to die with me, I began to hope that you belonged to me, that you had been returned to me and would never leave me again. In my heart I began once more to think of you as my fiancée. It would have been too much happiness to possess you here on earth—or maybe not enough—but the dreams of my childhood will come true in God's bosom. That is where you will finally love me, Indiana. That is where your perceptions won't be colored by all the lying fictions of this earthly life, where you'll be able to do justice to my lifetime of sacrifice, suffering, and self-denial. That is where you'll be mine, Indiana, because you and heaven are one and the same, and if I've been worthy of heaven, I've been worthy of you. And that's why I asked you to wear this white dress—it's your wedding gown, and this rock that juts out over the lake is our altar."

He stood up, walked over to a nearby thicket, plucked a sprig from the flowering orange tree, and laid it on Indiana's black hair. Kneeling at her feet, he then said, "Make me happy, Indiana. Tell me that your heart agrees to this marriage in another world. Give me eternity, and don't force me to pray for everlasting unconsciousness."

If you haven't been moved by the story of Ralph's inner life, if you haven't come to love that good man, it can only be because I haven't been a skillful enough medium for his memories or been able to convey the power of a man who is truthfully expressing his most profound feelings—nor do I have the help of the melancholy light of the moon, the song of the waxbill, the scent of the clove tree, or any of the other voluptuous seductions of a tropical night. Also, you may not be aware of how the thought of imminent suicide can give rise to strong and unusual sensations, or of how the curtain that covers the feelings and events of everyday life is lifted, allowing them to appear as they truly are just as one is about to leave them behind forever. It was just such an instantaneous, fateful revelation that suddenly illuminated all the corners of Indiana's heart; the blindfold, which had been working itself loose for some time, suddenly dropped from her eyes completely, and once she was able to see things in their true light, she saw Ralph's heart as it really was. She also saw his features as she had never seen them before: the exalted mental heights to which he had climbed had galvanized him, freed him from the paralysis that had frozen his eyes and voice. Clothed in all the glory of honesty and goodness, he was much more attractive than Raymon, and Indiana felt that he was the man she should have loved.

"Be my husband in heaven and on earth," she told him, "and let this kiss bind me to you for all eternity!"

Their lips met, and surely the love that comes from the heart must be more powerful than purely physical desire, because that kiss, on the threshold of another life, contained within it all the ecstasy of this one.

Ralph carried his fiancée to the point from which he would plunge into the torrent with her in his arms. . . .

CONCLUSION

*To J. Néraud**

ONE hot, sunny day last January, I left Saint-Paul to spend some time wandering idly through the wild woods of Bourbon. I thought of you during my rambles, my friend, because for me those untouched forests were still permeated with your presence, the ground was still marked with the imprint of your footsteps, and everywhere around me I could see all the marvels you had described to me during our wakeful evenings together so long ago. Then I wished you could be here instead of in old Europe—where you're able to live and work in happy, modest obscurity because no friend has been treacherous enough to tell the world of your intelligence and worth—so we could enjoy them together.

I had set off on a walk to one of the highest and most deserted parts of the island—the Brûlé de Saint-Paul.

When a large segment of the mountain caved in during some long-ago volcanic disturbance, the collapse must have shaped a kind of amphitheater, one that now seems to display a multitude of rocks that look to have been flung about in whimsical, haphazard, almost magical disorder. Here a large boulder balances precariously on small stones; there a wall of thin, light, porous rocks rises in airy arabesques; beyond, a basalt obelisk, its sides seemingly carved and polished by an artist, rests on a crenelated bastion; and in yet another place a gothic fortress crumbles alongside a bizarrely shaped pagoda. It's almost as though this magnificent assembly, formed by chance and destruction, had been responsible for the creation of every possible rough draft of a painting or architectural sketch for a building so that in the future every genius of every nation from every century might come

To J. Néraud: George Sand's acknowledgment to her friend, Jules Néraud, who had traveled in 1814 to Bourbon and given her permission to use his memoirs as a source of information about that island, which she had never seen.

here for inspiration. Those completely fortuitous, elaborate, lace-like structures over there could have given birth to Moorish architecture and design, just as the tall vacoa found in the heart of the forest, with its hundred arms branching out from its main trunk and anchoring it to the ground and its festoons of fronds high above, might have inspired one of art's most beautiful creations—the cathedral supported by airy flying buttresses. Yet all these shapes, all these different kinds of beauty, all these light-hearted or daring ideas, were the result of one stormy eruption at the Brûlé de Saint-Paul. The spirits of fire and air must have presided at that night's diabolical happenings, for they alone could have piled up and created these effects; they alone could have given them the awesome, capricious, unfinished quality that distinguishes them from the works of man; they alone could have set down these enormous boulders, moved these gigantic masses, played with these peaks as if they were grains of sand, scattered about these extraordinary prototypes of every conceivable art form, created these sublime contrasts impossible to copy—and all as if to defy the audacity of the artist and say to him mockingly, "Try to match that!"

I stopped at a sixty-foot-high column of crystallized basalt that looked as if it had been faceted by a gem-cutter. At the top of the odd monument there was what looked like a large inscription seemingly drawn by the hand of some immortal. This is not an uncommon sight on these volcanic rocks. Long ago, when they were still soft and malleable from the fire, their heat-softened surfaces must have been host to various insects, shells, stones, and vines; and as the rocks subsequently hardened, those accidental contacts left impressions that today look like strange puzzles, curious hieroglyphs, mysterious characters—cabalistic signs of some supernatural being.

In the foolishly childish hope that I would be able to discover the meaning of those peculiar marks, I stood there for a long while, and during my profound but fruitless meditations, I lost all track of time.

When I returned to myself, a thick fog had already gathered around the mountain peaks and was rapidly moving down the sides and hiding their outlines. It reached me before I had gotten halfway down the plateau, making the area I was crossing completely impenetrable. A moment later a strong wind rose and swept the fog away, but a moment after that it was calm again and the fog returned—only to be swept away once more by even stronger gusts.

Looking for some protection, I found and took refuge in a cave, but then another plague joined that of the violent wind: torrents of rain that swelled every stream and river, all of which have their source at the top of the mountain. Within an hour everything was inundated, and the whole massif, water pouring down every side of it, was nothing but one enormous cascade furiously rushing toward the plain below.

Two days later, after some hard and dangerous walking, I found myself—guided by Providence, no doubt—at the door of a house located in a particularly wild spot. The simple but pretty cottage had been protected from the storm by a rampart of overhanging cliffs that acted like an umbrella. A little lower down, a waterfall plunged turbulently into a ravine and formed at the bottom an overflowing lake canopied by groves of beautiful though storm-battered trees.

I knocked eagerly, but the face that appeared at the door made me step back. Before I could ask for shelter, the master of the house had silently and gravely motioned me to come in, and when I had, I found myself face to face with Sir Ralph Brown.

In the year since the *Nahandove* had brought Sir Ralph and his companion back to the colony, he hadn't been seen in town more than twice, and as for Mme. Delmare, she lived in such seclusion that many people were not even sure that she existed. I myself had landed in Bourbon at about the same time they had, and this meeting with Brown was the second one of my life.

The first, which took place down on the coast of Saint-Paul, had left an indelible impression. At first I had not been particularly impressed by his face and bearing, and when I questioned the colonists about him, it was only out of idle curiosity. Their responses, however, were so strange and contradictory that I became more interested in the recluse of Bernica.

"He's an uneducated clod," said one. "A nothing, a boor, a man whose only good point is that he doesn't talk much."

"He's extremely well educated and a very profound philosopher, but he thinks too much of himself," said another. "He's arrogant, and he feels so superior to everyone else that he considers the few words he exchanges with ordinary people a total waste of time."

"He's a man who doesn't care for anyone but himself," said a third. "He's not stupid, but he has only moderate ability. A truly self-centered person—to the point of being completely unsociable."

A young man brought up in the colony and as narrow-minded as any other provincial said, "Don't you know? He's a lecherous, cowardly villain who poisoned his friend in order to marry his wife."

That statement so stunned me that I turned to yet another

colonist, an older man whom I knew to have a certain amount of common sense.

He could tell from my expression that I was eager to hear the solution to these riddles, so he said, "Sir Ralph was once a well-respected gentleman. He wasn't very well liked because he wasn't very communicative, and that's all I can tell you about him because I haven't had anything to do with him since the unfortunate events—"

"What unfortunate events?" I asked.

Then I heard about M. Delmare's sudden death, his wife's flight during that same night, and Sir Ralph's departure and return. The investigation carried on by the authorities had thrown no light on any of the obscurities surrounding those circumstances, but there was absolutely no proof that the fugitive had committed any crime. The law had refused to prosecute; but everyone knew that the judges were partial to Sir Ralph, and they had been strongly criticized for not having, at the very least, given the public an explanation for events that left the reputation of two people clouded by suspicion.

What seemed to confirm those suspicions was the furtive return of both the accused, and their subsequent mysterious retreat to the wilds of Bernica. The rumor was that they had originally fled Bourbon to give the gossip time to die down, but that public opinion in France was so strongly against them that they had returned to take refuge in the most isolated part of the island in order to satisfy their criminal lust in peace.

I began to think, however, that every one of those versions of what had happened was equally unlikely because some people, who seemed in a good position to know, insisted that Mme. Delmare had always been cool and distant to her cousin Sir Ralph Brown—almost as if she positively disliked him.

After hearing all this, I examined the hero of these bizarre stories very carefully—I might even say conscientiously. He was sitting on a bale of merchandise, waiting for the return of a sailor he had sent on some kind of errand. His eyes—steady, frank, and blue as the sea—were looking thoughtfully at the horizon. Every feature was in harmony with every other, and his sinews, muscles, and coloring seemed healthy, robust, and in such perfect working order that I could have sworn he was the victim of an intolerable injustice—that there was no crime anywhere in his past, that he could never have even thought of one, and that his heart and hands were as pure and innocent as his expression.

He suddenly became aware of me staring at him with rude and undisguised curiosity, and like a thief caught in the act, I lowered my eyes in embarrassment—though not quickly enough to avoid seeing his stern disapproval. I had often thought of him since then, and he had even appeared in my dreams; whenever he came to mind, I felt vaguely uncomfortable—which is often the way we respond to someone with an extraordinary character or destiny.

Obviously I was very eager to know Sir Ralph, but I felt as if I had wronged him, and I would have preferred to observe him from a distance and without his knowledge. The crystal-clear transparency of his eyes was chilling, and he was so clearly a remarkable person—either much better or much worse than other people—that I felt very small and ordinary next to him.

His hospitality was neither irksome nor ostentatious. He brought me to his room, lent me some clean clothes, then led me to his companion, who was waiting dinner for us.

When I saw how young—she looked barely eighteen—and lovely she was, and which I had admired her grace, her charm, and her soft voice, I knew unquestionably, and with a stab of pain, that she must either be very guilty or very unfortunate: guilty of a dreadful crime or besmirched by a dreadfully unjust suspicion.

The overflowing rivers, flooded plains, wind, and rain kept me in Bernica for a week, and when the sun came out, I didn't even think of leaving my hosts.

Neither of them exactly sparkled. They weren't very witty — probably not witty at all—but they had something that enabled them to express themselves powerfully and humorously: they had intelligent hearts. Indiana is ignorant, but it's not the narrow, vulgar kind of ignorance that springs from intellectual laziness or indifference or incapacity; she's eager to learn everything she hadn't had the opportunity to learn before, and she may even have been pretending to know less than she does in order to be able to question Sir Ralph and allow him to display his truly impressive, wide-ranging knowledge.

I found her cheerful but lacking in vivacity; she has some of the languorous melancholy of the Creoles, though in her its charm seems more profound. Her eyes especially are incredibly soft; they speak eloquently of a life of suffering, and even when she smiles, they somehow remain sad, with the kind of sadness that comes from thinking about the nature of happiness or from feelings of deep gratitude.

One morning I told them I was finally going to leave.

"So soon!" was their response.

Their regret sounded so sincere and was so touching that I found the courage to ask Sir Ralph to tell me his story. I had promised myself that I wouldn't leave without questioning him.

but because of the suspicions that had been planted in my mind, I was very reluctant to introduce the subject and found it hard to conquer my timidity.

"Listen," I told him, "people are nasty, and they've said some terrible things about you. Now that I know you, I'm not surprised. It's because your life is obviously very enviable that they tell so many lies about it—"

I stopped short when I saw Mme. Delmare's genuine surprise, and I belatedly understood that she must be completely unaware of the atrocious stories being circulated in the colony. Sir Ralph looked at me haughtily, with unmistakable displeasure, and his expression reminded me so much of our first silent meeting in Saint-Paul that I was filled with shame and prepared to leave immediately.

Dismayed at having made that fine man feel as he now did about me, and deeply regretting that I had repaid the happy days I owed him by hurting and angering him, I began to sob, and I burst into tears.

"Young man," he said, taking my hand, "spend another day with us. I can't bring myself to let the only friend we have in the whole country leave like this"—Mme. Delmare had left the room—"and I'll tell you my story. But not in front of Indiana— there are some wounds that should never be reopened."

That evening we all went for a walk in the woods. The trees that had been so fresh and lovely two weeks earlier were completely leafless, but already covered with large gummy growths; the birds and the insects had repossessed their kingdoms; the dead flowers were being replaced by young buds; the streams were busily ridding themselves of the gravel that had accumulated on their beds. Everything was returning to life and joy and health.

"Look at the astonishing speed," Ralph said to me, "with which this fertile nature repairs its losses! Doesn't it seem as if she can't bear wasting any time and is ready to expend an extraordinary amount of energy to do a year's work in a few days?"

"And she will, too," replied Mme. Delmare. "I remember that a month after last year's storms, there was no sign of them."

"It's exactly the same with a broken heart," I said to her. "When happiness returns, it bounces right back and immediately begins to grow younger and flourish again."

Indiana gave me her hand and looked at Sir Ralph with an indescribably tender and radiant expression.

When night fell, she went to her room, and Sir Ralph and I sat next to each other on a bench in the garden while he told me his story up to the point at which we left it in the last chapter.

Then he paused for a long time, seeming to forget my presence completely.

I was so interested that I decided to break into his reverie with a final question.

He started like a man being awakened, then said with a pleasant smile: "My young friend, there are some memories that lose their bloom when we talk about them. It's enough for you to know that I was quite determined to kill both Indiana and myself, but heaven had obviously not yet recorded that sacrifice in the celestial archives. A doctor would probably say that a very understandable attack of vertigo made me lose my sense of direction and take the wrong path. I, who haven't the least pretension to being a doctor in that sense, prefer to believe that the angel of Abraham and Tobias—that beautiful, blue-eyed angel of our childhood, dressed in white and girdled in gold—came down to earth on a moonbeam, floated over the waterfall's mist, and spread his silvery wings over my gentle companion. All I can tell you for sure is that the moon sank behind the high mountain peaks without any sounds of calamity having disturbed the peaceful murmur of the waterfall, that the birds on the cliff didn't fly off until a white band of light appeared on the horizon, and that the first ray of sunlight which fell on the grove of orange trees found me on my knees blessing God.

"And don't think that I was quick to accept the unhoped-for happiness that changed my life so completely. I was afraid of the golden future that was opening before me, and when Indiana woke up and smiled at me, I pointed to the waterfall and said, 'If you're not sorry to have lived until this morning, then we can both say in all truth that we have experienced happiness to its fullest—and that may be another good reason for dying now, because my star may dim by tomorrow. Who can say? If we leave this particular place, this inspiring situation in which thoughts of love and death have somehow made me eloquent, I may revert to being the detestable clod you disliked as recently as yesterday, and if I do, won't you blush with shame when you see me that way again? Oh, Indiana, spare me that heartbreaking agony. That would be the final blow, the complete fulfillment of my dreadful destiny.'

"Don't you trust your heart, Ralph?' she asked, with a lovely, tender smile. 'Or is it mine that you don't trust?'

"Shall I tell you the truth? I wasn't happy at first. I didn't doubt Madame Delmare's sincerity, but when I thought of the future, I was frightened. For thirty years I had had so little self-confidence that it was hard to believe that anyone could find me attractive or be able to love me. I had periods of doubt and fear and terrible uncertainty. Sometimes I was sorry that I hadn't thrown myself into the lake the second after Indiana had spoken the words that had made me so happy.

"She must have had times when she was depressed, too. It was hard for her to get over the habit of suffering, because the heart becomes accustomed to unhappiness—it takes root there, and isn't easy to weed it out. In all justice to her, though, I must say that she never had a moment's regret for Raymon—I don't think she even remembered him well enough to hate him.

"Finally, as always happens when people are truly and deeply in love, time made our love stronger. Every passing day gave it an added intensity because every day showed us more reasons for respecting and being grateful to each other. One by one our fears evaporated, and when we saw how easily those causes for distrust disappeared, we both smilingly agreed that we each felt we didn't deserve the other but would accept our happiness like complete cowards, without trying to understand it. From then on, we were completely confident of our love."

Ralph paused; then, after a few moments during which we were both absorbed in our thoughts, he continued.

"I won't say anything about my happiness. Just as there are unseen sorrows that cover the soul like a shroud, so there are unspoken joys that remain buried deep in a man's heart because no human voice can express them. Besides, even if some heavenly angel were to alight on one of these flowering branches and describe those joys, you couldn't understand them, young man, because you haven't been bent by the stormy blasts or beaten down by the raging tempests. How can the heart that hasn't suffered understand happiness? As for our crimes—"

"Oh!" I cried, my eyes wet with tears.

"Listen, monsieur," he said, interrupting me, "you haven't spent much time with the two criminals of Bernica, but even one hour is enough to understand how they live. All our days are the same. They follow one another calmly, peacefully, swiftly, and as innocently as in the days of our childhood. Every night we thank God, and every morning we pray to Him for the sunshine and shade of the day before. Most of our income is devoted to buying the freedom of poor, sick blacks, and *that* is the main reason the colonists hate us. Would that we were rich enough to free all those who live in slavery! Our servants are our friends. They share our joys, we ease their troubles. And so we spend our lives—without anxieties and without guilt. We rarely speak of the past or the future, but when we do, it's without bitterness for the one or fear of the other. If we sometimes find ourselves with tears in our eyes, it's because great joy occasionally calls for some tears, whereas great misery is always dry-eyed."

"My friend," I said after a long silence, "if those who accuse you could see you here, your happiness would be answer enough."

"You're very young," he replied. "Your conscience is still innocent and pure and unsullied by the world, so the fact that we're happy is proof to you that we're good. In the eyes of the world, however, it's a sign that we're criminals. Never mind—solitude is fine, and the loss of society isn't worth a single regret."

"Not everyone accuses you," I told him, "but even those who respect and admire you blame you for being proud and arrogant and contemptuous of public opinion."

"Believe me," Ralph answered, "there's more pride in that reproach than in my so-called arrogance. As for public opinion, monsieur, judging by those it holds up as models and examples, don't you think that what we should really do is extend our hands in friendship to those it treats as outcasts? People say that one's reputation is an important part of one's happiness, and those who believe that should indeed respect public opinion. As for me, I sincerely pity anyone whose happiness depends on its irrational and capricious judgments."

"Some moralists criticize your seclusion, claiming that every man is part of society and that society has a claim on him. They say you're setting a dangerous example."

"Society has no right to demand anything from the person who demands nothing from it," Sir Ralph replied. "And as for the power of example, I don't believe in it, monsieur. It takes too much determination and energy to break with the world, and too much suffering to acquire that kind of force. So let our secret happiness, which would only make people envious, remain hidden. Go follow your own destiny, young man—have friends, a profession, a reputation, a country to call your own. I have Indiana. Don't break the chains that bind you to society, respect its laws if they protect you, accept its judgments if they seem fair— but if someday society slanders and spurns you, have enough self-respect and pride to be able to do without it."

"Yes, a clean conscience will allow us to endure exile," I said, "but to make us love it, we would need a companion like yours."

His smile was indescribable as he said. "You can't imagine how I pity the world that despises me!"

The next day I left Ralph and Indiana. He embraced me, and she wept a little.

"Adieu," they said to me. "Return to the world, but if it casts you out someday, remember our cottage."